SACRED HOLLOW

SACRED HOLLOW

John Harris

Library of Congress Control Number:		2009910471
ISBN:	Hardcover	978-1-4415-8072-6
	Softcover	978-1-4415-8071-9

This book was printed in the United States of America.

To order additional copies of this book, contact:
Xlibris Corporation
1-888-795-4274
www.Xlibris.com
Orders@Xlibris.com
66470

Author's Note

This book is dedicated in loving memory to my daughter, Nicole A. Harris, who passed away in the autumn of 2002. Nikki was my first editor, who provided loving encouragement as only a daughter can do for such a project. She often referred to this book as "your new endeavor." She was particularly interested in the chapters that were set in Washington, D.C., my birthplace, and the place where she lived before she passed. Nikki loved Washington, D.C. We love our daughter and will never forget our firstborn. She is greatly missed.

I would also like to acknowledge the loving support provided by my wife, Sandi, and my daughter, Amy, who, along with Nicole, have character roles in the book.

I would be remiss if I left out my brother, William Harris, who currently resides with his family in Fort Lauderdale, Florida. Bill was with me on several sight visits in the mountains of Virginia and in the middle of the Gulf of Mexico to do research for this book. He provided valuable insights and suggestions that one can only obtain out in the field for a project of this magnitude. I am also grateful to Richard Elwell of Chevy Chase, Maryland, for providing much needed editing support.

This novel is a work of fiction. The character names and incidents depicted in the novel are a product of the author's imagination. Any resemblance to actual individuals is purely a coincidence.

About the Author

John Harris was born in Washington, D.C., and raised in the nearby Maryland suburbs. A career federal civil servant and student of Okinawan Goju-Ryu Karate for fifteen years, John retired in the autumn of 2002. He was awarded a black belt degree from Mr. Thomas Boddie of New York City in 1979.

PROLOGUE

Shenandoah National Park, Virginia—Skyline Drive near Stony Man Mountain

Stony Man reminds us of cold times 10,000 years ago when the glaciers covered much of North America. This area was much colder then. Cold climate plants covered the land. Then the temperature began to rise on top of Stony Man. Glaciers retreated northward, and other plants adapted to a much warmer climate; but in the coolness on top of Stony Man, a few cold-weather plants survived. Native Red Spruce and Balsam Fir persist there today.

-Inscription on the plaque at the Stony Man Overlook

Driving on the "Highway to the Sky," Skyline Drive, nearly forty-two miles into the Shenandoah National Park from the park's northern entrance, one will come across Stony Man Mountain, the second-highest mountain in the park. One will be in a mountain range that once exceeded the highest of the Rocky Mountains to the far west. Stony Man is some 4,000 plus feet above sea level at its highest point and is one of a number of heavily forested giant gems that lie in the midst of 196,000 acres of federal parkland that fall between the Shenandoah Valley to the west and the Piedmont region of Virginia to the east.

Shenandoah—where did that name originate? Local lore has it that the original native Americans who lived in the region hundreds of years ago were mesmerized by the reflection of the stars at night on the Shenandoah River, which meanders close by. "Daughter of the Stars" or "Shenandoah" was their chosen name for the valley. Another legend has it that the name derived from an Indian phrase, "mountains to the stars" because the mountains seemed to climb to the stars. Not too long ago, human beings once lived in these mountains.

He saw the image of the man in the mountain as he pulled off Skyline Drive into the scenic overlook parking area in the shadow of Stony Man Mountain. His heart skipped a beat. He turned off the engine and walked to the edge of the overlook glancing sideways to his left at the peak of Stony Man. After looking down at the inscription on the plaque mounted at the edge of the overlook, he understood why this mountain had been named Stony Man. He could clearly make out the face of a man high up on the peak, indeed, a face of stone. Nearly straight ahead out past the overlook, directly down in the valley was a small lake surrounded by rolling forest with some fields cleared by the farmers who lived down there.

Looking at his notes, he realized that the area he would be most particularly interested in would be somewhere between that small lake and Stony Man. Since this was his first time being in this area of the park as an adult, his search at this point looked to be much more expansive than he could have ever envisioned.

He glanced back up to his left at Stony Man again and then turned his head nearly ninety degrees to the lake, panning from left to right. He began to grow frustrated. *How the hell am I supposed to find Ma and Pa in all of this? I have no coordinates to go by.* A tear trickled down his cheek as thoughts of his parents still hung heavy. He squinted at the bright blue sky, not really noticing the blazing sun. Then, in a moment of stern determination, he thought, *I am going to find them even if I have to spend every spare moment of the rest of my life looking for them.*

Part 1

The Beginning

Sanchin—Three Battle—Concept of threes—
All techniques are performed in threes

Chapter 1

Virginia Military Institute—Lexington, Virginia—Mid August

Lying in the southern sector of the Shenandoah Valley, approximately a four-hour drive from the nation's capital, Washington, D.C., stands the site of a former military post that was once utilized shortly after the War of 1812 as a major storage depot for the western part of the Commonwealth of Virginia. This site in the rolling valley of Rockingham County in the northeast quadrant of Lexington, Virginia, has been the home of the Virginia Military Institute since its formation in 1839. Before its inception, the storage depot had been manned by approximately twenty soldiers who were observed by the local townsfolk to be lacking in discipline and other matters of military etiquette. Accordingly, spurred by Lexington attorney John Thomas Lewis Preston, legislation was initiated at the Virginia General Assembly establishing the Virginia Military Institute, with the expressed goals of creating a military college at the site and infusing more discipline and character into its students.

The Institute has accumulated a long list of accomplishments and kudos since its inception. One of the Institute's early professors was Thomas Jonathan Jackson, a distinguished member of the faculty from 1851 until 1861 when he once again returned to military service, this time in the Confederacy. Of course, he has been known since then as "Stonewall" Jackson. Ten VMI cadets were killed and forty-seven wounded in the Battle of New Market where they helped turn back the Union forces that were pressing south in the Shenandoah Valley. Legend has it that when General John J. (Blackjack) Pershing visited VMI, he voiced words to the effect that VMI was not the West Point of the South—West Point was the VMI of the North.

The main barracks of the Institute stand out in gothic relief with the mountains of the Shenandoah in the background.

"Pop to when I talk to you, Rat!" barked an upperclassman at Joseph Allen Lynch, an incoming freshman from suburban Maryland, just outside of Washington, D.C.

It was mid summer and the freshman class of cadets was in the process of going through the famous "ratline" at VMI as initiation into the Corps of Cadets. Joe Lynch, a rather slim and smallish cadet with light brown hair and blue eyes at five foot seven inches tall practically standing on his toes, had graduated at the top of his senior class the prior June. He was excited about the prospect of becoming an officer in the U.S. Army, heavily influenced by his mentor and science teacher in high school. His father had been impressed by his visit to VMI earlier in the year and was very happy that his son had chosen the Institute for his college education since he was a Navy man himself. Nonetheless, he had cautioned Joe to at least consider attending a civilian school considering his major was going to be pre-medicine.

His father had dropped Joe off on a hot mid August day at the Institute, and Joe had just completed his registration paperwork. Things seemed to be relatively civil at the time. Most of the upperclassmen and faculty who were primarily officers in the U.S. Army and Air Force actually seemed quite pleasant and affable. Joe thought that this was going to be a cool experience. Although, it didn't dawn on him at the time, he was fully into academic burnout and hadn't the slightest idea what was boiling in the subconscious of his mind.

"I said pop to when I talk to you, Rat! Are you sleepwalking, Rat?" the upperclassman continued with his hazing.

Joe noticed that the upperclassmen wore black shoes that were polished to such a gloss that one could literally make their faces out in their shoes. They wore summer whites with the distinctive VMI garrison hat. The brass on their belts, as well as the Virginia state symbol and the letters "VMI" in the front of their hats, was shined to a bright gold color.

Before he could yell out the mandatory, "Sir, no, sir," which, while politically correct, would often be turned by the upperclassmen into a paradox for the typical rat at VMI, Joe was accosted by several other upperclassmen. Unable to respond to all of the demands of several upperclassmen in his face simultaneously, Joe addressed the initial question from the first upperclassman to greet him. "Sir, no, sir," replied Joe. Responding with a "sir, yes, sir" would have led to further hazing for admitting to sleepwalking. It was really just a game of words to bewilder the rats and keep them on their toes.

The upperclassmen continued with the onslaught. "Rat, I say you are sleepwalking. Are you calling me a liar?"

Joe hesitated and replied, "Sir, no, sir!"

"Get down and give me twenty-five, Rat, now!"

Joe dutifully dropped on the concrete barracks floor where he was attempting mightily to move through the gauntlet of screaming upperclassmen to reach his assigned barracks room. "Don't you dare touch the floor with your chest. Do you hear me, Rat! Don't do it; don't even think about doing it. Do you get my drift, Rat! You are making me sick; you can't even do twenty push-ups!"

Joe was striving to keep his chest off the floor with the small of his back arched in the process. He and the other rats were being harassed, hazed, bullied, and browbeaten so heavily that most were numb from the onslaught. The cadets with the proper frame of mind knew that this training was necessary. They seemed to understand that to one day be in the line of fire and be able to keep their wits about them, they would have to first be broken completely down—and built back up by the harsh discipline and treatment they were experiencing as rats. While it seemed almost impossible to Joe and the others to understand that concept at the time, days would come in the future for many, when under the onslaught of an enemy charge with withering fire, they would be thankful they had endured the "ratline" at VMI.

As Joe was stumbling to his feet to recover from his push-ups, another upperclassman jumped into his face. "I need change to buy a pack of rubbers tonight, Rat. I'm going out with the senior class president at Southern Seminary tonight. Don't worry, Rat, it's a female school. You got change for a twenty, Rat? I need a ten and two fives."

Joe reached back quickly to his wallet to look for the change.

"I don't have all day, Rat. I don't like to be kept waiting." The upperclassman was now nose to nose with Joe, and Joe could feel the heat and spittle coming from the upperclassman. Joe opened his wallet and showed two twenty-dollar bills to the senior cadet. "Rat, you don't have the proper change! Get down and give me twenty-five, now!"

"I have change, sir!"

The senior glanced over to see another rat with short reddish blond hair volunteering to help Joe out.

The senior cadet sneered at the rat, James Mackenzie from Luray, Virginia, who had offered his help. "Did I ask you to butt in, Rat?"

"Sir, no, sir," Mackenzie replied.

Looking at his temporary nametag, the senior cadet walked so hard and fast into Cadet Mackenzie that he practically head butted him in the process. "Get down and give me twenty-five, Rat, for interrupting my conversation with Lynch!"

Mackenzie did not flinch or appear intimidated in the slightest. He was a country boy, rock solid at 185 pounds, just shy of six feet tall, from rural Virginia and had been used to the rough life, hunting in the woods to put food on the table for his aunt and uncle. He had a short reddish crew cut and a bull neck honed from hard farm work as a youngster. His uncle had driven him hard, almost to total exhaustion. He believed in tough discipline. Jimmy was a southern woods boy who had come to the Institute prepared. He pumped out his twenty-five push-ups and bounded up immediately, hardly breaking a sweat, and had a slight smile on his face.

"Are you mocking me, Rat?" the senior cadet yelled.

"Sir, no, sir," Jimmy replied.

"Give me that change now. Don't keep me waiting, Rat!"

Jimmy whipped out the ten and two fives, and before moving off to harass another rat, the senior slapped the twenty into Jimmy's hand.

Finally making their way through their first "ratline" experience, both cadets Joe Lynch and Jimmy Mackenzie ended up in the identical barracks room. As it turned out, the rooms were assigned alphabetically by last name, and the rat that had helped Joe out ended up being his roommate.

"Where you from? I'm Jimmy Mackenzie from Luray, Virginia," drawled Jimmy as he reached out to extend his hand to Joe.

"Just outside Washington, D.C. Joe Lynch, pleased to meet you."

Jimmy laughed. "Oh, you one of them Yankees, huh?"

"I guess so," replied Joe.

"Aw, that's okay. Hell, I understood that George Marshall was from Pennsylvania. Guess you all ain't all bad any time you want to come to the Institute."

Joe smiled. "You know, I never gave it much thought."

As Jimmy and Joe began to wander around their room, Jimmy turned serious. "Joe, you seemed like you were intimidated a bit by those upperclassmen. Don't be. You know they got a job to do to get our butts straight."

Joe glanced intently at Jimmy and noticed that this country boy looked very tough. His hands were scarred, and he looked as though he would not back down from anyone. Joe had noticed how he had stood toe to toe with the senior cadet and had not flinched. That was impressive. Joe had grown up in a sleepy suburb, and his parents had literally given him anything that he had wanted. All he had to do was study and get good grades. While he was a fairly good athlete, he had never had to get "down and dirty" with tough physical work such as farming or hunting all hours of the day and night as Jimmy had. Joe knew almost immediately that a number of the southern rats did not appear as intimidated by the harsh yelling and discipline being thrown at them. Indeed, most of the senior cadet leaders, the squad lieutenants, and the company captains had southern accents. He never forgot the deep southern drawl-driven cadence as Joe and the other rats marched during drills on the Institute's twelve-acre parade ground.

"Lay-oft—righta—lay-oft—righta—lay-oft—righta—lay-oft."

"I guess you're right, Jimmy. I am just wondering how the heck I am going to handle getting good grades at the Institute and all the military training."

Jimmy bounced a quarter on his rack and replied quickly to Joe. "Hey, man, the last thing I am worried about is getting good grades. I plan to learn the military stuff as fast as I can and take the easiest courses I can find. I am majoring in U.S. history. What's your major?"

Joe frowned as he told Jimmy pre-medicine.

Jimmy lit up. "You got to be shitting me. Pre-med—holy shit—you got to change that as soon as you can, Joe."

"What's for supper mess, Rat?" A week had passed, and an upperclassman had spotted Joe walking away from the posted menu for supper mess call. "Don't make me wait too long, Rat!"

Joe thought for a second and blurted out. "Sir, mashed potatoes, spinach, hamburgers, rolls, milk, iced tea, or coffee—sir!" Satisfied, the upperclassman walked away without responding.

At supper mess call in the VMI dining hall, there was no break from the harsh regimen of being a rat. Rats were required to sit with their backs perfectly straight and their chins tucked down into their chests. There could be no deviation from that posture even while a rat chewed his food or passed food to other rats or the squad lieutenant sitting at the end of the table.

"Goddamn it, tuck your chin in, Rat! Look at you; you're so damn fat you can't tuck it in!"

Joe felt sorry for Cadet Simpson. He had come to the Institute grossly overweight and puffy. Freshmen such as he almost always received the wrath of the upperclassmen, and many were often seen running extra laps to get in shape.

"Lynch, quit looking at Simpson before I make you eat six hamburgers in six seconds!" Lieutenant Johnson from Arlington, Virginia, was glaring hard at Joe who immediately attempted mightily to eat with the proper etiquette required while having his chin severely tucked.

"Sir, yes, sir!" Joe shouted to Johnson. His roommate Jimmy was somehow able to gorge his food and retain the perfect bearing necessary to satisfy the lieutenant.

"Simpson! Get down on the floor and give me twenty-five, now!" The lieutenant had a definite hard on for Cadet Simpson. He appeared to view him with abject disgust.

Another week went by with the freshman class striving to adjust to the rigid rat discipline being thrown at them. One day they all thought they were going to drop when after doing a number of laps around the parade field in full battle gear with M1 rifles carried in both hands, they were required to undergo a mandatory physical exam with push-ups, pull-ups, sit-ups, and still more running. Joe acquitted himself well, having participated in the cross-country team at his high school for several years and staying in relatively good shape with intramural touch football and softball.

Nonetheless, he was amazed at the stamina and fortitude of Jimmy Mackenzie . He and his classmates watched in amazement as Jimmy jumped up to the bar and pulled his body up an incredible fifty times. *Damn, that country boy is in some shape. He better be careful. I notice he smiles at the upperclassmen every time he pulls off one of his physical stunts,* Joe mused to himself.

CHAPTER 2

Virginia Military Institute—Lexington, Virginia—Two Weeks Later

As Joe and Jimmy began to settle in to the academic regimen at the institute, they quickly learned to favor certain professors over others. The overwhelming majority of the instructors were U.S. Army officers, primarily captains, majors, and some lieutenant colonels. Some of the instructors were gruff, presenting a stiff bearing, and others were almost friendly.

"Okay, cadets, for homework tonight, I want you to read chapters four through six of the Poets of the Victorian Age and do the written questions at the end of each chapter."

Major Cliff Johnston, the professor of English Literature I at VMI, was a good old boy from Louisville, Kentucky, and one of the cadets' favorites early on. He sported a huge stomach and a larger smile to go with it. He was a kindly gent, unusual to find at the Institute, and would often spend the last five minutes of class reminiscing about his experiences as a cadet at VMI before getting his commission and serving his tour of duty at a number of Army posts out west, primarily as an instructor of one discipline or another wherever the Army could fit him in.

"I know a number of you cadets probably are wondering why the heck you even came to a place like this when you could be chasing coeds at a civilian college like UVA or Richmond U. In time you will come to appreciate the Institute for what it has to offer. Nowhere in the United States can you receive the kind of care and training that you can at VMI. Believe me, I've been around. I've attended classes at a number of schools around the country. In the beginning, I felt a lot of apprehension here when I first entered the ratline. After a while, you'll gradually understand what it's all about and what we're trying to accomplish. It's not always readily apparent and may even appear to work against your obtaining a college education. By the time you graduate and are ready to move on, you'll come to miss the Institute and will be filled with many memories. Class dismissed."

As cadets Lynch and Mackenzie walked with the other freshmen to the military science class, they appeared somewhat glum, if not mildly amused at the prospect of attending the next class after leaving Major Johnston behind.

"You know, Major Johnston is a good old dude," Jimmy said to Joe.

"You're right, Jimmy. He is about the only guy at the Institute that can reach cadets like you and me. I think it's good to have a few like him here to help some of the marginal rats get over the hump. He might be the difference between staying here or going to a civilian school."

Jimmy frowned. "I don't think I would like any other place. I like the military discipline and structure. The uniforms are sharp, and you can get a lot of women as a cadet."

"Maybe you're right," Joe replied.

As they bounded up the few steps to the military science building, they both began to smile slightly. Joe spoke first. "Old Stonewall. That dude is living back in the Confederacy, don't you think?"

"Yeah, I believe he is. You know that don't bother me none. I'm a southern boy born and bred; every drop of my blood is Dixie. I am following the traditions of the South with their young manhood getting a righteous military college education."

"All right, Jimmy, I get your point," Joe replied with a "whatever" look.

As Jimmy, Joe, and the other students in the Military Science I class settled into their chairs, they had to wait for Professor Thomas Jackson to make his grand entrance. Dressed in his dress green Army uniform, Lieutenant Colonel Thomas Mosby Jackson, a paratrooper in the U.S. Army's 82nd Airborne Division during the Vietnam conflict, strode in through a side door wearing his trademark airborne paratrooper beret and high, shiny black jump boots. At six feet, two inches on a chiseled frame with eyes that seemed to want to pop out of his head, he kept a stern visage, sporting a bright red handlebar mustache that somehow had not brought the wrath of the superintendent down on him.

When one considered that this man had single handedly wiped out a machine gun nest of six Viet Cong soldiers in South Vietnam years ago while rescuing his company commander and receiving the Distinguished Service Cross and the Silver Star as well as the Purple Heart in the process, it was no wonder that all bowed in deference to the man from the Shenandoah—Virginia's finest.

Thomas Jackson, often referred to smugly as "Stonewall" by the cadets due to his penchant of referring to confederate soldiers as "us" during his long-winded narrations of battle strategy and military history during the Civil War—though it was forbidden at the Institute to call him by that revered name—was a daunting presence. There was only one Stonewall Jackson in Virginia, and

Thomas Jonathan Jackson had died in the service of Virginia and the Institute over a hundred years earlier.

Professor Jackson had chosen to cover his war injury with his thick, fiery-red handlebar mustache. After killing all of the Viet Cong soldiers in the machine gun nest, he had temporarily slung his M1 carbine on his shoulder to help his wounded company commander. A wounded Vietnamese had viciously slammed Jackson in his face with a foxhole shovel, obviously the only weapon at his disposal. Various accounts recorded Jackson as spitting out several teeth and a dollop of blood before calmly dispatching his enemy with a single .45 caliber slug between the eyes with his sidearm, after which, he once again resumed administering to his captain.

"Cadet Mackenzie , what state in the United States grows more generals than any other?"

Jimmy stood at attention immediately. "The state of Virginia has more generals, sir."

Professor Jackson smiled down at his class. "I'm mighty glad you cadets have been coming up with the right answers lately. I was beginning to wonder bout you all.

"Today we are going to discuss the origins of guerrilla warfare as first practiced by another great Virginian. As a matter of fact, all you have to do is look at the plaque on the outside of this classroom at my middle name to know the answer.

Cadet Lynch, who am I talking about?"

Joe Lynch immediately stood at attention. "Sir, Colonel John Singleton Mosby, the Gray Ghost of the Shenandoah Valley, sir!"

"Very good for a Yankee," replied Professor Jackson with a smile.

After a discourse on the tactics and heroism of Colonel Mosby's group of hit-and-run raiders during the Civil War, it was nearing the end of class. "I just want to remind you cadets that here at the Institute, you will be frowned on if you don't join the Virginia Military Historical Society your freshman year. We don't necessarily expect you to stay in the Society your entire tour at the Institute. Nonetheless, upperclassmen do get wind of those who don't show up for the meetings—if you get my drift." He reminded the cadets of the mandatory assembly one week from today, next Friday right after supper mess at the huge assembly hall just outside of the barracks' entrance adjacent to the parade grounds and dismissed class.

Two Hours Later

Senior Cadet Rock Granger from Ft. Worth, Texas, was an imposing figure in his own right. At six feet, three inches with a blond crew cut and muscular body on a rock-hard, 215-pound frame, he had once been the top running back on the VMI football team, fondly known as the Keydets, before too many concussions took their toll.

Forced to leave the team, he took out his frustrations on rats, especially rats that thought they were already tough enough for the "system."

Situated nearly in the center of the parade field, two squads of cadets were undergoing military drill procedures under the guidance and grilling of several first and second classmen.

"Mackenzie , you think you're a smart ass, don't you, Rat?"

Cadet Mackenzie had just bounded up briskly after whipping out a hundred push-ups on orders from Granger simply because he thought Mackenzie was too ugly for the Corps of Cadets. In reality, Jimmy had been handling every chore that Granger could throw at him on the parade field during close quarter drill routines. Granger appeared to take it personally that this cadet could deal with any physical punishment he would dump on him.

"Sir, no, sir," Jimmy quickly replied with a slight edge to his voice. Granger had been ragging Jimmy all afternoon on his posture, his drill techniques, and rifle inspection; he had really stepped over the line when he asked Mackenzie to explain why he was so ugly. This was getting personal for a number of the rats. It was interesting that after making the comment, first classman Lieutenant Johnson, Joe and Jimmy's squad leader, had called Granger over to whisper something in his ear.

Turning back to Mackenzie and the other rats, Granger laughed. "Lieutenant Johnson was just telling me how much pussy he is going to get tonight from those Southern Sem gals. Too bad you rats aren't going to get any pussy tonight. Guess you'll just have to play with yourselves."

Johnson heard that comment, shook his head, and walked over to the other squad of drilling cadets.

Granger continued with his drill lecture. "Port arms, port!" he screamed at the rats as they adjusted their rifles accordingly. "Now, two laps and report back to me ASAP. Slackers will do one additional lap. Get a move on, Rats!" he screamed again.

Huffing and puffing while attempting to whisper to one another, Joe and Jimmy hung close while jogging, their rifles held in front of their chests at an angle. Joe leaned toward Jimmy to offer some words of advice.

"Fuck, Jimmy, that guy has it in for you; you better be cool."

"I know," replied Jimmy.

"Shit, just try not to look so good in front of him. He's going to kill you before it's over with," Joe replied.

"That's hard for me to do. I think the other first classmen are going to get on this guy. I've been watching Lieutenant Johnson, and he is pissed. Granger will settle down, you watch," said Jimmy.

"Whew, I am sure looking forward to going downtown tonight," Joe said.

"Yeah, me too," Jimmy replied through quick breaths.

After supper mess, Joe and Jimmy were happy to head downtown to Lexington, a relatively small, sleepy college town. With Washington and Lee University bordering Virginia Military Institute, the town on weekends was teaming with college students and cadets. Jimmy and Joe thought they would browse through some of the tourist establishments and collect souvenirs for their families.

"Man, I feel like I just broke out of jail, Joe," Jimmy mused to his friend as they walked down the main drag of the town.

"Yeah, me too," Joe replied. Joe's mind, however, could not venture far from his concern regarding Granger's constant haranguing of Jimmy.

As the two cadets, spiffy in their dress gray uniforms, walked past Eckerd's Drug Store on South Main Street heading in the general direction of the tourist shops two blocks away, Joe brought up the subject that kept troubling him. "Jimmy, I shit you not; don't be a showoff with Granger. That guy has a hard on for you. I can see the anger in his eyes."

Jimmy waved his friend off. "Look, Joe, I ain't taking no shit from that dude or anyone else there. I figure I give one hundred and ten percent in the military and PT drills. I heard it through the grapevine that Granger took one too many hits in that big baboon forehead of his when he played varsity football and is feeling bad about himself not being on the team anymore. He's got an attitude—pure and simple. I figure he's taking it out on me because I am doing an excellent job with the drills. Can't say the same about the class work, though.

"Hey, man, let's grab a banana split at the soda fountain on the way back to campus. What do ya say?"

They knew that there was a soda fountain bar in Eckerd's, and Joe liked that idea. "Hey, I'm up for it, Jimmy," replied Joe.

As they walked leisurely down the main drag, they didn't bother to notice the Motel Six directly across the street from Eckerd's near the end of the block where Preston Street ran into South Main. Something would catch their eye about that establishment on their way back to campus though.

While browsing in Smith's Antiques, it was Jimmy's turn to be concerned about Joe. "It's funny, Joe. You're worried about my performance on the parade ground, and I'm worried about you in the classroom. You study too much, man. I mean you ought to lighten up. I know you mentioned you were a straight-A student in high school and all; you can't duplicate that in college, especially in a place like this. You'd have to be a genius plus be in top physical shape with just the right attitude to be able to pull off a 4.0 at the Institute. I've heard dudes have done it. But, they're the exception. I notice how you seem to have a worried look on your face in the barracks when you open your books. Just don't hassle with it, man."

Joe fingered a small ceramic structure that resembled the barracks at VMI. "You're right, Jimmy. I really appreciate you saying that. You're the only friend I have here at the Institute that can pick up my spirits. I don't know what I'd do without you. That's one of the reasons why I don't want you to get angry at Granger. They might expel your ass and leave me here alone."

Jimmy laughed. "Don't worry. I'll cool it. Man, we worry about one another like a couple of old mothers."

After making several small purchases, they both headed back out into the brisk, dark night to stop by the soda fountain. Joe had noticed that when the sun had gone down, even in September in the southern mountains of the Shenandoah, the temperature would drop quickly. With just an hour to go before TAPS at 2300 hours, they knew they had little time to waste.

Milling on the sidewalk with a fairly large crowd of people who were frequenting some of the town's bars, the two people about to enter the Motel Six in nondescript civilian clothes certainly did not notice the VMI cadets. The tall man sporting a casual tweed sport coat with suede elbow patches was stumbling slightly. He was in his mid fifties, and there was no mistaking this person with the thick, bushy gray mane of hair on his head. The woman was wearing an unusually short, black, and tight-fitting skirt with stockings and black pumps. They were arm in arm with her appearing to support the taller man by linking her arm in his. His gait suggested that he had had a few too many earlier in the evening.

Jimmy and Joe just happened to be gazing in the general direction of the motel when their observation of the goings on in front of the motel held them transfixed. There was only one man who looked like the inebriated gentleman in front of the motel—and he was the superintendent of the Virginia Military Institute. And, there was only one woman who looked like the sexy lady with the short skirt and pumps—she was a professor in the Department of Mathematics at Virginia Military Institute.

"Jesus Christ! Did you see that!" Joe whispered to Jimmy as they sat pawing away at their banana splits at the soda bar.

"Shit, man. I couldn't believe it. That's the fucking super, and he is drunk on his ass. Damn, guess he was going to get some tail from Professor Gadsden," Jimmy replied, referring to the superintendent of VMI, Major General Mark Betters and the much younger female professor of Mathematics at VMI, Captain Loretta Gadsden.

They both knew the super was married. During one of the assemblies, the super's wife had been pointed out by upperclassmen, and this lady at the motel certainly wasn't his wife. Incredible! The super was running around on his wife.

"You know, Jimmy, you'd think the super would be a bit more discreet. Shit, I guess after he got drunk, he didn't give a damn. Liquor will do that to you."

Looking at his friend, Jimmy had a few words for the wise. "I think we ought to keep this to ourselves, Joe. I mean the super fucked up; everyone makes mistakes. I just wonder if anyone from around here recognized him. Hell, you wonder if anyone in the motel lobby saw him. Maybe once they got in, they separated to make it look like they weren't together. She could have already reserved the room, and he could sneak up there after she entered first."

Joe nodded in agreement with a slight smile. "Don't worry; I didn't see a thing."

Looking at his watch, Joe sounded the alarm. "Christ, Jimmy, it's already 2245; we got to get moving!"

It was 0400 hours, two hours before wake-up call, and there was a loud rapping on their barracks door as cadets Lynch and Mackenzie were getting some much needed sleep. Screaming at the tops of their lungs, six upperclassmen banged away at Joe and Jimmy's barracks' door.

"Wake up, Rats, now! Get the fuck out of the rack, you weenies. Quit playing with yourselves and get the fuck up now! Wake up, Rats!"

Joe bounded out of the bed in his skivvies thinking that someone at the Institute must have seen them checking out the scene in front of the motel, and they were going to be physically reminded to keep their mouths shut. As he opened the door to the onrush of the upperclassmen, it became readily apparent to him that every rat's room in the barracks was being invaded in the identical manner. The entire main barracks was lit up with activity and screaming. This was "resurrection call"—getting a rude wake-up call during the middle of their precious sleep, another of the many rites of passage for rats.

Upperclassmen smoking cigars rushed in to the barracks and turned on the showers and faucets to the hottest temperature possible, creating a steam effect. They blew cigar smoke in the rats' faces as they taunted and harassed them to no end, yelling as loudly as they could manage. All Jimmy and Joe could do was yell the requisite, "Sir, no, sir" or "Sir, yes, sir," and accommodate the requests of the upperclassmen as best they could. It ended as suddenly as it had begun with the command for lights out.

Chapter 3

Virginia Military Institute—Lexington, Virginia—One Week Later

"I am here this evening to speak to you young men who have chosen to enter the hallowed halls of this great Institute to encourage you in the strongest terms to join the Virginia Military Historical Society. As you know, we have the largest chapter at VMI, even larger than that school over in Blacksburg." Lieutenant Colonel Thomas Jackson was referring, of course, to the Virginia Polytechnic Institute, a civilian/military school that had a substantial Corps of Cadets in its own right. The rat class laughed in unison. They were attending a mandatory session of the Historical Society chaired by Professor Jackson himself at the large assembly hall adjacent to the parade grounds on a Friday evening right after supper mess. Jackson had a booming, intimidating voice that rang with a deep southern drawl. He was, of course, once again decked out in his favorite paratrooper uniform: dress greens with shiny black jump boots, a chest of medals, and the distinctive beret cap.

"Now, the reason why we strongly encourage you at the Institute to join our society is that we firmly believe that the experience will enhance your education. As many of you surely know, the history of the South is one of a great military tradition. There has always been a preponderance of military colleges in the South to prepare our young men to be citizen-soldiers. The need was recognized long ago by our forebears, and thanks to them and almighty God, we have kept the tradition going. One can easily tell by the bearing of a VMI man or a Citadel man that he is a young man of fine training and background: strong yet polite, firm yet willing to lend a hand to a lady in distress, spit shined and spiffy, bold and bodacious, chivalrous and courageous, ready to take up the cause if necessary. That's been the tradition of the young man in the South. We know that many of you are not from this region. Being southern men, though, we do tip our hat to you for choosing the Institute to further your education and accept our values as your values. A big part of that acceptance is to know the history behind the cause. Even though you may be from New York or California or Missouri, you're here getting a military education at the flower of the South's military college, the Virginia Military Institute. There is no finer military college in the land.

"Yes, I know about West Point. I also know that it was General Blackjack Pershing who once said that West Point was the VMI of the North! The General of the Army, George Catlett Marshall, was from Pennsylvania. Where did he get his education? That's right; he marched right here on the same parade ground where you young men have already spilled your sweat, blood, and guts. General Marshall strove to learn about the southern military tradition—and that made him a better cadet for it."

After an hour of uplifting oratory, Lieutenant Colonel Jackson asked the cadets to stand and recite the oath of the society. Joe stole a glance at Jimmy with his eyebrows raised as the rats spoke as one, repeating the oath word by word after Jackson spoke each sentence.

You know, this isn't supposed to be mandatory. They haven't even signed us up, and we're already members whether we like it or not, he thought.

After completing his closing remarks, Professor Jackson noted that next Sunday there would be an open house at his quarters on the post, and that it was "highly recommended" that all attend.

The Following Monday

After completing several laps around the parade field the following Monday at 1100 hours, senior cadet Rock Granger called the squads to formation. Many of the cadets were still out of shape and struggling to keep up with the rest. Jimmy, of course, stood out for the opposite reason. He was in superb condition and could take anything the upperclassmen threw at him.

"Okay, Rats, listen up," Granger barked to the group of sweating men, most of them out of breath after doing their mandatory laps. "We're going to practice hand-to-hand combat drills. As some of you know, there may come a time when, due to circumstances beyond your control, you will not have a weapon in your possession. A bullet, an explosion, or any of a number of reasons on the battlefield can cause one to lose his weapon. So, you must be prepared to improvise with whatever capabilities you have at your disposal if that scenario should occur. Quite often, it's just these," he noted, smacking his knuckles together.

"Smith and Hodges, front and center".

"Rodgers, hold their weapons," Granger ordered with Cadet Rodgers gingerly taking control of the other cadets' rifles.

"Now, I want Smith here to show me how he is going to take down Hodges when Hodges throws a punch."

Both cadets looked at one another with a puzzled expression, not knowing what to do or expect. "Don't worry, Rats. I am going to show you pussies how it's done".

"Face me, Smith," Granger commanded the tall blond lanky cadet.

"Now, don't warn me; remember, no one gets a warning on the battlefield. You must be prepared at all times. Just surprise me by trying to punch me in the face. I mean full force; try to knock me out. If you don't, you're going to pull extra time out here on the parade field while everyone else gets to go to lunch. Do I make myself clear, Rat?" Granger poked his finger harshly in the rat's chest to make his point.

"Sir, yes, sir." Smith had gotten the point well. No sooner had Granger finished his poking when Cadet Smith swung hard and fast at the upperclassman's face. Smith didn't know what hit him. In a flash, Granger had parried the punch, stepped into Smith, and had flipped him completely over his shoulder. Smith landed in a heap on the hard parade ground, the wind completely knocked out of him. He was completely stunned and lay paralyzed for several minutes while the rats looked on.

Jimmy made the mistake of going over to Cadet Smith to lend him a hand. Granger lashed out at Jimmy. "Rat, did I tell you to help him up?" Granger harshly inquired of Jimmy.

Jimmy stood immediately at attention yelling somewhat defiantly at Granger, "Sir, no, sir!"

Granger now had an opportunity that had come sooner than expected to further harass Jimmy. "Front and center, Rat! Now, it's your turn. I've been watching you, and I know that you would love to take me out. You have an attitude problem, mister. Christ, I don't know what's worse, your attitude or your ugliness."

That last comment drew the ire of Jimmy, and the cadets standing in formation taking the scene in were none too pleased. "Okay, Rat, here's your chance; slug me, and don't warn me, or it's just going to be you and me out here all day. Don't think I don't have the power to do it either!"

Jimmy pulled a fast one on Granger by deliberately aiming his punch for the senior cadet's shoulder rather than his face. Granger was big, strong, and fast—and was more than a match for any rat who aimed a face punch at him. Jimmy thrust his right fist as fast as he could, connecting with Granger's left shoulder. There was a sickening smack as Jimmy's fist landed, knocking Granger backwards in surprise and anger. Wincing in pain, yet tough as nails, it didn't take Granger long to figure out Jimmy's ploy. His face now shrouded in menace, he stepped into Jimmy and attempted to throw him hard to teach this upstart rat a lesson. He was going to make this rat pay for stinging him like this in front of the other rats.

Jimmy was crouched using the strength in his legs and hips as leverage against the attempted throw. Granger couldn't throw him and was seething with anger at the "strong arm" technique of the rat.

"Oh, I see, Rat. You're trying to make me, your squad drill leader, look bad in front of these other rats. Is that it?"

Jimmy stiffened and replied, "Sir, no, sir."

"I think you are. That calls for punishment drills. The rest of you rats report over to Lieutenant Boyers for rifle drill. Mackenzie , I want three laps in full gear—and you're going to wear the medicine rucksack." Granger was referring to the knapsack that had fifty pounds of sand that was used by the upperclassmen for slackers or discipline problems. Most cadets could barely do a lap, let alone three, with it slung on their backs with full field gear and rifle.

After completing two laps, Jimmy was just about out of gas. Joe kept a wary eye on him as best he could from a distance while appearing to give total attention to the instruction from Lieutenant Boyers. What was apparent to Joe was that Granger had been running along side of him continually berating and hazing him about Jimmy's facial appearance and attitude problems.

Goddamn, that fucking Granger sure has it in for Jimmy. Shit, I told Jimmy not to show off, and now he's gone and made Granger look like a fool trying to throw him. I told him! Jimmy looks like he is going to flat pass out!

It was exasperating for Joe. Jimmy was his last lifeline at the Institute—his one and only buddy, the only motivator he had, and he was afraid that this whole thing was about to unravel in front of his very eyes.

"Pay attention, Rat!" Lieutenant Boyers had spotted Joe gazing at Jimmy in the distance, vomiting, stumbling, and weaving like a drunk while Granger screamed at him.

Joe had no sooner turned his attention back to Boyers than a number of cadets on the parade field began shouting in the general direction of Granger and Mackenzie and waving their hands. "Stop that now; stop fighting! We have to break that up! Get that rat off Lieutenant Granger!"

Unbeknownst to most of the rats and upperclassmen on the field that thought Lieutenant Granger was administering some much needed discipline to a rat that sorely needed it, what was taking place between the upperclassman and the rat had fast slipped out of control. While Jimmy had been struggling to finish his laps loaded down way beyond what was recommended for such a field exercise, Granger, hugely embarrassed by his failure to flip the rat in front of a group of rats, was losing it. He had screamed profanities at Jimmy that even a rat was not supposed to have to endure at the Institute, insulting Jimmy and his family to the point where it had struck a very raw nerve with Jimmy.

In his mind he was questioning how this upperclassman could insult his dead parents. He was saying how ugly his parents must have been. He had clearly gone over the line; and while Jimmy was nearly spent, when he came around the bend to begin lap number three and Granger was spitting invective and spittle in his face, that was the last straw.

Jimmy stopped dead in his tracks, slipped off his medicine pack, laid his rifle down—a cardinal sin at the Institute—and assumed a look that could only be described as a look of death.

As Granger bore into him to chastise Jimmy for his latest sins, Jimmy decked Granger with a vicious right punch to the nose, splitting Granger's nose like a busted watermelon, the blow knocking Granger backward and down for the count on the hard turf. Jimmy savagely jumped on the upperclassman, held his shoulders down with his knees, and pummeled Granger's face and head using the ground as a backstop with a rain of unrelenting blows. All of the fury of his days of being singled out by an upperclassman with issues, only because he was a very good cadet, was focused into each and every blow.

By the time the upperclassmen and rats drilling on the field had pulled Jimmy off, Granger was in grave danger of not surviving the attack.

Joe was in a very somber mood as he left his barracks to attend the open house for the Virginia Military Historical Society, hosted by Lieutenant Colonel Jackson at his post quarters. The quarters were located at the far left end of the parade field very close to Washington and Lee University. As he saluted the occasional officer whom he passed on his way to the open house, he was extremely troubled in two widely different areas. His most immediate concern was for the welfare of his fellow rat, friend, and roommate, Jimmy Mackenzie . The word was out that Jimmy was most certainly going to be expelled from the Institute for his violent attack on senior cadet Rock Granger, who was still in the hospital after the attack a week earlier. Jimmy was being confined on post by the authorities and had been allowed to see his aunt and uncle, as well as a high-powered attorney that his uncle's money had bought.

Joe had been allowed a brief visit, and Jimmy had mentioned during that visit that he was being verbally harassed by some of the upperclassmen that had been friends with Granger. There had been words to the effect that "We're going to get you for this, Rat" or "You're going to pay for this, Rat."

While Joe was worried about losing essentially his only support system at the Institute over this incident, his more immediate concern was what Jimmy had mentioned to him. The authorities in Lexington, the town cops, and the Virginia state police were looking into filing criminal charges against Jimmy for his assault. Joe knew that at some point in the near future Jimmy would have to face the Honors Committee at the Institute, and expulsion would be the outcome of that meeting.

Closely tied into this mess was Joe's concern about his own situation at VMI. He had already experienced some bizarre feelings of burnout whenever he sat down to study or do homework. It was as though he was being turned off by the academics. Somehow, his penchant for academic perfection that had held him literally in knots in high school was not meshing well here at the Institute. He thought that the academic load was heavy, and trying to balance that with the constant drilling and physical exercise regimen at the Institute was weighing heavily on him. He had relied on Jimmy to put things in perspective for him and had really missed Jimmy this past week as his study time became ever more intense.

Jesus, if Jimmy is out of here, I don't know what I am going to do. I'm glad I'm not in his shoes, though. Shit, now they're even talking criminal charges! Poor Jimmy. That son of a bitch Granger put unbearable pressure on him. Jimmy was just an innocent victim. I hope he has a good lawyer. Somehow, I need to get him some help.

As Joe walked into the opened door of Colonel Jackson's quarters, he tried to put those recent thoughts behind him to concentrate on what the colonel had to say about Virginia's finest.

"I'm mighty glad to see you cadets this evening at our open house," Colonel Jackson announced in the rather large, elaborate ballroom in his quarters. The colonel lived alone in his quarters, having lost his beloved wife of five years, Deborah, a number of years prior when she had passed away suddenly from a brain aneurysm. A huge ornate chandelier hung from the ceiling in the center of the ballroom. The colonel was once again resplendent in his dress greens and sipping on a yellow liquid in a cocktail glass. Cadets, of course, were not permitted to indulge in alcohol on post. Judging by the crimson face of the colonel nearly matching the color of his bright red handlebar mustache, there was a high probability that he was feeling no pain from an alcoholic drink of some sort.

Joe had heard many rumors concerning the colonel around the Institute. It was well known that he was a decorated veteran of an armed conflict having won both the Distinguished Service Cross as well as the Silver Star in combat. He was also quite vain almost in the manner of a Douglas MacArthur. Thomas Jackson was a serious student of military history and felt in many ways that he was not acknowledged by the powers that be at VMI for what he had brought to the military college. He was a native Virginian, an esteemed professor at the Institute, a combat veteran, and officer—really a throw back to the glory years of the military when the officer corps had been on a much higher pedestal than even its current stature. He was grandiose in his dress, appearance, and vocal offerings.

In many ways some of the cadets gravitated to him because his leadership qualities were mesmerizing to them. Here was a military officer in the flesh, a true son of Virginia, who had confronted a powerful enemy on foreign shores and had turned the tables on them. His DSC medal and Silver Star stood out prominently on his chest. Here was a tried and true leader of the United States Army in their presence.

There was no mystery that a number of cadets lingered around the colonel as he held court in his lavish quarters. There also had been rumors that if any of the cadets, especially those who were members of the Virginia Military Historical Society, had encountered trouble, the colonel was a good man to know. He was at constant odds with the superintendent on many issues concerning VMI such as his role in the top administrative meetings held to determine the Institute's policies and procedures, as well as the funding that was allocated for the colonel's favorite activity, the Military Society. Nonetheless, his contacts in the military outside of VMI more than made up for his lower rank and the fact that the super was his boss. The Vice-Chairman of the Joint Chiefs of Staff at the Pentagon, who wore three stars, just happened to be his good friend and hunting partner when they chose to get together during hunting season in the George Washington forest.

Joe had been made privy to all of this through his conversations with classmates. He knew that the colonel was frequently at odds with the super on administration issues at the Institute, and perhaps more importantly, Joe knew that the colonel was a man to have behind you in this place.

There were approximately one hundred rats milling about as the colonel clapped his hands for silence. "Cadets, make sure that you sign in on the society's membership roster and that you have taken all of the handouts and fliers at the front desk. These items will give you all a background and history of the society and what we're trying to accomplish. I am happy that you all came this evening."

Gesturing to his right, he pointed out his aide, Captain Henson, as a point of introduction to the cadets. "One of the problems that we have been facing at the Institute is funding for the research that we carry on here in the society. I am striving mightily with the superintendent to correct his lack of concern in this area." Colonel Jackson spoke with a trace of irritation in his voice.

After a half hour of going over the history of the society and its mission, he reminded the cadets that there was plenty of punch and snacks available for them before they left his quarters to return to the barracks.

Joe was beginning to have feelings similar to some of the cadets that felt the colonel was their idol. As he sipped on his punch with the cadets beginning to disperse, his mind drifted to the subject that worried him the most. *I wonder if the colonel could help Jimmy out? I know he doesn't particularly care for the super, and the word is out that the super is angry with Jimmy for assaulting a senior cadet—the nerve of a lowly rat to do such a stunt. The super probably doesn't know jack about how Granger was trying to destroy Jimmy. I also know that Colonel Jackson has contacts outside of the Institute. I need to speak with the colonel; he even mentioned tonight that if any of us members of the society felt like we weren't being treated properly or had a beef, we should speak with him.*

Well, here goes nothing.

With those last thoughts, Cadet Joseph Lynch eased over to where the colonel was holding court with his aide and two cadets. Joe stood just outside of the group; about to take a major gamble that bringing this issue up with Jackson just might backfire on him. He had to do it for Jimmy—and, yes, himself. Joe felt that Jimmy's future one way or the other would impact his at the Institute. He wasn't sure how long he could remain a cadet with Jimmy gone.

Joe continued to linger in the area, periodically glancing at the colonel before Jackson waved him over.

"Come over here, cadet," Colonel Jackson beckoned to Joe. "I see you have something on your mind." With his offer, both Jackson's aide and the two cadets went their separate ways, leaving Joe and the colonel alone.

Trying mightily to retain his composure in front of the great one, Joe cleared his throat. "Colonel Jackson, sir, can I speak privately with you concerning a matter here at the Institute?" Joe inquired.

Jackson's face lit up with a broad smile, and he placed his hand on Joe's shoulder. "Follow me, son."

Joe followed the colonel through an archway into the main quarters. He led Joe to his study where a fireplace was roaring, and the walls were filled with shelves of books on military history, accounts of battles, and military strategy.

"Have a seat, son," the colonel said.

After freshening up his drink, the colonel was interested in what Joe had to say. "What's on your mind, cadet?"

Joe squirmed a bit in his chair, overawed by the presence of the colonel and his charisma. "Colonel Jackson, sir, I have a serious problem. I am not sure if you can help," Joe said.

The colonel took a stiff belt from his fortified scotch and leaned in the direction of Joe. "Spit it out, son. I just might be able to help depending on what you have to tell me. Don't hold back; I need to hear every last thing you have to say."

Joe proceeded to go into the background of his problem—how he and Jimmy were good friends and roommates, how Jimmy was from Luray, Virginia, a comment that caused the colonel to beam. How Granger had harassed Jimmy, a good country boy from Virginia who just happened to be a strong cadet, to no end, and what had finally transpired. By the end of his narrative, the colonel had finished his second drink and was on another. He seemed to appear troubled when Joe described how well Jimmy had performed and been mercilessly chastised by Granger for his efforts.

There was a long pause after Joe had finished that seemed to last for five minutes before Jackson spoke. "I'm profoundly troubled by what you have just told me, son. You see, I used to be a rat at VMI a long time ago, and I was a young country boy from not too far from where Jimmy is from. And, yes, I was very good at handling everything the upperclassmen threw at me here. I remember they tried to break me several times with excessive PT and drilling. I didn't break, though, and that really pissed them off.

"That's been one of my issues with the boss here. We're all human; and while for the most part the upperclassmen do a commendable job with you rats whipping you into shape, I know from my own experience and what I've heard around here in recent years, that some of the first and second classmen have personal axes to grind because of their own failings.

"I used to watch Granger play ball, and he was a damn hard-nosed running back for us. I heard what happened to him. Hell, the officers here were wondering as much as the Corps what the hell had happened to Granger, how come he just stopped playing when he was only a third classman after scoring all of those touchdowns. We thought it might have been an academic or discipline issue and only learned later of his medical problems with all of those concussions.

"I have also received numerous complaints from rats here at the society about his behavior. Almost always, the complaints are from cadets who are known to perform exceedingly well on the drill field. I'm disappointed that with his stature as a first classman, he has these issues. Of course, the assault by Cadet Mackenzie adds a whole different dimension to this case.

"While I greatly sympathize with both Jimmy and yourself as his concerned friend and fellow rat, this will be an awful tough nut to crack, son. Between you and me, there is no chance that Jimmy will remain at the Institute. He is gone; there is nothing I can do about that. Now, if Granger can be persuaded not to file criminal charges against him, that might alleviate the damage that could be done to Cadet Mackenzie 's career—even outside the Institute long after he has left. I must say that might take some doing to bring about. As a member of the society and considering what you have told me about Cadet Mackenzie , I do feel an obligation to help at least with the criminal charge aspect."

The colonel leaned very close to Joe; almost appearing to resemble the caricature of President Lyndon Baines Johnson in one of his backroom power chats to get what he wanted out of some person or organization, and spoke in a hushed vein to Joe.

"Just between you and me, and not a word to another soul, this is our sacred trust. The only way I have been able to make any progress on administrative issues here is to use leverage against the super. Don't say a damn word to anybody about this. That son of a bitch has been a thorn in my side since he assumed command two years ago. He is from Illinois and has no more interest in the society than that Viet Cong I shot between the eyes years ago. He has been an obstacle to my getting ahead at the Institute. I've been up for full bird since he got here, and you think that son of a bitch has bothered to support me? Fuck no! We have to rid the Institute of him. The only way I have been able to move him is to let him know on occasion that I am privy to certain personal aspects of his life that he would rather not make public.

"Let me think on this a bit more. You be sure and come to the next meeting in a week, and we'll talk once again about a strategy to help Mackenzie ."

Thanking the colonel for his time and efforts, Joe stood and briskly saluted Jackson before he left. He headed back to the barracks in the dark of night with some newly found hope.

Whew, the colonel sure had a heavy whisky breath. Interesting, I wonder if Colonel Jackson knows about the super's messing around on his wife? Joe mused to himself as he lay in his cot, his hands clasped together behind his head.

Chapter 4

Virginia Military Institute—Lexington, Virginia

Colonel Thomas Mosby Jackson sat in front of his fireplace puffing on a large corncob pipe eerily similar to the one that General of the Army Douglas MacArthur had once smoked at the height of his Pacific Theater campaigns during World War II.

Goddamn, ain't that something. Granger got his ass whipped for hazing a rat—by the rat himself! That sumbitch probably deserved it. I've seen him out there dogging some of the better rats. That prick got what he deserved, picking on a nice Virginia country boy like Mackenzie . I bet old Betters is fit to be tied just waiting to make an example of another Virginia boy. I've nailed that bastard before, and just maybe I can use this episode to get him again. I'll make a deal with him. If he will recommend me for full bird and give me the grants I need for the society, I won't try to disrupt his drumming Mackenzie out of the Corps in disgrace and encouraging Granger to file criminal charges. I know damn well that's what he has on his mind. If he balks on this deal and calls my bluff, I am going to recommend a course of action to cadets Lynch and Mackenzie that will frost that sumbitch's balls.

With that trail of thought tailing off, Colonel Jackson tapped his pipe out for the evening and slugged down the last of his scotch with a very broad grin on his crimson, mustachioed face.

The Following Monday

"Aten Hut!" Captain Loretta Gadsden walked to the front of the freshman math class. "At ease, cadets," she said in a businesslike tone. There was a shuffling as the rats sat in unison in their chairs. "I will be your freshman math instructor for today. First Lieutenant Buxton has been given a special assignment by General Betters and will return as your instructor at 1400 hours tomorrow."

Cadet Joseph Lynch glanced up at the lady that he and Jimmy had seen in front of the motel a little over a week ago. *Damn, she is fine. I can sort of understand the super wanting to pork her. I bet she would be a good lay. She has the sweetest legs and tits I've seen in a while since I left home.*

A brief thought of Jimmy, however, put a damper on Joe's lusty musings. *Shit. I sure hope the colonel can speak with someone. Maybe he could ask the super to call the dogs off Jimmy. I guess I have to face the fact he is going to be expelled from the Corps. I sure would hate to see them bring criminal charges against him. That could ruin his life.*

As Professor Gadsden dived into her lecture going over college algebra, Joe tried to concentrate on the lecture. In high school he used to daydream much of the time during a teacher's lecture knowing full well that he could just study his books at night and get an "A" on an exam. However, at this level, the professors threw a ton of material at the students, and it really behooved a student to take copious notes in conjunction with hitting the books in the evening hours during study hall. He began to feel those unpleasant feelings once again and basically tuned the lecture out.

After class, he began to feel depressed for a number of reasons. His best friend was clearly on his way out of the Institute, and he just could not get into the proper frame of mind to concentrate on the academics. He performed well with the cadre during drills receiving rare kudos from the drill instructors for his efforts.

Near the end of the day at 1900 hours as he commenced studying for upcoming quizzes in his math, history, and English classes, he began to really doubt how much longer he could stay at the Institute.

The Next Day

"How are you today, young lady? Is the boss around?" It was time for Thomas Jackson to make his deal with the superintendent, and he hadn't wasted any time in going after the man at the top.

Linda Cropp, the general's fifty-something secretary with a platinum hairdo and overly made-up face, responded brightly to the colonel's inquiry. "Yes, Colonel Jackson, as a matter of fact he is. I will buzz him."

After she buzzed the general, Colonel Jackson walked up to the general's door and knocked.

"Enter," replied General Mark Betters, Superintendent of the Virginia Military Institute.

Colonel Jackson strode confidently into the general's office and stood at attention. General Betters held the colonel at bay for several minutes while he finished writing a letter on school stationary. Looking up to face Jackson with his mane of gray-streaked black hair, appearing to be disheveled with weary eyes, he did not appear to be happy to see Jackson.

"At ease, Colonel; what can I do for you today? Since I didn't call you in, you must have something on your mind. Looking for more money?"

Jackson winced at the sarcastic comment from Betters. There had long been an element of mutual hostility between the two men ever since Betters had made superintendent. While Brigadier General James Kelley was the official second in command at the Institute as the Commandant of Cadets, in reality he was nothing more than a paper figure. Even though he outranked Colonel Jackson by two levels of rank, Brigadier General Kelley was nothing more than a paper pusher who did not care to place himself in the line of administrative fire. He preferred to stay in the background while the real second in command, Lieutenant Colonel Jackson, sparred with the boss for control of the Institute. With Jackson's connections in the Pentagon and with his advertised aspirations for promotion and eventual full command of the Institute, General Betters frequently made it a point to tread lightly on his decorated and popular history professor.

Betters was, however, combative in nature; and while he couldn't or wouldn't bring the ax down on Jackson's head whenever they had a difference of opinion, he could make life unpleasant for Jackson. Betters did not ask Jackson to sit, an act that was a dig at the colonel and did not go unnoticed by Jackson.

"No, sir, I am not requesting funds for the society at the moment," Jackson replied equally sarcastically. "However, I do have a favor to ask of you, General, if you don't mind."

Betters sneered at Jackson and cut him a short reply. "Do I have a choice?"

Jackson would have loved to cold cock the bastard, yet he knew his time would eventually come when he just might let the world know about this philandering prick and close his career out on a downer.

"General, it has come to my attention that one of my society members, a rat named Jimmy Mackenzie , is being held in confinement because of a violation here at the Institute."

Betters had become weary of Jackson's preferential treatment of his "society" members, especially the rats from Virginia. Every time an issue came up over discipline and it was one of his people from Virginia, this guy wanted a sit rep. Betters took a sip from his mug of coffee before responding.

"Colonel, I don't really have the time to waste concerning routine matters of discipline here at the Institute. If a cadet is deemed to be in violation of any of the tenets of the Honors System or has committed a heinous act such as what I have heard regarding Cadet James Mackenzie , it's really none of your concern. It is the concern only of the top levels of administration here at VMI.

That includes General Kelley, his aides, and immediate staff, as well as the superintendent, his aides, and staff—and, indeed, the proper authorities that will administer the kind of justice that Mackenzie deserves for nearly killing first classman Rock Granger.

"I really don't have the time to go over issues of privacy such as this with you. It is none of your business, and I am ordering you to mind your own business and stay the hell out of high-level administrative affairs here at the Institute. Is that clear, Colonel?"

Colonel Thomas Jackson felt as though he had been kicked in the face. He really wanted to jump over the general's desk and strangle this prick right now. However, he held his temper in check. "Yes, sir, I do get your drift. However, it is my duty to go on record and state that it is, in fact, my prerogative to inquire into exactly what happened concerning one of my cadets. I don't really expect you to honor my request. Perhaps there is another request that you might honor."

Looking impatiently at Jackson, Betters replied wearily, "Make it quick, Colonel; you're beginning to grate on me and ruin my day."

Since Betters continued to be an ass about his meeting with him, Jackson decided to dig in and slug it out. He walked up to the edge of Betters' desk and looking the general squarely in the eye with both hands on the general's desk in a clear show of disrespect, one hand containing a sheet of paper, the colonel let it all out.

"Look, Markie, here's the deal. I know you people are going to drum Mackenzie out, and there ain't a damn thing I or anyone else can do about it. However, I've heard about Granger, and he has issues that he takes out on our best cadets. I do want your job one of these days, the sooner the better. And, I damn sure am not going to let first and second classmen here with attitudes fuck over our promising rats, especially if they are society rats.

"So, Markie, like I said, here's the deal. I've been a nice guy. I have it written down on a piece of paper for you so you can understand it."

With that last stern statement from the colonel to his boss, he tossed a sheet of paper at the general and abruptly walked out of the office of the superintendent.

After the colonel had closed the door behind him, General Betters, still red and shaken from being insulted by a subordinate, gingerly opened up the piece of paper. What he read only deepened the shade of red on his face.

After reading the list of demands from the colonel, he buzzed his secretary to bring him a glass with three ice cubes. His hands were shaking slightly as Mrs. Cropp passed the glass to the general. After she returned to her desk, Betters twisted in his chair to open up the credenza behind his desk and pull out a decanter of Johnny Walker Blue Scotch, one of the most expensive scotch whiskies at two hundred something per bottle. He poured himself a full glass, took a stiff belt of the fiery liquid, and mulled over what the colonel had requested on his list.

That stupid idiot! He is demanding that I recommend immediately that he receive promotion to full colonel and that I give him virtually unlimited funds for his society. If I don't do so, he will inform the local newspapers including some of the big ones on the East Coast, The Washington Post and The New York Times, that the superintendent of VMI has been seen hustling females, in effect, cheating on his wife, Mrs. Betters, which reflects a horrible example for the cadets of VMI who cannot lie, cheat, or steal, or else face expulsion. That son of a bitch is trying to bribe me for a promotion!

Fuck him. I am going to call his bluff. I am going to send a note to that bastard and tell him if he so much as leaks a drop out that Mark Betters is getting trim on the side, I will fire him on the spot on the grounds that he made this up and is bribing me into recommending him for full bird. I'll fix that creep!

Taking another stiff belt, he felt his old combative spirits returning. No one was going to bribe him. He was the top dog, and he didn't get to this position by being a wimp.

CHAPTER 5

Virginia Military Institute—Lexington, Virginia

"Colonel, sir, I have a written document for you. Looks like it's from topside." Captain Henson, Colonel Jackson's aide, had just rapped on the door of the great man's study. Jackson had been relaxing on a Monday evening with his drink and corncob pipe winding down from a full day of lecture on military history and battlefield strategy as related to World War I.

Since he had delivered his written demands to the superintendent of VMI last Friday, he was feeling good about himself. He knew that he had the goods on the general. He had long ago brought in several of his senior and most loyal cadets and told them to keep an eye out for Captain Gadsden and the super. Jackson had seen them a few times in the administrative offices when he had been up there campaigning for funds and noticed the telltale signs of obvious affection that came from every look, wink, and slight brush that was supposed to go undetected by others. The colonel knew they were up to no good.

Having had a history of hostile dealings with the general over the importance of Jackson's role at the Institute on many occasions, Jackson had made it a priority to try to find out just what was going on between the math professor and the super. To that end he had made it a point to follow the general in his comings and goings around Lexington. Jackson began to realize what a golden opportunity he just might have to use as leverage against the general should Betters kick him one time too many. With the constant activity in and around the general's offices, Jackson felt it highly unlikely that the two officers would engage in a tryst in Betters' office behind locked doors; a moan or a muffled scream might be heard and would raise eyebrows and suspicion.

One late Saturday night, Jackson just happened to be coming out of a local bar on South Main Street when he thought he noticed a male and female bearing a strong resemblance to the couple firmly in his mind at the time. They appeared to be in disguise and coming out of the Lexington Inn, a bed-and-breakfast establishment. Jackson was puzzled as to the boldness of the general in not at least traveling some distance from Lexington to engage in his trysts, although in that regard Jackson was aware of two things: Betters found it difficult to escape from the demands of his job at the Institute for any lengthy period of time, and General Betters felt he was immune from being found out to the point where he thought that if his identity were discovered, people would simply look the other way.

To enhance his spying on Betters, he had enlisted the support of his closest and most loyal cadets. He had given them notes of what to look for, the identity of the parties in question, photos of each in civilian clothes, photos of the vehicles each used, and establishments the couple had been known to frequent. He wanted all the dirt he could get on the general, including more notes and pictures. He even promised the cadets a thousand dollars apiece if they could clandestinely film the general and his mistress having sex.

Yes, as he sipped his drink and puffed contentedly on his pipe, he knew that the general would have no choice. Colonel Thomas Jackson would soon be a full colonel, and the Virginia Military Historical Society's coffers would be full. Those were pleasant thoughts.

"Enter," the colonel replied. Captain Henson walked over to the corner of the study where Jackson was gazing out onto the darkened parade field and passed the leather-bound package to Jackson. "Let me take a look at the document, Captain."

After taking the package and noting it was from the offices of the superintendent, Jackson dismissed Henson.

Smelling the rich leather and fingering the package first, he became almost gleeful, and a broad smile began to form on his crimson face. He was like a kid with a new toy. This was no doubt the general's immediate response to his list of demands.

Damn! I am going to make full bird! Jackson happily mused.

He gingerly removed the straps, flipped open the cover, and pulled out the contents.

He began to read the letter and was not happy at what he read. In effect, General Mark Betters had called his bluff. The general stipulated in the letter that as superintendent of VMI, he would not be browbeaten, blackmailed, or blackballed into recommending a promotion to an officer under his command, especially a "country bumpkin joker" who was not deserving of such. Furthermore, if he received any further threats from the colonel, he—General Mark Betters—would personally fire Jackson on the spot and have him discharged from the U.S. Army posthaste for conduct unbecoming an officer. As of this moment he was relieved of all administrative functions at the Institute and would have to forward his request for funds through the proper channels, e.g. Brigadier General James Kelley, the official second in command at VMI. Kelly would have full discretion to deny Jackson the funding on his own authority.

After reading the letter, Jackson stuffed it back into the leather case and threw it across his study. He walked over to the liquor cabinet and poured himself another stiff drink, seething with rage.

That no good slimy son of a bitch. That philandering bastard. I will get him one way or the other. He can call my bluff on the promotion; maybe that was a stupid move on my part. Probably shouldn't have sent him a list on paper like that. That is evidence of blackmail. He probably won't take it any farther, though, if I don't press the issue. That idiot is aware of my connections. Shit!

He tapped out his pipe and stuffed it once again with an expensive brand of Turkish Latakia tobacco one of his Air Force buddies had smuggled stateside to him while stationed at the Incerlik Air Force Base in Turkey. After lighting up and taking several stiff belts from his glass, he began to engineer an alternate strategy. As he thought about Plan B for several minutes, the old smile returned once again, and the colonel began to take copious notes for the next two hours on his next course of operations.

The Next Evening—1900 Hours

"In summary, cadets, it appears that the administration is going to deny us additional funding for the remainder of this semester. Accordingly, our field trips to the Manassas and Antietam battlefields will have to be temporarily canceled. While I know that you all are disappointed, certainly no more than I am, we will prevail in the end. I have developed some plans to enable us to continue in full with our activities here at the society. Cadets Lynch, Mickelson, Schmidt, and Graves, front and center. The rest of you I will see tomorrow in class. Dismissed."

Before the administration had got wind of it, the colonel had put out the word through the Corps of Cadets, starting with the senior leadership, that he was summoning society members to a special closed-door session during the middle of the week, Wednesday, after supper mess. He was winding down the session and needed to speak with Joe Lynch, his troubled cadet, as well as the three cadets who were most loyal to him. Indeed, they had accumulated much information on the activities of the general and his mistress.

As the four cadets hustled close to the colonel, he directed them to his study in his quarters. Closing the door behind him, he was about to present his next course of action against the super.

"Gentlemen, be seated. As you have known for some time, the superintendent has been a PIA, a real thorn in my side, indeed in the side of our society here at the Institute. I believe just between us that he would like nothing better than to dismantle our operations. I won't allow that to happen. While I dislike having to bring up personal issues to use in this instance, I believe that when certain questionable activities committed by the super run counter to the goals and moral fiber we are attempting to instill in our cadets here at the Institute through the Honors System, I have no choice but to act.

Accordingly, here is what I have on my mind. You all know about Cadet Mackenzie 's clusterfuck here at the Institute."

The cadets nodded in unison.

"Now, Betters is looking to make an example of a society cadet, a damn good one if I might add, by drumming Mackenzie out of the Institute for assaulting Granger. I know Betters; he has a major beef with me, and he would like nothing better than to denigrate the society and what we all stand for. He is threatened by my aspirations for a top leadership position here at the Institute.

"After drumming Mackenzie out, I believe it likely that he will meet with Granger and have Granger file criminal charges so that Mackenzie will be jailed in downtown Lexington awaiting charges after he has been kicked out. Betters will announce to the local papers that Mackenzie is an example of how we operate here in the society. That we are a bunch of warmongers who can't remain in line here at the Institute, and that as the superintendent, he had no choice but to rein in a rogue cadet and send him home packing.

"Gentlemen, we can't let that happen. I will not let that stand. It has gotten so bad that Betters even sent me a letter threatening to fire me on the spot for no good reason!" With that statement all of the cadets looked down at the shiny wood floor of the colonel's study in apparent depression.

"Here is what we are going to do. Lynch, I know you told me that Mackenzie has a very good attorney that his uncle has procured for him." Handing Joe a package of materials enclosed in a sealed folder, Jackson proceeded to outline his plan to the cadets. He knew that Mackenzie was going to be called in front of the Honors System to face expulsion from the Institute the following Monday at 1100 hours.

Although there had been no word yet from Granger or his representatives, the colonel was virtually certain that criminal charges would be filed ending any chance that Mackenzie , a true son of Virginia, would ever be able to enter military service. The colonel thought that was a shame. He knew Mackenzie had great potential as a soldier and that Granger had driven him over the edge. Hell, any man could be driven over the edge by forces beyond his control.

He instructed Cadet Lynch to call Mackenzie 's uncle in Luray that evening from the colonel's quarters and to ask him to meet with him this weekend to receive these materials of evidence to be used at the Honors Committee meeting. He instructed Lynch to tell the uncle that the contents would eliminate the possibility of his nephew receiving criminal charges and to call Jackson if he needed clarification. Upon receiving the documents, the uncle was to request a meeting with his son prior to the Honors Committee meeting and slip the package to Mackenzie . Colonel Jackson explained to Joe that the package contained a cover letter to the Honors Committee and the superintendent detailing the contents, and that if Cadet Mackenzie were issued criminal charges based on his conduct here at the Institute with regards to Cadet Granger, copies of the contents would be distributed to the *Lexington Star,* the *Baltimore Sun,* the *Washington Post* and the *New York Times,* among several other prominent newspapers for distribution to the general public.

The contents contained among other damning evidence against General Betters a roll of eight-millimeter film revealing footage and sound of Betters and Gadsden engaging in rough sex interlaced with foul language. Parts of the film showed Captain Gadsden riding on top of General Betters, both totally in the buff in their room at the Lexington Bed and Breakfast in Lexington, Virginia. Her buttocks with several prominent stretch marks could be clearly made out as she wildly humped the general while stimulating her own breasts with each hand. While this activity was taking place, she was moaning and yelling at the general to move faster in grossly foul language. Another portion of the film had the captain engaging in oral sex with her partner. Still another revealing piece of footage had the general's head burrowed in Gadsden's crotch with both of her legs wrapped around Betters' back. The only items of clothing she wore were black silky stockings and shiny black pumps. While the footage showed Gadsden's face, there were only glancing shots of the general's visage. However, his cap depicting the two stars of his rank was clearly visible on the edge of the bed.

Cadet Graves had spied on the two lovers from the very moment they had entered the Lexington Bed and Breakfast. Unbeknownst to the proprietors of the establishment, the individual who worked at the front desk was on the colonel's payroll as well and had greatly facilitated Graves' spy operation by lending the cadet a key to the general's room. When the lovers were spotted in the lounge next to the Lexington Bed and Breakfast having drinks during a break from their tryst, Graves had sneaked into the room before the general and his mistress had returned. He waited for the most intense and passionate periods of lovemaking to get underway where both sex partners would be oblivious to their surroundings as they made furious love to one another.

Graves had used an expensive and newly developed camcorder, clandestinely filming the action quickly as he moved in stealth around the lovers' room in dim light. Since the room was unusually large, the cadet had zoomed in on the action while squatting in different corners of the room masking his presence behind different pieces of furniture. The colonel had presented Graves a thousand dollars in cash for his brave actions under potentially hostile conditions. Indeed, Cadet Graves had no doubt risked his career at VMI and perhaps beyond by undertaking an operation that could have brought him great harm if he had been caught in the act himself. If the public and the military became aware of this film detailing the sexual misconduct of Betters and Gadsden, both would no doubt be immediately relieved of their duties at the Institute, thereby paving the way for Colonel Jackson to move up the chain of command.

If Jackson couldn't directly blackmail the general for his promotion, he could certainly go about it in an indirect manner with the added benefit of perhaps saving Mackenzie 's career outside of VMI.

After passing the package to Joe, the colonel summarized the plan. "Thanks to some outstanding black OPS surveillance from Cadet Graves, we have come up with some evidentiary materials that should alleviate the possibility of criminal charges being filed against Cadet Mackenzie . Furthermore, the administration just might view us in a different light. Gentlemen, I view this as win-win. The cover letter is not signed, and none of you are privy to these materials for obvious legal reasons. Lynch, you are not to open the package. Instruct Mackenzie and his uncle not to open the package. Cadet Mackenzie should present the sealed package to the Honors Committee chairman Monday at 1100 hours. Mackenzie will indicate to the committee that he was presented the package in confidence; the identity of the individuals presenting the package cannot be revealed due to issues of privacy and legality. This should occur when Cadet Mackenzie is asked if he has any evidence on his behalf to present."

Smiling broadly, the colonel strove to end this session with his loyal cadets on a positive note. "Gentlemen, I think we have a viable plan that will bring about the necessary changes here at the Institute that will greatly benefit all of us. It is a damn shame that we will lose Mackenzie . He is a damn fine cadet. He was shafted. However, he and the Virginia Military Historical Society will have our day in court, and it will be a new day, indeed.

"Cadet Lynch, follow my orders to the T! Is that understood?"

As the cadets shuffled to their feet with Joe holding the prized package, Joe snapped a brisk salute to the colonel. "Sir, yes, sir. I will follow your orders exactly as you have issued them, sir."

Jackson stood in his dress greens and trademark beret, his newly found bravado in full bloom once again. "Dismissed," Colonel Thomas Mosby Jackson barked.

Chapter 6

Virginia Military Institute—Lexington, Virginia
The Following Monday—1100 Hours

Much had transpired over the past two weeks at the Institute, not all of it a cause of celebration for the Virginia Military Historical Society. After Cadet Mackenzie was summoned to the Honors Court, he had, in effect, been verbally humiliated by all present. He was told he was a disgrace to the Institute for committing one of the gravest violations ever witnessed at VMI—nearly mauling to death a senior cadet, one of the football team's greatest running backs who had given it his all on the playing field. As nasty as Granger's reputation had become in the past two years on post, upperclassmen and professors who had seen the hard-nosed cadet in action helping his team upset bigger, stronger, more talented squads from civilian universities still professed an admiration for his courage and fortitude on the field of battle. Indeed, Granger in his freshman year had become a legend in his own right with his relatively quick mastery of the military drills and PT exercises required by all rats to perform.

While he was a merciless and unsympathetic senior cadet who ragged on rats constantly, there was great consternation that a rat—the bottom of the totem pole at the Institute—had the audacity to put one of their own in the hospital. Cadet Mackenzie was told he was to never set foot on the campus for the rest of his life; he was variously described as a rogue, an out-of-control freight train gone wild, and a loose cannon among citizen-soldiers.

Sneering at Cadet Mackenzie , the senior cadet in charge of the honors proceedings, Lieutenant Jacob Byers from Athens, Georgia, lashed out at him in his deep, southern drawl. "Mackenzie , after carefully and deliberately ruling on your case, the Honors Committee has recommended that you be terminated effective immediately from Virginia Military Institute. If you so much as even think about setting foot on post, you will be detained forthwith and turned over to the authorities for trespassing. Don't even think about sending any of your sons here; they will not be welcome. The Institute will keep an eye out for you from this point on. We are watching you, mister.

"It is my understanding that Cadet Granger is going to file criminal charges for your chicken-shit attack on him when his guard was down. That was a cowardly act—the stunt that you pulled, Rat. Did I call you a rat? My mistake, you are no longer a rat; you are less than a rat, mister. You are a disgrace to the Institute and to the state of Virginia. I don't know where you are going to go or if you will somehow be able to get these charges dismissed. Believe me, if the military or any civilian agencies, even a drug store or filling station, asks us for a recommendation, I think you already know what you are going to get from us—a big fat zero, Mackenzie .

"Now, is there anything you would like to say for yourself before you are sent in disgrace away from this post?"

Jimmy Mackenzie knew beforehand that he was going to be verbally chastised and humiliated by the Honors Court. Yet, after the visit by his friend, Joe Lynch, and his uncle, just two days before his session at the court where Joe had not followed the colonel's instructions to the T as he had been commanded, Jimmy could not wait to shove the sealed package Joe had given him into the face of the Honors chairman. Joe had strongly alluded to the fact based on a whispered conversation from Cadet Graves, a statement of profound gravity, what they had on the super was going to cause the Institute's entire case against Mackenzie to be thrown out. Joe told Jimmy about the graphic pictures that were in the package. They had laughed all night in their respective barracks over the incident. Wow! Captain Gadsden riding the super as if she were riding a bucking bronco! Jimmy and Joe had been amazed that the colonel, as well as other cadets, was aware of the general's messing around on his wife.

Jimmy walked up to the Honors chairman and slammed the briefcase he had been carrying into the chairman's chest. "What I have to say is in this briefcase. Just make sure that you and the super see it before I send copies to all of the newspapers on the East Coast."

Lieutenant Byers appeared stunned by Jimmy's sudden and emphatic action. Recovering quickly, he barked at Cadet Mackenzie . "Stand down, mister! I see you haven't learned your lesson yet. I am thinking of confining you for another week based on this behavior."

Jimmy responded almost immediately, pointing his right finger at the senior cadet. "Jake, just open the fuckin thing now or you will regret it. If you don't, *you* will be the one facing charges by the super, if you get my drift. You can detain me if you want, but I don't think you will be around much longer if you do. If I am not let out of here by tomorrow, my attorney—you all may have heard of him, Ignatious Marcellus Rain—is going to immediately conduct a press conference in downtown Lexington and show all of the pictures in that package to the press." Jimmy had alluded to the popularity of one of the country's finest criminal lawyers based in Roanoke, Virginia.

He continued with his rant. "And you know what? He is going to go to the Pentagon and hold a press conference there to offer the news services the roll of film and documentation. You better slow your roll and check out them pictures now, boss man. I just hope you got a good film projector."

The Honors chairman, his face flushed with embarrassment at being dressed down by a rat in such a manner and body slammed with a briefcase to add insult to injury, was stunned by this sudden development. He retreated to the panel and opened the package in full view of all of the committee members. There was a collective gasp at what they saw—lewd pictures, documentation describing each of the film sequences and the damning roll of film itself. The committee took a full ten minutes to look over the materials before Cadet Lieutenant Byers once again summoned Cadet Mackenzie to appear before the panel front and center.

"Cadet Mackenzie , don't do anything rash. We will get back to you within two hours regarding the contents of this package. Dismissed," the Honors chairman squeaked as Jimmy was taken back to his cell.

Within one hour, two upperclassmen had delivered a letter on administration stationery signed by Superintendent Betters to Jimmy with words to the effect that while the Institute deeply regretted having to expel Jimmy over his assault of Cadet Rock Granger, Granger had elected not to file criminal charges against Jimmy over the incident. No permanent record would be retained of the assault, and VMI would administratively expunge any references to the incident. Jimmy was free to leave the Institute with no hard feelings. He could apply for any job, join the military, or apply to another college without any worries of the incident being brought up. As a matter of fact, the superintendent had on file a glowing recommendation of Jimmy that he would use should the Institute be asked to provide a reference. The official word was that Jimmy had to resign from the Institute due to a serious illness in his family that required his continued presence.

"Here's to Colonel Jackson, Hoo-rah!" shouted Cadet Mickelson to the group of rats assembled in Lieutenant Colonel Jackson's quarters for a meeting of the Virginia Military Historical Society. "Hoo-rah!" shouted the throng of rats in unison.

At the center of nearly one hundred cadets jammed into the banquet room of Jackson's quarters the atmosphere was indeed festive. Jackson was once again beaming and holding court for the cadets.

Within one hour of seeing the contents of the folder that had been passed to him by Lieutenant Byers, General Betters had cleared everyone out of his office while he made a phone call to Cadet Granger and hastily prepared a letter to be delivered immediately to Jimmy Mackenzie . After completing the letter, he had poured himself a double Johnny Walker Blue neat and dialed the personal phone number of Colonel Jackson. Jackson had picked up the phone in his study. "Colonel Jackson here," he spoke firmly into the receiver.

"Jackson, this is General Betters," he hissed. "I hope you are satisfied. I know good and damn well what you just pulled. You are the lowest of the low, Jackson."

Before he could continue on his rant, Jackson interrupted him. "I am the lowest of the low? I think you got it wrong, Betters. I have no idea what you are talking about. The only thing I am going to say, sir, is that you have some nerve to say I am the lowest of the low. I know otherwise. You are a disgrace to the Institute and should be replaced. I heard rumors from some of my people of what you are alluding to. I heard you let Mackenzie leave with no criminal charges. That was sweet. How about Colonel Jackson? What is his fate if I might ask, General?"

There was a long silence on the other end of the line. Finally, after clearing his throat, the general slurred his response, and Jackson could hear the ice cubes jingling in the general's glass. "Colonel Jackson, I have recommended you for a promotion to full colonel ASAP; the paperwork has already been cut. Furthermore, regarding any future outlays of funds, I have given you carte blanche to request the funds for your society directly from me. That is all."

Before Jackson could respond, the line went dead.

Looking around at the throng of cadets and savoring his soon-to-be promotion to full bird, Colonel Jackson spoke. "Tonight, cadets, I bring you excellent news. The superintendent, our own General Mark Betters, has decided to recommend me for promotion."

As the yells and clapping began, Jackson motioned for the cadets to be quiet. "And, the general has given me full authority to demand all of the funding we need to keep the society going at full tilt."

The cheers and shouting continued in such force that even across the parade grounds at his residence, General Betters, nursing his fourth drink of the day and clearly intoxicated, could hear the celebration before passing out on his couch.

Chapter 7

Route 81—North of Lexington, Virginia—One Week Later

If there were ever a time in his young life that he had felt this low, Joe Lynch could not remember it. Two days after the celebration at the colonel's quarters, something came over Joe that he could not get a handle on. His feelings of being overwhelmed at VMI turned into bouts of depression as he obsessed over his friend Jimmy leaving the Institute even though Jimmy himself seemed to accept his fate with humor.

Jimmy had dropped by the barracks as he was checking out of the Institute with his duffel bag to bid farewell to his fellow rat buddies. Joe remembered Jimmy's wry smile as he stood at the door to his room. "Hey, man, going to miss you, Joe," Jimmy said as he casually leaned into the doorway.

"I am not sure how long I am going to be here myself, Jimmy," Joe somberly replied.

Jimmy frowned at Joe and then lit into him. "Look, Joe, we have talked about this before. You have got to settle yourself down, get your major changed, and just concentrate on the basics here, dude. You don't have to get a 4.0 here. Just settle for a C average. Learn the military shit, do what the fuck they tell you to do, and just get by," Jimmy pleaded to Joe.

Exasperated, Joe had thrown both of his arms in the air as if totally resigned to his fate. "Naw, man, I know enough about myself that I can't settle for just being average. Jimmy, I just can't do this! I can't do what I did in high school! I am locked in to a way of thinking and don't know how to get out of it.

"As long as you were here, I felt like I had a buddy to go through this with. Now I don't have jack shit."

Jimmy nodded slowly. "Well, Joe, I can't change you; you will have to do what you have to do, buddy. Your shit is too complex for me. I just feel lucky to have survived the mess that Granger started. The sumbitch ruined my career here at VMI, egging me on, egging me on. That dude was a no good prick, and he got what he deserved."

Joe smiled weakly at Jimmy. "That's the one thing that I can smile about. You got vindicated. Thanks to the colonel; he made things right."

Jimmy tried yet another approach with Joe to get him to reconsider leaving VMI, yet suspected that it was useless to try to continue to persuade Joe to stay. "Joe, why don't you talk with the colonel about how you feel? I know he could motivate you to stay."

"Naw, Jimmy," Joe replied. "My mind is made up. I have already called my parents, and they are heading down here to pick me up."

"What did the lieutenant say?" Jimmy inquired.

Joe shrugged his shoulders. "It was kind of confusing. After drills yesterday on the parade ground, he told me he was sorry to see me go. He said I would have made a helluva cadet. Then, this morning he was ragging on me for quitting. Captain Johnson called me into his office and tried a similar tactic. He lit up a big cigar and told me that I could be a great officer in the Army. Then when I told him I still planned to leave, he got pissed off and called me a quitter. Guess he was trying to motivate me into staying. The entire Corps looks upon me with disgust. I've gone through too much in the past few days to turn back now, Jimmy. I'm outta here."

Jimmy grabbed Joe's hand and gave him a hefty shake, pumping his arm up and down vigorously. "Well, Joe, you take care and stay in touch, partner. You have my uncle's home phone number."

"Don't worry, man; I will call you. See you around," Joe replied with a hint of emotion in his voice.

Jimmy had then hurried away from Joe's barracks to meet his uncle waiting for him outside of the barracks. Joe wondered if he would ever see Jimmy again.

"What are you going to do now, Joe?" Joe's mother had turned around to look at her son in the backseat of their Oldsmobile as they headed back to their home in Maryland north on Route 81 in the Shenandoah Valley. Joe had been gazing up from the valley where the meandering road snaked between mountain peaks that seemed to reach to the sky. He shrugged his shoulders, later recalling that on that ride home, he had felt a plethora of wildly different emotions.

While relieved to be away from the pressure, most of which he had brought upon himself, Joe felt as if he were being literally overcome by a massive anvil of humiliation and depression. Just months ago at his high school graduation as the president of his senior class, he had been so upbeat. Now he was so low he wished he could just fly away to somewhere far from here, though he was in desperate need of love and support from his close-knit family. If there was a feeling of being dysfunctional, Joe felt that he had truly reached the horrible abyss of confusion and chaotic mindset that only a horrific emotional blow could take on the soul of an individual.

I just need to go home to my bedroom where I can think and get some rest, he thought to himself.

Glancing toward his mother, he really didn't feel much like talking at the moment. "Ma, I don't know. Maybe I can still get into one of the other schools I applied to."

His dad spoke with equal consternation. "Christ, Joe, you have a tendency to go to pieces when things get tough. You've got to get a better handle on how to deal with these things."

His mother chimed in once again. "God, Joe, we were mortified when we found out you wanted to leave VMI!"

About the only silent support Joe received was from his siblings. His younger sister Anna was sitting between her parents in the front seat, and his brother Bill, much closer in age to himself being just two years apart, sat opposite Joe in the backseat. Anna and Bill had looks that Joe could only remember as bewildered at the time.

Finally, after several moments of uncomfortable silence, Joe's dad sought to somewhat ease the pain for everyone. He glanced briefly in the rearview mirror at Joe before mentioning words that Joe would never forget. "Well, son, we can't let this get us down. You'll have other opportunities to get beyond this; there are other schools. You're going to be okay."

Joe felt a bit of hope and relief after hearing his dad's words. He understood perhaps for the first time in his life that despite his father's stern discipline and rugged constitution, his dad was really a man who truly loved his son.

Joe leaned his head back, relaxed for the first time in a month, and nodded off as the Olds headed home.

Chapter 8

Virginia Military Institute—Lexington, Virginia (Colonel Jackson's Quarters)—Six Months Later—Tuesday Evening—1730 hours

Colonel Thomas Mosby Jackson opened the faculty newsletter that Captain Henson had just handed him. After quickly glancing at some of the highlights on the front page, one short article quickly grabbed his attention.

"I'll be damned," Jackson muttered to no one in particular.

As Henson stood near his desk, he became curious at the colonel's short remark. "What is it, Colonel?" Henson inquired.

"Cliff is getting out effective 30 June. Shit, that's next month," Jackson replied. He continued to read on. "Says here that he has his twenty and is looking forward to retirement." The colonel was referring to the professor of English Literature at VMI, Major Cliff Johnston.

Looking suddenly angry and noting that it was nearly 1800 hours, the hour he normally used as a marker for his first drink, he abruptly left his chair and walked over to his wet bar where he hastily made a Chevas and soda over rocks. He took a swig of the golden liquid and squinted with another bout of developing anger and frustration at Captain Henson. The captain began to understand why the colonel's cheeks were turning scarlet.

Colonel Jackson knew that once he had officially been approved by the chain of command at the Pentagon for full colonel, this also would be a newsworthy item in the faculty newsletter, although he would have known many days before the publication of any issue announcing his promotion to full bird. This was just another reminder that the superintendent or the chain of command, hell, somebody was holding up his damn promotion.

"You know, Captain, I sometimes wonder if Betters really recommended me for a promotion to topside." Taking another hit off his drink, he warmed to the subject. "I mean Betters told me months ago—Christ, he called me on this very phone and told me he was recommending me for full bird. I hope he isn't up to any monkey business."

Henson looked perplexed. "How so, sir? He told you he was cutting the paperwork; that would be a flagrant lie if he didn't follow up on what he promised."

Jackson looked Henson squarely in the eyes, his red mustache quivering with anger. "I know Betters, and he is a conniving son of a bitch. Sure, he could say he recommended me for promotion on the phone; however, I have asked him on several occasions in the past few months how the promotion was going only to have him say it is tied up at the Pentagon. Apparently, they have bigger fish to fry, so says the general.

"Henson, I have been too complacent about this. I've gotten full of myself and caught up in a false rush I am afraid. Seeing this newsletter once again just reminded me of how many months have gone by without a word from that bastard. He is a wicked man. I know that he absolutely hates the fact that I have got him by the balls. I need to ring up my contact at the Pentagon, General Gibson, who just happens to be next in line for the top job there and see if he can find anything out about my paperwork."

Captain Henson was about ready to leave for the day as the colonel washed down the last of his drink. "Well, sir, I am going to call it a day. I certainly wish you the best regarding your promotion. You deserve nothing but the best, Colonel."

His consternation replaced by a brief smile, Jackson patted Henson on the back. "Goodnight, Captain."

The colonel's phone was ringing off the hook. Jackson was slumped over in his chair in his study when the constant ringing finally awakened him with a start. Feeling a wetness on his right thigh where his hand held a partially tipped over scotch and soda, he groggily raised his head off his chest and stared at his smoldering fireplace; then, he glanced just above the mantle of the fireplace where his old Westclox clock was located.

"Shit! It's 2200 hours, and I've pissed away the evening. Now, I know I shouldn't have taken that third drink," he muttered to himself. Shaking his head and feeling as if he had just come out of surgery with a heavy dose of anesthesia, the colonel reached for his phone. "Colonel Jackson here," he managed to forcefully mouth into the phone.

"Colonel, this is General Betters. Got some good news for you." The general was literally barking into the phone, somehow extremely upbeat at this ungodly hour. Other than the occasional staff meeting and the routine business of the Institute, there was little or no interplay between the superintendent and the colonel. Ever since Jimmy Mackenzie had left VMI and General Betters had been literally blackmailed into expunging all references to the incident that had brought Mackenzie down and been forced to recommend the colonel for a promotion, there had been an uneasy and distant relationship between Betters and Jackson.

Having to clear his head and assume a command persona was nothing new to Colonel Jackson. He had been knocked senseless in combat on more than one occasion; and with his life and the lives of his fellow soldiers hanging in the balance, he had shown remarkable ability to bounce back to an alert status. The situation with the general commanded no less. The colonel held his silence, having no earthly idea what the general wanted.

"Colonel Jackson, I hope I haven't disturbed you at this hour," Betters barked once again into the phone.

"Why no, General. As a matter of fact, I was just getting ready to turn in," Jackson lied.

Betters continued to nearly shout into the phone with somewhat of a ring to his voice, almost as if he were in a celebratory mood. Jackson wondered what the hell this was about two hours before midnight. As the general spoke, he had to place some distance between his ear and his phone.

"Colonel, as you may be aware, Major Johnston has decided to hang up his guns. He has been a magnificent professor for us here at the Institute, and I am truly sorry to see that Cliff has decided to take the option to retire 30 June." There was a hesitation on the line as if Betters were waiting for a reply.

"Yes, General, I saw as much in the faculty newsletter today. I greatly admire Cliff," Jackson sputtered.

Betters cleared his voice and resumed in his booming voice. "I have been in touch with some of my friends at the Pentagon as well as some staff here, and we want to take the major out for a celebration of sorts. Retiring from the armed services is a tremendous milestone in our lives and one that we cannot let go lightly. Cliff and his wife are moving back to Arlington just outside of D.C. this summer, and he and Joan often go up there on weekends to work on their new house. I thought it would be a wonderful idea to throw a party for him, say at a really swank restaurant and have some of our top staff along. I thought that you would love to join us."

Jackson's brow furrowed as he mulled over the general's last statement. While he had known Major Johnston as a fellow staff member, there were a number of other instructors who were much closer to the kindly English professor than he. Johnston had several weekend golfing buddies that the colonel was aware of. Why would Betters want to include him? He really did not want to kill a weekend up in Arlington over this.

Sensing hesitation on the part of Jackson, Betters piped in once again. "Colonel, I know you and Cliff were not close associates; however, the key reason why I thought it might be a good idea for you to attend Cliff's celebration is that some of the fellows present are friends of mine from the Pentagon. As you know, and I apologize once again for this, your promotion has been unfortunately mired in a logjam of paperwork topside. These days, it is damn tough to get noncombatants upgraded, even one as deserving as yourself. Shit, I am sure you remember the good old days when you were fast tracked," the general paused for effect, alluding to the colonel's combat tours of Vietnam.

"The other problem they're facing at the Pentagon is that the Institute is, as you know, a state institution, and we have restrictions on staffing and promotion that the Virginia state legislature has to approve. For example, even if the Pentagon were to approve our staff for, say five generals—of course, that would never happen—nonetheless, the state legislature would frown on that development. No doubt a situation like that would impact the approval of additional funds for the Institute.

"Informally, the two work together on these things. Even if the Pentagon approves you for full bird, they have to then kiss a little ass in the right places to make things happen for us, if you know what I mean. So, here's the deal," the general rambled on without waiting for a reply. "A few of my friends just happen to know state senator Rob Schmidt from the tidewater area. They are friends with him, and he is joining us to celebrate the major's retirement.

"Think about it, Colonel. This would be a grand opportunity for you to make an impression on some of the Pentagon people, as well as on our boy, Rob. He just might be able to pull the right strings to push your promotion through. You and I both know that's how things really work at the top levels of government. We both understand what it takes to pull strings."

The general paused once again for effect, Jackson not missing the sarcasm in Betters' last sentence. After all, the colonel had played the general like a lowly puppet, literally holding the general's career in balance over a potentially explosive personal issue for Betters, his wife, and his superiors. Nothing stimulated the front pages in the Washington area more than a general who had strayed from the expected straight and narrow path and had gone astray either morally or ethically.

Jackson thought for a full minute and replied, "General, you do make an excellent point. I'll be happy to join you, sir, to celebrate the major's retirement."

Jackson thought he almost heard a squeal in the phone and thought that this could not be so. "Excellent, Colonel. I have already made reservations for our staff at a suite in the Marriott in Arlington for next weekend. The staff van will pick you up at your quarters at 1000 hours sharp next Saturday. It is about a four-hour drive that should give us ample time to rest a bit and freshen up before we go to dinner. I am asking each staff member to contribute fifty dollars toward a gold-plated replica of the Institute's cannon."

"No problem, General. I will see you then," Jackson replied. The line went dead.

The colonel made himself a small scotch and soda and sat down to mull over the latest news from the super, thinking out loud. "I wonder why he would go to all this trouble to invite me to Cliff's retirement? Something stinks about this. And, why would he call me for something of this nature at this hour? I know that sumbitch hates me, yet I feel I must take him up on this offer. Maybe he wants to mend fences and is worried that I may yet spill the beans."

With that last comforting thought, Colonel Thomas Mosby Jackson quickly downed his drink and turned in for the evening.

Chapter 9

Vicinity of Winchester, Virginia—Route 50—1300 Hours

Shit. I knew I shouldn't have come along for this ride. Why the fuck did he have to bring Loretta and suggest that we all sit together like this? I am going to need a very stiff one when we get to that hotel, Colonel Jackson thought to himself. He was squeezed in between General Betters on one side of him and none other than Captain Loretta Gadsden on the other side in the very last bench seat of the staff van. In Jackson's mind, there was no doubt that Betters had planned this all along. It was his way of letting the colonel know that he hadn't forgotten about the blackmail. Moreover, Betters knew damn well that Jackson had seen footage of the captain and himself having wild sex.

I wonder what kind of woman is this who would go along with Betters knowing full well that I have seen her having sex with the general? Jackson mused.

A dozen individuals, most of whom were instructors at the Institute, occupied the first several rows of the fifteen-passenger van. The silence and tension in the backseat of the van as it meandered through the rolling apple country in Winchester, Virginia, was causing the colonel to sweat profusely. He only hoped that the air conditioning would mask his rising body odor. Indeed, he would need a long hot shower and a stiff scotch after he arrived at the hotel.

Glancing over at Gadsden, the general sought to make conversation. "Beautiful country don't you think?" The colonel couldn't help notice that Loretta's olive drab military-issued skirt was nearly six inches above her knees. He was sure that Betters was not missing any of the show.

"Oh, General, it is so beautiful in this part of the country," she replied to the general's comment.

Jackson frowned. *This is like in your face. That damn guy; he is literally flaunting his affair. I bet he and Loretta get it on up here. That bastard gives me the creeps! I don't know what this prick is up to,* he thought.

All the colonel could do was steel himself for the remainder of the drive; this was just another of the many challenges that he had had to face in his military career.

The general had reserved an entire wing of the hotel for the party from Virginia Military Institute. After checking in to their separate rooms, Colonel Jackson checked his timepiece and noted the time was fast approaching 1500 hours. According to the general, their van would pick their party up in front of the Marriott at 1800 hours sharp for a twenty-five-minute drive out Route 7 to Bailey's Crossroads where they had reservations for dinner at the Peking Gourmet restaurant, one of the best Peking Duck restaurants in the Washington, D.C. area. They would meet up with Major Johnston and his wife, Joan, as well as the entourage from the Pentagon and the Virginia state senator.

While the colonel had spoken with his friend, Lieutenant General Gibson, at the Pentagon regarding Betters' invitation for Jackson to join in the retirement celebration, Gibson was not privy to the goings on at the Peking Gourmet.

The colonel glanced longingly at the cocktail bar in his room before helping himself to a Dewars Scotch and water. He wondered if he had made a big mistake coming to this event; yet, he still held out a modicum of hope that just maybe it would be to his benefit to make a good impression on the attendees.

Peking Gourmet Restaurant—Bailey's Crossroads—1830 Hours

As Colonel Jackson and the contingent from VMI entered the restaurant and asked to be directed to the table reserved for Major Johnston and his entourage, Jackson quickly became impressed by the ambiance of the restaurant. Even though the establishment was located in a nondescript, unimpressive suburban shopping mall, once one entered the restaurant with its busy atmosphere of uniformed waiters and waitresses scurrying about to serve their considerable clientele, it was readily apparent what all the fuss was about.

The establishment was formally attired with walls displaying countless autographed photos of dignitaries including notable military personnel, as well as some of the more recent Presidents. One President had often dined at the Peking Gourmet, ranking it one of the better restaurants in the Washington, D.C. area. In fact, it was literally his personal favorite.

General Betters and his female companion, Captain Gadsden, were the first to reach the table. Major Johnston and his wife as well as several officers, mainly majors and colonels, were already seated and enjoying their first cocktails.

Betters beamed a wide smile at the attendees. "Major, Joan, good to see you on such a wonderful occasion. Senator Schmidt, great to see you again." Nodding in the direction of the officers from the Pentagon, Betters extended his greetings. "Good afternoon, ladies and gentlemen—how are you on this fine day?"

Introductions were made all around as everyone was finally seated. Once cocktails had been ordered, the conversation picked up demonstrably. After downing three Dewars miniatures in his hotel room, Colonel Jackson had made up his mind that he would need to be proactive among the Pentagon crew, as well as with the senator. Most of the attendees had huddled up in their own separate conversation groups dictated primarily by whether the officers knew one another from prior assignments and missions. General Betters seemed to be behaving himself and not attempting to use his rank to his advantage. He seemed quite animated in the conversations he shared with Captain Gadsden and several of the Pentagon officers with always a hint of a smile on his face.

Leaning in the direction of the bald, portly senator to his right who was nibbling on an appetizer of Chinese spareribs, the colonel thought now was as good a time as any to schmooze up to the politician; however, Senator Schmidt beat him to the punch.

"Colonel, before today I don't believe I have had the pleasure of personally meeting you. I have heard great things about you. The talk around the legislature for years whenever the subject of Virginia Military Institute comes up, almost always shifts to one story or another about your exploits in combat that us politicians love to repeat. The Institute needs more like you. Having a war hero on the faculty is a big plus for us and adds stature to our community and the state of Virginia. More importantly, the command influence you bring to the table for your cadets is the type of example we like to see whenever we think about approving a budget allocation for VMI."

The colonel raised his eyebrows slightly. *Shit, this sumbitch is making it damn easy for me. He already is touting me as a reason for funding for the Institute. I need to work on this boy,* he thought.

Opening up a large smile under his red handlebar mustache for the benefit of the senator, the colonel warmed up to him. "Why Senator Schmidt, I am honored that you feel the way you do and the kind words you have just spoken regarding myself. As a son of the Shenandoah, I have tried my best, sir, to do honor to my ancestors, indeed the ancestors of our great Commonwealth."

Before he could continue, the senator interrupted him. "It's not only myself, Colonel. Your exploits and what you mean to this state have become legend."

Jackson sipped from his Chevas before continuing, his voice lowered considerably. "Senator Schmidt, there is one matter that I hope you can help me with." The senator's political antenna immediately stood up as he sensed the colonel was about to ask him a favor. There was just the hint of a frown from the senator as Jackson continued. "You see, Senator, I have many years under my belt and have really, through no fault of anyone, been at a standstill as far as my military career is concerned.

"Now, I understand that you all in the state senate approve legislative matters pertaining to VMI, and I understand from my superior officer, General Betters, that you all take a look at promotions approved by the Pentagon as related to how much in the way of funds you might approve for the Institute."

Before the colonel could continue, Senator Schmidt held up his hand after gulping the last of his Jack Daniel's down. "Colonel, I take it you must be up for full bird. Am I correct?"

"Yes, sir, as a matter of fact, I am," Jackson replied.

"Well, I hate to disappoint you, Colonel Jackson. We don't have any impact on approving promotions. You guys are approved by your chain of command, the powers that be at the Pentagon. We don't get into that. All we look at is the budget, financial allocations—things like that for our state schools. As you know that also includes UVA, VPI, and a number of smaller schools. If it were strictly up to me and I were in the Pentagon chain of command, hell, yes, I would promote you to full bird in a heartbeat," Schmidt said.

The colonel's face began to flush perceptibly. *Betters, that prick. That sumbitch told me that the Virginia state senate did have some influence over promotion issues at VMI and other state-funded institutions. I thought that sounded fishy. I've been put in an ugly, embarrassing situation. Look at Betters. He is stealing a glance my way with a sly smile. He knows I am working on the senator. Shit!*

Once dinner had been well underway and everyone had had their fill of good food and drink including the signature dish of the restaurant, Peking Duck, that had been expertly carved at their table for the guests, the celebratory aspect of the retirement party began to take shape. While briefly eyeing the colonel as Loretta slipped off her shoe to play footsy with the general's legs under the table just before turning to toast the major, General Betters stood to offer a cheer for Major Johnston. "Major, I want to personally offer my congratulations to you and Mrs. Johnston for a job well done. Not only the Institute, but indeed, the entire Army owes you a debt of gratitude for over twenty years of fine service."

Betters held his glass high to a resounding chorus of, "Here, here" to honor Major Johnston. After presenting the major with his parting gift, a gold-plated replica of the canon at VMI, the general continued.

"Before turning the floor over to the major, I have a brief announcement to make to all of you. This may come as a bit of a surprise. Major Johnston isn't the only one retiring."

There was a hum of anticipation around the table as most of the attendees appeared incredulous at his last statement.

Holding his hands out for the crowd to be quiet, he continued, not once taking his eyes off Colonel Jackson. "I have announced my retirement effective 31 December. In the interim, I have been offered a position by the Pentagon as an adjunct professor at the National War College here in Washington while my retirement is being processed."

Smiling broadly while Captain Gadsden looked up at him as if he were a god, the general raised his glass and led the salute to himself. "Here, here," he beamed broadly.

This time the colonel could not conceal his anger and embarrassment, finally knowing full well why he had been invited to this event. He excused himself from the table and slipped out of the restaurant in an apparent daze. Noticing a cab, he was able to flag the driver down. "Where to, sir?" the cabbie inquired as Jackson settled into the backseat.

"Just find me the nearest bar where I can get a drink in peace," he uttered to the cabbie.

Chapter 10

Chevy Chase, Maryland—Three Months Later

Thomas Jackson sat in his spacious kitchen mulling over the past few months with a cup of coffee. After the humiliation at the hands of General Betters at the Peking Gourmet restaurant in Arlington, Virginia, he had scurried off to find a private watering hole where he could drown his rage in booze and assess his situation. Sitting in Jay's Lounge, just a few blocks down from the Marriott, he realized that Betters had gotten the best of him—at least for the time being.

There could be no mistake about Betters' intentions regarding the colonel's promotion. In effect, the general had suddenly requested retirement; the manner that General Betters had shown at the dinner eyeing Jackson with a smug, sarcastic smile would have only been evident to Jackson. It was blatantly obvious that by announcing his retirement prematurely, Betters knew that he would not be able to follow up on all of his paperwork. More likely, Jackson wondered if the super had even put in for the colonel's promotion at all.

The man is not stupid. He knows full well that by retiring, he makes it increasingly likely that it will be difficult for me to destroy his career. He never had any intentions of having me promoted. This has all been a scam to buy time, promising me a promotion to prevent me from exposing his scandalous activities with women, he had thought, sipping on his scotch in the bar.

He had continued to mull over the issue further when a smile began to form on his face. *It will be a while yet before he actually leaves the service. I should have enough time to air out his dirty laundry while he is at the war college. What I need to do is tell Gibson something I should have told him months ago, but I couldn't risk it, though, with my promotion on the line. Now, it makes no difference. I need to spill the beans to General Gibson. Just maybe Gibson can help me destroy this bastard's career; maybe Betters can be drummed out in disgrace.*

Now that I have decided to retire, the issue of my promotion is no longer on the table anyway. I believe I know what I need to do.

Just a few months ago indeed Colonel Thomas Mosby Jackson had had a few tears streaming down his face, as he had packed his gear and headed back to Lexington in a rented car. He had no intention of riding back with Betters and his entourage; he had indeed decided to request retirement himself. His mission as a civilian would be to seek the undoing of General Betters before he was able to escape to the safety of retiring as a civilian. The only way he could accomplish his goal successfully would be to stay close to the general and look for opportunities as they developed. He could accomplish this by retiring immediately, thereby freeing himself of the requirement to stay on a given post as ordered by the military. Yes, he would be free to roam and stalk his victim at will.

He had thought then he must immediately search for a new home and relocate somewhere in the Washington, D.C. area. As soon as he got back to his quarters, he had contacted real estate agents in or around D.C. and aggressively sought to leave the Shenandoah region and start a new life in the nation's capital. He would also be close to his good friend, General Gibson in the Pentagon. Not only would it be much easier for them to rendezvous several times a year for their hunts and fishing excursions, but they could also plan together how to bring down Betters while he still wore Army green.

Jackson looked around at the boxes, still stacked several feet high all around him. He had inherited a pile of money from his uncle in Luray; and in his haste to move, had literally grabbed the first house available in the D.C. area that was in a neighborhood to his liking. He had contacted Gibson and told him of his plans to relocate to Washington after retirement. He had literally slipped out of VMI, avoiding any celebrations on his behalf. Many of his true admirers, including Captain Henson and the colonel's loyal cadets, had been aghast at Jackson's stunning decision to throw the towel in and retire.

One of Jackson's first tasks shortly after he moved into his Cape Cod home, a house far larger than his needs, was to call his old aide and inform him of his new address and phone number. He also asked Henson to keep him posted regarding any developments of note at the Institute.

Jackson stared at one box that contained papers from his uncle's home in Luray. He had never bothered to look at the papers. It had been too painful to contemplate after his uncle's passing. He must find a way to rejuvenate his spirits, and he felt that the next phone call would have to be to General Gibson.

Sure, he could take his case to the *Washington Post* regarding Betters. Though, it would be far more rewarding to have the military court martial the bastard since Betters had gone to such great pains to humiliate the colonel.

Now the shoe was on the other foot, and Betters would face ultimate disgrace at Jackson's hands no matter what the cost.

Well, I moved in just last week and have made damn little progress. Maybe this would be a good time to open up my uncle's box as well. There just might be some old family heirlooms and pieces that just might go well in my new house, he thought.

Jackson made a mental note to call Josh Gibson later in the day, downed the last of his coffee, and started on his first box.

Chapter 11

Chevy Chase, Maryland—Two Weeks Later

"Damn, that hits the spot, Colonel Jackson, if I might say so," remarked General Josh Gibson in describing his first sip of Jack Daniel's whiskey Jackson had offered him. General Gibson was a relatively short bull-like man at five feet, eight inches tall, with bushy dark gray eyebrows and a mane of closely cropped black hair interwoven with streaks of gray.

The general and the colonel went way back before the Vietnam conflict. They had come across one another as young first lieutenants in the 82nd Airborne Division at the division headquarters officer's club while in Danang, awaiting to depart north to lead their respective units in a coordinated combat drop designed to provide a diversion for the secretive impending invasion by the Army and Marines along the Ho Chi Min Trail.

In actuality, it was a very rare coincidence for Jackson and Gibson to have met once again as they had long ago been mortal enemies on the football gridiron. For three years, Josh Gibson, a cadet at the Virginia Polytechnic Institute, and Thomas Jackson, a cadet at the Virginia Military Institute, had slugged it out on the gridiron. Josh had been a fireplug of a running back at 210 pounds on his short frame that had proven nearly unstoppable for many of VPI's foes.

In those days the football rivalry between the two schools was one of the best in the land for small college competition. Thomas was a hard-nosed, though smallish, middle linebacker who stood six feet one and weighed 215 pounds. They would constantly harass one another during the games; with Jackson threatening to knock Josh out from a hard tackle and Josh yelling back at Thomas that he would run over him. The two football players were probably among the first to invent trash talking on the college playing field.

By the time they had become senior cadets, a grudging admiration had developed between the two combatants; and after their last game during

Thanksgiving week in November of their senior year, they had parted with a long, warm handshake. Amazingly, on the night before they were scheduled to move out many years later in Danang, they had run across each other. Lieutenant Jackson had sauntered up to the bar to order his first drink at the officer's club, casually glancing around the O club to look for unattached females, and had spotted Josh at the end of the bar fully inebriated. He had never forgotten that face. The two had spent the whole night drinking and catching up, exchanging addresses and vowing to stay in touch.

Gibson's father had held four stars, a situation that normally imbued connections in the military for offspring that also chose the armed services as their vocation; and while an excellent combat officer in his own right, he had been fast tracked through the ranks, thanks to his father who just happened to be a retired general with friends in high places.

While Jackson went on to become a war hero with his exploits in Vietnam, Josh had been promoted to captain and major in short order, leading ever larger contingents of men in battle. By the end of the war, Josh Gibson was a full colonel in the Army, and Jackson was a mere captain.

Gibson, however, treated Jackson as his equal. He secretly envied Jackson's bravery and thought him a superior combatant; though, rather than becoming naturally jealous at such an outcome, he had warmed up to his friend who still remained several ranks below him many years later. They had found ways to keep in touch, and Jackson's phone call to him two weeks ago to request his presence at his new home in Chevy Chase had not been totally unexpected—only the circumstances surrounding the conversation between the two men.

Gibson had known about Jackson's sudden retirement though he was confused over the colonel's motivation and future plans. That was a cloudy issue he hoped would become clearer once he went over to Chevy Chase to see his old friend. Gibson's wife, Marlene, was away for an extended period to tend to her mother who was in a retirement home in Florida.

In actuality, Jackson had asked his friend if they could keep this get together strictly to themselves as Jackson had some very sensitive issues to discuss—another question in Gibson's mind as he savored his drink.

"Happy that it works well with your palate, General," Colonel Jackson replied to his friend.

"Your new house is fabulous if I might add," Gibson continued, looking around in admiration at the colonel's new digs.

"Any problem finding me?" Jackson asked.

Gibson shook his head. "Not at all; it really was a straight shot down from the beltway onto Connecticut Avenue. Then, I made the left like you said onto Thornapple Street, and here I am at your new house on Fulton Street. Seems like a quiet, well-mannered neighborhood, as most Chevy Chase neighborhoods are, I suppose."

"I have to admit that it is quiet, though not nearly as much as my old stomping grounds in Luray," the colonel added.

General Gibson and Colonel Jackson were facing one another in wicker chairs on Jackson's porch located on the right side of his house, given ample privacy by the thick strands of wisteria hugging the screen-shrouded porch, located just outside of his small living room. So far, the only items in Jackson's living room were a small Persian oval rug located directly in front of the fireplace, as well as a couch and two chairs. Jackson had placed a small table between the two men to accommodate their drinks and the smoked trout and crackers that Jackson had bought at the local deli as appetizers.

The general took another drink from his Jack Daniel's and eyed Jackson squarely. "You know, Thomas, all of this has hit me broadside. I had thought you were on a roll at VMI with an impending promotion, and the next thing I hear is that you are suddenly retiring—just like that. And, moving up here to the Washington area—that really threw me. I never thought you would leave your beloved Shenandoah Valley. Tell me, what's been going on with you, man?"

"Josh, I know that all of this is a big surprise to you. In truth I haven't been very revealing in what has been happening with my career at the Institute, and I do apologize," Jackson replied, sipping thoughtfully on his drink as Gibson made himself a smoked trout cracker sandwich and listened intently. "What you don't know is that there has been a great deal of animosity between my former boss, General Betters, and yours truly. I have long found him to be a bit pompous, and I don't believe he has thrown himself into the business of VMI as he should have."

Gibson raised his hand slightly and spoke. "No need to apologize, Thomas. Hell, when things aren't going right in a man's life, one does not have the time or luxury of expounding on his misery. We improvise and overcome. Years ago when I was a major in Japan, my boss, Colonel Roger Sharp who thought he was sharp as a tack became a real thorn in my side. We did not get along very well at all. It was simply a matter of a personality conflict between the two of us. I think he was jealous of my combat record being the career paper pusher that he was, and he used to just pile on the unnecessary bullshit paperwork. Guess he thought I was going to get bored with his staff job while awaiting my next combat assignment. I was so damn miserable that I started drinking heavily in the evenings at the O club. Once that asshole got orders to report to Germany, I was one happy camper."

Speaking of camping, are you still up for that trip to Assateague Island in a week or so that we talked about on the phone?"

Taking a bite out of a trout sandwich, Jackson responded, "Absolutely, Josh. I really need some airing out time," the colonel replied.

"Tell me about this godforsaken animosity between you and Betters. I don't know much about the man—can't say I ever met him," Gibson said as he lit up his pipe, eagerly anticipating what Jackson had to say.

Washing his sandwich down with the last of his scotch and soda, Jackson began to warm to the subject. "It's been a long-time thing, Josh. It started out years ago when the sumbitch took command and didn't want to allocate any substantial funds to my society at the Institute—I did tell you about that, I believe, some time ago?"

Gibson nodded as he sat back in his wicker chair and puffed contentedly on his pipe, filling the screened-in porch with the intense, sweet aroma of vanilla an instant before the evening breeze would take it away. "Yes, you told me you were pissed off at him because he didn't seem to care whether or not your historical society existed at the Institute."

Jackson's face flushed as he continued. "Josh, it's one thing to not tend to the business of the Institute, and it's entirely another to be occupying yourself with strange women as a superintendent of one of this nation's finest military schools," Jackson sternly said.

The general immediately took his pipe out of his mouth and sat up erect in his chair. "Hold that thought, Thomas, I need to go to the head. By the way, I won't hold it against you if you freshen up my drink." Gibson placed his pipe back into his mouth and excused himself as he got up to go to the bathroom.

When the general returned, he began to drink at a quicker pace as his lifelong friend proceeded to go over all of the events that had transpired at VMI between General Betters and himself. Between Jackson's narration of Betters' blatant philandering and the blackmail efforts on the part of Jackson; added to that the effects of his stiff drink, Gibson felt as if he were becoming wired as the evening wore on.

Once Jackson had completed the volatile history between Betters and himself, it was time for Gibson to speak up. "Thomas, I can certainly understand how you feel. You asked me if I wanted to see the tape of Gadsden and Betters. I think I'll pass on that for now. Though, in my position as Deputy Chief of Staff at the Pentagon, I must confess that I am perturbed at the allegations you speak of. Who the hell does that pompous ass think he is? Running around blatantly poking women and masquerading as the superintendent of a great institution such as VMI. The son of a bitch is guilty as hell."

"As your friend and confidant, I just hope that you haven't made this vendetta of yours a pariah that has shot your career to hell. Dammit, Thomas, sometimes you just have to accept things as they are in the military. There is a helluva lot of truth in the old adage that you can't fight city hall. I realize this is water behind the dam; however, in retrospect I think that if you had brought the tape to me in the first place, I could have had Betters court marshaled for conduct unbecoming an officer. I am sure Mackenzie got screwed. Yet bringing Mackenzie into the equation to try to save his career beyond the Institute and dangling the tape out as a threat—well, I am afraid all of that only made Betters a tougher adversary for you, Thomas. Rather than advertise a threat, it's much better to just nail your adversary without warning. Throwing that letter at Betters was a mistake, I am afraid, Thomas. And now, your emotions unfortunately have placed you in a position where you felt you had to prematurely retire, thereby robbing yourself of a just end to your career so that you can destroy this SOB as a civilian."

Casting a weary eye at Jackson, Gibson continued with his rant. "I am thinking you came up here to keep an eye on Betters. Don't get me wrong; in the heat of battle we sometimes don't think as thoroughly as we should. I suspect from what you are telling me that you felt that blackmailing Betters was, in your mind, the quickest and surest way to a promotion.

"I hate to say this to you, Thomas, but while strategically it might have worked for you, you underestimated the tenacity of your enemy, and it became a tactical disaster. The scope of your objectives became too narrow, and this has turned out to be a fubar.

"Thomas, please don't do anything rash with Betters—it just isn't worth it, for Christ's sake."

Gibson paused and washed down the last of his drink. "Colonel, I am going to make another drink and think over this a bit. Can you provide me with a copy of that tryst between Betters and Gadsden?" he slurred as he hurriedly got up to make another run to the bathroom before refilling his glass.

When Gibson returned, a copy of the tryst had been placed on the table they shared on Jackson's porch.

After a meal of carryout pizza and a bottle of Chianti, both men made hasty preparations to wrap up for the evening. Feeling tipsy on a Friday evening and having the weekend off, Gibson took Jackson up on his offer to spend the night at his house.

The next morning during coffee Gibson told Jackson that he needed a week or so to think about what might be the next best move for his friend. Getting him a promotion was a thing of the past with Jackson now a civilian. That was sadly a moot point at this juncture. However, the sweet justice of having Betters nailed for what had happened to make his friend become obsessed with Betters to the point where his blackmailing of the general had forced both Betters and Jackson to prematurely retire, thereby curtailing Jackson's bright career—that greatly disturbed Gibson.

After saying their good-byes and agreeing to meet up at Jackson's house in a week to saddle up for a camping and surf fishing trip to Assateague Island, the more Gibson thought about Betters dragging Thomas up to Johnston's retirement party to humiliate him, the more he thought that maybe he just might be able to help him. He felt that his lifelong buddy had become a victim of a slick, slimy manipulating bastard. Even worse, Gibson feared that Jackson's obsession was taking him to another level—perhaps a very dangerous level.

The fact that the colonel had moved to an area he had never before expressed an interest in bothered Gibson as he drove back home over the American Legion Bridge. There had been no mention of a job or teaching offer in his conversations with Jackson. Gibson mused—*Was Thomas intending to stalk General Betters?*

Chapter 12

Assateague Island National Seashore—One Week Later—2130 Hours

Assateague Island is a barrier island, as it represents a "barrier" between the angry, boiling waters of the Atlantic Ocean to the east and the mainland of the eastern United States, specifically the state of Maryland, a few miles to the south from the eastern seaboard resort town of Ocean City. The eastern edge of the island faces the rough Atlantic, and the western edge faces a far calmer, more pristine collage of marshes as well as the relatively calm Sinepuxent and Chincoteague bays that connect with the mainland.

The National Park Service manages the national seashore area of the island, whereas other areas of Assateague Island are managed by Maryland's Department of Natural Resources. The island and the strip of land that borders it to the south known as Chincoteague are a national wildlife refuge.

Shortly after crossing the bridge that connects the mainland with the island, one almost always runs across a stray pony, part of a herd that lives wild on the island along with a herd of deer. No one knows for sure how and where the ponies came to be found on the island. Speculation has it that they came ashore from a shipwreck of a Spanish galleon during the sixteenth century—quite probably the only survivors—and have made the island home ever since they piled out of the broken warship in a panic.

Colonel Thomas Mosby Jackson, USA retired, and General Joshua Gibson were finally reasonably comfortable in their tent at site number 62 at the Ocean Side Walk Up campsite managed by the National Park Service. Fortunately, the two men had done their homework on the area and had taken note of the fact that during the summer months, the mosquitoes on the island could prove to be particularly aggressive and insidious for prospective campers. They had worn light fabric clothing with thin gloves, the sleeves and leggings tied at the wrists and ankles to keep the tiny attackers from setting up shop on their bodies.

Moreover, they had worn jungle hats with netting sewn and zipped all around the area of their necks to the collars of their jackets to keep the angry bugs out.

Between the drinks they had made while setting up camp, the mosquito body spray they had used before coming to the area, and their clothing, they were well protected considering the circumstances. They had bought citronella candles to use in their tents during the evening hours to help retard the few mosquitoes that might work their way into their tents. Of course, the downside to the extra clothing was that between the efforts undertaken earlier in the afternoon to set up their tent and campsite, prepare a dinner of grilled steaks and corn on the cob, and fuel themselves with the drinks they had eagerly consumed in the process, each man was, to put it mildly, "ripe" for the cold showers they would need before turning in for the evening.

Josh Gibson puffed on his pipe as he stared directly across at his tent companion, Thomas Jackson. Both were lying in their tent propped up by their elbows on the floor of the tent. The wind had picked up perceptibly over the past hour since sunset, and the roar of the Atlantic surf just over the other side of the dunes was nearly drowning out their conversation.

"Talking about roughing it, Thomas. I thought we had left those days behind in combat. Been a long time since I've been bivouacked like this," Gibson said.

"Yes, sir, reminds me of the forced march I had to do in those woods around Fort Campbell twenty some years ago. Man, while we were pitching tents after our march, the mosquitoes were all over us. We were camped out near a lake so we sort of expected it. It is a dang shame they don't make these campsites just over the other side of the dunes, up from the shoreline. You could have them set up just near the dunes. Give you a little distance from the Atlantic, and the bugs wouldn't be nearly as bad with the wind coming off the ocean," Jackson added.

"I agree. Perhaps there are some reasons why they have these campsites set up on the western side of the dunes. What we may not realize is that the stability of a campsite that close to the top of the dunes factored in with the ocean wind could make camping prohibitive there. You have to admit that these campsites, while in the wet bushes near the marshes in these small valleys where the mosquitoes thrive, are probably much more stable and secure, especially when the weather gets up around here," Gibson said.

Between the smoke of Gibson's pipe and the odors from Jackson's Dominican cigar, as well as the scented candle and the booze that each man had consumed over the course of the evening, the mosquitoes were rapidly becoming a past issue.

When they had first arrived, the spirits of both men had been extremely upbeat. It was exciting to be in the wild with the roar of the surf in the distance, the prospect of surf fishing awaiting them the next morning after a camp breakfast, the sand, and the dunes on a thin strip of land that separated the awesome ocean and the mainland. In Jackson's mind, while he preferred the forests of the Shenandoah for hunting and fishing, this was the next best thing.

Gibson and Jackson had quickly made their tent and set up a campfire to keep the bugs somewhat at bay. They had each arrived at the campsite with cups of Jack Daniel's and Chevas Regal Scotch, respectively. Jackson had not brought up the issue of what, if anything, Gibson had done with the copy of the tape he had given him a week earlier at his Chevy Chase home. He wondered how long Gibson was going to remain silent on the issue.

Reaching over to his Coleman marine cooler, he opened the lid and placed four cubes of ice into his plastic cup and glanced over at the general. "General, more ice?" Jackson asked.

"I'm okay, Thomas, thanks," Gibson replied.

Jackson poured himself a healthy round of Chivas, shook the drink slightly, and took a large hit off the elixir. Steeling himself, he thought it was as good a time as ever to bring up an ugly subject once again. "General, I hate to bring this up. Have you decided at this point what I might be able to do with that tape I gave you last week?"

Gibson cleared his throat, looking uncomfortable in the process as the pounding crash of the surf continued relentlessly in the background beyond the dunes. "Thomas, I think I will take some more ice after all," he said before addressing the subject at hand. After receiving several cubes from Jackson, Gibson had reached over and poured himself a healthy dose of Jack from his bottle and proceeded to stir his drink with his right index finger. He took a swig and addressed his friend's question.

"Thomas, we did take a look at the tape. I must say some of the boys couldn't get enough of it. Amazing, a female captain of the reputation of Loretta Gadsden performing like a porno queen. Anyway, I swore those of my staff and a few others to secrecy on this matter. Two of my officers are lawyers, and they wanted to keep the tape for a few days to fully analyze it for whatever value it could bring in regards to your wishes—hell, our wishes—to have Betters' ass on a sling for his callous behavior at the Institute."

Gibson paused for an uncomfortably lengthy period of time as he sipped his drink. Taking a long puff from his cigar and another stout hit off his scotch, Jackson sought to break the ice and get to the point of their conversation. "Well, Josh—if I might ask—what has been the outcome? I mean, do your lawyers think we would have a case to bring the bastard down?" Jackson wined.

Gibson squirmed on the floor of the tent before responding. "I hate to tell you this, Thomas, but according to my legal aides—unfortunately, you don't have a case," he sternly replied.

Raising his right hand with his cup and cigar held between the fingers surrounding his drink and holding up his left hand as if pleading, Jackson began to turn angry. "What do you mean, I don't have a case? We caught the prick red handed, screwing one of his staff live and in living color!" he nearly shouted over the roar of the distant surf.

"Come on now, Josh," he implored. "What do we have here, another case of the officer corps protecting its own? How many officers is Betters blowing topside? This shit stinks," Jackson said in disgust.

Gibson held up his hand to calm his angry friend. "Dammit, Thomas, calm down for Christ's sake. What you failed to realize was that in that entire tape there was not one clear picture of Betters' face. Sure, there is no doubt that the man in the tape was a two star as evidenced by his cap on the bed. There is no doubt as to the identity of the female participant, Captain Gadsden, of course. The problem is one doesn't get a clear view of the man.

"Think about it carefully, Thomas. Do you recall actually seeing the face of General Betters? No. My boys went over the tape again and again, front and back. Unless we have his face on this particular piece of evidence, it will not wash in court on an Article 32. Case closed, I'm afraid. I was as pissed as you are now."

The wind began to howl, knocking the Coleman stove the men had used earlier from the small table onto the sand in front of their tent. Gibson decided now just might be a very good time to step out of the tent and check on the stove. When he returned, he noticed that Jackson had refilled his drink and was literally chugging his scotch down. Gibson closed the tent flap and picked up where he left off. "Thomas, I didn't want to watch any of that tape. After my lawyers told me we didn't have enough on Betters to hold water in court, hell, we couldn't say definitively that he was the male on the tape; I took it upon myself to watch the tape.

"Sorry, Colonel, we can't bring Betters down using this tape. In actuality, my guys did mention to me that even if Betters' face was in this tape, you and your cadets could have gotten yourselves in legal hot water, as well.

"Look, don't you think that Betters and his lovers' rights just might have been violated by your actions? This is America; and here you have, in effect, a spook spying on the man so that you can get a promotion. Thomas, what were you thinking? I've gone over this a million times to myself, and, man, while I know Betters is morally repugnant, this just isn't the way to obtain justice. Sooner or later, he will bring himself down. Believe me, Thomas; I don't get any satisfaction out of this clusterfuck. Face the facts; do you think he really wanted to retire at this juncture? He may have had an opportunity for a third star. Maybe that is a small victory for you in and of itself. You forced the superintendent to step down, Thomas, all by yourself."

Jackson proceeded to plead once again to Gibson. "General, maybe his face wasn't clearly depicted in the film; I will swear on a stack of Bibles that was him in there with Loretta. I've been around the man enough to know what his body looks like. I believe I have some photos of Betters in action with Gadsden. Maybe I can use those."

Gibson held up his hand as if to negate that idea. "Thomas, at this point, to use old pictures or films even if you can prove it is Betters smacks of sleazy stuff. You are so bound and determined to bring the man down that you have lowered yourself in the process. The bottom line is—it makes no difference—Betters cannot be identified in the film, period. Case closed. Even if he were clearly identifiable in this film or any other photos or footage, you have no idea how many lawyers Betters could troop into a courtroom, screaming invasion of privacy. Christ, Thomas, you could have been sent to Leavenworth in a heartbeat!" the general emphatically said.

After an uncomfortable period of silence between the two men, Jackson appeared shaken by the general's diatribe, and his face appeared to take on a strange bewildered demeanor as he slowly got up from the floor of the tent. He seemed almost as if he had gone into a trance. "Josh, I think I am going to take that shower. I will be back," he said.

General Gibson stared at the flickering candle in a bucket that Jackson had brought to give them light and ward off the mosquitoes. He had made himself another stiff drink after his friend had left for the showers approximately one hundred yards from their campsite. He had felt himself becoming dizzy and had decided to lie down on his back to steady himself from the effects of a long afternoon and evening of drinking. Telling his lifelong friend that in effect giving up on his career in the Army had been a waste might certainly not have helped matters.

Josh Gibson awoke with a start. There was a screaming wind raking the island that was frightening. Their tent was barely able to stay intact and was buffeting wildly. He was in total darkness and thought that he and Thomas should seriously think about taking their tent down before it was destroyed and retreat to the relative safety of his Chevy Tahoe with their equipment in tow, waiting it out until the morning.

Forcing himself to his knees in their tent, he shouted to his friend. "Thomas, I think we need to decamp and book it to the Tahoe—pronto!"

There was no response to the general's suggestion—only the whistling of the wind and the crashing of the surf in the distance. "Godammit, Thomas, wake up; we need to get the hell out of here before my fuckin tent gets blown out into the Atlantic!"

He received no response. *Shit, he must be really out of it, poor fellow. I have got to find my flashlight, get his ass going, and check the time,* he thought furiously to himself. He had made a mental note of where he had placed his police-length MAGLIGHT flashlight in the tent and reached over to retrieve his flashlight. Flicking on the beam, he checked the time and noticed that it was 0300 hours—3:00 in the morning. More significantly, glancing around his tent, Gibson discovered he was the only person in his tent, and he began to immediately worry about the whereabouts of this friend.

Christ! It was about eleven when he went to the shower. Where the fuck is he? Gibson wondered.

Concerned that his friend had gone to the showers unarmed and that perhaps Jackson had been accosted somewhere on the island, Gibson reached over under his pillow and pulled out the pistol rug containing his stainless Colt .45 Gold Cup pistol. He opened up the rug, retrieved his pistol, and placed it snugly in his belt, pulling his jacket down to conceal the weapon. He slid out of his tent and proceeded to follow the path to the bathhouse where his friend had supposedly gone nearly four hours ago.

An hour later he returned having found no trace of his friend, scouring the nearby mosquito-infested brush along the path. He knew that if Jackson had merely gone for a walk, this was way past a reasonable time when he should have returned. *That poor guy is worrying the hell out of me. I wonder if he walked into the ocean and committed suicide. He certainly is way off the edge on this one,* he warily mused.

He decided he would take one last check on the beach side of the dunes. He had barely been able to stay erect along the dark, desolate beach—struggling mightily against the wind and sand beating him and his clothing mercilessly at an ungodly hour. Gibson had even walked partially into the surf to look for a body—anything out of the usual. There was no sign of Jackson anywhere. The only thing he could do now was to take his tent down and stow all of their gear in his Chevy Tahoe. He would ride by the park service headquarters on the island and report his friend missing. That really was all he could do at this juncture. He decided he would take a roundabout trip to the park service cabin and see if he could locate his friend wandering the island aimlessly, perhaps in the middle or western bayside of the island.

Driving the next day over the bay bridge, Josh Gibson had done all he could to find his suddenly vanished camp companion. He had searched the island, reported his friend missing, and the local police had been contacted. Thomas Jackson was not to be found—anywhere. All he could do now was to go home and hope that somehow Jackson would gain his senses and call him—if he were alive to do so.

Alexandria, Virginia—Two Months Later

General Joshua Gibson slumped into his favorite chair in the study of his colonial home located in Old Town—Alexandria, Virginia, a block off King

Street, fingering a drink his wife Marlene had made for him after he arrived home from a long day at the Pentagon. There had sadly been no confirmation of the fate of his old friend, Thomas Jackson, since that fateful night two months earlier on Assateague Island when Jackson had literally disappeared into the night. The strangest thing about Jackson was that officially he was not a missing person. Gibson had tried calling Jackson's home several times, even driving by his house in Chevy Chase, stopping and knocking on the door, but to no avail.

Yet, on two occasions when Gibson had queried Jackson's neighbors about his whereabouts, they had insisted that the colonel was alive and well, having seen him come and go recently a number of times after their camping trip to Assateague—though not within the past several weeks.

When he had driven by the previous Saturday, he had noted that the colonel's Chevy Blazer was not parked in his driveway. Of more concern was a statement made by his immediate neighbor next door to Gibson that Jackson had indicated he was going to be away from his house for unspecific and frequent trips, and to please keep an eye on his house for him.

Gibson had called the local police in Berlin, Maryland, the nearest city to Assateague, and they had indicated that the individual who Gibson described had never been missing in the first place.

"Freshen up your drink, honey?" Marlene sweetly asked the general.

"Why sure, babe, thanks," replied Gibson.

After Marlene had gone to the kitchen to refill his glass, Gibson lit both his pipe and the newspaper in his fireplace, uttering to no one in particular. "Thomas, where the hell have you gone, and why didn't you talk to me?"

Fredericksburg, Virginia—One Month Earlier

Colonel Thomas Jackson took the right off Route 95 at the Route 3 Fredericksburg exit. Unbeknownst to General Gibson, the colonel indeed had made it off Assateague Island safely the night Gibson and the police had thought he had disappeared into thin air. Jackson was a warrior in his own right, and no one was going to take him out on the island.

He had made an immediate decision to leave Gibson at their campsite, in effect to part ways with the general for the rest of his life. He felt that Gibson had been too hard on him, blaming Jackson for the way he had handled the travesties committed by Betters. The colonel had become disillusioned and angry that Gibson had not been more proactive with his colleagues at the Pentagon over the behavior of a general officer. *Well,* he decided, *I will take matters into my own hands.*

He had merely walked out of their campsite arriving hours later at the nearby town of Berlin, Maryland, by dawn. The colonel had been well protected with a thin profile Browning 9 millimeter automatic pistol tucked into an inside-the-belt holster. He had found a car rental agency and rented a car that had him back home by midday.

The colonel had decided from that point on to maintain a low profile, essentially going undercover while still officially living in Chevy Chase. He kept his blinds closed and went out at night only after several minutes of careful surveillance of his dead-end street.

Within a week of returning home, he had responded to a voice mail message from the Berlin Police department indicating that he was indeed alive and well; the messages left by Gibson were not returned. He had contacted Captain Henson at VMI and asked him if he could use his contacts on campus to find out the current address of one General Mark Betters, a professor at the National War College. He requested that Henson keep their conversations, as well as the colonel's whereabouts in confidence, a request that the captain would gladly honor.

A day later, Henson had called with two addresses. One was an apartment in Rosslyn, Virginia, on Wilson Boulevard; the other was an address on Lawyers Road in Fredericksburg, Virginia, near where the Civil War Wilderness Battlefield was located. Jackson had decided, for the time being, to merely keep an eye on Betters. He really wasn't sure what he was going to do at the moment although he had made up his mind to send anonymously copies of everything he had on the general from still pictures to films, regardless of whether Betters' face was clearly depicted or not, to the administrative offices of the National War College. His theory was that he had nothing to lose and everything to gain from individuals at the college who just might become perturbed at what they saw.

Who knows? He thought. *Just maybe they will initiate an investigation—and just maybe old Betters will come crashing down ignominiously off his high horse.*

As Colonel Jackson rode west on Route 3 past the battlefield signs, he smiled for the first time in months at that thought and abruptly made a left onto Orange Plank Road. Henson had told him that Betters normally spent his Mondays through Fridays at his Rosslyn residence just across the Potomac from his job at the war college and the weekends at his farm in Fredericksburg. The colonel thought for obvious reasons that it would be easier to sneak and peek on the comings and goings of the general operating in a rural environment where he could blend into the surrounding forest with surveillance equipment. He was, after all, a country boy, and the area he was presently driving through bore a strong resemblance to his home grounds.

He drove past the general's farmhouse on Lawyers Road, noting that it was an old, probably pre-1940 model, yet in good repair. Smoke was drifting lazily out of the smokestack, and Betters' Toyota Land Cruiser was parked at the far end of the driveway, two good signs that the general was home.

It was late afternoon, and the colonel had decided that it would be best to complete his observation and surveillance mission before darkness had set in. He didn't want to make this first operation a risky one; this was just a probing mission to check out his adversary from a distance and take notes.

Jackson took a number of narrow asphalt paved roads in and around the general's residence before deciding that perhaps he should park his vehicle on a back trail that appeared to be largely unused. From that point, he would take his Nikon camera with zoom capability along with his trusty Browning for protection and move closer in to the perimeter of Betters' property.

After backing his Chevy Blazer as far back as it could go in an area clustered with a few trees adjacent to the trail he had entered, the colonel turned off his engine and emerged from his vehicle fully clad in military camouflage with his equipment. He waited for several moments merely listening to the sounds of the forest to be absolutely positive he was the only individual in his area of operations. Jackson quickly applied green and black war paint to his face and slipped off his "boonie" hat, tossing it into the backseat of his nearby Blazer, leaving only a camouflage bandanna to cover his head.

He crept silently in the direction of the general's farmhouse; however, with the thickness of the trees and brush in the area typical for the eastern seaboard of the United States, he had to rely on his compass for any directional moves he would take with this surveillance op.

He proceeded cautiously in a low crouch, occasionally fingering his cocked and locked Browning automatic in a nylon shoulder holster rig for reassurance as he moved steadily toward Betters' house in the direction indicated by his compass. He began to smile once again. *Hell, this is just like the good old times on maneuvers when I was a young paratrooper right after a jump.*

The colonel gained confidence as he thought he could begin to make out the white siding of the general's farmhouse in the distance through the maze of trees and shrub.

He had just begun to finger his Nikon hanging directly in front of him to commence his picture-taking session when he froze in his tracks from a familiar sound. *Craaack! Craaack!*

"*Jesus H. Christ! That's fuckin rifle fire*," the colonel whispered to himself. He immediately dropped prone to the forest floor for protection from incoming fire and whipped his Browning out of its holster. Placing the pistol in both hands directly in front of him, he scoured the forest in all directions for hostile fire. The slow rhythmical rifle fire continued, yet there was no indication that the shots were directed his way. He began to relax once again, remembering that in this neck of the woods, as was often the case back home, residents were able to shoot freely for fun or target practice on their own property. Jackson decided he would edge closer to see exactly what was happening just ahead of him.

After ten minutes of creeping forward, he thought he could make out a stack of logs directly in front of him. It only took him a few seconds to realize that he was in the direct line of fire on an outdoor target range.

"That damn Betters! That sumbitch is target shooting! Shit! I am behind the backstop of his outdoor range. I need to get the fuck out of here ASAP before I get nailed by that sumbitch!"

He had no sooner uttered those thoughts than a stray round whistled through the brush too close for comfort. In a panic, the colonel tripped over a branch, falling to the ground onto a tree stump that jutted into his groin eliciting a loud scream of pain from Jackson.

As General Mark Betters loaded another magazine into his M-16 assault rife, he heard a scream from the area of his range backstop. His instincts immediately told him that there was an intruder on his property, possibly armed. He switched his rifle to full auto mode and retreated behind the cover of a large oak tree in a crouch near where he normally stood to fire at his targets.

"Who goes there!" the general yelled at the top of his lungs while peeking from behind the protection of the oak. Hearing no further sound, he yelled once again. "Whoever you are, you are on my property! Drop your weapon and stand with your hands raised! I am armed and ordering you to surrender immediately!" the general screamed.

Jackson was hurting from his fall, yet no way after hearing those words was he going to let Betters find out who his intruder was.

Shit, that bastard actually wants to take me in. You'd think he would have been content with just letting me go. I am going to have to back my butt out of here.

As the colonel scuffled around in the brush to make his escape, Betters heard the ensuing cracking of branches and noticed movement at the edge of his range; he proceeded to open up on the mystery intruder with full automatic fire, raking the trees and brush around Jackson.

Jackson froze for a moment, quivering from fear—he was not the man he used to be. His instincts told him that he was in deep trouble, and he must return fire to have any chance of halting the automatic fire he was taking.

Flicking the pistol's safety lever downward with his right thumb, he steeled himself to sit upright behind the cover of the nearest tree and took careful aim at where the rifle fire was coming from. As the bullets rapidly zipped through the trees and brush all around him, he held his weapon in both hands and willed himself to empty the Browning's magazine at his enemy. One round after another went in the direction of where Betters was kneeling.

Though none of Jackson's shots found their mark, the return fire forced Betters to cease firing his rifle and take cover behind an oak tree. In mere seconds, he made a run to his farmhouse for more protection and to call the police.

Finally, the automatic fire ceased. Totally wet from perspiration and literally frightened out of his wits, Jackson tucked his pistol into its holster and moved quickly toward his vehicle. It was imperative he extricate the area immediately to avoid being taken by the enemy.

Jackson found his Chevy Blazer, tore off his camouflage clothing, leaving on only a pair of nondescript blue shorts and white polo shirt that would not attract attention. He literally threw himself into his Blazer, tossing his camouflage outfit into the backseat and spun his tires to quickly leave the area. By the time he had turned onto Route 3, he had been able to wipe most of his facial war paint off and had settled low in his vehicle, hoping with all of his heart that he could safely clear the area before the police were sufficiently alerted to view him with suspicion. With luck he would be heading north on Route 95 buried in a familiar line of heavy traffic by the time the local authorities had mobilized to investigate the violence that had occurred on Betters' property.

As darkness rapidly settled on the area, he felt the old familiar pangs of being totally humiliated and beaten once again by Mark Betters.

Part 2

Ten Years Later

MU-SHIN—Concept of No Mindedness—
The Mind Is Empty of All Thoughts.

Chapter 1

Front Royal, Virginia—Early Autumn

Front Royal, Virginia, was first discovered in the late sixteen hundreds by a German doctor and an English settler. No one really knew for sure just how this relatively small town hard by Manassas Gap received such a name. One of the stories handed down that seems to be the most prevalent was that the tiny outpost was the most distant of the "royal" territories at the time. It was at the very "front" of the territories then under control of Great Britain. British custom dictated that when naming a village, the location be placed in front of, rather than following, the actual name. Hence, instead of "Royal Front," they called it "Front Royal," nestled just to the west of the hilly Piedmont region of Virginia, and beginning the climb to the northern most entrance to the Shenandoah National Park now known as Skyline Drive. The nearby, pristine Shenandoah River with its twin forks and background mountain setting meanders its way north towards Harper's Ferry to empty into the Potomac.

Jimmy Mackenzie had a weathered face, what little you could see of it. Most of it was covered with a fierce shock of red beard with interwoven gray streaks. Now in his thirties and standing five feet eleven and 185 pounds, he gave all appearances of a rock-hard body honed by years of conditioning.

Jimmy was originally from the area near Luray, Virginia, about a half-hour's drive south on Route 340 from Front Royal. He was not known around town socially; nor did he appear to be active in any of the town's politics or the many functions that typically occurred during the autumns in the region when the town became flooded with tourists looking to check out the foliage in the nearby Skyline Drive.

No, Jimmy was an introspective sort who pretty much kept to himself and his small cadre of friends and work associates. Much earlier in his life Jimmy had been in the Navy as a SEAL, an acronym for SEA, AIR, and LAND—the environments where they functioned best.

This is a special branch of the service commonly referred to as SPEC OPS where only the nation's best dare train with any hope of making the grade.

A combat injury to his jaw line and lower left side of his face that had occurred while in the service had left that area of his face an ugly, scarred mess. Needless to say—it was a stumbling block in Jimmy's pursuit of women.

Before joining the Navy, he had briefly attended two colleges, one of which was the Virginia Military Institute. Jimmy had been forced to resign after brutally assaulting an upperclassman that had been mercilessly hazing him during parade ground drills. Although he left the Institute in disgrace, no permanent record of the incident had been left to impede his career.

Jimmy now owned "Jimmy's Sporting Goods", a small establishment located on Commerce Street near the intersection of Route 340 that ran astride the Shenandoah River south of town. When he had returned home from his stint in the Navy to handle the affairs of his aunt and uncle who had passed away, he had inherited several hundred thousand dollars from his guardians who had, for the most part, raised Jimmy. His parents had passed away while he was still a very young child, and his aunt and uncle had gladly filled in as his parents.

Jimmy had used a portion of his inheritance to purchase the store from Bob Miller who had not been a very good proprietor and had to sell his store to financially break even. Jimmy's store bore a striking resemblance to the much larger "Galyans" located in more populous areas of the state. There were areas devoted to hunting equipment and supplies, rifles, handguns, ammunition, and a large section stocked with camping, fishing, and hiking gear.

After an honorable and distinguished career in the service, along with his experience growing up with a frequent exposure to the great outdoors, it seemed only natural for him to take advantage of Mr. Miller's sale. He had little competition in the region and worked diligently with his staff to maintain his retail enterprise at a very high level.

Of course, with the location, it was no surprise that some of his biggest selling items were hunting rifles for the locals who frequently hunted in the nearby George Washington Forest. With the incredible popularity of Skyline Drive and its enormous tourism draw, Jimmy had many out of town customers vying for his camping and hiking equipment as well.

Just south of town right off Route 340 on the Shenandoah was the "Shenandoah Canoe Company," which rented canoes and rafts and provided customers with fishing gear and licenses for a frolic on the river.

It was about an hour before his store was due to open at 10:00 a.m. when Jimmy, coming out of his small office in the back of the store, spotted his right-hand man, Mike Stoner, coming in through the front door. "Mornin,

Mike," Jimmy said to the much younger and equally fit dark-headed man with the square jaw and countenance of an outdoorsman as he strode in and hung his jacket up just behind the main counter of the store.

"Mornin," Mike replied.

"Have we received that shipment of 444 Marlins yet?" Jimmy inquired.

"Should be any day now," Mike replied.

"Okay, can you follow up with Bluestone on that?" Jimmy asked.

"Will do," Mike again responded.

"Bluestone Supply" was one of a number of wholesale suppliers that Jimmy regularly did business with to stock his store. They were based in St. Louis, Missouri, and Jimmy had received many requests regarding the Marlins. These lever-action "brush bustin" rifles were very popular in the densely forested mid-Atlantic region among deer hunters. Typically available in 444 or 450 Marlin calibers, as well as the equally potent 45/70 round, these guns could hang with the best in heavy brush country. It was rare in the region to take a deer farther out than 100 yards, unlike Colorado where Jimmy and Mike had gone on several hunting safaris with their Redfield scope-mounted Winchester Model 70 300 magnums to bag mule deer from several hundred yards.

As Jimmy and Mike went through some of their pre-store opening routines, tidying up the place and making sure that all of their display weapons were properly locked down, Jimmy's mind still was hanging on his Marlin question, fast slipping into a hunting mindset. Since Mike owned a square mile of land just off Route 522 in Hampshire County, West Virginia, about an hour's drive northwest from Front Royal, he and Jimmy had made much use of this private property. It was an ideal hunting environment with no competition from the annual horde of hunters who swarmed the forest every autumn beginning in late October. This large plot had once been a homestead for Mike's great grandparents and had been passed down through the family to him. He had expressed an early interest in deer hunting and had roamed the posted property for many autumns before being hired by Jimmy at his store in Front Royal. They developed a fast friendship and were able to balance the business aspects with their friendship keeping both in proper perspective.

Mike had early on in one of his discussions with Jimmy offered his boss a chance to hunt unimpeded on private land, and Jimmy had jumped at the opportunity despite some initial misgivings regarding mixing business with friendship.

Jimmy and Mike had built a small hunting cabin with a wood stove and bunks in a cleared-out area of Mike's property. With the rustic setting and rolling hills permeating his property, there were few hunting setups that topped this area of paradise. They would typically set up camp in the cabin after the store closed on a Saturday and camp out, hunting Sunday and Monday. Since

Saturday was Jimmy's last workday of the week, he had insisted on a two-day "weekend," electing Sunday and Monday as his "weekend."

Adding to their hunting equipment were the two Bushmaster tree stands that Jimmy would bring on their hunts. He and Mike would set the stands high up in the big oaks well above any worries about deer picking up their human scent. Typically, the tree stands were set up in the two largest oaks near the edge of the forest where a clearing began and stretched about 35 yards to a small natural lake where the white tail deer often went for water.

They sat up in their trees with the woods thick among them, a heavy scent of oak, chestnut, and pine all around. They would take a swig of George Dickel Tennessee whisky now and then as they raised their heads toward a powder-blue sky in the brisk morning light to augment the experience.

Well, let's just say that Jimmy and Mike were two solitary souls enjoying a little bit of heaven. Being positioned hard by the lake where the deer typically were vulnerable once they broke free of the protection of the thick forest to move toward the shore line for liquid sustenance was definitely an added benefit to hunting the wily and amazingly difficult to bag white tail deer, despite popular opinion that it was a piece of cake to bag one.

Switching back to where he was now, Jimmy's mind still hung on hunting. Mike had mentioned last Saturday that he might hang out at his cabin on his property for the weekend to check on what the deer were up to since they were right in the middle of the mating or rut season.

"Mike, see any deer in Paradise over the weekend?" Jimmy asked.

"Hell, yeah, shit, they were all over the fucking place. Man, I was tempted to take one, but ya know with hunting season not opened up yet, I figured I better not. Be my luck that the state would get wind of it, and my ass would be grass."

Jimmy smiled a bit at first, and then his face wrinkled into a frown. "Yeah, man, don't ever do that. That would be all we need to mess up a great situation we have up there on your property. I really don't want to get back into the public hunting scene with those drunkin assholes shooting wild and acting crazy out there.

"I thought I was in a fuckin war on one hunt before we hooked up. I was over in Rockingham County two years before I hired you 'bout four in the mornin in a crouch thick in the brush waitin on the deer near Lexington when all of a sudden all hell broke loose. There were bullets flyin all over the place. Shit, I had no choice but to take cover in a mound of rocks near Spit Creek. It's one thing to be in civilian life with these drunkin fools out here, but another to be with a trained squad of dudes who will cover your six, if you know what I mean."

Mike nodded with understanding, remembering that Jimmy had briefly discussed some of his combat episodes while in the Navy years ago.

With that thought Jimmy's mind wandered back in time. When it came to being shot at, it seemed as though it hadn't been too long ago when he had gotten his face fucked up in the Navy.

Chapter 2

Southwest of Destin, Florida, in the Gulf of Mexico—Five Years Earlier

It had been two long years since graduation from Basic Underwater Demolition/SEAL Training School (BUD/S) at the Naval Amphibious Base in Little Creek, Virginia. Petty Officer Jimmy Mackenzie was finally going to see some action. He sat with his boat crew, consisting of twelve combat Navy SEALS, looking out at the wide expanse of the Gulf of Mexico facing a stiff breeze aboard a Sea Chrome Marine Conquest Navy patrol boat making haste in a southwesterly direction at 35 plus knots in a stiff headwind. Their destination—an old ESSO oil rig—planted deep on the bottom of the Gulf that rose upward nearly 7,000 feet from the ocean bottom to its highest most point located at coordinates 100 miles roughly southwest of Destin, Florida.

Huddled up at the starboard side of the boat stood the team leader, Lieutenant Commander Chuck Brockton, and his second in command, First Lieutenant Joseph Broderick.

The boat crew was equipped with a full array of combat weaponry and demolitions. Every SEAL carried the ultra reliable and superbly accurate Heckler and Kock MP-5 nine-millimeter submachine gun, as well as a polymer framed H&K nine-millimeter pistol. Both H&K weapons were among the finest in the world for the types of operations that SEALS and other special forces often engaged in—wet, rugged conditions. Their arsenal of demolitions consisted of various types of C-4 satchel charges that came in handy for various aspects of most SEAL missions.

There was nothing like sitting back at a safe distance and watching a boatload of bad buys get blown to bits. Their mission was to board the ESSO oilrig and provide protection for its current residents. The oilrig itself had been determined for some time to be a defunct operation since the particular pocket of oil from which the rig drew was—well, empty. The U.S. Department of Interior had been participating with the University of New Orleans Department of Marine Biology in a study of marine life surrounding depleted oilrigs with a view toward developing artificial reefs to enhance the marine environment in the region. It had been determined that the marine ecosystem greatly benefited from the presence of oil rigs in the Gulf.

The oilrigs become fertile fishing grounds supporting the economy of the region; moreover, the Red Drum species of fish alone provided a total economic impact surpassing 100 million dollars to the state of Texas. It seemed as though the fish enjoyed hanging around the oilrigs with all of the underwater plants flourishing and supporting the smaller fish upon which they fed. The whole marine ecosystem had amazingly been supercharged indirectly by petroleum—paradoxically one of the worst polluters of the earth's atmosphere with offshoots of environmental degradation everywhere. "Acid rain" and the damage the environment incurred from it was one prime example.

Spurred by the federal government, the idea was to set up marine scientists, their equipment, and supporting staff on this particular ESSO oil rig, using the well-kept facilities for scientific research to study the effect of marine ecosystems caused by the presence of offshore oil rigs.

The word had long been out to the oil companies that Gulf fishermen made a point of extensively fishing the rigs, and the harvest was nearly always bountiful. Plus, it was very costly to the oil companies to remove the depleted rigs.

A few top oil executives had gotten together in Washington to lobby their interests over drinks one day with the deputy Secretary of the Interior, and the rest is history. Why not keep the rigs around? That would save the oil companies many dollars and staff the platforms with research scientists whose efforts could pay wonderful dividends to the country's economy. It seemed like a win-win proposition.

The only problem was that the Gulf was a big, wide expanse of water filled with predators, not all of which were barracuda and sharks. The Coast Guard had been aware of problems with rogue Cubans prowling the waters in the Gulf looking for targets of opportunity. Innocent fishing boats and their crews had reported being robbed at gunpoint by the Cuban pirates. The problem for the Coast Guard had been that while they were effective at interdicting individuals attempting to smuggle drugs and/or people into the United States, they were not specifically trained in combat operations out in the open waters where the need to defend an oil rig demanded specially trained individuals such as the Navy SEALS.

Some of the depleted rigs that had been staffed with scientific research teams had already reported being boarded and robbed by the pirates in the dead of the night. Even more ominous were the reports of rapes and, in one case, the deaths of two scientists who attempted to resist the bad guys.

Enter the U.S. Navy with its specially trained group of SEAL team special operators (SPEC OPS) evolving from the Underwater Demolition Teams (UDT) first trained on the Treasure Coast of Florida near Ft. Pierce. Some SEAL team crews had received advanced training after graduation in specialized offshore combat operations similar to their present mission. So far, the ESSO had been lucky. The government did not want this study or the lives of those involved compromised in any way and had directed the Navy to support the Coast Guard in protecting the ESSO.

Jimmy looked over at their main demolition man fondly. He was known among the crew as "Demo" Mike Maloney. "Hey, Mikey!" Jimmy yelled above the roar of the diesels and the blowing gulf wind.

"What the fuck's up, big Jim?" yelled Mike back to his buddy.

"Goddamn, looks like we're finally going to get a chance to fuck up some pirates out here in the big blue."

"Fuckin aye! I'm definitely looking forward to blowin anyone's ass out of the water that's fuckin with my country. It will beat the fuck out of shootin holes in paper behind the barracks in Destin."

"Yeah, man," Jimmy laughed. "We get to shoot assholes instead of holes," he added. They both cracked up over that one and looked out over the bow for any signs of the oilrig.

Coming up fast now as Jimmy and his crew squinted toward the horizon was an enormous structure jutting out of the ocean. He could see a helicopter pad at one end of the rig and what appeared to be a housing/office complex at the other. Most of the rig appeared to be a jumble of cables and pipes in between.

Lieutenant Commander Brockton glanced quickly at Lieutenant Broderick. "Lieutenant, see that the craft is tied up and secure and instruct all hands to gear up and prepare to board."

Jimmy and his mates had a hell of a time doing just that. Not only had the Gulf turned rough at this juncture, but also the sun was fast setting, and the wind was becoming an absolute bear. There had been a forecast of a fast-moving storm approaching the area of the ESSO; however, there had been no indication of a direct hit on their present position.

"Fuck this weather," Lieutenant Commander Brockton muttered more to himself more than to anyone else.

Jimmy turned again to Lieutenant Broderick. "Lieutenant, looks like they have some sort of contraption to help us with that. Let's climb up and tie those ropes on the pulleys you see up there to the boat and board this rig."

A huge wave rolling through the rig supports unceremoniously banged the boat into one of the rig supports, nearly dumping Brockton into the gulf. "Let's get a move on before we lose the craft and all of our gear," the skipper yelled as he grabbed onto the boat's handrails to stabilize himself.

After working in unison under dangerous conditions to secure the craft in place under the oilrig, the boat crew and officers scampered up the access ladder with their gear in tow.

"Are we ever glad to see you guys. I'm Bill Carpenter," Dr. William Carpenter of the University of New Orleans said as he extended his hand to the skipper with a wide smile. Dr. Carpenter was the senior marine biologist on the ESSO.

"Glad to give you a hand. I'm Lieutenant Commander Chuck Brockton, team leader for my crew, SEAL Team 15, out of Destin, Florida, at your service. I would like to introduce my boat crew to your staff."

After the boat crew was introduced to the staff, they were shown to their quarters and received chow in the small mess hall on the rig. The skipper and his second in command then proceeded to form the crew and issue orders. These orders included assignments for two-man teams among the crew to be stationed around the clock at different points on the ESSO for deck observation, ocean surveillance, and other duties that came with such an operation. One such planned duty was to periodically take the *Conquest* out with a skeleton crew to patrol a perimeter around the ESSO. That was one of the main reasons why they had used a boat in lieu of a chopper for this OP.

Hands on his hips, Broderick barked orders to Jimmy. "Mackenzie , I want you and your telescopic surveillance crew to have eyes-on-scopes from 0 to 24 hundred hours every fucking day of the week. Is that clear? I mean I want eyes glued to the scopes! Anyone who falls asleep on the job—his ass will be mine."

"Aye, sir," Jimmy said sharply. As a petty officer, Jimmy was the top enlisted man on this boat crew and occasionally funneled orders down from the officers to his men. He directed who would man each of the four observation scopes that would be used to scan the horizon from the four sides of the ESSO.

The telescopes were specially made, extra powerful Zeuss monocles equipped with the recent technological advance of night vision and were fixed with tripods that Jimmy and his crew would use to look for signs of approaching trouble. Based on information previously provided to Lieutenant Commander Brockton and his boat crew, the monocles would fit nicely onto the railings surrounding the deck area of the oilrig.

Jimmy never forgot the night that the wind and rain wracked the ESSO so horrifically that the telescopes were rendered useless and were stowed below deck to prevent damage or loss in the stormy seas. That scenario, of course, would result in losing their most important surveillance tool.

The boat crew had been on board for two whole weeks with no signs of trouble. Lieutenant Broderick had suddenly shouted in Jimmy's ear on the deck just barely above the roar of the wind, rain, and sea.

"Mackenzie , sound general quarters. Make sure all of the scopes are stowed in the storage shed and have all the boys geared up for combat including MP5s and side arms. The skipper wants two mags per weapon per man. Make damn sure every man is in his designated security position to repel possible boarders. Is that clear?"

"Aye, sir," Mackenzie replied.

Among the first instructions the crew had received was where to position themselves during general quarters.

"The boss thinks we may be in deep shit with this weather, and it may provide an opportunity for the bad guys to move in on us. Now, get a move on!" Brockton added.

"Yes, sir," Jimmy said.

Of course, what really worried the skipper was the timing that the weather might play in any surprise attack. Both Lieutenant Commander Brockton *and* the enemy knew that weather played a major role in the outcome of any combat situation where it could be a factor. He knew that the enemy was aware that his crew would be most vulnerable having to put away their surveillance equipment due to weather—and that a critical juncture would come in that window of time waiting for the weather to clear. It was imperative that *Brockton's Bad Asses,* as they had been dubbed back at Little Creek, Virginia, get their surveillance gear and men into position pronto to resume normal surveillance once the weather cleared. The question was, could they beat a fast-moving crew of pirates steaming in under cover of darkness from out of nowhere?

As the night wore on, the storm began to abate ever so slowly. While Lieutenant Broderick conferred with the skipper on the next course of action, there were several loud thunderclaps out of nowhere. Or, was that machine-gun fire?

"Fuck! We're being boarded," shouted Mike Maloney from the northwest corner of the rig. Before "Demo" Mike could get his act together, he stumbled forward gushing blood out of his torso and mouth. He was dead before he hit the deck.

Jimmy and several of the crew observed the action just as they burst out of their quarters, weapons at the ready.

Alarm and fear spread quickly throughout the rig. The scientific and support crew, some of whom where asleep and others who had been alarmed by the intensity of the storm, were unsure what to make of the loud, sharp cracks of noise. In a panic, they began to scurry about yelling for the SEALS.

In the confusion a group of five menacing looking Cubans wearing black bandannas apparently had been able to secure rope ladders to the northwest corner of the rig and climb up and over into the deck area. They scrambled out onto the deck, machine guns drawn and waving in all directions, and yelled in Spanish.

"You sons of bitches!" Jimmy said.

Turning to three team members, he screamed, "Joe, Kenny, Ron—hit the deck and cover my six with fire."

While the three SEALS did as he ordered, sending staccato bursts of machine gun fire with their MP5s toward the boarders, forcing them to take cover, Jimmy zigzagged around a cluster of empty oil drums directly to his left, taking cover behind the drums while attempting to outflank the pirates.

Fuck me, Jimmy thought. Mike was a bar buddy. He and Mike had raised many a ruckus in the Destin bars while they had been temporarily stationed there at a makeshift barracks awaiting final orders to the ESSO. One night they had gotten into a drinking contest with a couple of good ole boys at the "Destin Rides Again" bar, and after doing tequila shooters all night, only Mike had been left standing. Just before the bar closed, their buddies had to drag Jimmy and the two farm boys out of the establishment by their feet. Once out on the sidewalk, the drunken SEAL and their farm boy friends had been revived with three coolers of ice and water.

Damn that was brutal. Jimmy wanted to smile, yet sighed, realizing what had just happened to his fellow SEAL. Mike was going to be missed.

Suddenly, all firing ceased as both sides appeared to take a breather and reconnoiter the scene. Jimmy figured he had the goods on them. All he needed to do now was dash quickly to the end of the oil drums and rake the bastards with murderous fire from his MP-5 as they lay vulnerable on the deck.

The next thing he remembered was waking up in the hospital at Pensacola Naval Air Station with a throbbing headache, an aching jaw, and his face totally wrapped, with slits made for his eyes and nose. While his mates had eventually been able to kill all of the boarders, Jimmy would never look or feel the same again.

Chapter 3

Foggy Bottom, Washington D.C.

Foggy Bottom, located in Washington, D.C., had once been a very muggy swamp during summers long before the present grid of concrete monuments and government buildings had been constructed. Out of that area near the Potomac River, which meanders in a southeasterly direction from a tiny creek far northwest of the city on the border between Maryland and West Virginia, it has become a center where some of the most critical decisions and policies affecting hundreds of millions of individuals around the globe are made.

Such key institutions as the White House and the Old Executive Office Building border Foggy Bottom and the Department of Interior, Office of Personnel Management (formerly the Civil Service Commission), and the State Department are all tenants of Foggy Bottom. George Washington University and numerous other buildings and organizations combine to form the concrete cluster hard by the Potomac.

"Ouch!" screamed Ann Cohen, as she launched an incorrectly formed karate chop at Joe Lynch just as he rounded the corner from the hallway to enter his cubicle. "You hurt my hand, Joe!" Ann cried with a slight smile on her face.

Joe had quickly raised his right arm in a defensive karate block to protect himself from this sudden "attack" from Ann, and her hand had received the worst end of the clash.

"Ann, haven't I told you to quit playing around like that? You could get hurt," Joe said.

Ann was one of a number of Joe's coworkers at the Civil Service Commission (CSC) in Foggy Bottom; she frequently chided Joe regarding one of the most important aspects of his life—Okinawan Karate.

Joseph Lynch worked for the CSC as a computer programmer/analyst with the automated data processing division. The Civil Service Commission had been established in 1883 to create and manage personnel policies for virtually all federal employees in most agencies. One of its earlier locations had been in the old pension building downtown before the present facility had been completed in the early sixties in Foggy Bottom. The new building had been placed between 19th and 20th Streets with E Street and Virginia Avenue intersecting near the State Department.

Of course, like most federal agencies or self-contained work establishments, there needed to be a payroll system to duly compensate its employees for their efforts. And, like many organizations at the time, the field of automated data processing (ADP) was just getting underway, and the need for support personnel was blossoming.

At the time there were very few universities or colleges in the United States that offered a computer science degree in automated data processing or information technology. Many employees in the federal sector who had college degrees in other disciplines such as English, history, mathematics, or business had entered the computer field for the pay and benefits. Likewise, many others who did not have the benefit of a degree found themselves at least initially on an equal playing field with their college-educated colleagues in the ADP field. All individuals who eventually became programmers or analysts in ADP had received extensive technical training in the languages they would be required to master to perform their jobs at a high level.

Joe and Ann were among seventy-five other employees, who made up the ADP support team for the payroll, accounting, recruiting, and examining departments of CSC. Typically, these employees would field requirements from their "users" or clients in the subject departments and design and program systems to accomplish their clients' end objective.

Joseph Allen Lynch had originally been born in Washington, D.C., at the old Providence hospital located on the southeast sector of Capitol Hill. His family raised Joe in the nearby Maryland suburbs just across the district line where he had grown up to be a rather serious and studious individual. He had always had a penchant for numbers and minute details and was a perfectionist. While that was his greatest attribute and would manifest itself with a 4.0 academic grade-point average as a high school senior, it would eventually become a demon for him, contributing to his feelings of academic burnout shortly after entering college at the Virginia Military Institute in Lexington, Virginia. He dropped out of school, an emotional wreck with his confidence at an all-time low at the time, and landed a job, based on a recommendation from a friend's father, with the Civil Service Commission as a clerk. While more than qualified for that position, at least he had a job that was largely free of stress, and he had time to think about his next career move.

He was eventually able to take advantage of a "career ladder" transition program whereby clerks who showed promise and aptitude with logic could have their positions changed to a "professional" grade series, lining them up for a much more lucrative career. Joe was told by a friend in the general counsel's office at CSC where he worked that the ADP field was wide open and that as a college dropout, it might be his ticket to a more lucrative career, while he contemplated the next step of his future. He completed an application and was hired as a computer operator trainee, eventually impressing his superiors enough to work his way up to the systems and programming division.

His first mentor in computer programming, Patrick Sedgwick, had carefully and patiently brought Joe up to speed on the techniques of programming, and Joe had been sent to a number of training courses to augment his development as a programmer analyst. Now after seven years on the job, Joe still worked closely with Pat on the payroll system.

"I think Joe is right, Ann. We have a lethal weapon here in the office," Pat Sedgwick said with a smile. Pat was frequently referred to as a "goody two shoes" around the office because he would say "darn" or "doggone" rather than "damn," and he appeared to be religious. He was a very thorough mentor who emphasized writing, planning, and organization whenever a project was undertaken.

Typically, if Joe were tasked by his supervisor to develop a system to either replace an antiquated one or create a new system entirely from scratch based on criteria presented by clients, Joe would develop his strategy and then proceed to write a block diagram of the logical flow of the client's requirements as one of the first steps in his user requirements analysis process.

Pat stole a sly glance around the office at those who were looking on, including Ann, before gazing at Joe. "You better watch out for this doggone guy," he said with a smile and a wink.

Joe's face began to flush, and he felt the need to respond. "You guys ought to just stop it. You act like what I do over at the State Department is something freaky. Don't believe everything you see in the movies. We don't jump over cars or possess any mystical killing skills. If you ever observed any of our classes, you would probably be bored to death."

Ann playfully slapped Joe on the shoulder. "Oh, Joe, we're just kidding around. You're always so serious," she said.

"Whatever," Joe replied happy to change the subject.

Turning to Pat, he addressed a work-related issue. "By the way, Pat, I think I have finished that flowchart showing all of the functionality of the payroll edit program if you would like to take a look."

Pat had assigned Joe the job of rewriting the payroll edit program from an old version written in assembler language to the more easily understood COBOL language.

COBOL was a recently developed computer business language where each statement was written in an English-like form as opposed to assembler language where each line of code was quite often a hodgepodge of difficult to understand symbols and abbreviations. His goal was to have all of the programs in the payroll system written in one language for consistency and easier problem resolution.

"Okay, man, good deal. I'll check it out, compare it to the functional edit document that Dottie left us, and I will definitely let you know if anything doesn't jive—at least from my perspective," Pat replied.

Dottie Logan, another of the employees in the ADP section, had written the original edit program in assembler and had just retired. Pat had requested that one of her last duties before leaving the agency would be to document edit functions of the assembler version of the original version of the program.

It was getting near close of business for the day, and Joe felt good. After a couple weeks of pouring over Dottie's write-up, he thought he had performed a creditable job in developing a flowchart to depict the logical flow of the program. A real sense of accomplishment seemed to envelop him.

"Well, I'm off to class," he muttered to himself. Joe grabbed his coat, said good-bye to Ann and a few coworkers closest to his cubicle, and walked out of the south entrance of CSC to head to karate class at the State Department.

Chapter 4

Foggy Bottom, Washington D.C.

Joe Lynch smiled to himself as he crossed Virginia Avenue and stood facing Main State. *My God, when I think about what I have accomplished in just five short years, it's amazing*!

As he approached the guard's desk at the "employee" entrance lobby, he flashed his U.S. Civil Service Commission ID and proceeded to move to the corridor that led to the diplomatic side of State. After a few minutes, he came to the "diplomatic" entrance of State. With its curved line of floor-mounted flags representing all of the countries of the world and shiny marble floor, this entrance was considerably more formal when compared with the "employee" entrance. Numerous heads of state often passed through this very lobby to tend to international business and policy issues.

On the way, Joe had passed the entrances to the cafeteria. As a long-time employee of CSC, Joe and many of his fellow employees had long been attracted to State, primarily because of its cafeteria fare. The prices were reasonable for lunch, and the food was just plain tasty with cuisine from all over the globe available depending on the special of the day. With the enormous size of State connecting Virginia Avenue to 23rd Street, it had been an education for Joe just to get around the building.

In the beginning, there had just been *the* State Department. A major addition called "New State" had been added over the years as the world and its set of problems had grown.

Joe walked past the flags to the elevator and pushed the "SB" button taking him to the subbasement of the building. Like CSC and many other government buildings, the basement or subbasement levels were normally used to house a variety of operations. Printing facilities, mail handling and processing operations, snack bars, mainframe computer operations—with the need for raised flooring and special environmental considerations—as well as employee recreation clubs for their use during the lunch hour were frequently found on this level.

Joe slipped his castle key into the slot at the front door, pushed the door open, and entered the Department of State "Okinawan Shorei-Kan Karate Dojo." Every time he went through this rudimentary exercise, memories beginning from five years ago would flood his brain.

Five Years Earlier

"Hey, John, how is that special order of tapes I requested coming?" Joe said to one of his coworkers and friends, John Hernandez. They had been milling around the office of the chief of ADP operations when Joe popped the question. John was one of tens of thousands of individuals who had migrated to the Washington, D.C. area seeking work in the federal government. At that time in the early seventies with automated data processing literally exploding as a new way of life in the work force across the nation, there were many new areas of functionality also opening up throughout the government and the private sector that required ADP support. This spawned a burgeoning need for people with mainframe computer skills to meet the demand. John was one such individual from New Mexico who had learned valuable new telecommunications and computer software/hardware skills while in the Air Force. He had been hired at CSC primarily because of his background in relatively new areas of information technology.

One of John's duties had been to set up an inventory system for the tape library system at CSC and to develop backup procedures for the internal mainframe direct access systems disks (DASD) files that included the software that actually ran the computers in the CPU (central processing unit). Backup systems were also needed for the various applications that loaded millions of characters of data onto the disk files within the computer. The Civil Service Retirement System (CSRS) alone contained tons of personal information for all federal government retirees and produced their monthly annuities. It was one such system that utilized a large chunk of DASD. Imagine a computer crash with *no* backup to that critical file affecting millions of Americans!

John had not only developed a set of daily backup routines for CSRS; he had also been charged with developing backup software that was required by all of the programmer analysts at CSC for their specific applications.

"Joe, I backed up your accounting system files last night. As a matter of fact, unless you indicate otherwise, your original written request to begin backing up your files will stay in place every night. I've put it in the automatic scheduler," John replied.

"Hey, thanks, man, I really appreciate that. You want to do lunch at the Governor Shepherd today?" Joe asked.

That was certainly okay with John. "That would be super, Joe. I'll meet you at the E Street entrance around noon—same place we always meet."

The Governor Shepherd was one of the few restaurants in Foggy Bottom where employees could be served a decent lunch and a cocktail. They had some of the best crab cakes in the area. For some bizarre reason there were very few eating establishments in this area of Foggy Bottom, where many government agencies were located, other than the individual agency's cafeterias. Maybe it had been planned that way so that employees would not be tempted to take too long for lunch and be less productive.

Of course, there was an added plus for employee production in that no alcohol was served in the government cafeterias. The Shepherd even had decent drinks. Employees from State, CSC, Interior, and GSA, as well as students and faculty at the nearby George Washington University, were among the many customers at the restaurant.

The waitress led Joe and John into a booth facing the sidewalk in front of the restaurant. "What'll it be, guys?" she asked.

"I'll just have a Budweiser," John said.

Joe thought for a moment. "Likewise."

"So, Joe, what do you do for stress release other than sex?" John asked his coworker with a grin.

Joe had to smile at that one. "Actually, nothing. I used to run cross-country and track in high school, and I tried jogging a bit when Sandi and I first got married. Kind of miss the workouts," Joe added.

The waitress brought their beers, placed two frosted mugs on the table, and poured their drinks.

Sipping thoughtfully on his beer, John posed a question to Joe. "Well, have you ever considered getting involved in karate?"

Joe's eyebrows raised slightly in acknowledgment. "As a matter of fact, I have. For some reason I was always very good in wrestling in high school. I seemed to have great balance and very good speed. I have been checking out some of the Bruce Lee flicks, and it does seem interesting."

Starting to feel some effect from the beer, John responded, "Well, you ought to check out the club over at the State Department. I have been in it for about six months now. I don't like to bring it up at work because people can take it the wrong way. They think you are into some 'killer shit' if you know what I mean. We emphasize a classical style of karate, actually ninety percent hand techniques."

Joe assumed a thoughtful expression. "Wow, with all of the jump kicks and flying leaps you see in the movies, that's hard to believe. To be honest, I don't know that much about karate."

"Well, you ought to drop by and at least observe a class. The sensei is a cool guy; he is a sixth-degree black belt in Okinawan Shorei-Kan Karate, and he learned it in Japan while he was stationed over there in Tokyo as a foreign service staff officer."

"What's his name?" Joe asked.

"Sensei Huffman. His first name is Mike. You just need to call him Sensei; that means teacher in Japanese," John said. "Sensei Huffman is amazing. He has a Ph.D. from Georgetown in Political Science and travels several times a year for his job and to visit his home dojo in Tokyo. What's so cool about him is that he gives you, the student, all of the history behind each *kata* that he teaches and all of the techniques you learn," John continued.

"What is *kata*?" Joe asked.

"*Kata* are forms or sequences of punches, blocks, kicks, and moves which simulate combat. It is really the core of the style. The most important *kata* is *Sanchin*. You have to see it to believe it. A student must move slowly and deliberately with this *kata*. The emphasis is on the yoga-type breathing and strengthening of the abdominal area. Some of the black belts there have rock-hard bodies. You can throw your hardest punch while a student is doing the *kata* to no effect."

"Man, that sounds like what I might be interested in," Joe replied.

"Well, let me write down this number for you, and you can call the sensei," John said. He proceeded to write down the number of the dojo on a napkin and handed it to Joe.

"Thanks, John," Joe said.

After a lunch of crab cakes with a grateful Joe paying the bill for both John's work for him at CSC and the useful information regarding karate, John and Joe headed back down toward E Street to their building. Joe was thinking very hard about John's conversation at lunch.

Joe was still thinking about his lunch with John when he parked his late model Honda in the lot directly in front of the Rustic Woods apartments located in Wheaton, Maryland, about five miles just outside of D.C. He and his wife, Sandi, and two young daughters, Amy and Nicole, had moved there just two years ago from Silver Spring right across the border from the district. They were looking for a larger apartment to accommodate the recent arrival of Amy. Joe, in particular, had loved the setting of the apartments with the Wheaton Regional Park just a stone's throw away from their balcony with its jogging trails and picnic areas.

"Hi, Hon," Joe said to Sandi.

Sandi was originally from southeastern Louisiana, and her mocha complexion revealed her Creole heritage. Her hair, done in a soft bush, was brown, though it was dark enough to appear black. She had met Joe on a blind date set up by their friends and coworkers. "Hi, how was your day?" Sandi replied.

"Well, actually very interesting," he replied.

"Hi, Dad," Nicole said, smiling at her dad and then happily going back to her coloring books without waiting for a reply.

Nikki had many of the Creole features of her mother and was a strikingly beautiful child. Joe smiled at his firstborn and peeked into the small bedroom at little Amy who was obviously having a sweet dream with a big smile on her face. Amy possessed the lighter features of her father, and her hair had blondish-red highlights that appeared golden in the sunlight. Amy was also a gorgeous gift for her parents.

Trying not to awaken her, he gave Amy a small peck on the forehead. Joe and Sandi sat down in the living room with two glasses of a *Pinot Grigio* white Italian wine, to relax from their day.

Sandi worked as a kindergarten teacher in the nearby elementary school. Glancing over at her husband, Sandi wondered what had been so interesting about his day. "So, what made this day so fascinating?" she asked.

Joe took a healthy sip of wine, smacking his lips in approval. "Definitely not the work. I am trying to get started rewriting the payroll edit program and having a hard time with it. Anyway, I know you're not interested in the particulars of that. What was really interesting was a lunch I had with John. Remember me telling you about John Hernandez, the guy they hired about six months ago?"

"Oh, yes, you had mentioned that CSC had hired this guy from the Air Force and that he was very good," Sandi replied.

"Well, John was telling me at lunch that he has been working out in karate recently. He started about six months ago. This was my first time hearing about it. John is a bit private and said he didn't want to spout it all over the office because he was concerned that our coworkers would make fun of him. You know, the karate yells and calling him 'killer,' stuff like that. I don't really blame him. I was very intrigued by his description of the class. Nothing like TV or the movies."

"How so?" Sandi inquired.

"Well, according to John, there are many styles of martial arts, and this particular style that he is studying originated in Okinawa. They emphasize hand techniques and abdominal breathing, and it seems to be really an interesting art form with much discipline involved," Joe explained.

Sandi took a sip of her wine. "Are you thinking of getting into it? I know you have mentioned several times that you really missed being involved in an exercise program and considered looking into some of the karate schools in the area."

Joe took another long sip of his wine. "What I like about the situation downtown is the convenience—right across the street at Main State. They have a recreation association there, and classes start about an hour after close of business."

Sandi got up to go to the kitchen turning her head slightly toward her husband. "Dinner is just about ready; we're having baked chicken tonight," she said.

"Great," Joe replied.

As he sat later that night in front of the TV, the only family member still up watching the late night news, his thoughts drifted to the idea of perhaps checking out a class first before he made up his mind. He was not one to quickly make a decision. Once made, though, Joe knew that he would pour one hundred and ten percent into the effort.

Chapter 5

Foggy Bottom, Washington, D.C.

The next morning, Joe hopped off the metro at Connecticut and K Streets and proceeded to begin his existing exercise routine, a fast walk to his office of approximately fifteen minutes duration southeast of one of the busiest intersections in the district. He entered CSC from the E Street side.

After the usual morning greetings from his coworkers and wolfing down a sweet roll with his coffee, he settled into his latest programming assignment. Mulling over his flowchart, he started writing down the main steps that would have to be addressed in his program on a legal-sized sheet of paper. Joe was very intense once he got into a project, and this was no exception. The time would literally fly by when he immersed himself into a project.

"Damn, almost lunch time," he muttered to himself. *I ought to call Mr. Huffman up and see if it would be okay to drop by after work and watch one of his classes,* he thought.

He had long ago decided with the arrangement of the cubicles in their ADP department that he would have no privacy with any personal phone calls made from his desk. It was just too natural for coworkers to want to listen in on the conversations of others. He made a mental note of where he was in his logical thought processes with the program and then bounded down the stairwell at the end of the building to the first-floor lobby where the nearest pay phone was located across from the credit union.

"Huffman," the person on the other end of the phone line answered in a clear, nondescript manner.

Remembering John's admonition regarding the use of the title of the karate instructor when addressing him, Joe began the conversation. "Hello, Sensei, my name is Joe Lynch, and I work at the Civil Service Commission. A friend and coworker of mine, John Hernandez, indicated to me yesterday that he was a student of yours and recommended me calling you. I am interested in observing one of your classes."

"Drop by anytime, Joe. We are always looking for new people. John is a very dedicated student. If you have a few minutes I will give you a brief background of the style," Sensei said.

"That would be great," Joe replied.

Huffman continued, "We teach the classical form of Okinawan Goju-Ryu karate. Master Miyagi developed the style, basing it on techniques he had studied in China many years ago. The style incorporates Zen and Yoga breathing exercises with a heavy emphasis on hand techniques and form. A hallmark of the style is a form called *Sanchin* that develops upper-body strength, giving the student an ability to withstand blows from an attack. Don't worry; it's not as brutal as it sounds. A student is brought along gradually.

"I became fascinated with the art when I was stationed in Tokyo about ten years ago as a Foreign Service staff officer. I am still performing the same duties, though I spend most of my time in D.C. these days. With this style of karate, one can learn some interesting breathing and relaxation techniques, as well as self-defense. Our classes start at 5:30 sharp."

Joe thought that was interesting. "Okay, thanks, Sensei. I will definitely have to drop by and observe a class. Thanks for your time," he replied.

After saying good-bye, Joe thought how intellectual and soft-spoken Sensei appeared to be.

After lunch, Joe was back working on the logic steps required for his new program. When he looked up again, he had worked way past close of business. *Shit, it's 5:25. I will be late observing the karate class if I go over to State now, and that would be a hell of a first impression to make to Sensei. Guess I'll pass on it for today.*

He made a mental note to call Sensei and try to reschedule another appointment to observe the class.

Several months passed before Joe finally made up his mind to observe the karate class. One thing had led to another, and watching a karate class had faded from Joe's mind. John Hernandez had left CSC for a promotion at the Department of Defense in the Pentagon and had mentioned to Joe that he would unfortunately have to give up karate for the time being.

It was now February and frigid in Washington, D.C. and Joe was concerned about the ten additional pounds he had gained during the winter months and what he could do about it. *Yes,* he thought, *it is time to observe a class.*

Sensei had been out of town on an intermittent basis, and Joe had had difficulty hooking up with him. Once they were able to connect, Joe apologized for not following up on Sensei's original invitation and made plans to attend the class tonight after work.

With the light fading and the temperature hovering at twenty degrees, he bundled up and walked across Virginia Avenue past the steam grates billowing surreal clouds of steam into the cold, late evening air under the street lights and ambled over to the "employee" entrance of Main State. Following the directions he had received from Sensei to get to the karate class, he walked down a side corridor of the building past the diplomatic entrance and got on the elevator heading to the subbasement of the building.

Since Joe was not a member of the recreation department and merely a visitor, Sensei Huffman had told him to pound hard on the front door of the dojo several times when he came by to observe a class.

Wanting to give a good first impression, he arrived early. It was approximately 5:00 p.m. when he knocked and was let in by one of the students, Dick Stickler. Dick was fully dressed in his karate uniform known as a *gi,* wearing a brown belt with three black stripes taped on each end dangling downwards to form an arch up to the belt knot at his navel area. In this style of karate, the brown belt and black stripes denoted Dick as a 1st brown belt or 1st *kyu,* the highest class or *kyu* in the style before obtaining the rank of Sho-Dan or first-degree black belt.

"Good afternoon, glad you could drop by and observe a class," Sensei Huffman beamed as he rushed to grab Joe's hand.

Joe was a bit taken aback by Sensei's appearance. Sensei was wearing only his *gi* pants with a two-inch wide tattered black belt that appeared to be more off white than black from age and extensive wear, sprinkled with faded gold oriental characters. That belt had been around for a while, Joe guessed.

Huffman was only about five feet seven; however, this relatively small man definitely had an edge with him. His torso was well muscled though not in the "weightlifter" manner. His body had a lean, sinewy appearance defined by many years of the specific training inherent in karate.

As he looked down at Sensei's hand to enclose it with his, he could not help observing that Sensei's first two knuckles on both hands were swollen grotesquely. In fact, both hands were heavily callused.

Gesturing to the black belt to his left, Huffman introduced Richard Stickler to Joe. "This is Dick Stickler, one of our top students.

"Dick, Joe Lynch from CSC. He is interested in joining our club," Sensei said.

"Welcome, happy to meet you, Joe," Dick responded.

"Come on into the office and pull up a chair," Sensei said as Dick proceeded to the main workout area to stretch and loosen up before the class started.

Joe had started to pick up on a loud, whacking sound from the far end of the dojo and noticed a tall, lanky black belt punching what appeared to be a board that was mounted vertically onto some form of platform on the floor with the top portion covered by a thick canvas block. That canvas block was the area where the black belt was punching.

Noticing Joe's apparently keen interest in his student's incessant pounding of the *makiwara,* Sensei sought to explain. "I see you are watching Keith over there on the *makiwara.* That is one of the tools that we use here in the dojo to develop punching power, build calluses on the two large *kento* or knuckles of each hand, and develop martial spirit."

Joe grimaced a tad at each hit and wondered how the fellow, even though he was a black belt, could stand the pain.

"You really lucked out. What you are going to observe tonight is a promotional exam. We are going to test Dick for first-degree black belt. These events are always monumental occasions for us. We generally do promotional exams every six months or so depending on the progress of the student. Dick has been a very dedicated *karateka,*" Sensei said, denoting the term used for a karate student in Japan and Okinawa. "Please take a seat in the second row over there. The judges, who will be myself and three other black belts, including Keith, will be sitting in the first row once we have completed the warm-up portion of the class." Sensei pointed out the rows of folding chairs directly in the front, center area of the workout area with a long table serving the judges in the first row.

Joe worked his way over to the rows of folding chairs and was immediately struck by the symbolism in the dojo. On the wall directly above where Sensei was now standing to start the class was a large flag; it was bright red with some form of five-pronged black star with a large left enclosed fist and oriental characters to the top and just above both sides of the fist. Sensei would later explain that this was the Okinawan symbol of Shorei-Kan representing Master Toguchi's fist. This was a revered symbol by all who studied this martial art. On the plaster walls surrounding the dojo were martial arts weapons of various sorts that Joe had seen used in various martial arts flicks. He had no idea what the names of the weapons were or what they were used for other than obviously to hurt somebody. The only weapon he was vaguely familiar with was the *nunchaku,* which consisted of two wooden sticks connected with a nylon cord. He had seen Bruce Lee use it to great effect in some of those karate flicks he would occasionally check out. There was also a wall with a pyramid of pictures with an Asian fellow, probably Master Toguchi, at the very top. Among the pictures were Sensei and other black belts.

"*Kioske!*" screamed one of the black belts, standing in the group of approximately twenty students. Joe noticed everyone coming to attention much as one would witness a squad of soldiers called to attention by their leader. Another command was shouted, and Sensei and his students bowed to one another before sitting in the lotus position with their backs erect and eyes closed.

Sensei spoke next. "Close your eyes. Visualize a calm, clear lake. Remove all thoughts from your mind. Meditate and inhale slowly through your nose. Exhale out of the mouth." Then there was silence in the dojo for what seemed like several minutes. Sensei then called everyone to attention once again and directed all of the students through a series of stretching and pre-arranged warm-up drills using a five-count Japanese cadence: "*Ichi, Ni, San, Chi, Go,*" moving on to the next set of drills progressing from the feet and ankles up to the torso, limbs, and finally the head and neck area.

Then a thunderous command in Japanese to hit the floor and do knuckle push-ups shook Joe from his trance. What followed was the sickening smack of twenty students with closed fists simultaneously banging the hardwood floor in unison. Sensei was right down there with them.

Jesus, Joe thought, *I'm not sure if I can get into this. It's a wonder they didn't break their knuckles*!

Sensei again counted out in Japanese as the students were admonished not to let their chests touch the floor. After a series of sit-ups where two-man teams took turns holding each other's ankles down to assist in the exercise, the class immediately jumped up and began a series of punching, blocking, and kicking drills.

Joe could not help but hear the whip-like crack of the punches coming from the brown and black belts. That was impressive.

"*Yasume!*" commanded Sensei, which indicated the students were to relax. All of the students then proceeded to sit in the lotus position with the three black belts taking a seat in the front row as judges for the soon-to-be-commenced promotional exam. Sensei joined the judges sitting in the empty folding chair reserved for him in the middle of the other black belts. On the table in front of all of the black belts were notepads that had been placed there to be used by the judges to score the exam.

Dick Stickler was commanded to appear front and center and bounded to the area just below the Shorei-Kan flag. He bowed to the judges.

Sensei announced to all that the exam was for first-degree black belt and that the exam would be divided into several segments. The first segment of the exam would consist of a series of techniques to be executed by Dick that would be initiated upon Sensei's command—primarily various forms of punches, blocks, and kicks. The next segment of the exam would consist of *kata* or forms Dick would have to perform where a series of techniques combined with movement in all four directions would be required.

Dick would be judged on the precision, focus, power, and speed of his *kata*. For this exam, Dick would be tasked to perform nearly all of the *kata* he had learned from his very first start in the dojo as a ninth *kyu* (lowest class) white belt up to and including some of the black belt forms he had recently been studying. As he began each *kata*, Dick would announce the name of the form.

"Very good, Mr. Stickler," Sensei said.

"Now, we will begin the kumite segment of the exam. First, *Kiso Kumite Number 2*—begin!" commanded Sensei. "Shihan Mobley will assist you."

Shihan Mobley, a second-degree black belt, was the fellow Joe had seen whacking the *makiwara* when Joe had first entered the dojo.

After coming to attention facing one another, Keith and Dick proceeded to execute a series of swift, powerful punches and blocks moving from head level to torso and then to a lower level near the groin. Joe noticed that both combatants appeared to be at the top of their game with the rhythmical smacking of their *gi*-enclosed arms going at a staccato pace. After going through a number of fast-moving kumite with Keith, Sensei announced that *jyu-kumite* would begin the next segment of the exam.

While most Shorei-Kan schools frowned on *jyu-kumite* or free sparing, believing that time spent on free sparing was too valuable and should be more properly allocated for *kata* training, Sensei felt it was a necessary element of training to reduce the natural anxiety his students might experience if called upon to defend themselves or others against a physical attack.

Another of the black belts was then called to center stage with Dick, and they both bowed to the judges and then to one another. At the command to fight, Dick and the other black belt assumed a fighting stance with each facing one another at an angle to protect their torsos. Each combatant held both hands up in an open-handed *shuto*, or knife-hand position, before striking or blocking with their thumbs tucked into their hands. The thumb tuck created the necessary tension in the hand to enable it to be rigid enough to be an effective striking and blocking tool for the practitioner. Since ninety percent of the individual's weight was located on the rear leg, the front leg was in a position to snap out a quick front kick to the groin area of an onrushing attacker.

As Dick and the other black belt began to fight, Joe began to cringe. *Damn, Dick just took an awful blow to his stomach that damn near doubled him over. Christ, he has blood running from his mouth from a punch he barely was able to deflect—I don't know about this shit. They're not even using protective equipment like I've seen in tournaments on TV.*

As it was, other than the slight hit to his front jaw area, Dick was able to acquit himself quite well despite taking damage in the fight. Joe had looked away from the carnage for a second. When he bravely peeked once again at the action, Dick had nailed the black belt with a wicked, spring-loaded roundhouse kick from the top of his right foot to the black belt's left rib cage area, which appeared to knock the wind out of him. The black belt doubled over appearing to be temporarily stunned from Dick's powerful kick. He stood still and appeared to be unable to move, wheezing to catch his breath. Then, he started to cough.

Perhaps to save face for one of his best black belts, and indeed himself as the chief instructor, Huffman called a halt to the action. Both combatants bowed, and the black belt went slowly back to the judges' table, attempting to appear unhurt as the judges began to write furiously.

Sensei then announced the final segment of the exam, *Kata Sanchin. Sanchin* was a form that was the heart of the Goju system. It had been said that in the old days, students would be required to study *Sanchin Kata* for three years before they could move to other areas of the system.

At a command, Dick was instructed to remove the top portion of his *gi* so that he had only his *gi* pants and brown belt on. Joe noticed that Dick appeared to have a rock-hard abdominal area with the "ripple" stomach look. As Dick came to attention and began the form, inhaling and exhaling with a prominent, hissing sound almost like the roar of a lion with each slow, dynamically tensed strike and withdrawal, Joe became alarmed when two of the black belt judges rose from their folding chairs carrying two-by-four pieces of wood. Each black belt began to beat Dick about his abdominal areas with the pieces of wood.

One of the black belts then abruptly dropped his board and at various points of the *kata* where Dick would tense, proceeded to pound Dick's midsection with vicious punches from the horse stance. By now Dick was sweating profusely with his body showing signs of damage as the thick red welts and bruises began to appear prominently on his body.

Joe felt as though he was going to puke. *Oh, no, they are actually kicking him with the heels of their feet on his thighs! Poor Dick! His goddamn knees are buckling. I can't believe I am sitting here watching this shit!*

In actuality, Dick, indeed, appeared to be in duress from the punishment, especially given the fact that he was already practically exhausted from the earlier segments of the exam. It appeared to Joe from looking at his eyes that he was pleading for a stop to this madness. Mercifully, Dick concluded the form and bowed to the judges.

Sensei then asked the sweat-soaked and bruised Dick to stand with his hands behind his back in a relaxed manner. Joe took in the scene with a numbed expression on his face. After what seemed like ten minutes while the judges conversed among themselves and tallied their scores, Dick was instructed to appear front and center under the red flag.

Sensei spoke. "Very good, Dick. You made quite an impression on us. One thing you have to work on. We noticed that during *kata*, you were still showing a tendency to pick your feet up too high as you changed stances. You could find yourself swept by an opponent's leg, taken down, and defeated with those habits.

Remember for maximum balance, we must always keep our feet moving in a semi-circular manner close to the ground. Otherwise, great job."

Sensei then walked to the front of the class, holding a certificate and black belt, and called the class to attention. He then turned to Dick, who was now standing at attention on the left side of the red flag.

"Congratulations. You are now First-Dan," he said as he shook hands with Dick and handed him his "sheepskin" and new black belt.

"*Domo arigato,*" replied Dick, signifying his humble thanks. He then proceeded to take his brown belt off and proudly covered his waist with the black cloth mantel signifying excellence in martial arts.

After class was once again called to attention and meditation was complete, Sensei dismissed the class.

Sensei walked over to where Joe was getting up from his chair. "Well, what do you think, Joe? Are we going to see you in class on Monday?" he asked.

"Sensei, I really appreciate your letting me observe the class. I will think about it. I am also quite interested in pursuing tennis. I am just not sure where I want to go with exercise at this point."

"Well, think it over and let us know; we'll be here," Sensei said.

With the students milling about offering congratulations to Dick, Joe sauntered on out of the dojo. As he left Main State and walked back in the direction of the metro on 16th Street, he thought, *Damn, I don't know about this karate shit. I don't mind the exercise and learning how to defend myself, but the beatings I can do without. I had no idea they were into that kind of violence. I think I'll contact the YMCA on Monday and look into their tennis course. Spring is coming up, and this is a good time to get into it.*

Chapter 6

Front Royal, Virginia

As Jimmy and Mike finished tidying up the store in anticipation of the coming day's business, a few customers began to arrive and browse. From his position behind the counter, Jimmy looked up from a stack of firearms approval documents they had just received from the Virginia state police and noticed Buster Fahey, one of his long-time customers. Buster was looking at the boxes of ammunition that were neatly stacked on the shelves to the left of Jimmy. He was an avid deer hunter in his early forties and lived about a half hour south of Front Royal outside of Luray where the famous caverns attracted many tourists year round.

"Hey, Buster, how ya doin?" Jimmy asked.

"Aw shucks, I'm doin okay, Jimmy," Buster replied. "Been fightin allergies is all. Hate it with the ragweed this time of year and huntin comin up, if you know what I mean."

"Sorry about that, man," Jimmy said. Noticing that Buster was keenly looking over the boxes of ammo, Jimmy walked out from behind the counter and shook Buster's hand. "What can I do you for today, partner?" he asked.

"Well, I'm kinda low on .30-30 ammo," Buster replied. "Lookin right now for some practice ammo. I need to go out back of the house and re-sight that Model 94 I bought from you last year." Buster was referring to the Winchester Model 94 lever-action rifle he had purchased from Jimmy. "The dang thing fell off my gun rack in the back of my pickup 'bout two weeks ago over yonder, and I'm dearly afraid it won't shoot good when I get that buck in my sights," he added.

Jimmy thought for a minute. "Well, I think I have just the ticket for you, Buster. Winchester has recently developed some USA brand practice ammo for just that purpose—practice and sighting in your weapon."

Buster picked up a bottle of Hoppe's gun solvent as he came over to the counter. "Okay, Jimmy, gimme six boxes of that USA ammo, and I want this gun cleaner too," he requested.

"You got it, Buster. Before you shoot your Winchester, I would recommend that you check your scope out and make sure your scope supports are tight around the base mounts. They may have come loose when your rifle fell off the rack."

"Good idea, I'll do that," replied Buster.

Seeing that Jimmy was tied up, another customer, Billy McClintok, who had just walked through the front door, made his way over to where Mike was setting up a display of Columbia brand backpacks on a revolving stand. "I'd like to take a look at your .45's if you don't mind," he said.

"Are you interested in a particular make or model?" Mike asked.

"I just want the best you have. I don't know if its true or not, but I heard a rumor at the barbershop the other day that a hiker was reported missing up off Skyline Drive near Route 211, and that is dang close to where my apple farm is located. Might be a crazy out there somewhere in the mountains looking to hurt people, you never know. I'm just down the mountain in Spencerville, and I don't like to hear that shit. Got a thirty ought six, but that's just for huntin. I want something where I could blow that fool away fast if in he tried to come into my farm."

Mike hesitated for a minute and said, "Hate to say this, but you wonder 'bout those hikers and if some of them ain't up to mischief up there. I was up there with my girlfriend on a picnic two years ago, and we seen a couple fellers with backpacks on who was drunk as skunks walking into the woods at a trailhead. They could have been up to no good. Whenever we go up there, we always bring a gun even with the park rangers around. One side of my family had ancestors who used to live in the national park and was plum run out a long time ago by the state or government, can't rightly remember which."

Switching back to address Billy's original question, Mike pointed over at the glass counter where the pistols were displayed. "We do have a very nice selection of .45's. Come on over to the counter there, and we can fix you up with what you need."

Billy and Mike moved toward the counter with Mike taking up a position behind the gun display and Billy facing him on the other side of the counter. They both viewed the display of handguns under the top glass of the counter. "The three makes I like most are the Kimber, Para Ordinance, and Springfield Armory. They will give you outstanding service and are damn near match-grade accurate right out of the box," Mike explained.

"Well, which one do you recommend?" Billy asked, scratching his beard.

"If it were me, I'd take the Kimber 'cause of the price, and it is just as good as the others. The Para would be nice if you liked double action only and were doin a lot of carryin. It's got a smooth double-action trigger pull that is a nice safety feature as well. If you want a great .45 that won't break your bank, though, and want something powerful and damn accurate, I'd take the Kimber," Mike added.

Billy began to gaze intently at the Kimber and said, "Okay, Mike, lemme take a look at that Kimber, then."

Mike unlocked the counter where the handguns were stored and pulled out the Kimber, racking the slide before presenting the gun sideways holding the grip to Billy. Billy proceeded to look it over and depressed the slide stop with his thumb, slamming the slide home with a metallic ring. He then racked the slide several times before pointing the pistol in a safe direction to take aim. "I really like this. Great balance, and it is a damn good-looking piece. How much?" Billy asked.

Mike pulled out the price book and began to search through the pages. As he reached the correct page, he scratched the side of his face briefly. "Okay, here we are. You're talkin 795 dollars and 95 cents including tax," he replied.

Billy's face lit up. "Could I put a deposit down on it and get you the rest in a couple weeks?"

"That would be fine," Mike replied. "What we can do is get started on the paperwork right now. Once that is completed, we'll send it to the state police for their background criminal check, and they'll send it back approved or not approved."

After reaching under the cash register for another folder, Mike proceeded to begin the paperwork. "What is your full name?" he asked Billy.

After Billy deposited one hundred dollars to hold the weapon and had left the store, Mike filed away the paperwork for mailing. Noticing that Jimmy had finished with Buster, Mike walked up to Jimmy. "Ya know, Jimmy, this is the second customer this week been asking about a handgun for protection because a hiker has been reported missing in the park," Mike said.

"That right?" Jimmy replied.

"Yeah, most folks round here ain't into handguns much, just long guns for huntin," Mike noted with ready agreement from Jimmy.

"That's true. Tell you what though. With our .44 magnums, I don't think we have anything to worry about." Jimmy was referring to the Ruger Redhawk handguns that he had ordered for both Mike and himself last year from Bluestone Supply when the guns had first come out using the innovations Ruger had incorporated in their GP100 line of .357 revolvers.

"Shit, you're right 'bout that, boss," Mike replied.

As twilight began to descend on Front Royal, Jimmy and Mike's thoughts turned to wrapping up for the day. They locked the store, said their good-byes, and went their separate ways back home for the evening.

Jimmy was heading down U.S. 340 going south in his late model Jeep Cherokee toward his farmhouse near Luray when his thoughts turned toward fishing. The Shenandoah was just a stone's throw away on his right, and one of his old friends, Buddy Parsons, was the owner of the "Shenandoah Canoe Company" just around the bend. The boat company rented canoes and rafts for use on the river and sold fishing gear and licenses. He thought that maybe he would drop by for a chat.

"Hey, Buddy," Jimmy said as he climbed a few steps to the entrance and saw Buddy sitting on the front porch of the establishment.

"How ya doin, Jimmy?" Buddy replied.

"Well, been okay. Business has started to pick up with the huntin season comin around. Can't complain; it don't do me any good," Jimmy said.

"I know what you're sayin," Buddy replied.

"What's the fishin been like lately?" Jimmy asked.

"Not all that much to brag about," Buddy replied. "Problem is with the drought and all, the damn water levels been too low. We figure the small mouth and perch probably headed up north toward Harper's Ferry to deeper waters."

Jimmy gave that a bit of thought when he asked another question. "So, you think if I wanted to go out and toss a line, might be better just to try my luck with waders?" Waders were the waterproof hip-length rubber boots that covered one's body from the feet up to the waist area enabling fishermen to walk out into a river or a lake without getting wet and fish.

Buddy opened up his pocketknife and began to pick at his nails. "Yep, I think you may be right about that. Of course, a lot of the folks who go out in the river to fish end up taking a canoe so that they have the best of both worlds. They can get to any point they want along the river fairly quickly; then they just park it, hop out, and fish."

Jimmy thought that sounded reasonable as he started toward the front steps. "Well, I just might take you up on that—maybe in a week or two. Anyway, good to see you, Buddy.

"Trust the family is fine?" he asked.

"Oh, we're doing okay; thanks for asking. You take good care of yourself. Come to think of it, I guess your business may be picking up for other reasons, too."

Jimmy stopped and turned slightly while raising his eyebrow slightly. "How so?" he asked.

"Well, I know this feller who is a state policeman who loves to go canoeing. He's down here every chance he gets, and he told me the other day that several hikers have disappeared up in the park over the past couple months. Nobody's figured out what happened. He even said the FBI's been called into it. It's starting to be talked about all over town. I know a lot of people are a little uneasy that there might be some feller or group of fellers up to mischief in them mountains. With that situation and all, seems natural that folks would want to protect themselves. I know I've been bringing my .357 to the store and keeping it behind the counter just in case."

Jimmy narrowed his gaze to Buddy. "That's interesting. Come to think of it, my assistant at the store did mention that rumors were beginning to appear about hikers missing. Anyway, got to run—check you later and be safe." Jimmy bounded down the steps toward his Jeep as Buddy waved good-bye to him.

Jimmy turned left off U.S. 340 onto a gravel road where his mailbox was and slowly headed up an incline toward his farmhouse, originally built in 1930 by his Uncle Ronny. His uncle and Aunt Ruthie had lived there virtually their entire lives while running an apple orchard in the back. They had had a decent inheritance left over from Ruth's family and were able to eke out an existence living off the land with Ronny able to make a small profit from selling apples to a local distributor. Most of their table fare consisted of venison, squirrel, and rabbit that Ronny shot on his many forays into the forest along with vegetables that Ruthie had planted in her garden on the side of the house.

Like many farmhouses in the area, after driving into the driveway, you could pull on around to an area in back of the farmhouse that was between the house and a garden or apple grove. Ronny and Ruthie had taken in young eight-year-old Jimmy after his parents had passed away and raised him well, sending Jimmy off first to college and then on to the Navy. After Ronny passed from a massive heart attack, Ruthie died of a broken heart two years later. Ronny's passing was a seminal event in Jimmy's life and triggered his departure from the Navy to return home.

Jimmy turned off the engine and stared at his house in the dim light, still in great shape thanks to the upkeep Jimmy and his uncle before him had put into it. It was a sturdy, wood-frame house that had been covered with pale white aluminum siding and had a concrete and brick foundation. While it had a front door easily seen as one pulled into the driveway on the left side of the house, it was seldom used. The back of the house, facing what had once been an apple grove, now faced a well-mowed field stretching out toward the edge of the woods. Like many settlements in the area, this one was on an incline near the base of a mountain.

Jimmy walked up the few steps, unlocked the door to his enclosed back porch, and walked into the small kitchen with the wood stove on his right. He grabbed a beer out of the fridge and walked back out to his porch to sit on his old brown tattered cloth couch. Taking a swig of brew, he gazed out over the field into the edge of the forest. A fleeting memory of Uncle Ronny near the top of his ladder with his picking sack covering his front and leaning into the apple trees as he plucked Granny Smiths, quickly dropping the apples into his sack, passed through his mind. A tear rolled down one cheek as his mind began to fade into the past. He just couldn't remember much about his life as a child; the earliest memories were of his aunt and uncle. Uncle Ronny had said his parents had died in some kind of freak accident on their farm. It apparently had burned down one night, and he was the only survivor.

Jimmy had enjoyed his childhood on thc apple farm eagerly participating in the harvest and throwing rotten apples at trees for target practice. He had been a good student in school; and influenced by his uncle and his fondness for the military, he had entered the Virginia Military Institute in Lexington, Virginia, to pursue a college education and get a commission in the Army.

After an unfortunate incident at VMI where he was kicked out of school, he had decided to follow his high school sweetheart, Cindy Smith, to junior college in Roanoke. She was into agricultural studies, and Jimmy thought that college was the thing to do at the time. He had quickly grown bored with school and had stopped by the Navy recruiter's office in Front Royal to inquire about joining that branch of the service. His aunt and uncle were heartbroken when he told them one night after dinner that he wanted to drop out of college and pursue the service. By then, the fire had gone out of his and Cindy's courtship, and they had gone their separate ways in college. Later, after Jimmy had signed the necessary papers and taken his physical, his aunt and uncle had come around to the idea of his joining the Navy. In a way they could understand his desire to see the big wide world and not spend the rest of his life in a backwater town.

He quickly got up to stifle the memory and went back into the house as night descended. He had been shooting in his backyard the prior Sunday and had some weapons to clean.

Jimmy had assembled a large bundle of oak logs he had chopped down on his property to use as a backstop to protect against anyone who might be in the forest behind his property. He would shoot at either tin cans placed in front of the backstop or mount a collection of paper targets stapled on large segments of cardboard. Developing a fondness for weapons while in the Navy and, of course, being the owner of a sporting goods store where his biggest intake of revenue was from the sale of firearms, it was natural that Jimmy would have a sizable collection at his farmhouse.

With thoughts of a human predator perhaps lurking nearby in the woods, he double-checked his windows and doors finishing up with the front door in his living room. He placed a few well-seasoned, dark brown logs that he had stored in a small bin in his living room into his fireplace with some newspaper and a few strips of lumber and started a fire to take the chill off. He seldom turned on the heat in his house until late in the evenings.

Grabbing his Boswell pipe and stoking it with black Cavendish, he gathered his recently fired weapons to clean. He placed his Browning Mk III Hi-Power

9mm pistol on the newspaper along side his Ruger Redhawk. His Browning automatic rifle, popularly known as the famous BAR, stood leaning up against his much used and aged maple coffee table, originally built by his uncle. As he lit up, he proceeded to clean his weapons and then charged each handgun with a premium hollow point load and the BAR with the best federal .30-06 soft-point load he had available.

Placing the Hi-Power in his nylon shoulder holster that he often wore while in his farmhouse and then grabbing another beer from the fridge, he began to eat dinner. The left over chili he had heated up on the wood stove made him feel warm all over. His recently cleaned and loaded weapons gave him a sense of security. He relit his pipe and sat back in his rocking chair in front of the fireplace. Startled by the heat he was now feeling from the fireplace that was fast warming him, thoughts of the past once again came rushing in.

Christ Almighty, it is fucking hot in this place, trainee Jimmy Mackenzie thought, as he stood dressed in fatigues in the sand in a line with the rest of his SEAL team class at the Naval Amphibious Base in Little Creek, Virginia. It was July, and SEAL team training was in full swing.

After dropping out of junior college in Roanoke, he had entered Navy boot camp at the Naval Training Center (NTC) in Norfolk, Virginia, and wondered as the blowing sand literally sand blasted his face how he could have been so stupid to volunteer to in effect do boot camp once again. Only this was at a very different level. Running around the parade field in Norfolk in the autumn holding an M-16 with both hands in full gear had been tough, but this training was something else entirely.

Boot camp graduate Jimmy Mackenzie had read the bulletin posted on the board in the hallway of his barracks announcing an opportunity to become a Navy SEAL. He had grown excited reading that the SEALS were very special, and only the best need apply.

Jimmy was intrigued about the concept of operating with a small unit of guys who would be sneaking up on hostile beach areas, blowing up obstacles, or jumping out of airplanes ready to wreak mayhem on the bad guys. He had never expected such an opportunity in the Navy. Like everyone else, he had joined the Navy to see the world, indeed, to get out of his small shell of a life back in a country town in Virginia.

"MacKenzie! Get your head out of your ass," shouted Chief Petty Officer Jim Snowden. "You will remain alert at all times. I don't want to see any of you pukes glassy eyed. Do you read me!" he yelled.

"Aye, aye, sir," Jimmy replied.

Staring Jimmy down as the wind whipped his face with stinging sand, Snowden yelled, "Drop and give me twenty-five!"

Jimmy handed over his M-16 to the fire crew leader and dropped quickly onto the hot sand to do the push-ups.

"Recover," shouted Chief Snowden.

Jimmy quickly scrambled to attention, taking his M-16 that had been thrust into his hands by the instructor.

"Now, the first ten trainees starting from my right fall out and double time to the range. The rest of you pukes report to Chief Petty Officer Michaels at the surf area double time and be at attention beside your IBS. You trainees are going to enjoy surf passage training. Chief Michaels will be waiting. Don't keep him waiting!" Snowden commanded.

The IBS or Inflatable Boat—Small, was one of the boats that BUD/S trainees would be required to guide through the rough surf with a minimum of spills and was an integral part of their training. Indeed, the IBS would be a key delivery and extraction vehicle for many of their future missions.

After Jimmy and the nine other recruits had reported to the range with its manmade wall of logs and sand set up as a barrier to prevent bullets from going out of the area, they were issued handguns and began to take target practice as ordered with the Beretta 9 millimeter pistol. No sooner had trainee Mackenzie loaded his weapon and prepared to sight-acquire his paper target down range when Chief Petty Officer Snowden jumped into his face once again. "Stop! Freeze! Don't move a fucking muscle!"

Jimmy literally froze in his tracks as Snowden slowly and gingerly pried Jimmy's trigger finger from the trigger of his Beretta and took the weapon from him. He then proceeded to drop the magazine, eject the live shell from the chamber into the cup of the hand that had racked the slide, and visually inspect the pistol, rendering it safe.

"How many fucking times have I told you to keep your finger off the trigger until you are ready to fire the weapon! You are disgusting! Drop and give me fifty!" Snowden screamed.

Once Jimmy had completed his push-ups, Chief Petty Officer Snowden proceeded to call a halt to the activities at the range, admonishing all of the trainees about the importance of keeping their trigger fingers off the trigger until they had acquired their targets.

All of the trainees on the range had then been sent running to the beach to endure "surf conditioning," a form of torture where the students wormed their way through the sand, crawling while rubbing their knees and elbows raw as the surf boiled in and around their bodies.

Man, am I ever glad I survived that, Jimmy mused as he walked to his bedroom and prepared to call it a night.

Chapter 7

Washington, D.C.

"Hey, Joe, how's it going," Pat Sedgwick said as he walked into his cubicle just down the aisle from Joe's cubicle in Systems and Programming.

It was 8:00 a.m. sharp, and employees were beginning to pour into the building to begin another day managing the personnel arm of the federal government. While Joe had been a computer programmer for nearly two years, he still deferred frequently to the knowledge and wisdom of his original mentor, Pat.

"I don't know, Pat. I'm kind of discouraged right now with this rewrite of WR100," he said. WR100 was the name of the only assembler language program remaining in Pat's Work-Reporting System, a system that tracked the number of hours per project that each employee worked during a pay period. Tom Akron, Pat and Joe's supervisor, had recently tasked Pat with converting all remaining assembler programs in his system to the COBOL language. Both Pat and Tom thought it would be an interesting challenge for Joe to rewrite this particular program in COBOL. WR100 was a complex program, and this would be a fitting assignment considering the great progress Joe had made in the past two years under Pat's tutelage.

"I'll tell you what, Joe. Let me go down to the subbasement and get a cup of coffee, and we'll take a look at the doggone thing when I get back."

"Thanks, Pat, I really appreciate that," Joe replied with a forced smile.

Once Pat had returned with his coffee, he proceeded to give Joe some additional verbal background on the functionality of WR100. It was an interface program that performed complex calculations based on the number of project hours reported by all CSC employees in the agency on their time sheets and the corresponding accounting codes that the employees charged for their various projects. Then Pat drew up a rough flowchart to provide Joe with a logical picture of the program's functionality to reinforce the verbal summary he had just given to Joe. When Pat had first discussed this rewrite with Joe a few weeks earlier, he had quickly gone over the program's functionality, and Joe had taken notes. Now that Joe was really digging into it, he had come up with many questions that needed answers before he could continue with the rewrite. With Pat's additional enthusiastic input provided this morning, Joe began to relax for the first time in the several weeks since he had been tasked with this latest project. He now began to actually feel good about his ability to complete the task.

After Pat finished his rough flowchart, he passed it over to Joe. "Okay, Joe, do you think you have a handle on it now?" he asked.

"I think so, Pat, thanks a lot," Joe replied.

"No problem. Hey, if you get stuck, just come on over." Pat motioned in the direction of his cubicle just down the aisle.

Joe gathered his notes together and proceeded to organize his thoughts once again to focus on the task. As the lunch hour approached, his thoughts temporarily drifted to the sport of racket ball. After observing the karate class just before Thanksgiving last year and thinking to himself, "*Thanks, but no thanks*," he had indeed looked into the county YMCA near where he lived in Wheaton, Maryland, with the idea of taking the indoor tennis course. While at the Y to sign up for the tennis course, he had observed a racket ball contest being played out in another area of the building and had been impressed with the workout that the contestants were getting. Sweating profusely with the constant "whack" of the ball back and forth against a wall going in all directions, those guys seemed to be getting a hell of a workout, and they weren't getting their butts kicked doing it!

Aware that the Department of the Interior across 19th Street from CSC had a recreational association similar to State's with a number of racket ball courts, Joe had elected to join that program and put tennis and karate on the back burner for the time being. He was a fledgling player who labored every day during the lunch hour to get the type of workout he craved. While for the most part enjoying the mental challenges he faced every day as a mainframe programmer, he was by nature an intense person and needed a release to escape from the pressure, in actuality more his doing than anyone else's. With that in mind, he left the office for his daily workout.

After his workout, Joe grabbed a greasy hot salami and cheese sub from the subbasement snack bar and returned to his cubicle with his lunch to pick up where he had left off with the program rewrite. Since he had been floundering for the past several weeks really not making any progress at all, he stopped his supervisor in the hallway, Tom Akron, to inquire about working overtime to catch up.

"Hey, Tom, would there be a problem if I stick around after close of business to work on the assignment that Pat gave me?"

Tom smiled at Joe. "You mean the rewrite of that assembler program?" Tom asked.

"Yes, sir," Joe replied.

"Joe, I don't have a problem with you working overtime on that. Work as much overtime as you need; you have blanket authority from me on that. Just make sure to note your hours in the overtime column of your time sheet. As you know, one of the big directives from my boss is to get rid of all of the assembler programs. It has already been decided that we are going over to the IBM 3090 beginning early fall, and it will be a lot easier to convert a totally COBOL Honeywell system to the IBM platform. We don't want to have to worry about those assembler programs still out there that need to be rewritten during the actual conversion process. We want all of those converted to COBOL by the end of spring."

"Thanks, Tom," Joe happily replied. This would give Joe a chance to fatten up his paycheck considerably.

When Joe looked up from his newly developed block flowchart, he noticed that it was 3:00 p.m. already. He would have to let Sandi know that he would be late getting home. Since no one appeared to be nearby, he picked up the phone on his desk and dialed home.

"Hello," Sandi said.

"Hi, Hon, I'm going to have to work some overtime this evening. Just found out from the boss that I can work as much overtime as I want on this new project. I can pull the Honda into the garage under the building after close of business."

"Well, that's great, Joe; we can certainly use the extra money. Just use good judgment coming home through the city at night. Remember, Rock Creek Park is closed because of major road work, so you will have to go through the city."

"I will; I'll just come up 16th Street. I hope to be getting out of here by nine." After saying good-bye to Sandi, Joe picked up a caffeine-laced soft drink in the snack bar and returned to his cubicle eager to continue working on his project.

"So, Joe, you're going to stick around and work on WR100, huh?" Pat asked as he walked past Joe's cubicle while pulling on his trench coat to leave for the day.

"Yeah, figured I might as well stay with it while my mind is fresh. Tom said it was no problem to work extra on it," Joe replied.

"Well, great, Joe. If you don't have it rewritten by midnight, I would take off," Pat laughed.

"You don't have to worry about that. I'm out of here by nine at the latest. Have a good evening."

"You too," Pat replied.

There was one thing Joe had noticed about himself whenever he was totally absorbed in work. Every time he looked up from the task at hand, it would seem that the clock had bounded forward an hour or two. Joe noticed that it was almost nine, and he called Sandi to let her know he was on his way home. However, no sooner had he hung up from the phone than his mind once again became totally occupied with figuring out the next logical path of his code, and he found himself immersed again in his work.

The phone rang, and it was Sandi. "Where are you?" she asked.

"Damn, Hon, my mind is so consumed with this, I just let the time slip away." Joe glanced quickly at his watch and noticed it was now 10:30.

"We'll, don't you think it's time you headed home? I am worried about you," Sandi pleaded.

Joe responded quickly, "I will wrap this up in a half hour. I just can't leave right now; I have to write down some fresh ideas I just came up with or I will have to start over in the morning," Joe explained.

Sighing on the phone, Sandi told Joe that she would leave dinner out on the stove for him to heat up when he arrived home.

He went about the process of writing down his recent ideas, made a note of the time, and grabbed his leather jacket as he headed down the hallway on the sixth floor where his office was located.

"Shit, it's damn near midnight. I've got to get my butt home," he muttered to himself.

As he sauntered down the hallway toward the elevators, he thought he heard a phone faintly ringing in the distance. He was in too much of a hurry to worry about it. He waved at the guard in his booth just outside of the CSC cafeteria on the ground floor that led to the multi-level garage where employees parked their vehicles.

Getting into his Honda, he was a bit startled when his car appeared to be difficult to start. He mused, *"Damn, I wonder what's the matter?"* After depressing the accelerator pedal furiously multiple times, he attempted over and over again to start the car with no luck. Finally, after waiting several minutes, he turned the engine over once again, and it came to life with the familiar sound of the Honda ignition system, improving his mood considerably. With a sigh of relief, Joe went out of the garage entrance directly facing the Department of Interior on 19th Street.

It was a frigid February night, and the wind was howling. Since 19th Street was a one-way street going in the direction of the Tidal Basin, Joe worked his way around Interior to 18th Street near Constitution Avenue and began to head north towards K Street where he would eventually run into 16th Street heading toward his apartment.

Along the way he passed some homeless people wrapped in their rags hovering around the steam grates for warmth. While he felt sympathy for them, like many federal employees and their private sector counterparts who worked in Foggy Bottom, he had been the victim on more than one occasion of verbal abuse. There had even been the time when he was heading over to the bank a block away from CSC to cash a credit union check, only to find a homeless man suddenly right beside him on the curb. For some reason, the homeless man yelled something in Joe's ear, and then shockingly pushed Joe on his left arm with his dirty open hand as they both took off to cross 18th Street. Joe had been alarmed by that and remembered at the time how much of a wimp he had felt. He should have turned around and shoved the dirt bag.

Thinking about that as he made a left onto 16th Street only made him feel vulnerable again. *Christ, here I go again. I hate feeling intimidated. That's the one problem I have not fixed. Racket ball's a great workout, though it sure doesn't help with my intimidation problems.*

Joe worked to stifle those feelings of ineptness as he passed by the Trader Vic restaurant with its tasty Hawaiian fare located in the Shoreham Hotel on his right. I *wonder what Sandi has prepared for dinner? She had said she was going to do red beans and rice with her special simmered pork chops last weekend for one of the dinners this week. Forgot to ask her. Maybe she'll surprise me when I get home*, he thought with a smile.

He drove slowly up 16th Street past the Federal City College with some thoughts once again of insecurity and anxiety beginning to seep into his mind. Using public transportation for the most part during the daylight hours to go in and out of the city for his job, Joe normally didn't dwell on what was going on in the city at night. He knew that there were some areas where he would definitely not want to be once the sun set. He had always been leery of this particular segment of the 16th Street corridor, especially once one got out of the scene downtown on K Street where the businesses and restaurants were located, many of which were highly recommended by the restaurant critics.

From where he was now near M Street, all the way through the Adams Morgan area at the location where Arkansas Street crossed was the segment that bothered him the most. On those rare occasions when their money situation permitted, he and his family would be driving home from dinner at the "Hogates" restaurant in southwest DC on the waterfront coming through this area to go home, and the old fears would haunt him again. Naturally, he never told Sandi of his worries.

He attempted mightily to stifle these thoughts when suddenly he noticed that there was a detour sign, and those few cars that were on 16th Street in front of him were making a right turn to follow the detour. Since he had been deep in thought and driving slowly, he had not noticed the faint glow of red on the instrument panel of his car that was attempting to warn Joe that his engine was beginning to run hot. Losing track of the cars ahead of him, he made a right turn at the detour sign and found himself on T Street. At this point there were no cars ahead of him. With his mind wandering, he must have lost track of where the cars went.

What the hell? Wonder where those cars went? Joe asked himself. While a long-time resident of the Washington metropolitan area, having been born in the District and raised in the nearby Maryland suburbs, Joe had seldom ventured out into the city late at night and had only vague familiarity with this area of town. He had heard that this location was a haven for prostitutes, drug dealers, and winos.

He slowed down and crept forward, slowly trying to get his bearings as he neared 16th and Swann Street. Then out of the blue he heard a sharp crack.

Shit! Wonder if that was a handgun going off? Joe thought with a shiver. His question was answered when he turned to the left and noticed a large branch approximately two inches in diameter lying on the sidewalk to his left. *Hmm, the wind must have knocked it out of the tree*, he thought. His only goal now was to get the hell out of this neighborhood as soon as possible.

As he moved past 16th and Swann and began to approach the drug-infested 14th Street area, he noticed a group of what appeared to be prostitutes huddling with heavy coats on the corner of 14th and T Streets. *Jesus, they must be desperate to make money tonight*, Joe thought. They were young women with pretty, hard faces. Despite the coldness of the night, he noticed that a few had on skintight leopard-patterned leotards with black "fuck me" pumps on. In a moment of weakness, Joe had to admit that the girls where damn sexy. Shivering from the cold, they merely stole a quick glance his way. Anyway, cruising for whores was the last thing on his mind tonight.

He was more than halfway up the street when a lump began to throb in his throat. Joe had noticed suddenly a stark red glare coming from his dashboard and felt his Honda begin to sputter.

Oh, shit! This damn car is quitting on me. I can't believe this shit. What the hell am I going to do now in this godforsaken place? This is what I get for being so stupid, getting myself caught up in my work. When am I ever going to learn?

There was a "poof" sound that came from under his hood followed by a bellow of steam beginning to emanate from his radiator as he attempted to will his car forward. Finally, the Honda just wouldn't move another inch.

Joe sat there feeling totally helpless in an area of town where he definitely was not comfortable. As the cold wind kicked up, he noticed that there appeared to be only one street lamp per block dimly glowing now—a far cry from the lit-up portions of 16th Street near downtown. His mind became cluttered with fearful thoughts.

What should I do, now? Hell, I just can't sit here and wait for the cops to come by. They never seem to be around when you need them. Wasn't there a place somewhere on U Street called Ben's or Ben's Chili Place—something similar to that? Maybe I should just get out and try to find it and call Sandi and a tow truck from there.

With that thought in mind, he took his keys out of the ignition, buttoned his coat up tightly to his neck, and gingerly stepped out of the Honda, closing the car door very slowly and locking it so as not to attract attention. There was just the smallest room for vehicles to get around his stalled car on T Street.

He had thought that Ben's was located in the vicinity of 14th and U Street, so he turned around and headed back toward where the prostitutes had been, thinking he could just go north from there on T Street to U Street. As he walked toward where he had seen the whores, his face began to feel the sting from the cold wind. Fortunately, he had a great pair of leather gloves to protect his hands; Sandi had just gotten them for him at Christmas. Unfortunately, knowing that he had a car for work today, he had only worn his thin leather jacket with no lining to protect him from the elements.

Suddenly, he stopped dead in his tracks. He thought he had heard some people talking loudly coming directly down the sidewalk halfway up the block from him. *Oh, well, all I can do is pretend I am not afraid and ask them if they know where Ben's Chili whatever is*, he thought.

He picked up his walk slightly, holding his head up and staring straight ahead as the distance between Joe and the people he had heard began to close. His heart sank as he noticed that the group of people coming down the sidewalk appeared to be a rough bunch of young men talking loudly as they walked.

One of the young men with a Navy pea coat and a heavy woolen, dark-blue skullcap pulled down over his ears holding a large, clear bottle of "Olde English" malt liquor, fondly referred to in the street as a "forty," spoke first. "Look what the fuck we got here! Man, what you doin in the hood?" he asked of Joe as the old familiar tingles of fear began to make Joe's skin crawl.

Joe cleared his throat as the group came up to within a few feet of him. These were, in fact, rough-looking young men dressed for the cold with heavy nylon jackets and woolen skullcaps of various colors. Before Joe could answer, the smallest one in the group with a prominent set of protruding front teeth moved aggressively toward Joe and began to thump him shockingly in the chest with his right index finger. The young man's beer breath was foul, as spittle sprayed all over Joe's face and coat. "Answer the man! What the fuck is you doin in my hood? You Five O, chump? Answer the man 'fore I kick your ass!" he yelled as Joe felt a sensation of fear he had never experienced as he stepped back from the street dude thumping his chest.

He broke out into a cold sweat, and his throat appeared to constrict. The hair on the back of his neck stood out like porcupine bristles as he began to mumble words to the effect that he was looking for "Ben's Chili" restaurant.

"Man, you are in the wrong neighborhood. Ain't no "Ben's Chili" restaurant round here," the short one pressed, spittle again spraying into Joe's face.

Joe tried to put on an appearance of being strong. "I had heard Ben's was somewhere up on U Street," he responded.

Turning to the others in the group, the short one spoke up at an ominously higher note. "I'll be damned; this dude be callin me a liar. Time for an ass whuppin, chump. Which one of you home boys wants a piece of this mothafucka?"

Before Joe knew what had hit him, the short man had charged into Joe and smacked him hard on his left ear with his open palm, breaking Joe's eardrum. Joe fell back, nearly stumbling over his own feet. With his ear ringing and then rapidly becoming numb from the blow, Joe raised both hands in a defensive posture to protect himself.

The dude who had spoken first handed his malt liquor to another of the street dudes and laughed. "Aw, this chump want to do battle now. I'm going to have to knock him out," the short man said. With that expression, the young thug suddenly moved forward and kicked Joe in his groin with a sickening thump. Joe thought he had lost all sensation in his body at this point as his eyes rolled back into his head, and he crumpled to the sidewalk. Before it was over, the street thug had kicked him on his cheek as he lay defenseless on the sidewalk, splitting his face open like a cut melon and proceeded to beat him around his head and body with the fallen branch that Joe had seen just a few moments earlier.

After they had rifled through his pants and jacket and taken his wallet and new Seiko watch, another of his wife's recent Christmas gifts, the short dude kicked Joe in the side again for good measure and spat out his final, angry diatribe. "Fuck that, asshole."

Losing consciousness as he lay in agony on the mean streets of DC, Joe weakly muttered his wife's name. Then, the lights went out for Joe Lynch in the cold, lonely asphalt jungle.

Chapter 8

Shenandoah National Park, Virginia—Stony Man Mountain Overlook

I am going to find them even if I have to spend every spare moment of the rest of my life looking for them.

With those thoughts he wondered where in all this expanse of mountains and forest he was going to start. Once again, he stared back up at the summit of Stony Man, high up on his left rising above the group of trees that walked their way up the side of the mountain from the lake far below. Then, he looked out again from his perch on the overlook panning the wide vista straight ahead and up. The sky was a conglomeration of blue-and-white haze that met the land far out there somewhere on the distant horizon. He whispered to himself. "Ma, Pa—where are you?"

For the first time, he was keenly aware that there were several other vehicles on this overlook. He wasn't alone. There was a family, probably a mother and father with their young son, only thirty feet or so from him, standing along the stone barrier that ran along the edge of the parking area.

A tear rolled down his cheek. He wiped away the tear and tried to pull himself together. He had been greatly challenged in his life in a number of arenas and situations that he had overcome. So, he was not going to be beaten by this. This was something he *must* do at all costs. As he had willed himself in the past to clear his thoughts and focus on the task at hand, he would do so now. He wondered where he should start his search.

He remembered that in his first trip up here just to sit on the overlook and think, he had driven down the road toward Stony Man and pulled into a parking area to the right. There he had come across the Stony Man trailhead. This was the beginning of a nearly two-mile hike to the summit, an easy hike according to the information provided on a plaque provided by the park service. He had to start somewhere. Maybe he would have a better perspective from the summit. He certainly couldn't just step over the stone barrier on the overlook and start trekking down the mountainside. What would people think? More importantly, what would park rangers think that happened to be in this area?

Pulling into the parking area where the trailhead began, he proceeded to gear up for his hike. By all appearances, he was just another of the many of thousands of hikers who had gone this route before. He slid on his full-sized Columbia backpack, extending from his shoulder area all the way down to the small of his back, locked his vehicle, and proceeded to the trailhead. He had stuffed his backpack with provisions that hikers normally take with them such as several bottles of spring water, a flashlight, several power bars, a sandwich tightly wrapped in aluminum foil enclosed in plastic, and a compass—certainly nothing questionable.

What was unusual were the additional items he packed: his seven-inch, razor-sharp hunting knife, a fifty-foot strand of rope, extra clothing for an overnight stay, a Philippine-made machete for clearing brush, a Ruger GP100 .357 magnum revolver stoked with 158 grain hollow points that rested in his Safariland leather shoulder rig, two hundred rounds of extra hollow points for backup, and a *tonfa*. The *tonfa*, also a gift from a long-lost buddy, was an old wooden Okinawan farm implement turned martial arts weapon, L shape in design, where the practitioner could hold the smaller end in his hand while the longer end fitted snugly to the arm riding up to the elbow. Using his arm this way as a guide, he could wreak havoc on his enemy by driving his elbow with the long end of the *tonfa* into the side of a person's face, literally crushing the cheek and skull with a single blow.

He started into the trail glancing at a large patch of fern plants to his left. The thought occurred to him that someone with evil intent could immerse himself into that patch of fern camouflaged and easily take out the unsuspecting hiker or park ranger. Holding that thought, he proceeded into the trail noting that any perception of elevation change was minimal.

He wondered if his parents had ever been in this area of the park. *Did they ever summit Stony Man?* They certainly would have seen the fern patch and the numerous large gray squirrels scurrying about looking for the tasty harvest of nuts and acorns supplied by the forested mountain.

The temperature was around forty degrees at 10:00 a.m., though it seemed much cooler here in the mountains in early March with a stiff breeze blowing nonstop. It felt invigorating to him, and he began to feel a renewed sense of purpose about his mission. Walking slowly up the trail, he spotted a large white tan doe, sitting in the brush with its ears occasionally flickering. He walked a little slower to not disturb the animal in its natural habitat. It was interesting to note that the deer seemed not the least bit alarmed with his presence. He knew that had certainly not been the case back in his Ma and Pa's day.

Something cruel had happened to his parents in these mountains. Sinister thoughts of revenge began to creep into his consciousness. His thoughts were abruptly interrupted when two big fellows with loud voices brushed by him on their way to the summit. Then one of the intruders made a comment that turned his stomach.

"Man, too bad I didn't bring my gun; we could have wasted that fuckin deer." Then they paused to relieve themselves directly on the path, rather than walking into the brush nearby. The doe quickly jumped up and ran through the brush in the opposite direction to get away from the disturbance.

Those pricks, he thought, *just like the enemy. I ought to take them sumbitches out now.*

He quickly collected himself and stifled his rage. He could not let incidents such as this detract from his objective. No, that wouldn't be a good idea this close to a frequently used trail. He would be in danger of bringing too much attention to himself; he would never complete his search if he were behind bars for the rest of his life. He let the men put distance between them and himself as he lagged behind.

Continuing onward, he came to an intersection where he remembered this being the point where the Appalachian Trail crossed the Stony Man summit trail. A posted sign indicated that he was now over 3,800 feet above sea level. Creeping forward slowly, he was able to obtain a glimpse through the top of the trees on the side of the mountain in the direction of the lake and could make out distant mountain ridges. He paused for a minute to savor this sight and understand perhaps for the first time how lucky his family was to have made this area their homestead.

With that thought, sadness again invaded his consciousness. *Shit, with every good thought I have, a larger negative one settles in to interfere—fuck.*

Then he heard voices, young women in their twenties with pigtails looking like Austrian alpine hikers out doing their hike for exercise and adventure with their backpacks and Timberland hiking shoes, waving and saying "Hi" quite pleasantly to him as they headed for the summit.

The wind was picking up at this elevation, whistling easily through the mixture of red spruce, brush, and ferns. He felt a brief shiver moving forward and noted to the left of the trail that there were neatly stacked large, somewhat rectangular rocks. When he had been at the visitor's center browsing through materials a few weeks earlier, he had found out that there once had been a copper mine that had been worked for both copper and silver near the summit of Stony Man. From an outward appearance, it was impossible to tell where the shaft began, and if one could seek shelter in the mine, if it were needed in an emergency. He had no idea why that thought occurred to him. He wondered if his Pa or any of his family had ever worked the mine. He felt the familiar sadness once again.

At last coming out of the trail, he was on the top of Stony Man's head, which consisted of huge clumps of rocks contorted together. He noted the individuals he had seen along the trail joining several others already at the summit.

The two men he had seen earlier on the trail near the doe were sitting out on the rocks to his right while other hikers were snapping pictures of themselves at various points on the summit with the incredible vista that Stony Man presided over. Out on the rocks at the summit, the wind was more persistent. Thankfully, the two men rose and proceeded back into the trail. He gingerly got down on his hands and knees, semi-crawling to the spot on the summit he craved. This was where he wanted to sit and reflect, since he could now see the lake as he sat on the right side of the summit, definitely smaller at this distance. The buildup of haze had begun in earnest as it neared the noon hour. *Probably due to pollution from the factories to the south and west*, he mused. Squinting through the glare of the sun and haze, he thought to himself, *Ma and Pa, how am I going to find you out there?*

If the notes he had found were accurate, and he had no reason to think otherwise, he could at least narrow his search to this quadrant and give it a try. While he was not provisioned beyond two or three days for hiking into the deep brush with the slow, tortuous challenge such a task presented, he must begin somewhere. He could mark the trees in the thickets for two purposes. One, to ensure that he would not go over old ground unnecessarily in any future searches, and two, if a given search were to prove fruitful, he would have a marker in which to come back. He thought it might be a good idea to backtrack toward where the mine was located on the trail, and then he would linger by the mine and listen for any human sounds before making his next move.

He had been at the mine for nearly an hour trying to look interested and pretending to take notes as hikers continued to come and go from the trailhead to the summit, and he was growing impatient. Finally, there was some silence, as there seemed to be an inexplicable break in the activity. He checked his location with the compass and pushed himself across the trail from the mine, entering the thick brush. Since he was still relatively close to the trail, he would have to initially move slowly without aid of his brush-cutting machete. This took enormous patience and perseverance as the jagged twigs began to tear into his new Columbia nylon trail jacket and cut him about his hands, arms, and legs.

He must have gone fifty yards from the trail, taking nearly an hour to accomplish that task before he said to hell with it and slid off his backpack. Wiping the sweat from his face, he found that he was into the deep brush now, and the woods were thick with the smells of the forest: oak, pine, and leaves. It was intoxicating to him. As he licked a rather large abrasion on the top of his right hand, he glanced upwards and could barely make out portions of the sky.

He sat down in a clump of leaves to plan his next strategy while taking a badly needed break. He decided with this off-trail hike, he would start marking the trail beginning at his present location, using the waterproof trail marker he had bought at Hudson Trail Outfitters. He could easily remember during return trips where his off-trail browsing started.

He had just pulled out his machete when he began to hear some crashing in the brush to his left. In the mountain forest sound is as deceiving as being in a cleared valley. There develops a scary phenomenon where the individual has no earthly idea where the sound is coming from.

Fuck, I wonder if a bear is making that sound, he mused. The hair began to rise on the back of his neck—a certain signal of danger. The crashing became louder and ominously closer. He quickly pulled his .357 from his Safariland shoulder rig and slowly rose up, moving his head slowly in a circle right to left, gun at the ready, and then he quietly turned around performing the same technique hunters often used to look and listen for signs of their prey. He repeated this front-and-back check several times before hearing a snort and a growl. Then, he just barely made out a black bear as it bobbed its head in the brown and green thickets almost ninety degrees to the left of where he had been facing in a sitting position. This was too close for comfort. He very slowly plugged his ears with the rubber portable plugs attached with nylon he had slung around his neck for such a scenario, and without hesitation began to squeeze the trigger of his Ruger in the general direction of the bear. There was a deafening roar from the .357 with enough of a blast to nearly ignite the small leaves of brush lingering near the front of the muzzle of his weapon. The bear immediately twisted and crashed through the brush at full speed to put itself as far away as it could get from the horrible sound. He had no intention of wounding or killing the animal, just alleviating the threat.

With a sigh of relief, he holstered his weapon, thanking the Lord for guns, as he had done so many times before in his life. He knew that the occasional blast heard from a distance would not alarm anyone, not even the hikers doing the Stony Man trek. *Hell, people in this neck of the woods shoot all the time. The park is very close to farms and areas where hunting, legal or illegal, goes on year round.*

Checking his compass and continuing through the thicket, now getting somewhat more manageable in part because of the active swinging motion of his machete, he continued to walk in a southwesterly direction. He continuously hacked and moved brush, pausing occasionally to mark his newly formed trail. While it was obvious that he was forming a new trail through the deep forest as he moved toward the base of Stony Man, he doubted seriously if anyone other than himself would come across this area of the deep forest. It was just too way off the beaten path.

He had begun to work up a sweat, relentlessly pushing forward through the brush, when he noticed that the light was beginning to fade. He had been entertaining the idea of spending the night here in the forest when a thought gave him a shudder. *Fuck! I can't leave my Goddamn vehicle at the trailhead overnight. The fuckin park rangers may tow it away. Even worse, they will have my tag number and find out who I am. I've got to head back now.*

He turned abruptly to go back in the direction he had come from, using his compass and the markers on the trees. With the trailed cleared by his machete, he was able to move several times faster than when he had first entered this area of Stony Man mountain.

He began to think more positively about his aborted adventure with the realization that he had *finally* begun his search. Somehow while intending, if necessary, to stay overnight in the forest, he had completely forgotten about his vehicle. Thank God this potential dilemma had occurred to him before the night had gotten too old. He had just barely made it back to within fifty yards of the trail when his trail ended, and the heavy thickets once again became an issue. Of course, he knew that there was no way he could cut completely through to the trail. That would be inviting too much curiosity to hikers or even worse to park rangers, leaving his mission exposed. He quietly bulled his way through the thickets, and taking a quick peek both ways to ensure the coast was clear, he walked up and out into the trail facing the copper mine.

He had paused just before emerging from the bushes to listen for sounds, and with the late hour—darkness had just settled over the mountain—he turned sharply to his left and walked briskly down the trail to his vehicle.

While his was the only vehicle in the parking lot, there was no evidence that the park service had paid his vehicle a visit to leave a note or ticket or even worse, tow it.

Quickly sliding his backpack off and laying it on his backseat, he fired up his vehicle and drove back home. Smiling to himself, he had a pleasant thought. *Next time I come, I will have a better plan so that I can stay a long time.*

Chapter 9

Shenandoah National Park, Virginia—Skyline Drive Near Stony Man Mountain

Damn good idea if I might say so myself, he reflected as he drove his sport utility vehicle slowly up the old service road into the mountains. The park service had closed this road to the general public by stretching a linked chain between two concrete posts at the entrance. It led to an abandoned quarry that had originally been used in the construction of the park in the late twenties and early thirties. He had noticed the gated gravel road on the way back from his first mission to Stony Man a week earlier to find his parents. When he had arrived home and had a chance to reflect on the day's adventures off the beaten path, he had come to a number of conclusions. In his efforts to locate his ma and pa, he would probably have to circumvent any laws that were in effect in the park.

First, weapons were strictly prohibited in the park, though if pressed, many a hiker would readily admit to packing a firearm of some sort at least for that day-long hike to Old Rag Mountain. After all, there were hundreds of black bears roaming the park. *What do you do if you stumble upon a mother and her cubs, when all of the screaming and yelling in the world won't stop this particular bear as she continues to move menacingly forward, maybe taking a swipe or two at your face as you are steadily backing up? Do you permit yourself to be a victim when a mere discharge from a firearm in the air will most likely send her scurrying away at breakneck speed?* He would have to carry a weapon as he had experienced last week with the unexpected intrusion of the black bear interfering with his search.

Four-legged predators had not been his only concern. He had made an honorable pledge to the memory of his parents that he would find them at all costs. No individual or group of individuals, or any animal —not the park service, the police, or the military—would stop him. He *would not be stopped.* People would die in their efforts to thwart him from his search.

Second, his notes and commonsense told him he would have to make his own way in the park wilderness. The designated trails were wonderful creations of the park that were a great service to the public in their being able to safely enjoy the pristine forest and mountains, only an hour and a half from the nation's capital. For him the trails would be an initial means to an end. He was quite sure the park service would not approve of his moving off the designated trails and thrashing his way to God knows where with a sharpened machete made in a small town outside of Manila in the Philippines. An important part of this premise was once he was in the park and prepared to move off the main trails, he had first better have a plan to hide his arrival vehicle somewhere that was both convenient for insertion and extraction once a mission was completed.

Third, he knew that when he found his parents' homestead, he intended to claim it as his property by any means necessary. After all, wasn't this where he had been born and raised as a young child? This was his family home, therefore his by birthright. No state or federal government was going to usurp him on this point. He was a serious believer in the Second Amendment believing that every man had a right to possess a weapon to defend his hearth and home—and this was no different.

Fourth, he was almost certain that people were going to die before his mission was completed. Someone would be forced to pay the piper of justice. Moreover, he knew that he would not be alive to pay if his time came. Bottom line—he was not going to be taken alive.

He came across an area close to the end of the road where the quarry was located that was sparsely wooded, yet thick with heavy, tall brush wonderful for camouflage. He drove off the road, switching to four-wheel drive as he moved deep into the thickets and then shut his engine off. He paused for a few minutes with the windows down to listen carefully for any sounds. Other than the normal sounds of the forest, the busy shuffling of the squirrels, the slapping of leaves by the occasional mountain gust, the pecking of a woodpecker high up in the oaks—that was it—no sounds of any humans prowling and growling.

Feeling confident, he checked his shoulder rig and ear protectors just to be certain in the knowledge that he had not forgotten either and then bounded out of his vehicle. Opening the back of his SUV, he pulled out his extra-large Columbia backpack. He had included all of the provisions that he had brought with him on his initial search of a week earlier. He had also added extra food, additional clothing including a rain slicker, a rolled-up overnight sleepover bed, a sharpened hatchet with a leather cover, and a twelve-gauge, sawed-off Mossberg Model SP590 pump-action shotgun, nickel-plated to protect against the elements. This weapon, arguably the most lethal in the world at close range even against large and dangerous game, was his ace in the hole if necessary. He had brought two boxes of three-inch steel magnum no. 2 shot for the trip, and his Mossberg was already stoked with eight of those bad boys. Somehow, he had been able to fit all of his gear into the backpack.

As he neared the entrance of the gravel road from Skyline Drive, he peeked cautiously out onto the roadway for any signs of the park service. When he had first pulled up to the entrance to the gravel road, he had parked for ten minutes while he planned a quick maneuver to unhook the gate and drive his vehicle past the entrance some distance down the road from a visual sighting from Skyline Drive. He knew that this was one of the riskiest parts of his mission, and he had a plan for that as well. He would merely tell a suspicious park ranger that he had just assumed it would be okay for him to explore this part of the park and had failed to see the "Authorized Personnel Only" sign. While they would probably have a hard time buying it, he had planned to finesse the situation as well as possible. There had been no vehicle activity when he made his move during his earlier entrance.

Now seeing that the coast was clear on his way out of the road, he stepped out onto Skyline Drive moving to his left, appearing no different from any other hiker trudging up alongside of Skyline Drive looking for that special trailhead to plunge into.

After an hour of walking, he entered the Stony Man parking lot at the trailhead to his right and walked onto the trail once again. He had arrived early in the morning shortly after the park opened and had not seen any hikers on his way up to the defunct copper mine. He quickly slipped into the thick brush at the point of his last entrance a week earlier. Once he was ten yards from the trail, he paused to check his compass and proceeded ahead, bulling his way through the brush, although it was much easier the second time around.

After fifty yards into his makeshift trail, he saw his first tree marker and the evidence of more serious trail blazing he had first initiated a week before with his machete. His plan was to follow the exact same route into the forest in the general direction that his notes had indicated, looking for signs of an old homestead. Such signs would be the presence of large rocks and stones of various shapes and sizes that had been cleared from the land for farming eons ago. Also, the presence of heavy brush with occasional clusters of relatively small trees might indicate that a mountain family had once risen to a pot of coffee in this neck of the woods.

What had caused the heavy brush to grow? Once the original settlers had been removed or left the area of their own accord, the farms and houses had either decayed and/or been destroyed. The farmland had been grown over by heavy brush. In most cases when the settlers first arrived, in addition to clearing the land of the rocks, it had been necessary to chop down the numerous trees to clear the fields for farming.

This particular day was quite brisk with the temperature refusing to rise above the high thirties, though he could see the bright halos made through the crevices of the treetops by the sun peeking through. Within a couple of hours, he had completed the path he had created earlier rather uneventfully. No unusual sounds or bears.

Time to pull out his machete and start to work again. Based on his notes and compass, he theorized that the path he was beating was right around the middle of the quadrant that he wanted to search. Even if he arrived at the lake without finding his family, his plan was to backtrack and mark trees every fifty yards or so and then create multiple branches if warranted from that point on from his main path, and explore out and back from that point. It seemed like a good idea at the time. He knew he had to have a plan with all of this forest and just a very general idea of the location of his family. He had reasoned that it was unwise to just go out there and start thrashing around with no plan.

After clearing brush for what seemed like several hours, he pulled off his backpack and collapsed in exhaustion in the middle of nowhere. He could hear what sounded like a hawk squawking incessantly somewhere out there looking down on him with disapproval at his intrusion.

He looked up in the direction of the bird's cry and shouted—not too loudly—his disapproval. "Shut up, bird!" He couldn't blow his cover. He pulled out a handkerchief and mopped his brow. The bird must have heard him because the squawking stopped abruptly. Seconds later he noticed the hawk flying swiftly over the distant treetops.

Suddenly feeling the pangs of hunger, he ripped open his plastic foil-enclosed ham sandwich and began to gorge while taking intermittent swigs of spring water. As he looked upward through the treetops with the sun attempting to push through, he knew that his task was going to be difficult.

Shit, this ain't goin to be easy. I knew that before I started. I should rest here for maybe an hour and continue. I will break through this brush and find Ma and Pa!

Having nodded off, he was rudely awakened by a loud crack. As he cleared his eyes, it appeared that he was enveloped in darkness, and he quickly reached for his Mossberg for protection, wondering what was happening around him. *What the fuck is going on? Shit, what's happening?*

He began to feel a cool wetness descending around his head and hands. He had been sweating profusely after hours of thrashing around and had removed his corduroy cap to cool his head while he had lunch. Once his eyes had cleared and he had settled down from his sudden feeling of fear, he could see the flakes drifting down through the cracks in the treetops. *I bet that's thunder snow*, he thought.

He glanced up at the sky. *Ma and Pa, I know you are here. You woke me with a clap of thunder and sent the snow through the treetops to greet me. Since you did this for me, I will come to you—I promise.*

After the Alberta Clipper had passed through the area, darkening the sky and brushing the land with an inch of the white stuff, he had arisen from his lapse, pulled his gear together, and begun thrashing once again into the brush. Taking longer pauses to catch his breath now as twilight was fast approaching, he began to hear another sound that was difficult to make out at first. It almost sounded like a distant roar. Getting closer now as he hacked left and right, right and left, he finally understood what was causing the roar—a waterfall!

Knowing that he would have to soon think about bedding down for the night, the thought occurred to him that it would not be a good idea to sleep close to the waterfall, as the sound emanating from it could conceivably mask any hostile sounds which could spell his demise or capture deep in the woods. He knew that it was probably safe, though not one hundred percent so, in making a small campfire to ward off at least four-legged predators while he dozed in the forest at night.

Looking around at his present position, he began to relax. *This is as good a place as any to bed down for the night. I'll need to make a clearing, gather some twigs and branches, and make a fire. Deep in the woods where I'm at, I need to make this look from a distance no different from a fireplace smoking in a farmhouse.*

After making a clearing for his campfire and gathering the flammables he needed for the effort, he proceeded by the light of his campfire to settle in for the evening. He pulled out his shotgun to keep at the ready and placed his overnight roll so that the end was nestled against a chestnut tree and he could sleep in an upright position ready to spring up and defend himself if need be upon short notice. He kept only his food in his backpack and secured it against any hungry bears by looping a small segment of rope through one of the handles, tightening it in a knot, and throwing the other weighted end up and over a branch roughly ten feet above the ground under the tree. He then placed the bundle of twigs under a heavy rock to secure it in place while his backpack hung freely in the air safely above and beyond the reach of any wayward bear. He had even taken precautions with the food he had decided to eat for dinner, a clump of beef jerky that he chewed on as he gazed into his fire. He had been careful to leave the plastic that had enclosed his dinner in his backpack. With his shotgun by his side, his fire going well, and knowing his .357 rested reassuringly in his shoulder rig, he felt as secure as one could be under the circumstances.

The night concluded uneventfully for him. His campfire was no longer smoldering after he had shoved some of the damp forest soil onto it. He let down his backpack, grabbed a breakfast bar, geared up, and proceeded on his journey.

After working hard for nearly four hours, he thought he saw a clearing through the brush dead ahead. He sheathed his machete just in case any sounds coming from his trailblazing efforts would bring undesirable attention to him and pushed through the thickets toward the clearing, only to feel a tremendous sense of a letdown.

I'll be Goddamned. There is the lake. I have gone the entire distance from Stony Man to the lake and have found nothing. This stinks—fuck!

After steaming for ten minutes, he willed himself to settle down. *Well, I knew this could happen. I knew it wasn't going to be easy. Anything that's important to you in life, you have to pay a price for. I certainly can't go beyond this point because there are farmhouses over yonder and too many cleared fields. No way. I need to backtrack and branch off my main path at intervals, marking the trees so I know my location at all times.*

He turned around and pushed through the brush making it to the area where he had last used his machete. Instinctively, his hopes began to soar. *Okay, I am going to gamble that since the lake may have been here when my folks were here, and there is a waterfall somewhere nearby—just maybe that was a source of water for my family.*

He decided he would go back approximately twenty-five yards or so toward Stony Man and then make a new path perpendicular to his main path going to his right. Since he was in an area that obviously bordered farmlands with cleared fields, perhaps he could use those distant clearings as a guide to just how far he would need to push ahead on his branches from his main path. He knew that any move he made from here on out was a gamble with no immediate guarantee of success.

After backtracking the distance he desired, he set out to forge another path, carefully marking a tree before hacking away at the forest. He worked incessantly for several hours before noticing a clearing with farmland directly ahead. He had found no indications of a prior homestead here in the woods. He wondered if it were possible that all traces of his family were gone—that between the government and mother nature, his entire heritage had been wiped out over time without a trace. He dropped his machete and slumped to the ground in frustration and depression as the late afternoon began to turn into night.

Willing himself up, he walked in the pitch black back to the intersecting point of the new branch and the main path and forced himself to settle down from his emotional state. *Get yourself together, man! This is just the start; I've only done the main path. I'm still in the deep woods, and it is dark as hell in here. I am going to use my flashlight and head back to my base camp and regroup.*

He did just that, setting up his camp for the night in much the identical manner of his first night in the forest. With the combination of exhaustion from two days and nights of thrashing about the wilderness and total frustration, he drifted into a deep, though fitful sleep.

He awoke again with a start wondering what time it was as he checked his Citizen dive watch. *Christ, 5 o'clock. I don't feel a bit tired. I'm ready to go. Maybe this is my day*!

With that positive thought in place, he dowsed his campfire, pulled his backpack down from the tree, geared up, and headed back in the direction of the lake.

This time he thought he would try moving southward down his path to a point approximately fifty yards from where he was now and move into the forest at that point to his right. He had remembered that it was right around this area of his path where he had originally heard the sound of the waterfall. And, in fact, though greatly fatigued, he thought he had heard the identical sound on his way back from making his new "branch" path closer to the lake and farm areas further south.

He thought about this for a minute. *It would only seem natural that a family would want to start a homestead close to a water source. Maybe this will lead to something.*

Brimming with renewed hope now, he pulled his machete out and started making a new branch of his original path, this time going more toward the west rather than the east. He slugged away with his machete only to discover that the brush in this area was unbelievably thick and difficult to clear. He had only worked two hours and was near exhaustion, yet he sensed he was getting closer to the sound of a waterfall.

He had to take a break. The weather had warmed to nearly fifty degrees and was beginning to cloud over as he wiped the sweat from his face and neck. He slipped off his backpack and fleece-lined jacket—too much clothing for the physical labor he was expending. With this effort, he had no need for the extra clothing, so he stuffed his coat somehow into his backpack and picked up where he had left off.

Feeling a sense of relief from the body heat he had been generating, he picked up his efforts, working at a frenzied pace to forge ahead toward the sound of the rushing water. In some cases he had to pause because his machete would not cut through the really thick branches on his path. This would obviate the necessity for his sharpened hatchet riding in a holster at his waist level on his right hip.

This time he paused, though not for the fatigue he was feeling. The roar of the onrushing water had suddenly become much more noticeable. He stood stock still for five minutes, just listening.

Son of a bitch, I am close now. Wonder where that water goes to? Like maybe near a small pool or gorge? Wonder if it just goes into a creek bed? The only way he was going to answer those questions was to continue.

At this particular juncture for some inexplicable reason, the brush started to thin out—to the point where he did not have to use his machete. He sheathed the machete and sliced forward getting closer now to the cascade of the waterfall. Then suddenly he came upon a wide patch of ferns only several feet high where he could actually make out the waterfall just a stone's throw away. It was narrower than he had envisioned; however, the onrushing water was moving over the rocks at an amazing clip. He just stood there in admiration and stony silence. Then he gingerly started making his way through the fern patch to the waterfall to determine where it might lead.

Suddenly, all hell broke loose. Without warning, the ground suddenly seemed to rise up from under him, throwing him into a state of panic. *What the fuck! I am sitting on a goddamned animal! Fuck! Shit!*

He slid completely off the back of a twelve-point antlered, two hundred pound white tail deer known among hunters as a buck as it slung violently forward. Landing in the patch of ferns on his backpack hard, he could feel the pain from the slam of his shotgun barrel against his backbone beginning to smart. With the buck jumping around in a crazed frenzy twisting and turning in the fern patch just ahead while he lay there vulnerable with the wind knocked out and a numbness beginning to set in, he thought his time had come. *I'll be damned—I'm going to be killed by a fuckin deer!*

He struggled mightily to his feet only to be gored in the front from the deer's antlers as it abruptly decided to charge its adversary. Back down on his back once again he went as the buck continued to thrash around in the patch of ferns. He felt a tremendous pain in his stomach as he once again willed himself up, knowing that he would die if he stayed on the ground, and reached back to the side pocket of his backpack with all of his effort to draw his Mossberg. The pain was so severe now in his back and rib cage that he could barely reach back to his left and retrieve the shotgun with his right hand. He had to do something before this godforsaken, crazed deer got the best of him.

There—he finally got a grip on his long gun, pulling it back from the side pocket and across to be readied with both hands. All he had to do was to flick the safety off; he already had a round in the chamber. In his panic, he never thought to reach for his .357, an equally effective weapon at this close range that would have been much easier to acquire under the circumstances.

Flicking the safety off, his fear and panic now turning to anger and rage at this lunatic of an animal, he attempted to draw down on the buck as it continued twisting and turning in the ferns. *I am going to get you, you fucker! Damn—it's hard to get a bead on this sumbitch.* He moved the shotgun up and down and from side to side desperately trying to nail the deer. Finally the animal began to slow down just a bit. *Boom!* The twelve-gauge shell nearly tore the buck's head off with a rain of bright red arterial blood splattering the tops of the mossy green ferns all around. The deer, seemingly now in a seizure, walked a few steps with its head hanging grotesquely limp like the broken neck of a chicken, its antlers dangling down at its legs before crashing into the ferns with a sickening thud.

Taking a deep breath, he walked up to within a few feet of the dying animal and emptied his shotgun into the buck, covering every inch of the deer, one shell after another—the smoking, empty casings popping out into the cold night air with each stroke of the pump, leaving no doubt as to the outcome of this struggle.

After the fusillade, the deer's head had been completely shot off, and the torso appeared to have been mutilated with a giant meat cleaver. He then walked over to the deer's head and emptied his .357 for good measure. *Shit, if anyone heard this, maybe they'll think it was target practice,* he mused.

Then, gazing with extreme menace at the dead carcass, his eyes squinting and sweat pouring profusely from his forehead, he voiced his anger to the dead animal. "Nothing will stop me! I will kill any being, human or animal, who attempts to stop me!"

He staggered over to the receiving pool where the waterfall emptied and collapsed beside it, his shotgun in his left hand and his .357 in his right, a lazy stream of smoke coming out of both weapons.

He had begun to feel some relief after rubbing his face and torso with the cold water from the pool using one of the rags he had pulled from his backpack. He sat up before taking stock of his present situation to down nearly a fourth of the bottle of Jack Daniel's he had also brought with him, taking several long pulls to help him cope with the pain and his badly frayed nerves. Feeling the warm fire of the liquid as it went down, he knew that he might well have broken some ribs in the battle with the buck. He remembered reading an article in the *Field and Stream* magazine where the phenomenon of a male deer attacking an individual in the forest, though rare, could occur if the animal felt attacked or provoked. Walking practically on top of the buck, which might have been sleeping at the time, would have certainly qualified as a provocation to the animal.

He thought—*What should I do next? Christ, I feel weak; the day is almost gone. I am going to have to think about turning in early this evening before I run out of gas. My fuckin ribs and back are killing me!*

He decided before making his next move to brave the onset of the cold from the night and took his shirt completely off, dampening his rags once again with the ice cold water from the pool and applying it to his ribs and back. Between the Jack and the ice therapy, he began to feel somewhat invigorated.

After toweling off and regrouping with dusk fast approaching, he pulled out his flashlight and decided to follow the path of the creek that he had noticed emanating from the pool. Feeling devoid of energy after the horrendous fight with the deer, he had nothing left to whack away at the forest. He would follow this stream till just before dark and make his way back to his campsite.

At this point with the fight taken out of him and nearing total exhaustion, he was seriously thinking of calling it quits when he suddenly slammed first his right foot, quickly followed by his left foot, into a hard object, banging his shins hard in the process. He fell face down on the forest floor with his legs dangled over a foot-high wall of what he now realized were stones. He writhed again with a new source of pain from his feet and shins and turned over to look up at the dark of the trees above. *I have just about had it. I thought I was a tough SOB. Where the fuck am I now?*

He twisted his body over to his left and then right, reaching for his flashlight that he had lost with his sudden fall. He found it as he wrapped his right hand around it. The beam was shining at some sort of low wall made out of stone. He pulled himself up as a light rain began to fall, tapping through the trees above. It seemed as if he was in virtual darkness now as the weather began to inexplicably change to wind, rain, and darkness deep in the forest—way off the beaten path.

"Oh, God," he said as he panned his flashlight a full one hundred and eighty degrees around what looked to be a cemetery plot left long unattended deep in the woods and overgrown with blue-flowered periwinkle, a kind of vine used in cemeteries that covered the ground well and required virtually no upkeep.

"Oh, God," he cried again. He stood in this ancient cemetery realizing that just maybe his hope had come true.

Holding his flashlight at waist level, he saw two small gravestones together twenty feet directly in front of where he stood tilted almost all the way over. "Oh, God, it can't be," he cried. Walking up to the gravestones and sinking to his knees, he felt a severe migraine begin to come over him and began to tremble uncontrollably, the beam from his flashlight throbbing like an oscillating light as he strove mightily to control his hand and focus the beam on the stones.

Laying the flashlight down, he pulled his wet rag out and began to furiously wipe the gravestones covered with moss and dirt from fifty years of neglect. He shifted the rag to his left hand and picked up his flashlight so the beam would point directly at the faded writing in the stones. Making out for the first time the names of the man and woman buried here, he dropped his rags and flashlight, bursting into tears as he fell forward and wrapped his arms around his mother's tilted headstone.

The rain was falling furiously now with loud claps of thunder resounding through the forest. After nearly thirty minutes, he twisted around with his back facing his mother's grave, pulled his knees up to his chin, and sat facing out from his family cemetery. He stared straight out into the forest near where he had blown the deer's head off and pulled his .357 out with his right hand, cradling it like a baby. Swinging the cylinder out, he dropped six more hollow points into the gun with one movement of his speed loader.

His face became contorted with rage, and his eyes squeezed into small slits as the water rolled down his forehead. Then he raised his voice at the brush just outside the wall of the cemetery and growled to the forest standing mute. "Anyone even thinks of coming near my home, I will kill you, cut you up into pieces, and make you disappear. You will never be found again!"

Chapter 10

Wheaton, Maryland

Sandi Lynch sat on the couch with her husband, Joe, finally home after spending a week at the Washington Hospital Center near North Capitol Street recovering from his severe mugging in Washington, D.C. After his wounds had been stitched and his broken bones set, his doctor had recommended that he stay at the hospital for a few additional days for observation. His ribs had been so severely broken that he had experienced internal bleeding after the incident. Rest, medication, and his body's own healing mechanisms enabled Joe to recover to the point where his doctor gave the go-ahead for his hospital release. He was, however, ordered to spend at least a month at home before returning to his job at the Civil Service Commission in Foggy Bottom.

"Glad to have you home, sweetie," Sandi smiled.

Joe smiled weakly. "It feels so good to be home. Funny, every time I used to spend more than a couple days here, cabin fever would set in. You just take this for granted. After what I've been through, this is definitely where I want to be for a while."

Sandi could only partially agree with that assessment. "Well, knowing you as your wife, I am quite sure that you will start getting antsy and want to get back to work as soon as you are up for it. I just wish you hadn't gotten so caught up in your work that night. I mean—Joe, I don't want to rag on you about this, but when you get wrapped up like that, some things can go undone. When they first admitted you, the thing I kept thinking about was that you had kept saying that it was way past time for the Honda to be serviced. You know I don't know what to say to the auto mechanics. I don't know the lingo. The girls and I could have been right there with you on T Street or wherever you were."

Joe lightly rubbed his sore side. “Hon, I don’t want to talk about that now. It’s difficult to change the person I am; that’s just the way it is. I’ll try to do better,” he said.

“I’m sorry, honey. I just worry about you,” Sandi replied, trying to understand.

They embraced, thankful to be together again safe in their apartment. As they lay in bed together that night for the first time in nearly two weeks, Joe could not sleep. His frequent day naps brought on by fatigue and the pain medication had made an insomniac out of him at night.

After the beating on T Street, one of the hookers who had been amongst the group of girls Joe had seen huddled together that night, had lit a cigarette and gone for a short walk down Swann Street where she had heard what sounded like a group of young men talking in loud, threatening voices. Curious, she had eased herself a little closer to the action. Seeing a group of rough-looking young men now walking rapidly back toward her and realizing that her pimp was in Bar-Key’s lounge near the corner where she worked, unable to protect her against the thugs, she had immediately felt threatened. She thought the best thing she could do under the circumstances was to not appear suspicious. She started her “Ho Walk,” moving the best parts of her anatomy around in tempting fashion as she pranced slowly down T Street.

“Gimme some,” one of the young toughs yelled as they moved quickly by her, though none of them stopped to follow up on the one dude’s request.

She thought she saw something or someone lying out in the middle of the street. “Oh, Lord, what have these young thugs done?” she wondered out loud to herself. It only took one glance at the poor fellow lying beaten to a pulp before she quickly spun on her heels to head back to her corner as fast as her clacking pumps could take her. Arriving at last at her corner, she dashed over to the police cruiser parked across the street taking in the action and told the two officers, smiling at the hookers, what she had seen. They immediately fired up the cruiser, went to the scene of the beating, and called in a team of paramedics from the 14th Street Fire Station to assist.

Joe was taken to the Washington Hospital Center and treated for his injuries. After being revived and stitched up, Metro police had taken his statement, receiving a description of the muggers as best Joe could recall, given his condition.

After Sandi’s sister had come by their apartment to keep an eye on the girls, Sandi and Joe’s parents who lived in the area had arrived to check on Joe in the ER unit. His Honda had been towed to a maintenance garage on 13th Street where Joe’s dad had been able to take care of having the radiator and cooling system repaired.

Joe tossed and turned, going over and over the nightmare that he had incurred. Feelings of depression began to descend on him. He didn’t want to awaken Sandi and alarm her, but he thought he was going to lose it. Recovering from his physical injuries was not going to be a problem; he had already seen progress. He was not so sure, however, about the damage to his psyche. He knew he had been, in many ways, physically insecure, seemingly afraid of his own shadow at times. His parents had raised Joe to be a young man who would perform well in academics and climb "the corporate ladder."

Joe had always envied his dad who had been in the Navy and had been a prisoner of war in the Pacific Theater during World War II. His dad was a tough guy. If the Japanese couldn't break him, no one could. While his dad was not in the best of health these days, he still had a rock-hard constitution.

He talked silently to his dad as if he were with him, even though his parents were forty-five minutes around the beltway from where he and Sandi lived. It was too late in the evening to call his dad; he knew that his parents turned in early. *Dad, I just wish I could be strong like you. I feel like I am losing it! It's one thing to lack confidence in your physical abilities, but entirely another to have it violently stuffed down your throat. I feel so sad and humiliated.*

Joe began to cry, starting out as a quiet whimper and escalating to a wail causing Sandi to awake with a start. "Calm down, Joe! We are going to have to get you help. You can see someone. My God, honey, I had no idea this was going to happen to you."

Joe grabbed his wife's arm. "I'm sorry, hon. I'm still a wimp, aren't I?"

Sandi reached over to her husband to put her arm around him. "Joe, you are only a wimp if you let yourself be one. I don't know much about situations like this. I do know that no matter how much help you get, *you* are going to have to be the one to pull yourself up by the bootstraps. You can do it," she implored her husband.

Somehow, Joe was comforted and strengthened by her words. Between her uplifting words, the medication, and his injuries, he fell into a deep sleep.

"You have a good day, hon." Joe kissed his wife goodbye the next morning as she went off to her job at the Wheaton Daycare Center.

"Are you going to be all right, Joe? I left the number for the psychologist that Dr. Allen had recommended at the hospital."

"Thanks, hon. I'll be fine." Joe replied. He closed the front door and sat down on the couch with his coffee and turned on the TV.

"I'll be damned," Joe brightened up, his face breaking out into a full, though somewhat painful grin. "Jesus, that's John!" he cried. What Joe saw as the morning news was winding down was the last segment of the sports portion where results of the big East Coast Invitational Karate tournament held in Atlanta, Georgia, were being posted on the screen. John Hernandez, a third-degree black belt in Japanese Kempo Karate, had won the Grand Champion's trophy as the best fighter in the tournament. The news channel panned a large picture of John smiling with his trophy; he was wearing his karate uniform and black belt with gold Japanese characters running down both ends of the belt.

Joe was impressed. *Christ, that's a big tournament; they have over three thousand contestants from around the world*!

With his developing interest in martial arts in recent years, he had begun to follow the results of martial arts tournaments as well as the Bruce Lee flicks in the movies. Joe could envision John Hernandez confronting those street punks and kicking their butts. *Another tough dude just like my dad,* he thought.

Joe suddenly sat erect on his couch and made a vow to himself. *I know exactly what I need to do. I am not going to call a shrink. When I get back to work in a couple weeks, I am going to call Sensei Huffman.*

Chapter 11

Foggy Bottom, Washington, D.C.

After spending two weeks at home, Joe Lynch finally returned to his job at the Civil Service Commission. As he entered the building with some trepidation about returning to work after having taken so much time off, he expressed some private thoughts to himself. *I wonder if anyone picked up where I left off on my project? It's going to take me a while to get back into it.*

Getting off the elevator, he passed Ann Cohen walking down the hall holding a computer printout. "Joe!" she squealed. "We're glad you're back. We had heard about your car accident. I'm so sorry."

Joe had instructed Sandi in his then delirious state at the hospital to tell his boss, Tom Akron, that he had been in a horrible auto accident. He did not want his coworkers questioning him about where he was and what happened to him. With his fragile psyche, that would have been all he needed. He knew that some of the guys in the office had talked of riding through the 14th Street corridor and verbally harassing the prostitutes. It would be embarrassing to tell them what had actually occurred.

He would probably be the talk of the office—he could hear it now. "Did you hear about Joe? His car broke down while he was propositioning whores!" There would be a big laugh all around.

He smiled gratefully at Ann. "Hey, I appreciate that, Ann. Good to see you again. Trust you're not working too hard."

Ann laughed. "No way, Joe, I'm just taking it one day at a time."

As Joe was about to enter the Information Technology Section, he had the same thought. *Yeah, that's going to be me too. Taking it one day at a time.*

"Hey, man, how the heck are you? You don't look too bad considering that doggone car accident I heard about." Pat Sedgwick had glanced up as Joe rounded the corner on his way to his cubicle.

"Hi, Pat. I still have soreness in my ribs, and my cheek is still a little tender," Joe responded pointing to the bandage on his cheek.

"I'll bet. I'm real sorry to hear about that, Joe. Trust you are on the mend." As he rose from his desk chair and came over to shake Joe's hand, Joe relaxed immediately with Pat.

"After being out so long, I'm just trying to get my bearings right now. I don't even know if I remember how to write a COBOL program."

"Don't worry, man. You'll get back into it fine. Fortunately for all of us, they have decided to push back the date when we were supposed to convert our systems to the IBM 3090, so you can just take your time on that WR100 rewrite. Tom and the other bosses want to make absolutely sure we're ready when the conversion happens."

Joe was heartened by Pat's words.

After being greeted by several other coworkers including his supervisor, he went down to the snack bar and bought a large coffee and Danish, thinking that he was very lucky to have survived that mugging and to return to a wonderful family and work situation where people really cared. He did have a bit of a headache though, a little worse than the typical feeling he normally experienced on Mondays.

After he returned to his cubicle, he returned a few phone calls and proceeded to try to pick up where he had left off with his block diagram. At the moment, work was the farthest thing from his mind. He thumbed through his work phone pad and looked through the cards under the letter H tab. He smiled as he saw John Hernandez's work number at the Pentagon. He would have to call him and catch up—maybe do a lunch with him sometime. Joe thought that he would love to hear of John's exploits in karate.

After finding the number he wanted, he went ahead and dialed Sensei Huffman. "Dr. Huffman's office, Christine speaking. May I help you?"

Joe had talked with Christine Pearman several times when he had called Sensei in the past. "Hi, Christine. This is Joe Lynch at the Civil Service Commission. I don't know if you remember me. I used to call Dr. Huffman to inquire about his karate school."

"Oh, yes, I do remember that voice," Christine pleasantly replied. "You are in luck. Dr. Huffman just returned from Tokyo yesterday. I'll get him for you."

"Thanks, Christine, and good to talk with you."

"It was great to talk with you as well," Christine replied.

After waiting several minutes, Joe heard the familiar pleasant voice. "Mike Huffman here."

"Sensei, I don't know you if you remember me. I'm Joe Lynch at CSC. I observed a karate class last year," Joe replied.

"Yes, I do remember you, Joe. How are you? We were hoping that you would have joined our karate club by now."

"Actually, Sensei, I have been thinking long and hard about it and finally made a decision. Tennis just wasn't cutting it for me. I would definitely love to join your club. Guess I just needed some motivation."

That brought a question from Sensei. "I am always interested in what motivates people, Joe. What did it for you?"

There was an embarrassing pause on the line as Joe desperately attempted to provide a response. Mike decided to help him out. "That's okay, Joe. Everyone has reasons for wanting to get involved in karate. I have found with some people the interest is kindled because they want a combination of physical exercise and to learn defensive skills. Others get into it simply because they want to fight, especially in tournaments. We don't promote that here. Our philosophy, handed down from Master Toguchi, is that it takes a lifetime of practice to master our style of karate; there is little time for competition. People who just want to fight for trophies using protective equipment are missing the true, pure style of karate. Real karate is very difficult to master.

"Tell you what. If you are free for lunch today, we can explore this issue a bit further."

Joe didn't take long to respond. "That would be great, Sensei. Where would you like to meet?"

"I'll meet you in front of the Governor Shepherd at approximately twelve-fifteen if that is okay with you."

"Great, Sensei—I am looking forward to it," Joe replied. After hanging up, Joe smiled to himself and went back to his block diagram.

"I'll have an IPA," responded Mike Huffman, referring to the India Pale Ale they offered at the Governor Shepherd, in response to the waiter's cocktail inquiry.

"Same here," Joe piped in.

"So, Joe, where were we?" Answering himself as he took a pull from his ale, Mike continued, "Joe, I remembered that you had seemed to show a keen interest in Goju-Ryu when we first talked last year. After Dick's promotional, we didn't hear from you. That's not all that unusual. People need to take time making up their minds before getting into karate. While I was heavily involved in Dick's promotional, I did notice that you weren't masking your feelings very well. You appeared to cringe at some portions of the exam."

Joe smiled, somewhat embarrassed by the comment. "Well, Sensei, I don't know; it's just that I had not expected the workout to be so brutal."

Sensei nodded. "I can understand."

Joe was surprised to hear those words coming from Sensei. "With each student, I try to make a character judgment on where they are coming from. In your case, I sensed that you were intimidated by the workout. However, in a way you reminded me of myself long ago. Believe it or not, I was once quite intimidated by certain people, particularly big vocal guys.

"Look, Joe, I'm a small guy just like you, just a little over five feet seven inches tall. Bruce Lee was the same height and one hundred forty pounds soaking wet. I am going to share this with you only because I sense that you will one day make a very good student.

"As we talked about earlier on the phone, there are many different ways individuals are motivated to get into the martial arts. For me, I hate to admit this to you—the impetus came from my own father in a very negative way. When I was a young, frail, skinny kid growing up, he used to be verbally and physically abusive. I am not going to go into all of the sordid details other than to say that after my last beating at age sixteen, I made up my mind that there would be no more beatings. When my parents became separated, I was able to move out of there and live with my mom. After graduating from high school, I joined the Air Force and found myself stationed over at Kadena Air Force Base on the island of Okinawa. One day while talking with some of the guys on the base, I heard about this karate school, and the rest is history. I joined Sensei Toguchi's Goju-Ryu school near the base and received excellent instruction while I was stationed at Kadena for three years.

"I am guessing that maybe you are somewhat intimidated by certain kinds of individuals—that was the case for me back then—initiated by my father's behavior. So, I found that by immersing myself in the art, strengthening my mind, body, and soul, I became a better person for it. Eventually, I was able to go through college courtesy of the military and became interested in political science where I completed my doctorate at Georgetown ten years ago."

Joe had been steadily sipping his ale and was beginning to loosen up. "Well, Sensei, I really appreciate your sharing that with me. While my situation is much different, I have to admit that I was mugged several weeks ago. Between my horrible experience and hearing about John Hernandez's great tournament win in Atlanta last week, well, both events—one bad and one good—were the deciding factors for me wanting to join your karate club."

Sensei Huffman frowned on hearing that Joe had been mugged just a short while ago. "Wow, Joe, I am really sorry to hear that you were attacked. I empathize with you. Are you okay?"

After Joe responded with a nod, Sensei continued. "Normally, I wouldn't have suggested lunch with a perspective student whom I hardly know. However, I did sense something about you and thought that for whatever it was worth, it would be a positive experience for us to get together."

Joe warmed to Sensei's words. "I really appreciate your taking the time to share this with me, Sensei. While I am still a tad beat up, I am hoping within a week or two to be able to finally join the club."

"Super," Mike replied.

After they both split the lunch bill, Mike looked thoughtfully at Joe. "Joe, don't want to put a downer on our lunch, but I do need to mention that I don't want you to come away from this with ideas that we can be buddies. In our dojo, I am the sensei, your instructor, and you are the student. We must maintain the sanctity of that relationship at all times. There can be no deviation from it. While I do participate in some of the celebrations after some higher brown and black belt promotional exams, normally I make it a point not to fraternize with the students. Hopefully, you understand."

Joe nodded. "Yes, Sensei, no problem."

As Mike grabbed Joe's hand on the way out of the restaurant, Mike spoke first. "Before you come to the club, it would be a good idea for you to do two things. First, go over to State and join the recreation association. The fee is only twenty dollars a year, and, second, stop by one of the martial arts stores in the area and purchase yourself an all-white *gi* and white belt. No fancy uniforms in our style."

"Will do, Sensei, see you in a week or so," Joe replied.

It was nearly a month before Joe felt capable of starting karate school. While most of his injuries had healed ahead of schedule, it was difficult for him to get over the persistent soreness in his rib cage. The Metro police still had not found the perpetrators, and he was sure this was going to stack up as another unresolved case.

It was the spring in Washington, and with the sense of renewal that the season can often bring, Joe headed over to State after work one day to join the recreation association and become a member of the State Department Karate Club. He went through the entrance to the recreation association in the subbasement of the building, had his picture taken for his magnetic ID card, and paid the fee. He had brought his new karate uniform with him; and with it snug under his left arm, slid his new ID card into the slot to the right of the door. After hearing a *click*, he pushed his way inside.

"Hello," Dick Stickler said. He happened to be near the entrance to the club's office.

"Hi, I'm Joe Lynch, a new student. I spoke with Sensei a month ago about joining the club."

Shaking Joe's hand, Dick thought he might have remembered the face. "Joe Lynch, I believe I remember you. You came over last year to observe a class and were at my promotion exam. Sensei did say that we were expecting you to join any time, within a month or so. Anyway, welcome to the club. You're about an hour early, and a number of students have called in, so it looks like a small class tonight. Actually, Sensei himself won't be able to make it and asked me to run the class tonight."

Pointing to a doorway with a full-length black curtain stretching down from the ceiling much in the manner of a customer's changing room in a clothing store, he indicated that Joe would be able to change on the other side of the curtain.

Only three students in addition to Joe showed up for class. Stickler had the students bow in, do meditation, and then made a few announcements. "Since Sensei will not be able to teach the class tonight, and a number of students have called in as well, we will have a modified class and focus on the basics only—drills and *kata*. He has asked me to instruct for him tonight.

"First off, on behalf of Sensei and the club, I would like to welcome Joe Lynch as a new student." Dick and the other students proceeded to bow to Joe, and in turn he returned the bow from the lotus position.

"*Kioske*," Dick said as everyone stood up and snapped to attention. Joe sensed that Dick was new to being in charge. *He seems a little lower key than Sensei. Maybe it will be better for me to get a slow start the first time around, anyway.*

After leading the class in basic warm-ups, Dick slowed the pace down in order that the new student could keep up. This was not unusual in Sensei Huffman's classes. He felt that it was critical that a new student be brought along slowly. He knew that very good students with potential could fall by the wayside if they were not carefully nurtured in the very beginning stages of classes. He went over the basics of how to form a fist properly and instructed the students in the basic or "kihon" stance, sometimes known as *Sanchin* stance with the toes of both feet curved inward, rear toes in line with front heel. From this position, Dick instructed the students to execute soft, slow punches, and to utilize proper breathing while executing the techniques.

The emphasis with this exercise was on form, not power or speed. Then, using Japanese numbers to count off the sequence of punches, he instructed the students to punch with focus and power, concentrating all of their energy into the first two knuckles of each fist.

Joe was sweating profusely by the time one hundred punches had been completed for the three levels of attack—high, middle and low—and he thought how awkward the style appeared to be.

This is definitely nothing like I've seen on TV. Man, the rigid pigeon-toed stance—don't understand how one can jump around and defend oneself from these stances.

With his toes pointed inward and the knees bent slightly to assume the basic or kihon stance, he felt restricted in his movements. This was certainly nothing like the tournament fighting he had checked out on the tube where combatants were dancing around, feinting punches. He wasn't sure this style was for him, and he had to be constantly corrected by Dick.

It became obvious to Dick with the slight frowns on Joe's face that Joe was feeling frustrated. During the warm-ups he had nearly lost his balance while holding his legs together, twisting at the knees to loosen up the knee joints for kicking and movement. Dick called a halt to the drills; and pulling Joe aside, he instructed the other students to practice their respective *kata* and critique one another.

"Don't get frustrated, Joe. When you first begin this style of karate, it will seem awkward at first. There is a reason for everything you learn in the style. The hallmark of this particular style is the tremendous upper-body strength that one can develop from constant practice. There is no way that I would have been able to withstand the punishment I took in my black belt exam last year, as I'm sure you remember, without the constant repetition of the types of practice you have just begun to get into. This is nothing like what you've probably seen on TV. We believe in rigid adherence to the ground for stability—not jumping around, throwing high kicks where one can be exposed to a counter technique or be swept and taken down. In time you will understand."

Joe nodded, thinking about the beating that Dick was able to take in his exam and how he acquitted himself quite well. He also thought about the beating he took and how he had gone down from much less powerful blows. He was beginning for the first time to understand where Dick was coming from with his statements.

The two hours passed quickly for Joe as he attempted to grasp all of the techniques that had been thrown at him for the first time. When the class had taken off their *gi* tops toward the end of the class to perform *Sanchin Kata*, Joe had felt apprehension as Dick struck the other students hard in their abdominal areas. However, it became evident that Dick was not going to do likewise with Joe. Perhaps Sensei had told Dick that if he were ever on travel or unable to run the class and Joe showed up for his first class, to go easy on him the first time due to his injuries.

After class was completed and the students had bowed out, leaving Dick to pound on the *makiwara*, Joe was able to shake hands and introduce himself to the other students.

As Joe walked out of Main State, he expressed a sigh of relief. *That wasn't so bad. Sure, I've got a lot to learn. I've got to start somewhere. Damn glad Dick didn't throw any punches at my ribs.*

He also felt a sense in the still early, cool spring night that he was on his way to recovery, not only physically, but also more importantly, mentally. He smiled as he began his fast walk, gym bag with *gi* in hand, up to the train station at Connecticut and K.

Chapter 12

Shenandoah National Park, Virginia—Appalachian Trail Near Stony Man Mountain

The Appalachian Trail stretches for over 2,000 miles as a footpath that meanders through the forests and mountains along the eastern seaboard of the United States, traversing fourteen states from northern Georgia to Maine. Fondly referred to as the "A.T." by its many hikers, the Appalachian Trial was developed by volunteers, spurred by the vision of forester Benton MacKaye, and finally opened in 1937.

Whew, getting close to Stony Man Mountain—finally, Jim Gooden thought as he squinted into the distance at the craggy-faced mountain looming in the distance just north of his position on the Appalachian Trial. He had started his marathon hike on the A.T. near the southern entrance of the Shenandoah National Park at Rockfish Gap two weeks earlier. Not being in prime physical condition, Jim was now completely exhausted and dehydrated. He was a systems analyst at Parker Systems Development, Inc. in the Research Triangle near Durham, North Carolina, and had come up with the idea of long-distance hiking to control his weight. He had heard about the A.T. from some of the guys at the office who were into hiking, and one night after dinner he had announced to his wife and two young children that he was going to drive up to Virginia and hike a portion of the A.T. His goal was to hike for a couple weeks in the Shenandoah National Park, starting at the southern entrance, and finish up in the vicinity of Front Royal, Virginia.

He had contacted his brother in Front Royal close to the northern entrance of the park and asked him if he wouldn't mind driving him back to his car parked at the Humpback Rocks Visitor Center near Rockfish Gap once he had made it as close to Front Royal as he could manage. Jim had said that it would give them an opportunity to "catch up." Since his brother was retired with lots of free time, he had readily agreed to Jim's suggestion and knew he would be excited to hear of Jim's great adventures on the A.T.

He had requested and been approved to take two weeks off from the job and had gone to the local outfitter store to buy all of the best equipment for long-distance hiking. Indeed, his backpack was feeling a tad heavy at this point as he stared long and hard at the endless path ahead of him.

He had driven northwest from his home, eventually hitting the Blue Ridge Parkway heading north to Rockfish Gap to begin his great adventure. Jim's adventure was a stretch for a novice hiker.

Based on the trail markers, he now appeared to be in the vicinity of the park, somewhere close to the Stony Man area. He slipped his huge, bulky backpack to the forest floor by the trail and sat on a stump nursing his last bottle of spring water.

The trail was beginning to get the best of Jim. While he had lost twenty pounds in the past several weeks with a strict regimen of hiking and low-fat foods, this dramatic alteration of his normal dieting and exercise habits was taking a toll on him. He had started regretting this enormous hike just a few days into it, blaming himself for taking on more than he could handle.

Of course, that was Jim. He had made it through college, gaining his bachelor's degree in electrical engineering from Duke, the Harvard of the south, in three years.

God, I'm tired. Got to call Bob as soon as I get to the first visitor center I see in the park, he thought. He knew that he had to be close to the old Skyland Resort. His notes indicated that landmark in the park was very close to the Stony Man area.

As he rose to continue north on the trail, he suddenly began to feel dizzy and disoriented. He had enough sense to know that he absolutely must make it to the Skyland Resort as soon as possible or he could end up in serious trouble here in the deep woods.

The cold spring wind began to pick up, and the sky darkened with Jim now beginning to feel panicky. He had no idea what was happening to him, and he soon found it difficult to stay on the trail. *I'm probably getting dehydrated. Man, I am in deep shit. I've got to get some help!*

What's that? Could that be a waterfall? He thought that he heard the sound of a waterfall and decided to do the unthinkable—veer off the trail toward the waterfall.

Jim anguished over his plight. *I need something cold to wash over me and revive me. I'm losing it!* Perhaps he could just thrust his head under the falling water, and he would feel better. He had to try it.

There, I fixed you up real nice, Ma. Pa, you don't look so bad yourself, he thought. He had made many trips back to the little pod of blue periwinkle where his parents had lain neglected for so many years. Both of the gravesites had been spruced up considerably with his loving touch. There were bouquets of fresh red roses he had managed to cart into the forest on this latest trip, smothering the headstones to create a flowery rendition of two red halos upon a bed of blue. Indeed, there had been many conversations with his parents since he had first found them a month ago. *Don't worry, Ma. Your son is going to take real good care of you from now on. Me and Dad are going to stay right here with you and protect you.*

As he rose up from his squat in front of his parents' gravestones, he thought he heard a loud crashing in the brush nearby. With the hairs beginning to stand up on the back of his neck, he drew his .357 from his shoulder rig and set out to investigate. *Goddamn! It's those fuckin government people tryin to run us out of here again. I am going to lay low and ambush those sumbitches.*

Almost in a state of total delusion by now, Jim was now holding onto one thought—how he could save his life. He never knew what hit him as the butt of a heavy, stainless steel revolver came crashing down on the side of his head, sending Jim sprawling face first to the ground, blood dripping in rivulets down the side of his head.

The man at the gravesite turned over the unconscious intruder and easily pinned him down with a knee on each shoulder. Without hesitation, he placed the muzzle of his revolver into the unconscious man's mouth and pulled the trigger. The 158 grain hollow point blew the back of Jim's brain out. He tied Jim's arms and legs to the thick strands of surrounding brush with pieces of rope and pulled as tightly as he could, fully stretching Jim's limbs to their limits before rigor mortise would set in. Jim's body appeared to be hovering just inches above the floor of the forest. Whipping his machete out, he then hacked Jim's limbs and the remainder of his body into small pieces with the anger of a madman, methodically stuffing each piece into two large green trash bags.

Over the next two days, Jim Gooden's body was given up to the forest piece by piece as the bags were carried for many miles with a body part tossed here and there over a diameter of several miles of thick forest and brush. Within minutes of being tossed, the insects, birds, and other small mammals began to feast on the remains. Weather and time would take care of the rest.

Jim's brother never received a call, and no trace of Jim Gooden was ever found.

Chapter 13

Hampshire County, West Virginia

"Ain't this the life or what, boss?" Mike Stoner had just fixed Jimmy Mackenzie and himself a double Jack Daniel's whiskey in two tall glasses and topped off the drinks with ice and water. He handed the drink to Jimmy as they sat at the picnic table in front of Mike's rustic log cabin.

Jimmy readily agreed. "Shit, it doesn't get any better than this. Here we are in God's country with the sun just about to set and gittin ready to get into some rib eyes and fresh corn!"

Jimmy and Mike had closed the store in Front Royal at 4:00 p.m. and headed northwest towards Hampshire County, West Virginia, finally arriving at Mike's property just off Route 522 in one of the most deer-infested areas of the east coast.

Since hunting season had not yet opened up in West Virginia, they had planned to spend the weekend at Mike's cabin scouting for deer on their runs and sighting in their hunting rifles and pistols. Of course, eating and drinking copious amounts of food and liquor would have to figure into the equation as well.

Mike had immediately fired up his outdoor charcoal grill and made himself and Jimmy drinks shortly after arrival. They had stopped at the grocery store in Front Royal on their way out of town just off Route 340 and stocked up on food and liquor.

Jimmy had pointed out to Mike the day before at the store that it might be a good idea for both of them to bring their weapons, clothing, and personal items for the weekend outing so that they could readily load up Jimmy's sport utility and head north, losing a minimum of time.

"Hey, Jim, could you get those steaks for me, boss?"

"Now you're ordering me around, huh? Well, since this is your property, I guess I'd have to say you're the boss here," Jimmy replied.

As he took the marinated steaks from the dish with his tongs and slapped the meat on the grill, there was a loud hiss. He intended to sear the steaks over high heat to develop a crust and leave the middle blood red or "rare" to use the culinary term.

"What do you think about them hikers that's been missin in the park, boss?" Mike asked as he flipped the steaks with a loud hiss on his grill.

Jimmy took a stiff pull from his Jack Daniel's and thought for a few seconds. "Don't know really what to think. It's only been a few over several years. Maybe, they got lost and eventually died in the woods—its possible."

Mike looked over at his boss while poking at the meat. "Yeah, but damn strange. I just heard there was another hiker turned up missing after being in the park hiking for a few days. Hate to say it, but those folks from out of town been trashing the park for many a year."

Mike took the steaks from the grill and placed the meat on a warmer on the wood stove in his cabin. Then he gingerly placed the foil-wrapped corn onto the grill.

"Man, I don't know what's happenin out there," Jimmy replied.

After putting his tongs on the serving dish on the picnic table, Mike slowly pulled out his loaded Ruger Redhawk .44 magnum revolver and swung the cylinder out.

Jimmy looked at Mike as if he were crazy. "Fuck, Mike, you make me nervous when you do that."

Mike laughed at Jimmy. "Aw, boss, you know I just like to feel this piece now and then. My great Uncle Corbin used to live in a hollow in the park, and he used to tell us younguns just before he died that he thought he and his neighbors who lived in the mountains got a raw deal when they was kicked off the mountain."

Jimmy took another pull on his drink with Mike following suit.

"Yeah, I had heard that some of the mountain people were not ready to move. Let's face it; you lived your whole life in one of those hollows on the sides of the mountains, toiled your whole life with sweat and blood, raised a family in the mountain wilderness, and look what happened to you." Mike holstered his revolver and switched on the floodlight to illuminate the backyard. His face starting to feel flush from the booze, Mike continued on the theme. "It ain't right, I am telling you," he nearly shouted.

Jimmy just stared at the red-white coals in the grill almost as if he were in a trance. "Well, Mike, there ain't a Goddamn thing we can do about it."

Mike took another long swig. "I know one thing; if any of them state people comes on my property here in Hampshire County, they won't leave alive."

With the finality of that statement, they refilled their drinks and sat down to dinner in Mike's kitchen, the coals of Mike's grill starting to cloud over in a white ash.

"Fuck, I got a headache." Mike rubbed at his temples with his fingers.

"Yeah, me too. Probably the liquor," Jimmy said.

"You got that right, boss."

"Quiet! You're going to make us miss the deer," Jimmy admonished him.

"You're right, boss; we have to use stealth," Mike smiled.

Both men had walked into the forest just down from the ridge behind Mike's backyard after breakfast. They had planned to look for signs of deer rut where the bark was scraped off trees by male deer using their antlers during the mating season and get a feel for the deer activity a month before hunting season was due to open. Then they had planned to rig their tree stands down near the lake and just observe the comings and goings of the animals in the forest. Once in the tree stands, they needed to maintain absolute silence to not frighten the animals away. Their plan was to just enjoy the outdoors on a beautiful fall day.

Now in mid-October, the foliage was at its peak color with bright reds, yellows, and oranges lending a magnificent hue to the forest. They rigged their tree stands and spent a few hours scanning the forest, noting a proliferation of white tails in the area.

Mike turned his head directly to his right and shouted to Jimmy. "Hey, boss, you think we ought to head back and fix us up some grub?"

"Good idea, Mike. It's getting to be nearly four and going to be dark soon."

The next morning, Mike and Jimmy decided to do target practice. As a general rule, both men shot regularly throughout a given year using the town indoor range primarily for their revolvers and pistols, and they used Mike's property to shoot long guns. Mike had just bought a Browning automatic rifle or BAR in .30-06 caliber at the firearm dealer's wholesale price and was eager to fire the weapon. Jimmy had brought his trusty .35 Remington Marlin lever-action rifle along for the event. Both almost always carried their revolvers as backups in the woods.

While Mike owned nearly a thousand acres of prime forestland, he was also surrounded by public hunting grounds; and now and then, a hunter or group of hunters—some quite intoxicated—would wander over onto his posted property. Upon seeing the intruding hunters, Mike would draw his revolver and warn them sternly off his property. Tall and rangy at six foot four with a mangy black beard and fierce persona and presenting a very large magnum stainless revolver—well, that was all it usually took to encourage the lost hunters to take a hike.

As both men walked up to the backstop of heavy logs that Mike had created for his outdoor range, they stacked their weapons on one end and began to set up their cardboard and paper targets by nailing the long strands of cardboard onto the logs and then stapling the paper targets onto the cardboard. Mike and

Jimmy had long ago set up the shooting rules for Mike's fifty-yard outdoor range. Only one individual could be on the firing line at a time, and the other individual would not be allowed to handle a weapon while he was idle.

Mike smiled at Jimmy. "Boss, why don't you go first."

"Don't mind if I do," Jimmy smiled back.

After going through a dozen cycles of shooting a few rounds and checking on his shot placement each time, Jimmy nodded for Mike to take his place.

"Damn, Jim—not bad shootin,"

"All right, Mike, let's see what you got."

Mike hefted the loaded BAR up onto his shoulder and began to squeeze the trigger. Each crack of the round was simultaneously followed by the metallic click of the smoking, spent cartridge. Because his weapon was new, Mike took significantly longer on the range to carefully shoot and adjust his scope for elevation and windage after each cycle of rounds.

Finally satisfied, he carefully placed the BAR propped up at the end of the backstop and proceeded to tear off several of his paper targets. He then pulled out several human silhouette paper targets and stapled those to the cardboard. Pulling out a flask from his back pocket, he offered a hit to his boss.

"No, thanks, Mike, I'll get some later. You go ahead. Matter of fact, I'm pretty much done for the day. Take your time and shoot all you want. I'll just watch and enjoy myself."

Taking a stiff belt from his flask, Mike gleefully responded. "Boss, you're just too good of a dude. I got this Browning sighted in pretty good now, and I'm fixin to take some heads off."

Mike capped his flask and stuffed it into his back pocket and then picked up his BAR, loaded the weapon, and began to fire away. After putting several holes between the eyes of each silhouette target, he laughed, telling his boss that he had just killed one of those "state fellers."

Then a curious thing happened. Mike proceeded to blast away at what was left of the human silhouette targets, firing rapidly and replacing one loaded clip with another in an apparent state of frenzy. Jimmy looked up with a puzzled expression, taking a hit off his Jack as he observed the action.

After what must have been five boxes of ammunition, Mike finally put down his hot, smoking BAR. Only the very tops of the paper targets remained attached to the range backstop. As Mike turned up his flask, finishing off the last drop of the brown liquor, he turned to Jimmy with a sneer forming on his mouth. "I'm telling you, boss, I'll kill them mother fuckers if they come around here."

Jimmy merely nodded as they gathered up their weapons and gear and headed back to Mike's cabin.

Chapter 14

Foggy Bottom

Well, here goes nothing, Joe Lynch thought to himself as he crossed over Virginia Avenue and headed up toward Main State to the dojo to take his test for first-degree black belt. Joe was about to take one of the most demanding promotional exams in Goju-Ryu Karate after studying the art in a multitude of venues during the past three years. He had trained, of course, at the State Department dojo, yet had likely performed more training sequences at his apartment in Wheaton, Maryland. Joe had become very dedicated to his art. It had more than fulfilled his highest expectations. His manly confidence was soaring for the first time in his adult life. He had become one with his art.

Joe used to ask himself a question frequently asked by novice martial artists and non-practitioners alike. If one were attacked, would one use the skills and tools that he or she had learned in the dojo to defend oneself or revert to the primitive forms of self-defense that was all such a person had known prior to his martial arts training? He had only recently been able to honestly say to himself that he would indeed use the techniques that he had learned in the dojo.

Joe wiped the perspiration already on his brow, though he had been outdoors fewer than five minutes. It was late spring, and the weather had been unusually warm. In fact, he reminded himself that he had to make a mental note to tell Sandi to call the maintenance people at their apartment development once again to repair the air conditioning.

One of those training venues—his apartment—went through a major transformation every evening to become his home dojo. After arriving home each evening from the job, he would put on his *gi* and belt—the colors of his belt had changed over the years from white to eventually brown, with three black stripes as he stood ready to make his move for black belt. He would carefully remove the dining room table and chairs to the living room and unhook the wooden post dividers that he had made a few years back to separate the dining room from the living room area. Then, he would commence meditating, stretching, and the remainder of his training regimen. As a general rule, he had never received any complaints from his fellow apartment dwellers. He skipped the karate yells or Ki-I's, mandatory at the dojo, and avoided hard stomping and jump kicks in his *katas*. Also, while he had not set up a *makiwara* in his home dojo to train his hands, he had mounted a vinyl enclosed bag of sand in his bedroom doorway jam with four pieces of flexible nylon cord to toughen up his knuckles and practice focus with his punches. While this setup produced a nerve-racking noise for Sandi every time his fists crashed into the bag, the sound was, for the most part, confined to their apartment with Sandi once remarking that Joe could knock someone out with his punching power.

With the temperature in their apartment that spring frequently in the low nineties because of problems with the air conditioning unit and adequate cross ventilation, Joe often worked himself into a sweating frenzy. In fact, he was so driven with his art that after most practices, he would literally crawl in total exhaustion to his meditative stance at the end of his sessions.

Joe had also, on many occasions, taken his act outdoors in the nearby Wheaton Regional Park and had drawn a small group of onlookers—many initially doubtful that this smallish man was any more than a self-promoting charlatan. Once he started his *kata* though, the doubt quickly faded, and the snickering turned to polite, appreciative applause at the whip-like crack of his *gi* with every precisely executed technique. Now—today, he was about to be tested for Sho-Dan, first-degree black belt. He couldn't believe it! He had paid his dues. It was time to find out what he was made of.

Sensei Huffman stood directly under the red Shorei-Kan flag in line with three of his black belts: Dick Stickler, now a third-degree black belt or Third-Dan; Ron Gill, Sensei's top fighter and ranked Second-Dan, and John Trueworthy, a recently promoted First-Dan who was a *kata* champion in his own right. The student body, consisting of Joe and three other brown belts, as well as five green belts and twenty white belts of various class or *kyu* ranks, stood directly opposite the ranked color belts.

"*Kioske!*" John Trueworthy issued a sudden, thunderous yell for all to come to attention. At the command to meditate, the entire class sat in the lotus position in unison. Once meditation was completed, and all of the students were led through warm-ups and basic drills, the exam would begin. It was Sensei's position, unlike many other karate sensei, that since all students were required to attend promotional exams, all students should benefit; this was, after all, still a dojo workout; and they should receive the benefit of continuous instruction whenever they entered the dojo—exam or no exam. Since proper warm-ups and basic drills would benefit the student taking the exam, why not include all other students?

Sensei commanded all to sit in their designated positions and announced the exam for Sho-Dan to be administered to Joe Lynch. Ron Gill quietly excused himself for a few minutes to go to the restroom. In the interim, the other judges took their seats, and all other students including Joe sat in the relaxed position with feet crossed. Sensei commanded Joe to report under the flag immediately for his exam.

As he stood and prepared to bow to Sensei and the class, Ron Gill suddenly bolted from behind a curtained area at the end of the stage and leveled Joe with a vicious tackle. Joe certainly had not expected this, nor did the student body as they sat with expressions aghast at this development. Joe did not know what had hit him.

Ron then grabbed Joe by his hair with one hand and began to pummel Joe about the face and head with his other hand using various karate strikes such as the "hammer fist" and "knife hand" to great effect.

Somehow in the mayhem, Joe delivered—flat on his back with Ron's knees and legs pinning him to the floor—a wicked punch to Ron's abdomen stopping him completely in his attack. Ron rolled off Joe holding his stomach with a grimace on his face. Both men then immediately jumped to their feet and assumed a *jyu-kumite* or free-fighting stance.

While there had been a collective gasp from the student body at this sudden turn of events, neither Sensei, nor any of the other black belts, had made any attempt to intervene. They merely sat stoically in their chairs expressing no emotion. One side of Joe's face was red and puffy from Ron's violent attack. While Ron danced around very relaxed and confident in his fighting ability, Joe stood rooted to the ground with a grim and now angry expression on his face. He certainly had not anticipated or prepared for this attack and was looking for revenge.

After sparring heavily for three minutes with Joe holding his ground admirably against a three-time grand tournament fighting champion, even decking Ron with a surprise reverse back kick to the stomach at one point, Sensei stood up from his chair and yelled for the action to stop. The contestants were then commanded to face the judges and bow. At that point Ron moved quickly to his seat at the judges' table.

Joe's bewildered expression turned to a somewhat surprised demeanor as he began to realize just what had transpired. *I'll be damned! This was no surprise. Ron's attack on me was part of the exam. Now I remember Sensei saying over and over again from day one of our training to always expect the unexpected.*

The judges took a few minutes to scribble on their pads. Joe was taken through all of the requisite phases of the exam, performing at the same high level Sensei and the other students had long ago become accustomed to while observing and participating in Joe's three years of training in the dojo. He was totally exhausted by the time he was called to receive his certificate for Sho-Dan and his new black belt.

When the class gathered around Joe to offer congratulations, Ron forged his way to the front to shake Joe's hand and looked sheepishly at Joe. "Sorry about the attack, Joe. That was part of the program."

Joe produced a weak smile. "That's okay, Ron; I have to admit I was shocked when you came out of nowhere. You took me completely by surprise. I didn't know what the hell was going on. My only thought was to defend myself as best I could. When I realized it was you on top of me, I said, 'Oh, Man' to myself—Ron of all people—only the best fighter in town."

Ron smiled broadly at the comment. "Well, Joe, Sensei had instructed me to attack you as part of the exam. You know how he thinks. If an individual is about to become a black belt, he or she certainly should be able to defend against a surprise attack. I think what we wanted to see was how you would react to a sudden attack totally out of the blue where someone was intent on seriously hurting you. Would you resort to undisciplined, wild fighting, or would you present yourself as a thoroughly trained martial artist? We weren't surprised."

Sensei interjected himself into their conversation wrapping his arm around Joe and glanced around the swarm of students and instructors. "Ron, Joe, Dick, and the rest of the brown belts, let's shower up and report back here ASAP. We're going to the Golden Palace to celebrate. I think we all could use a drink."

Fingering his new black belt and the puffiness on the side of his face with the soreness from the abdominal blows he had absorbed beginning to take effect during the *Sanchin* portion of his exam, Joe knew that he could use something to ward off the pain.

As Sensei drove his van of advanced students down the H Street corridor toward China Town and turned into the parking lot across from the Golden Palace on 4th Street, Joe began to feel that familiar sense of bonding that is common among martial artists who strive as a team toward a common goal. While hard training, sweat, and blood were a given part of the equation, bonding over drinks and dinner and telling war stories, was another important part. Joe had attended and thoroughly enjoyed John Trueworthy's celebration in China Town when John had made first-black belt. It was Sensei's position that after any student was promoted to black belt, there would be festivities afterwards at Sensei's favorite Chinese restaurant.

He smiled at Joe, waving him over to the chair next to his at their table in the restaurant. "Joe, dinner is on me. You sit right here," Sensei said, padding the chair to his right.

After everyone had been served drinks, Sensei lifted his double Gray Goose Bloody Mary with all following suit. "Here's to Joseph Lynch, first-degree black belt in Okinawan Goju-Ryu Karate."

A resounding chorus followed. "Hear, hear."

Taking a stiff belt from his drink and watching Joe slowly sip his scotch and soda, Sensei leaned over to Joe. "Joe, your responsibility in our style of martial arts has only just begun this evening with your successful completion of your exam. You are now technically a sensei yourself. You are officially qualified to open up your own school, though I am sure you would agree that you don't have nearly the experience for such an endeavor."

Taking another stiff swig of his drink, Joe responded. "Sensei, as far as I am concerned, I am still a humble student and have much to learn in the system."

After ordering another round of drinks, their conversation continued with Sensei taking the lead. "It's a lifelong obligation for all dedicated students of Gojo-Ryu. When I made Sho-Dan in Tokyo over ten years ago, I thought I was the man. Then Rukio, Mr. Toguchi's son who was a Third-Dan at the time, began to show me some of the advanced *kata*, and I was once again humbled. I have always been lucky, Joe, I do believe you make your own luck. After making third black, I was ordered back to D.C. to work at the German affairs desk here at Main State. Master Toguchi had told me before I left to set up a dojo at Main State. He thought it would be a great idea considering the diplomatic mission of the State Department and the international clientele. So, I joined the recreation association and asked about setting up a dojo under their auspices."

His speech beginning to slur, Joe put his drink down. "Well, Sensei, how were you able to set up such a beautiful dojo? I was amazed when I first set foot in the dojo with all of the wonderful quality wood and oriental implements."

Sensei smiled at the question. "It wasn't easy at first, Joe. Talk about making your own luck. My initial karate classes were in the Dean Acheson auditorium on the stage—nothing but carpet. Of course, we already had a built-in mat which was great for sweeping techniques, though we could only manage about ten students at a time with the limited facilities."

Before Sensei could continue, Joe interrupted him. "I've seen that auditorium before—never dreamed you actually had a dojo there."

"Oh, yes, one of my first students was actually Daniel Schmitt, one of the assistant Secretary of States at that time. Amazingly, even though he was my student, and I must say he was a great one—my first black belt as a matter of fact—we became very good friends. Dan is now stationed oversees at the London office, and we still stay in touch. I suspect that when he returns in a couple years, he will rejoin us here at the dojo. I still keep him updated on what's going on here and in Tokyo at the head dojo. Dan was a good friend of the Secretary of State—they had attended the military academy at West Point together—and somehow Dan had talked him into financing the construction of our dojo based on my specifications. Don't ask me where he got the money. I suppose if you are an assistant Secretary of State and you want something, you are going to get it. I was just lucky enough to be the guy's friend."

At this point in their conversation, occasionally interrupted by Ron or Dick's input, Sensei was on his third double Bloody Mary and slurring badly. "Like I said, Joe, you make your own luck. Hard work and dedication and being able to bond with friends in a commonality of a goal can make great things happen." He then laid a heavy slap with his callused, open hand on Joe's sore shoulder much to Joe's chagrin.

After an excellent dinner of chicken and corn soup, fried rice, and an assortment of fine Mandarin fare, including stir-fried crab legs still in the shell, Sensei somehow drove his advanced students back to the garage at State where each went his separate way.

As Joe said good-bye to Sensei and scooted happily out of the van in front of CSC to where his car was parked at a meter, he felt the warm flush of success and the booze soothing his aching body. He thought to himself what a wise move it had been on his part to submit an annual leave slip to take the next day off.

Chapter 15

Shenandoah National Park—Dickey Ridge Picnic Area—A Few Weeks Later

Joe pulled his family Jeep Cherokee into the Dickey Ridge picnic area at the south end of the visitor center parking lot. Joining him for a picnic in the mountains were his wife, Sandi, and their two daughters, Nicole and Amy. They had browsed through the relatively small Dickey Ridge Visitor Center nearby—much to the chagrin of their two restless daughters, especially Nicole, now a pre-teenager with young Amy, just three years old tagging along. Joe had expressed a keen interest in the informative flyers on the people who had once inhabited the park before Skyline Drive had been constructed. He had noted that the Fox Family had once lived just across Skyline Drive from the visitor center in a "hollow" on the side of the mountain. There was a writing that had apparently been lifted from the gravestone of the patriarch, Lemuel Fox, who had passed away in the early nineteen hundreds, which stated simply "Gone but not forgotten" by his beloved daughter.

Joe had always been a history buff and sentimental when it came to the feelings of others. While still on a high from his recent promotion to black belt, he felt an immediate humility while reading the touching commentary. He bought several small books on the history of the mountain people before finally succumbing to the wishes of his family to cook a lunch at the nearby picnic area.

Nicole walked over to her father who had just started a small bonfire at the outdoor grill with his heavy dose of lighter fluid and mound of charcoal. "Dad, I thought you would never leave that place. It was boring over there," she said.

"Oh, Nik, I just got interested in reading about the people who once lived in this park. Believe it or not, there were quite a few families living right here in the mountains up until just before World War II," Joe replied to his oldest daughter.

Interestingly enough, that very statement took him back to his younger days as a freshman at the Virginia Military Institute where he had once befriended a young man who was also from the mountains of Virginia, probably not too far from where he and Nikki stood at the very moment.

"That's boring, Dad. Who cares; besides, I'm hungry," Nikki replied to her father.

All Joe could do was smile at this point.

With Amy pulling out her dolls and talking animatedly to herself, pretending she was one or another of her doll characters, Sandi and Nikki brought over their sodas and two folding chairs for Sandi and Joe. As her parents sat in their chairs, Nikki stood idly by for a few moments.

Sandi spoke first to her daughter. "You know, Nik, Dad did attend a college in the mountains south of here when he was a kid."

Picking up on that line of conversation, Joe jumped in. "Nik, a long time ago I went to a military college located in a town called Lexington, Virginia. It is about two hours from where we are now."

"Did you meet any friends there?" Nikki asked.

"I met a good friend who I haven't spoken with for years," Joe replied.

"Well, Dad, what was his name? Was he a hillbilly?" Nikki asked.

"No, Nik," her father said with a smile on his face. "Jimmy Mackenzie was his name. He was a nice guy who just happened to be a country boy from the mountains. I kind of forget, but I believe he may have been from either Luray or Front Royal. You might remember that we just passed by Front Royal on the way to this park," he said.

"Well, where is he at now? Have you talked with him?" Nikki asked.

"No, I tried calling Jimmy a couple years after I left school and just couldn't reach him. I really can't remember why. I ought to try to call him when we get back home."

"Joe, you could just get a hold of the operator for Front Royal, and they might be able to put you in touch with this guy," Sandi helpfully added.

At that point Nikki abruptly went over to the picnic bench where Amy had her dolls talking to one another and proceeded to tease her little sister.

Sandi turned to her husband who seemed to be in deep thought at the moment. "What are you thinking about, Joe? You seem really preoccupied in thought."

"Well, Hon, I hope I will be able to get in touch with Jimmy," Joe replied. Frowning a bit, he continued. "I couldn't help but wonder about the people that actually once lived in this park. When I was young, and Mom and Dad used to bring me down here to ride through the mountains and check out the sights, we never looked into whether any families once lived in this area. I don't know. I feel a kindred spirit with them for some strange reason."

"Well, Joe, that's just you. Ever since we first met, you've been talking to me about history. If you weren't talking about the history of our country and the revolutionary patriots who founded this country, you might be talking about the history of the Okinawan people who had to overcome being subjugated by the Japanese. You're just a history nut."

Joe smiled and got up to check the charcoal grill. "Well, guys, I think we're about ready to throw some steaks on the grill. Who wants steaks?"

In a unified chorus the whole family responded. "We do!"

While finishing up the last of his steak, Joe looked over at his wife who was sitting on the same side of the picnic bench. "You know, hon, I am intrigued by the idea of hiking that Fox Family trail, at least as a starter. Hiking is a good way to exercise."

Other than the occasional brisk walk, Sandi was not very much into exercise. She just let Joe do his thing, whether he jogged or worked out in martial arts. "You're not going to talk me into coming with you," she replied.

Nikki added her comment. "Me neither, Dad. No way am I going into those woods."

Little Amy piped in. "I'll go, Dad."

Joe broke out into a big grin. That was his little buddy. He knew he had to enjoy her as long as she was his little one. He had felt the same about his oldest at one time, though with her going through the pangs of being a pre-teenager with all of the rebelliousness it entailed, he could only hope that one day perhaps when she got older, she would come around and start to want to do things with her dad once again.

Sandi picked up her youngest by the sides of her *Oshgosh* jeans. "Ames, I think maybe for the first hike, we'll just let Dad do his thing, and he'll let us know how it went." She then gave Amy a peck on the cheek. Amy pouted for a second and then happily went about playing with her dolls once again. Nikki just shrugged her shoulders as if making a "whatever" statement without actually saying the words.

After packing up their cooking gear, chairs, and Amy's dolls, the family settled in to drive deeper into the park, finally reaching the Stony Man scenic overlook. No one except Joe seemed interested in exploring this area. He told his family he just wanted to read the plaque mounted at the end of the parking area.

It began with *"Stony Man reminds us of cold times 10,000 years ago when the glaciers covered much of North America."* There were a few additional sentences regarding the vegetation to be found on the mountain, and then Joe noticed a small warning sign posted next to the plaque. "Caution! Hikers beware! Due to several incidents that have been reported recently in the Skyland Resort region of the Shenandoah National Park, it is recommended that you do not hike alone. Please report any strange or unusual behavior exhibited by any individuals immediately to the park rangers in the visitor centers or patrolling the park."

Reading about the glaciers and this strange warning sent a chill up Joe's spine. *I wonder what they are referring to?*

Two weeks later, Joe pulled his Jeep into the Dickey Ridge Visitor Center, and with his small backpack containing a hunting knife and bottled water, he proceeded to cross over Skyline Drive near the flagpole and enter the Fox Family trail. He immediately noticed the large patches of a wheat-looking plant referred to as Golden Jewel Weed. Moving into the trailhead at the left, he slowly descended the path, eventually coming to a large mountain of stones that according to the flyer had been placed there by the family in the process of clearing their land for farming. The mountains in the region were pockmarked with large rocks presumably due to volcanic origins.

After a short walk, he came to the small walled family cemetery. He paused to pay homage to the remains of the family that once had lived there in a homestead in the early nineteen hundreds. The area near the cemetery was covered over with brush, a sign that the land had once been cleared for a homestead. It was amazing how the forest had taken it over, probably after the family had died or left the area. There was nothing there except thick brush and a few trees.

He couldn't help thinking about some areas along Skyline Drive that appeared to be more studded with trees, whereas this area and others were heavily brushed over. He knew that the large trees of a forest take years, even centuries to grow to their full size.

Emerging from his first hike back into the golden weeds near the ridge of Skyline Drive, Joe vowed to return to the park shortly to do more advanced hiking. On his way past Front Royal driving north up Route 340 to merge into Route 66 going east, he thought about the posted warning sign.

I am not afraid to hike this park alone. I really don't know anyone who is interested in doing a hike with me at this point, and I'm not going to worry about it. I really would like to duplicate Master Toguchi's feat of performing Sanchin under a waterfall in the forest.

He thought about the White Oak Canyon trailhead that he had driven past before coming back to the Fox Family trail. He had read somewhere that White Oak Canyon had been referred to as the "scenic gem" of Shenandoah. He was intrigued about the reported steep gorge with six waterfalls and thought that he must attempt this hike soon. His reinforced martial spirit would not let him dwell on any dangers that could be lurking in the forest.

Chapter 16

Route 66—Vicinity of Shenandoah National Park, Virginia

Bill, Gina, and Patty Hodge, a family of three who lived on Utah Street in Arlington, Virginia, were ardent hikers. A member of the Potomac Appalachian Trail Club for a number of years, forty-eight-year-old Bill was a Bank examiner for the Federal Deposit Insurance Corporation just down Washington Boulevard from his home. His forty-five-year-old wife, Gina, a computer specialist also worked at the FDIC. Their teenage daughter, Patty, attended the nearby Washington and Lee High School, once also attended by the famous actress, Sandra Bullock. Bill had made fast converts of both Gina and Patty to hiking as a form of adventure and exercise. Bill considered himself an advanced hiker, having completed most of the difficult hikes in the mountains of Maryland and Virginia, including a seven-plus hour affair in the Shenandoah National Park from the Weakley Hollow area to Old Rag Mountain. Both Gina and Patty were relative, though eager, newcomers to the sport. Gina and Patty had completed a few short hikes in the park, including the Fox Family and Stony Man summit trails. They had been eager to join Bill on a more challenging expedition.

At 5:00 a.m. sharp the family packed their hiking gear into their Volvo station wagon and headed out Route 66 in a westerly direction to connect to Route 211. Their destination was the Thornton Gap entrance to the Shenandoah National Park.

Sitting in the backseat, Patty leaned forward to speak with her father. "So, Dad, can you give me the deal again on just where we are going to be hiking in the park today? I know that you have gone over this before with us—I just kinda forgot where we will be hiking."

Her father smiled at her. "Well, Patty, as I may have mentioned before, I sort of thought that we would do a hike that is much more challenging than any either your mother or yourself have ever completed. I don't believe it will be nearly as tough as that Old Rag trip I took last fall. The trail is a lot more forgiving where we are going today. I'm sure you remember the tumble I took on those granite boulders I told you guys about."

Gina joined the conversation. "Oh, yeah, I remember that well. Your whole left side was one big blue-black mess. I honestly don't know how you completed that hike. Good thing you were hiking with some club members."

Her husband winced at the memory. "Hon, I really do believe I would have been in serious trouble alone that day. Thankfully, Tom and Butch practically carried me the rest of the way, and we were able to hitch a ride back to the station wagon. That's a prime example of why people should not take long hikes alone in the mountains."

Bill had almost forgotten about Patty's original question. "Patty, I thought we would drive to one of the entrances to the park you and your mother are not familiar with, the Thornton Gap entrance. The park has a number of entrances. The one we usually use is the northern entrance near Front Royal. There is a southern entrance called Rockfish Gap at the very bottom of the park. This one is a little over thirty miles south of the northern entrance. My plan is for us to park at the visitor center, gear up, and hit the A.T. near Thornton Gap, and then connect with an old trail that runs close by an area called the Little Stony Man cliffs. I thought it would be cool if we could finish up by climbing Stony Man Mountain."

Gina frowned. "Stony Man Mountain? That's a peculiar name. Where did that come from?"

"Actually, Gina, once you see the mountain, you will understand. From a distance the summit looks literally like a face of stone. We are going to go a bit off the A.T. and connect with what's left of an old trail called the Passamaquoddy Trail."

Patty piped in quickly. "Passama what? Where did that name come from and where did you find out about all of these funny names?"

"Well, Patty, you know I've been into hiking for some time, and I've done a fair amount of reading on the subject. I think it pays to really know the background and the particulars of any area of the park you may want to hike. You just don't go in blind."

Patty assumed a bored expression. "I know that, Dad."

Bill responded to Patty's inquiry. "A long time ago, at least this is from what I've learned, there was a man by the name of George Pollock who originally built the Skyland Resort in the park near where we are going to hike today. There is a creek in that area called the Furnace Spring that supplies water to the Skyland Resort. Mr. Pollock decided it would be a good idea to make a trail connecting Furnace Spring with Little Stony Man. Apparently, the spring runs partially under the trail going into Skyland. The actual name, I believe, is an Indian name that Pollock had borrowed from the Indians in Maine, which stands for 'abounding in Pollock,' a type of fish."

Gina smiled. "That's interesting, honey. Mr. Pollock created a trail in which the Indian word translates to—Pollock!"

"Yeah, babe, that is funny in a way," Bill replied.

An hour and a half later the family pulled into the visitor center at Thornton Gap and piled out of their car to begin preparation for their hiking adventure. They were easily able to get into the Appalachian Trail near the visitor's center to begin their foray into the mountains.

He sat in the folding chair he had brought for his latest visit to his old home, sweating profusely in the heat. It was early September near Stony Man Mountain, and at midday the temperature was hovering around ninety degrees. He took a swig of water, capped the bottle, and began talking with his parents.

"Ma, you still smoking that pipe, huh? Got that blue scarf still around your head like I remember. I remember those corn fritters you used to throw together. Man, were they the best.

"Pa, I remember how you used to come back from huntin with those coons hanging out of your backpacks. God, we worked hard in these here mountains. We've hardly ever seen any neighbors. Most of 'em were north of these here parts. I remember we worked like hell clearing the land, Pa. I don't believe I worked as hard in my life getting those rocks out of the ground so you could start up your corn. I think you worked too hard, Pa.

"Don't you agree, Ma? I'm sorry Pa you came down with a heart condition. I remembered you breathing so hard every time you lifted something heavy. Shit, there wasn't no people to help us out. We were all alone here. I remember Pa that your brother and his missus paid us a visit a couple times, but that was about it. You done just worked yourself to death, and I knew I was not old enough to help you like I would have.

"Shush! I believe I hear something."

Slowly sliding off his folding chair and stepping just outside of the cemetery to crouch behind the wall in the direction of the sound, he became alarmed. He whispered to his parents. "You all be quiet," he commanded.

"Oh, no! I hear that truck coming again and those voices. Those sumbitches are cursing and laughing. Get 'em, Pa. Shoot those sumbitches; they're trying to kill us! Oh, God! They done kilt Pa. He is bleeding bad from the head, and his eyes are open. What are they doin with Ma? She done pulled out a pistol and is tryin to shoot 'em."

"Ma! They shot my ma! Now they're coming for me!"

"Boy, don't you run; we have to take you away from here. Sorry about your ma and pa. You can't shoot at people and get away with it. We had no choice. We need to get you some help."

Flipping out the cylinder of his .357 magnum revolver to make an ammo check, he grabbed his hatchet and machete with one hand and went to investigate the sound he had heard.

"Don't you all make a sound; I'll be right back." He placed his finger on his lips with his free hand and silently crept into the forest just outside the walls of his family cemetery.

They had only been on the A.T. for an hour, and already the complaints were coming, starting with Patty first. "Dad, it's too hot—how much farther?" she moaned.

Noticing his wife continuously wiping the perspiration from her brow, Bill looked a bit sternly at his wife and daughter. "Look, guys. I know it's hot out here. We knew ahead of time what we were going to be in for. I mean it's a workout; we have plenty of water in our packs; and after we summit Stony Man in a few hours, we can catch a ride at the resort back to Thornton Gap. We'll freshen up at the visitor center and ride back home in the cool, air-conditioned comfort of our car."

"Oh, right, Dad, so we sweat it out for several more hours?"

Gina felt she should take Bill's side at this point. "Now, Patty, your father is right. We talked over and over about this hike and just how hot it was going to be this time of the year. He did level with us when we had our discussions. If you remember, he had suggested that we wait until October to begin the hike when it would be much cooler in the mountains. But, no, you said you wanted to do it right away."

Patty looked down at her hiking shoes and shrugged her shoulders. "You guys are right. I'm just hot."

Bill tried to pep his hiking crew up. "We're on the Passamaquoddy Trail now. I think I remember one of the club members talking about an ancient trail that connected this trail to the Stony Man trail going to the summit. I was hoping to circle back on the A.T. I have to admit it is damn hot and perhaps more risky than I thought. Up ahead about two hundred yards, we should be able to see this old, rarely used trail that will get us to the Stony Man trail. Let's see if we can find it."

They never made it. Finding themselves in deeper brush once off the Passamaquoddy trail, they were viciously attacked from behind by a man wielding a sharpened hatchet. Eyes blazing like a madman, he hit them from behind quickly and chopped and chopped until Bill, Gina, and Patty were three bloody pulps. Their screams were muted because of the blinding speed and savagery of the attacker as he alternately chopped at each family member. The life quickly drained from them with the ferociousness of the assault. The brush surrounding the poor victims was awash in blood and brain matter in less than two seconds.

The small family was slowly given up to the forest in very small pieces over a period of the next several days.

Alarmed at not receiving a call from their daughter at the appointed time, Gina's sister contacted the Virginia state police who began an investigation with the Department of Interior's Park Service. A team of FBI agents was also assigned the case to investigate the strange disappearance of the Hodges somewhere in the park without a trace.

Chapter 17

Hampshire County, West Virginia

As he brought his T5820 Motorola "talk about" two-way radio to his face, Jimmy gazed fifty feet to the north of where he sat in his Bushmaster tree stand at his hunting buddy, Mike, who appeared to be falling asleep in his tree stand.

It was November 25th; just four days before Thanksgiving, and both men were into the thick of the hunting season in West Virginia. The weather was bright and sunny, yet with a forecasted afternoon high of only thirty degrees, much colder than usual this time of year at this location in the West Virginia "panhandle." They had arrived the previous day, Sunday late afternoon, and had gone through their usual ritual of grilling steaks, drinking Jack Daniel's, and telling each other war stories.

Since this was the opening day of hunting season, like most hunters, they had anticipated some early kills with the deer running amok in the forest since last year's hunting season with no worry of being stalked. Jimmy had decided to bring his .30-06 Browning automatic rifle known in the trade as a BAR in lieu of his .35 Remington for the advantage of fast follow-up shooting in the confines of a tree stand. Under ordinary conditions, either stalking his prey or planted at a stationary stand on the ground waiting for the game to come to him, he preferred his Remington simply because he had used it as a hunting tool for twenty some years and was fast with the lever action. As a semi-automatic rifle though, the Browning could not be beaten for its speed of delivery with a superior cartridge in a tree stand. Indeed, both Jimmy and Mike carried BAR's today.

Jimmy pressed the button on his Motorola. "Hey, Mike, you awake over there?"

Mike sat up a tad in his stand and turned his head slightly in the direction of where Jimmy's stand was. "Hell, yeah, boss," he yawned.

Jimmy was curious as Mike appeared to be slumped over. "Well, you stay alert. Did you hear that rifle shot?"

"Boss, there's shootin all over this region during hunting season. Even though I own a lot of land, them rifle shots sound like they're just a hundred yards away."

Jimmy squinted into his two-way radio. "I don't know, Mike. I don't like the sound of it—seems too close to me."

Behind Mike's cabin there was a backyard area of approximately thirty-five yards between his cabin and a forested ridge that slanted downward into the thick of the woods. In scouting for white tail deer on Mike's property over the years, they had noticed that the deer liked to nibble at the vegetation on that ridge and occasionally bed down in a clump of pine trees at one end of the base of the ridge to rest and hide.

"Okay, boss, we'll keep an eye out for any assholes who have a hard time staying off my property."

"That's good, Mike. Remember, we're into surveillance mode. If you hear *any* sounds—twigs cracking or those shots sound like they're getting too close for comfort, it will be time for us to leave these stands and do some sneaking and peeking. We will be vulnerable up here in the stands if there are any crazy dudes around here. Out."

Mike nodded in the affirmative. "Got you covered, boss. Out."

John and Joe Kelly were brothers who liked to hunt as much for the action and drinking as anything else. They couldn't wait for the opening of hunting season. Working in an auto repair shop in nearby Romney, they had been known among the townsfolk as hell raisers, often closing several of the local bars by staggering out of the establishment and picking fights with anyone in their way. The scary thing about these fellows was that they were both excellent shots with their hunting rifles, could fight like hell with their hands, and consumed enormous amounts of alcohol, either in bars or out in the woods hunting. Somehow they figured that being in a bar hunting for women or hunting deer in the woods were both exciting adventures that needed to be stimulated even more by drinking.

The twenty-something Kelly brothers also possessed great physical stamina in spite of their negative nocturnal habits and would often hunt illegally into the night, blinding the deer with the search light attached to their pickup truck and picking the poor animals off one by one. They weren't of the mind to be stationary at a stand. They wanted action, and being still would not cut it.

Somehow—fueled by the booze in their flasks and the thirst to shoot something, they had both wandered over into Mike's property, failing to recognize or, more likely, just plain ignoring the "No Hunting" sign posted at the perimeter of Mike's property where a gravel service road separated his land from public hunting grounds.

It was approaching 10:00 in the morning, and Jimmy and Mike had been in the trees since 6:00 a.m. Both were feeling cold and stiff now and really needed to take a break to limber up. They were relatively close to Mike's cabin, having elected to set up their stands so that they would have a clear view of the ridge slanting downward into the woods. Their position was only fifty yards or so beyond the ridge behind Mike's cabin, enabling them to simply walk back up to the cabin for lunch or refreshments whenever the mood struck them.

Deciding that it was time to take a break, they both dropped rope ladders from their stands and gingerly ambled down, eagerly anticipating the roast beef sandwiches Mike had made that were sitting in the fridge and a shot of Jack Daniel's to warm their cold bones and wash their grub down.

As they entered Mike's cabin, he pulled the brown lunch bags from his fridge and placed two plastic cups on the table, pouring his boss and himself a hefty dose of Jack Daniel's whiskey. "Well, Jimmy, we haven't seen or heard anything suspicious, which is good."

Taking a stiff hit off the Jack, Jimmy scratched his red beard. "Like I said, we'll just keep our eyes and ears open. I know that you have run across people straying onto your property before. We just want to be careful. While being up in the stands gives us an advantage for hunting with our scent way above where the deer can pick up on it, I just feel confined and vulnerable up there."

"We'll be okay, boss; we're going to stay vigilant. You know I don't take a liking to strangers on my property. Intruders piss me off real bad."

In the interest of time, they decided to take their lunches and drinks back to the woods and eat before climbing back into the tree stands. After arriving at the base of their trees, they sat down together on a fallen log nearby with their BAR's stacked up close to where they sat. Just as they had begun to tear into their tasty roast-beef sandwiches, a man rudely interrupted their lunch with a shrill voice standing behind them.

"What the fuck you all doin here?"

Jimmy and Mike twisted around to see two burly hunters dressed in bright hunting orange, pointing rifles at their backs.

Mike's face contorted in anger. "What the fuck you mean, what are we doin here? This is my property, and you better get your butts off it. I don't want to have to tell you again."

John Kelly looked over at his brother and stumbled slightly with his rifle as he took a heavy pull off his flask of Jim Beam with his left hand. His face became a heavy flush of scarlet while he waved the rifle with his right hand, trigger finger at the ready.

"Hey, fuck you, man. Who said this was your property? You stakin a claim or something?"

Jimmy started to stand; however, he was taken aback by Joe's threatening sway of his rifle. "You just sit your ass back down, dude." Gazing more intently now at Jimmy, Joe continued. "What the fuck happened to your face, dude? Looks like somebody put a hurtin on your ass. Goddamn, you are one scary looking son of a bitch."

Jimmy's face turned beet red in anger and embarrassment.

Joe's brother John piped in. "We are going to use them tree stands, and we want you all to get the fuck out of here before we shoot you sumbitches. You hear? Now git. Don't be takin those Brownings with you either. We could use them up in the stands."

At this point, Mike was beginning to get very agitated; however, Jimmy winked slyly at Mike and remained very calm. "What you guys are doing is wrong, but you got the upper hand, and we don't want any trouble. We'll go," he said.

As Jimmy and Mike reluctantly rose and began to walk toward the ridge, they were stopped in their tracks by the loud crack of one of the brother's Winchesters firing into the air. They froze in place.

"Hey, assholes. Did I tell you to walk toward that ridge? Turn around and walk back out to yonder." Joe Kelly pointed toward the opposite direction into the woods.

After walking a distance far enough from the Kelly brothers where they couldn't be heard, Mike leaned into Jimmy with a hiss. "Why did you give into them like that, boss? Them mother fuckers got to go. They on my property drunk, done stole our BAR's, and fucked us over."

Jimmy whispered to Mike. "Quiet, Mike. I got a plan. I'm pissed too, but I think we can handle these bastards drunk as they are." Knowing the answer ahead of time with Mike's hunting coat opened at the front, Jimmy asked the question anyway. "Did you bring your Ruger?"

"Naw, boss, I plum forgot." As Jimmy unzipped his coat, Mike noticed Jimmy's stainless .44 magnum nestled in a leather Bianchi shoulder rig. "What you thinking, boss?"

A sly smile began to form on Jimmy's face. One thing Jimmy had always known about himself was that he had been brought up with a fair amount of courage. When he had been in BUD/S training, his instructor had motored Jimmy and a group of his fellow trainees out into the Chesapeake Bay indicating that he wanted to see how well they could swim. Jimmy and the others had assumed that they would be required to simply swim around the boat for a while, get back in, and head back to base. That was when they had received the bad news from the instructor.

"Now that we are a mile out in the open water, I want to see how good you trainees can swim. We've done you a big favor by giving you fins to go along with your masks." Pointing his finger in the distance at the Little Creek amphibious base that was clearly too far away to make out, the instructor had added, "The base is over there. Now get the fuck out of here, and I'll meet you at the base."

The trainees had looked intently out at the horizon in the direction the instructor had pointed for land, and they saw much to their chagrin only the bay meeting the sky. Jimmy and the other trainees' spirits had sunk as they realized they were nearly a mile out in blue water.

Noticing that some of the trainees had assumed a panicky look, Jimmy relaxed and just thought, *one stroke at a time*. He tumbled out of the boat backwards into the bay, aimed his body in the direction of Little Creek, and began to swim toward the base.

While he eventually made it safely to base, a number of his fellow trainees had given up and had to be rescued by instructors who just happened to be nearby.

Jimmy looked sternly at Mike. "Here's what we're going to do. We're about a hundred yards west of where the stands are. I am betting they are going to be stupid and drunk enough to get up in those stands and probably go to sleep. What we need to do is to surprise 'em, get 'em to their feet in the stands, and discombobulate 'em. I figure you can circle around to their rear and yell something nasty at them. Then, with all the rocks lying near the ridge, throw some rocks up at them to piss 'em off. They will have no choice but to turn around in the tree stands and wonder what the hell is happening. What I am going to do is to shoot the stand straps from the other side. That should break the straps and send those sons of bitches tumbling to the ground. They'll be out of the stands and ours at that point."

Looking at his watch, he continued. "Let's synchronize our watches. It's thirteen fifteen hours now. We will initiate hostilities at fourteen hundred hours sharp. Thank God, we have our mikes in our coats. When you hear the clicking sound from me, start yellin and throwin. Call 'em dirty names."

Mike looked a bit puzzled. "After you shoot 'em, then what, boss?"

"You leave that up to me, Mike," Jimmy sternly replied.

Mike knew that Jimmy was an ex-SEAL and was not surprised that he had been coolly planning revenge as soon as he and his boss had been humiliated by the drunken hunters. One thing about Jimmy, he was one cool dude under pressure and SEALS don't give up. "Damn, boss, you're something else."

"Don't worry about that, Mike. Just do as I told you and get a move on," Jimmy ordered.

"Okay, boss, I'll wait on your signal. Then when you hear me cussing at them sumbitches and throwin rocks, it's gonna be on you."

With their plan set, Mike hastily began to make a wide circle around to the other side of the tree stands while Jimmy checked his weapon. He swung out the cylinder and slowly turned it, smiling with confidence as he snapped it back in place with a click. His Ruger was stoked with six Federal Hydra Shok 240 grain hollow points, lethal for most any human or animal. That would be more than enough bullet to snap the straps that held the tree stands in place in the trees. Jimmy Mackenzie then started his slow walk to the tree stands.

John Kelly gazed in the distance at his brother Joe; both now up in the hijacked tree stands with the stolen Browning rifles, yelling as loudly as he could manage. "Goddamn these BARs is nice, bro. I always wanted one of these fuckers."

Lifting his flask and taking a hit of the fiery liquor, Joe responded, "You fuckin right about that."

It was very close to two o'clock, and the sky was beginning to cloud over with a stiff wind moving into the area.

Mike heard the brothers and muttered under his breath. "Those pricks. Them sumbitches have a nerve—just coming on my property and takin our shit. Goddamn them sum . . . ."

"*Click, Click.*"

Fuck, that must be Jimmy's signal.

Standing up from a crouch in the thickets, Mike yelled at the backs of the Kelly brothers. "Hey, you drunkin pricks, get the fuck out of my tree stands." At that point, he started picking up rocks and throwing as hard as he could at the tree stands.

Arising in surprise and anger from their drunken slumber in the stands, the Kelly brothers shifted quickly in the tree stands, attempting futilely to twist around and point their rifles toward the sound of Mike's voice while the stones kept pinging off the metal stands. Before they could fully engage their target, two sonic *booms* less than a second apart sounded from the other side of the stands.

Mike heard some panicky sounds coming from the Kelly brothers as they lost their balance and tumbled out of the stands. He had heard them alternately yelling "Fuck!" and "Oh, shit!" as their rifles dropped onto the forest floor ahead of their crashing with a very painful landing in the vicinity of the trees where once they had sat in drunken bliss.

What Jimmy had completed was an amazing feat. He had placed one shot each into the metal ring that locked into the tree to support the tree stands, snapping the ring open and causing each of the tree dwellers to lose his balance and tumble chaotically toward the ground.

Neither man had been hit by the gunfire from Jimmy's revolver, though both now writhed in pain on the ground with the wind having been knocked out of them, hurting big time from broken ankles. In Joe's case, his knee had been torn up in the process.

Mike walked up to the brothers. "Well, what do we have here? Two clearly inebriated hunters. Don't you dumb fucks know it's illegal to hunt drunk in these here woods? I ought to arrest you assholes, but I'll guess I'll let you go since as far as I know, it's only your first offense."

Looking over at Jimmy and seeing that he had put his finger to his lips and had begun to shake his head from side to side quickly, Mike became quiet. He had to assume that Jimmy thought it best not to reveal who they were to these rogue hunters.

Jimmy walked up to each and in a flash let each one of them have it with the butt of his six-pound revolver. The Kelly brothers slumped over, unconscious on the ground. He then proceeded to kick each in the ribs and back, breaking a few more bones in the process with the wicked, glazed look of a crazy person.

"Damn, lighten up, boss," Mike replied somewhat surprised by the viciousness of Jimmy's assault.

Satisfied with his work, Jimmy directed that they tie up both hunters' hands and broken ankles to large sticks which they used to carry each of the Kelly brothers separately off Mike's property, much in the identical manner that hunters carry dead deer from the woods. It was a time-consuming, though enjoyable process for both Jimmy and Mike as they dropped off the Kelly brothers in a heap sans their weapons just past the dividing trail into the public hunting area.

Cleaned up and back in Mike's cabin after their harrowing experience, Mike spoke first. "Boss, you SEALS know how to take care of people. You were so cool out there. I felt like I was so angry and scared, I didn't know what to do."

Jimmy's smile turned into a sneer. "Mike, I know this is your property, but I hate it when intruders just think they can come in and take over. We only had two choices the way I saw it. Either kill 'em or beat 'em badly and take 'em out of here. I figure if we shot 'em or killed 'em, we would have had some explaining to do to the state police. This way they learned their lesson. They won't be back. They're going to be in the hospital for a long time. Someone will find them, and they won't want to report what happened to 'em because they could get in a lot of trouble. After all, they started it."

Mike nodded in agreement at Jimmy. "You're right, boss."

Jimmy finished the last of his Jack Daniel's whiskey. "Mike, even though we still have another day, it might be best if we saddle up and head back to

Front Royal considering all that's happened today. We can fix those tree stands at the store."

Jimmy and Mike beat a quick retreat on Route 522 heading south, happy to put behind the violent events of the day.

As they drove south, Jimmy made a mental note to call back Joe Lynch. After checking his voice mail before he and Mike had headed to West Virginia, Jimmy had been happy to hear that an old friend from his younger days had finally tracked him down.

Chapter 18

Baltimore, Maryland—Little Italy

Sensei Mike Huffman and two of his top students, Dick Stickler and Joe Lynch, were very fortunate to find a parking place on Fawn Street in the Little Italy section of Baltimore. The east coast headquarters of the Okinawan Shorei-Kan Karate Association was located in a nondescript row house on Fawn Street just a few doors down from Sabatino's, one of Little Italy's finest restaurants.

Taking his keys out of the ignition of his van, Sensei pointed to the steps heading up to the row house just a few feet from where they had parked. "Okay, guys, this is it. Believe it or not, we are about to enter the Shorei-Kan East Coast Headquarters Dojo. I come up here every month for a practice with Master Hytaga. Afterwards, we go out and hit one of the many restaurants here in the neighborhood."

The senior master of the style on the east coast of the United States, Fumio Hytaga, had migrated to the states from Japan in the late sixties in part on orders from Master Toguchi. Mr. Toguchi was eager for his style of karate to gain a foothold in America, and what better way to accomplish this than to send one of his top instructors to the states. Fumio had already expressed an interest in relocating to the United States and bringing his culinary skills as well. Hytaga was a master sushi chef and had heard that Baltimore with its east coast seafood reputation might be a good place to start anew, utilizing his mastery in the martial and culinary arts to maximum benefit for himself and, indeed, for America.

He had been the beneficiary of a large inheritance from his father's estate after his Dad passed away in Tokyo five years before that had left Fumio a multimillionaire. It turned out his father had been the Chief Operating Officer of Hytaga Electronics, Inc., a firm that produced annually millions of cameras,

VCRs, televisions, and other electronic equipment that brought both him and his company millions of dollars in revenue. Fumio had bought a house in the Homewood area of Baltimore near the Johns Hopkins campus; and after presenting his credentials to the dean of the school; he had started a small karate club on campus. There he had met and fallen in love with one of his students and current professor of English Literature at Hopkins, Maria Scotti.

Maria, the daughter of Italian immigrants who had lived in several sections of Little Italy in Baltimore, had herself inherited a large row house on Fawn Street.

After a brief courtship, they married, and Fumio and Maria refurbished her row house in accordance with her husband's wishes and set up a karate studio in their home by extensively redesigning the entire first floor to be essentially a traditional Japanese dojo. There was a large workout area and an adjoining "office" for the sensei.

Fumio and Maria bought a townhouse in a neighboring suburb in Howard County to the south from which they commuted daily to their jobs in Baltimore. Fumio eventually was able to successfully ply both of his trades with his dojo in Little Italy assuming great popularity in part beginning with the martial arts upsurge of the early seventies.

He was hired by a group of enterprising Japanese immigrants, originally from the successful Osaka Group restaurant business in Tokyo, to work as the Executive Sushi Chef at the Sukaro Palace, an upscale establishment in the nearby Inner Harbor. Indeed, Fumio Hytaga had become an unqualified American success story.

Opening the door of his dojo approximately two hours before class began at six o'clock, Fumio Hytaga greeted his visitors from Washington, D.C. with a bow. "Greetings, Sensei Huffman and students. I see you have come today for training. I have heard wonderful things about your dojo at New State."

Bowing in return, Mike Huffman spoke. "*Domo arigato*, Sensei. It is a great honor, once again, to be welcomed into the headquarters dojo. May I introduce two of my top students, Dick Stickler, Second-Dan, and Joe Lynch who we promoted to First-Dan nearly a year ago."

Mike, Dick, and Joe all bowed to Sensei Hytaga and took turns shaking his hand. The master then motioned his visitors to join him in his office. "Please come into the office. We can talk and then start a preliminary workout before the class arrives. We have scheduled an advanced class for today—only first *Kyu* brown and black belts."

Facing Sensei Huffman, the master smiled broadly. "So, Sensei, as you had mentioned in your phone call the other day, I must visit your dojo at New State. I have recently spoken also with Mike Ogama in Tokyo who had trained at your dojo, and he said your dojo is one of the best in the world."

Smiling shyly, Sensei Huffman responded to the praise. "Oh, yes, I remember Mike. He was a student with our club a few years back before he transferred to the foreign-service liaison staff over in Tokyo. We were very fortunate to have a good infusion of funds to start the dojo in the first place. An assistant secretary of state just happened to become one of our top students, and he was able to request a very nice chunk of change from the budget. We have a traditional wooden dojo floor, the full complement of training gear, and a dressing room and showers, as well as an extensive array of Okinawan weaponry. It is rather amazing, if I do say so myself, and it is located in the subbasement of a government building."

Gazing over at Dick and Joe, Fumio smiled. "So, Dick, you hope someday to open your own dojo?"

Dick responded readily. "Actually, Sensei, at this point, I don't honestly know. I have a full plate with my present job in personnel at State recruiting new employees as well as a number of outside hobbies."

Looking over at Joe, he directed a question his way. "And, Joe, how about you? You have only been a black belt for a year. What do you hope to accomplish in our art?"

Joe squirmed a bit before responding. "Sensei, my interest at the present is purely as a student. I am in computer work at the Civil Service Commission and love it. I do have a fascination for Gojo-Ryu. It brings me great spiritual peace and happiness. For me it has provided a surge of confidence and allowed me to live life with new meaning."

Fumio nodded understandingly. "I like to hear that, Joe. Very interesting. What you have said in a nutshell is our mission. I am impressed with your comment."

Looking around at his visitors who had come already dressed in their *gi* pants, Sensei Hytaga spoke again. "Gentlemen, let us begin warming up for class. We are expecting six students to join us for today's session."

After leading his visitors in a warm-up session, Sensei Hytaga's students joined in, and class officially began. Going through the traditional workout program, Joe could not help but notice how "poker faced" Mr. Hytaga was directing the session. He displayed absolutely no emotion, yet led a spirited session. The training session increased in intensity with sharp kumite drills, and each student received an opportunity to do his *kata* and be critiqued by the master.

Joe was the last student who was commanded to perform *kata*. All of the other students sat at a command from the master. Joe thought this was rather strange. Nonetheless, he performed as commanded by his master. He began to perform a number of *kata*, beginning with some of the brown-belt classical *kata* and progressed to the Second-Dan qualification *kata*.

Sensei issued one final request. "Joe, now do *kata* Seipei."

Joe came to attention, bowed to the sensei and the class, and proceeded to deliver an explosive rendition of the *kata.* With precise breathing and catlike quickness, his heavily starched *gi* snapping like a whip with each hand technique, the entire class sat in awe during his performance.

"Joe, be seated," commanded Sensei Hytaga.

Noting Sensei's stony expression, Joe was convinced he had disappointed the master with his performance. Without saying another word, the sensei bowed and then left the workout area to enter his adjoining office. A full ten minutes passed before he bowed back into the workout area carrying a folder.

"Kioske!" Master Hytaga shouted. The class stood up and came to attention. Staring directly at Joe, he commanded, "Joe Lynch, step forward!"

Joe jumped up to stand at attention in front of his master. "Joe Lynch, I award you Second-Dan. You are now second-degree black belt in Shorei-Kan Goju-Ryu Karate."

Taking his certificate while rapidly shaking Sensei's hand and bowing to the master, the sensei followed up with praise. "Joe, that is best performance of *kata* Seipei I have ever witnessed in the United States. You are a credit to our style of martial arts. I have followed my conscience and the tenets of Master Toguchi who would on occasion promote a student on the spot for a magnificent performance. After class, we celebrate. Your Sensei Huffman and fellow students, you, and I celebrate this achievement."

Joe humbly bowed to Sensei and expressed his thanks. "*Domo arigato,* Sensei."

After class had ended, Sensei Hytaga took his guests for a short stroll down the block to one of Little Italy's most famous restaurants, Sabatino's. The sensei insisted on paying for dinner and had drinks ordered for everyone. Sipping on his double Chivas Scotch and soda, he turned to Joe. "So, Joe, what have you got to say about yourself? You come up to my dojo and get yourself promoted to Second-Dan."

Joe's face began to flush with embarrassment at Sensei's praise, as well as at the effects of his gin and tonic, and he just shrugged his shoulders. "I had no idea this was going to happen, Sensei. I am deeply grateful and honored to have received this award today. I don't know what else to say. The feeling that I have now is just too overwhelming to describe further."

Master Hytaga laughed aloud and slapped Joe on his shoulder. "You know, Joe, what you experienced today is very unusual. I had not dreamed I would ever do such a thing, yet wondered if the time would ever come. This same thing happened to me many years ago in Tokyo headquarters dojo. My sensei, Master Toguchi, told me that as a teacher one knows when to award such a spontaneous honor. You will feel it as a teacher, and you *must* award your student if he deserves the honor. To do otherwise—to ignore a *kata* that is a magical performance is a mistake and will not be tolerated. I had no other choice. You deserve honor. It is also reflection on Sensei Huffman's excellent instruction in class."

Beginning to slur his words, Sensei Huffman spoke next. "Sensei, we are deeply honored that you awarded Joe with a Second-Dan. I had always wanted my top students to visit our east coast headquarters here in Baltimore to experience training from our master. For that as well, we from the dojo at New State in Washington, D.C., are also deeply honored."

Master Hytaga smiled at his guests and raised his glass in a toast, his guests following suit. "Here's to Joe Lynch for achieving Second-Dan, and here's to the dojo at New State. Thanks to its founder and chief sensei, Mr. Mike Huffman, it is our only Shorei-Kan representation in the Washington, D.C. area. Sensei Huffman, it is a credit to you that your students, in particular Joe, have demonstrated their excellence in Gojo-Ryu to us in Baltimore today."

After touching glasses all around, Sensei Hytaga turned once again to Joe. "So, Joe, you said that you are in the computer business in the federal government. What types of other hobbies do you have?"

Joe put his drink down and turned directly toward the master. "Sensei, I have recently gotten into hiking as a form of exercise and mental relaxation to go with my martial arts training. I have already performed some short hikes in the Shenandoah National Park only an hour and a half outside of Washington, D.C. What I really want to do is hike in the White Oak Canyon region of the park where there are waterfalls and do *kata Sanchin* under the freezing waterfalls as a form of meditation similar to what I understand Master Togochi had performed many years ago."

Hytaga San nodded understandingly. "Ah, yes, I had heard of his feat many years before. He had performed *Sanchin*, standing under cold waterfalls with his *gi* top off. It was witnessed by several students."

Joe quickly responded. "Well, Sensei, my plan is to just bring my camcorder and record the event. I don't know anyone who is interested in or has the time to spare to do the hike."

After dinner and exchanging good-byes with the master, Mike, Joe, and Dick headed west on Lombard Street to connect with Route 95 heading south toward Washington D.C.

Thinking about his conversation with Sensei Hytaga regarding his future hiking adventure, Joe hoped that he had reached *the* Jimmy Mackenzie he had once known a long time ago; perhaps Jimmy would be willing to do the waterfalls' hike with him. He had finally found a phone number from an operator in Front Royal, Virginia, and left a voice mail message for his old friend to call him. Having him along would be interesting. They could catch up; and in that neck of the woods, Jimmy could be very helpful with what to look for or perhaps, more importantly, what to watch out for.

"Hello," Sandi said into the phone receiver.

"Hey, my name is Jimmy Mackenzie ; I'm an old friend of Joe Lynch from way back, and I am returning his phone call," Jimmy replied to Sandi.

"Hold on, please. I know Joe will be happy to hear from you," Sandi excitedly said.

"Honey, it's Jimmy on the phone for you," Sandi yelled to her husband down the hall of their apartment. He was toweling off after taking a hot shower to ease his muscles, sore from the workout in Little Italy.

"Tell him I will be there in a second," Joe yelled back. Tossing his towel over the rail in his shower and whipping on a Tee shirt, Joe walked briskly to his living room and took the phone from Sandi.

"Hello, is it really you? Is this the country boy I haven't talked to in too many years who used to be a *keydet*?" Joe exuberantly said.

"Hey, Joe, how the hell are you? Damn, been a heck of a long time since we parted ways at VMI. What have you been up to?" Jimmy inquired of his long-lost friend.

"Well, Jimmy—obviously, I never forgot about you, man. It's just that as you move along in life, lots of other things jump in to fill up your time. I got married; you talked with my wife, Sandi. I suppose you figured that I would drop out of school. I just couldn't hack it at the time, dude. I had let myself get way too overloaded mentally."

"Yeah, I do remember that you were awful uptight back then. I used to say what a damn shame that was. I mean—in my case—they just kicked me out because I couldn't control my temper. Oh, well, the past is past; we have to move on," Jimmy replied.

"Well, Jim, I ended up being a government worker. Got into mainframe computers. I really enjoy it. It pays well, and I receive great benefits from the government."

"Yeah, Joe, I heard about you government workers, getting paid to goof off," Jimmy joked.

"Hey, Jim, it really depends on where you work no matter what job you have," Joe said. "In my case I support financial and payroll operations. No way you can goof off with that type of responsibility."

"What have you been up to?"

"Well, Joe, I guess I lived up to my reputation. I tried community college for a spell, got bored of that, and joined the Navy to get the hell out of the woods and see the world. Got into a special branch of the Navy called the SEALS," Jimmy said.

"You're shitting me!" Joe excitedly replied. "Those guys are really bad dudes—some serious kick-butt guys from what I hear," Joe continued.

"Well, Joe, all I can say is it was very difficult to make the grade; it was the most challenging undertaking I have ever tried. Did well, though—saw some combat, and then I decided to leave the service to check on my family back home. My uncle wasn't doing very well anyway."

"So, you're a government worker. What else you been into?" Jimmy inquired.

"You're not going to believe this. I got into martial arts, actually Okinawan Karate and have really enjoyed it," Joe said.

"No shit, Sherlock!" Jimmy replied. "You a black belt? Can you break bricks and shit?" Jimmy inquired.

"Naw, Jimmy, we don't get into that. We are a classical style, though some of us fight in tournaments on the side," Joe explained.

Feeling a bit weary after his workout and the ride home, and not wanting to extend Jimmy's long-distance call, Joe decided to bring their conversation to a close for now. "Look, man, I just got back from a workout up in Baltimore and need to get some rest. I am thinking of doing a hike down in your neck of the woods real soon. It would be great if we could hook up and do the hike together with you being a backwoods boy and all," Joe said.

"I would like that, Joe. My problem is breaking away from the job. I own a sporting goods store in Front Royal and being the owner, well, I don't have a lot of free time. My assistant, Mike and I usually spend our spare time hanging out at his place on the weekends."

"Tell you what, when you pin down your dates, let me know, and maybe I can break free for a couple days and do it with you. Even if I can't break free—you see the busy time for us is coming up with the fall and all, you know, huntin and fishin—anyway, I will give you the address of my store and how to get there. That way, you could drop by either before your hike—got lots of hiking equipment I could give you a great deal on, and we could do a lunch—or after your hike, whatever," Jimmy said.

Once Joe had written down the coordinates for Jimmy's store and the phone number, they said good-bye to one another, vowing to stay in touch.

"Wow, Hon, it was great to talk with Jimmy after all of these years. The dude became a Navy SEAL and owns a sporting goods store in Front Royal," Joe said to Sandi.

"That's something. Maybe Jimmy can go with you on your hike," Sandi replied.

"I asked him that. His problem is he is very busy. We'll see what happens. Just maybe we can hook up," Joe said.

Chapter 19

Washington, D.C.—Vicinity of 16th and U Streets, N.W.—Three Months Later

"Okay, class, to review what we have gone over this week, CICS is the acronym for Customer Information Control System. It is the software platform that operates in the online environment that enables your programs to function. Remember that the concept here is totally different from the top-down concept that you have been using since most of you got into mainframe applications."

The instructor at the IBM Education Center near 16th and U Streets, N.W. in Washington, D.C. was providing his class a summary of their five-day course introducing the students to CICS online programming. Among the students were Joe Lynch and his coworker Pat Sedgwick from the Civil Service Commission, recently renamed the U.S. Office of Personnel Management.

With the rapid advance in mainframe technology over the past decade culminating with the introduction of Visual Interchange Projectors or VIPS, affectionately known as "dumb" terminals because they do not include "memory" or central processing units, the emergence of the need to enter and process data in a "real time" environment was fast becoming the trend in the industry. Clients were literally screaming for the capability. The old days of punched cards and voluminous computer-generated reports were fast becoming history. Many of the long-time COBOL programmers, entrenched in the ways of beginning their code by opening files and processing data somewhere in the middle of the code and then closing files at the end of the code, had a difficult time coping with the new concept of online programming. With this concept, one had to erase the "top down" methodology and think of screens that would appear with boxes or windows where data could be entered, computed, and displayed.

You are right about that. Getting adjusted to this new way of programming is going to take some practice, Joe mused as he raised his hand to ask the instructor a question.

"Yes, Joe, you have a question?" the instructor pleasantly inquired. Like many IBM personnel, the instructor wore a white shirt with a dark blue tie and dark pants. His hair was unusually short for the time period, and his glasses and frames were thick enough to border on being out of style. However, it certainly fit the corporate mode perfectly.

"Yes, I do," replied Joe. "My question is—are you saying you need EXEC statements every time you open up a screen or read and write to a file?"

The instructor peered intently at Joe to respond to his question. "Yes, EXEC or execute statements are needed whenever one opens a screen, reads a file, writes to a file, or closes a file. It's a matter of getting used to the code in lieu of the simple *open, read,* and *write* statements you have grown accustomed to with batch programming. Remember, before you code, just as you have been used to doing, a good practice is to block diagram your program. The major difference is your program will be screen driven rather than top-down driven.

"So, think in terms of the screens you have drawn on paper. You will probably have some sort of intro client screen with a number of options to give the user. Then, each option will spawn a separate screen with more specifics. Once you program the EXEC statements to bring up the screens, for the most part, the COBOL within the screen modules is exactly what you have always been used to."

"Thank you," replied Joe.

Joe Lynch and Pat Sedgwick had been designated by Tom Akron, their boss at OPM, to take the CICS intro course. One of the first questions they had was where the school was going to be located. Since their mainframe computer was an IBM 3090 and there were many education centers around the country, there was always the exciting possibility of travel to an interesting city such as San Francisco or Orlando, Florida, among many others where the students could build in additional "vacation" time to complement their class work. Mainframe computer programmers were constantly taking courses to update their existing knowledge to accommodate the frequent advances in computer technology. It was not unusual to take two courses per year.

Many employees such as Joe and Pat were also required to switch gears whenever their bosses decided to replace or upgrade mainframes with those of a different manufacturer. In Joe and Pat's case, they had upgraded to an IBM machine from a Honeywell 6000 computer within the past year. This required courses in the understanding of hexadecimal versus octal code and mastering a totally different rendition of job control language.

When Joe was told that the course was being offered at the IBM ED Center near 16th and U Streets, N.W., his heart sank. It was not so much because the location was not nearly as glamorous as a trip to an exciting city; this area was a mere two blocks from where he had been savagely mauled and humiliated by a gang of street thugs just a few years earlier.

When Joe arrived at the location, he had to stifle an old fear when he passed by "Ben's Chili Bowl" restaurant on U Street—just a block down from the training center. That thought was quickly put to rest by two new thoughts: first, he knew with his recent promotion to Second-Dan in Baltimore a few months earlier that he was not the wimpy fellow who had gotten his ass kicked in the hood a few years earlier. Moreover, U Street had been undergoing extensive renovations since his horrific experience. The area was now bustling with new commerce, businesses, and office workers. Joe had even noticed in the newspapers the mention of several prominent nightclubs in the area where well-known musicians and rock bands had performed, and he had heard upbeat conversation around the office from some employees who had frequented the area at night to party.

No, this wasn't the same area. However, he had no doubt that the exact location where his Honda had stalled a couple of blocks away was still not an area that one would want to hang out after dark. Still, he had psyched himself up to think positively the past Monday morning when he had pulled into the garage just a block down from the education center, happily paying the attendant to park for the day.

After another hour of course summary by the instructor, he gave the class a fifteen-minute break to relax, get coffee, and snacks or go to the restroom as they saw fit.

"Well, Joe, are you ready for the final exam?" Pat inquired of his coworker as they sat at a table in a lounge at the education center munching on bagels and coffee during their morning class break.

Joe glanced at Pat with a smirk on his face. "You know, I hate these short one-week courses. I would rather take a college course over a period of a semester any day. I mean, how do they expect you to absorb all of this material in one week?"

Pat nodded in understanding. "You're right about that. They can have these doggone courses. The problem is most colleges don't offer these types of courses, and our bosses can't wait a whole semester for us to get up to speed. This has been stressful."

As they finished up their breakfast, Joe patted Pat on the shoulder and leaned close to him. "You know, Pat, I know you're not much of a drinker. What do you say we have a couple beers after class at that "Sweet 16" bar and grill across the street after class today? Heck, it's Friday; I want to celebrate putting this course behind us."

Pat smiled. "Why not, I'm up for a beer or two."

Once class had been concluded for the day, indeed for the week, Joe and Pat sauntered over to the "Sweet 16" bar and grill.

The "Sweet 16" bar and grill was a rather new establishment with a mixed clientele: office workers, construction workers who were quite busy with the renovations that had been approved for the area by the D.C. government, and the locals who frequented the place later in the evening. Because of its close approximation to 16th Street and the frequent recent trips of the local university basketball team to the NCAA "Sweet 16" portion of the basketball tournament, it was no secret where the ownership had gotten the name for their new establishment.

Joe had noticed after leaving class every day at 5:00 p.m. that office workers made up most of the customers looking to get a release from their hectic days at work. There had been many days during the past week when he had been tempted with the stress brought on by the CICS class to drop by for a scotch and soda to unwind. After thinking about Sandi and the kids back home, he would quickly change his mind. He had decided to wait until Friday to pose the question to Pat.

The "Sweet 16" bar and grill, in fact, reflected much of what the name was all about. It had a long, curved dark wooden bar with comfortable stools, and the dark wood-paneled walls contained numerous photos of basketball players and NCAA tournament games. There was a large-screen TV mounted at the end of the bar permanently set to the ESPN channel. The liquor cabinet behind the bartenders was fully stocked with every brand and make of liquor and spirits from around the world.

Nursing a double Chevas Scotch and soda, Joe glanced over at his bar mate and ruminated on the past week's activities. "Tell you what, Pat. I am glad the dude didn't give us a final exam."

"Hey, man, you don't have to tell me. I was just thinking the same thing. That doggone guy was really jamming the stuff down our throats. I was holding my breath to the very end hoping he wouldn't give us a test."

Pat was sipping on Guinness Stout, a bit strong for him; yet he, too, had felt the stress of the class and was happy to have the course behind him.

Looking around the bar, Joe changed the subject as he thought about his experience a few years ago. "You know, Pat, this area isn't all that bad after all. You used to hear about this being a rough neighborhood."

Pat shook his head a tad to that comment. "I don't know, Joe. I don't think I would ever leave Centreville, Virginia, to move here," Pat replied, referring to his suburban neighborhood.

"I don't think I would leave Wheaton to move down here, though I have thought of maybe working with some of the local D.C. neighborhood leaders to establish a dojo in the area."

Pat finished up his Stout and ordered another and then addressed Joe's statement. "You gotta be kidding?"

"I'm serious. I have tried a few times to get a karate class started in Montgomery County where I live, only to be brushed aside because they don't want the competition. I have read about guys like myself with the skills who can also motivate young people to do the right thing by getting involved in learning the martial arts where you can learn discipline, control, and spiritual values. I have heard about guys taking old row houses—heck, even our chief instructor in Baltimore did the same thing—and fixing them up to be dojos. Because the school is located in a downtrodden area, the rent is cheap. I would accept donations from the students and community. If you get a base of support from the neighborhood, they don't view you with suspicion. You make it clear that all you want to do is help people—not make money. You want to spread your art to people who would have no chance to ever learn it because they can't pay out a hundred bucks a month to a lavish studio somewhere out in the suburbs," Joe said.

Joe had completed his first drink and was working on another. He clearly was on a roll and relished talking about anything other than work and mainframe computers.

Pat had to smile, noticing that Joe was slightly slurring his words. He had to admit, though, that Joe's idea was noble if not practical. "I guess you have a point. If you are an expert instructor and don't have a lot of money yourself to start a school, plus you're getting brushed off by guys who already have karate classes set up in their recreation association, I can understand where you're coming from. The tricky part, though, is getting that base of support for your endeavor."

Abruptly finding that he was thinking about his old school mate, Jimmy, Joe sought to share the good news of his reconnecting with Jimmy just a few weeks earlier with Pat. "Pat, I got some good news," he said.

"Yeah, what's that, man?" Pat asked.

"I looked up an old classmate of mine, and he returned my call a couple weeks ago," he said.

"That's great, Joe. What inspired you to try to reach him?" Pat inquired.

"Well, Pat, I've been telling you guys at work about getting into hiking and sort of thought that my old friend, Jimmy, could go with me. He is from the area where I am planning to do my hike. Plus, I've missed the dude. He is a country boy and a very interesting dude," Joe said.

"Is that right? How so?" Pat asked.

"Well, he always inspired confidence in me," Joe said eagerly warming to this line of conversation. "He tried to keep me in school when I wanted to drop out. It didn't work, but I appreciated his efforts. Also, he became a Navy SEAL and is an owner of a sporting goods store in Front Royal. It would be great to hook up with him again."

Pat squirmed a bit when Joe completed his second stiff drink and called the bartender over to order another. "Tell you what, if I were going to be hiking in the woods down there, I think I would want someone else to go with me. I thought I saw a short blurb on the tube the other night about some hikers turning up missing down there. Anyway, man, I think I've had it for the night; it's already seven o'clock, and I have to get home to Mandy and the kids," Pat said.

"Well, Pat, I enjoyed spending the week with you, man, in class. Glad I didn't have to do this by myself," Joe said.

"Me too. You have a good weekend," Pat replied.

With that, they shook hands, and Pat placed his tab money on the bar and slid off the barstool to make his way out of the establishment. Pat had been fortunate on this Friday to locate a parking spot in front of the training center, one of just several spaces that had been free in the morning. Joe, of course, was parked down the street at the public garage.

It was quarter to eight, and Joe was well along on this third drink. His spirits were soaring as he contemplated the end of a stressful week and a return to his familiar working environment next Monday at OPM. He glanced around the bar at the customers and noticed that the clientele had changed perceptively since Pat and he had first entered the establishment after class. There were few, if any, office workers in the bunch. While the ESPN channel was still showing on the overhead TV, the music had been kicked up to a louder volume with a definite edge to it. Joe noticed that groups of people seemed to be huddled in booths and that some very sexy women began to appear prominently in the bar area.

In his euphoric state fueled by three stiff drinks, he began to take in this new scene seemingly oblivious to the time. While feeling intoxicated, he had enough awareness about him to notice two things. The males in the crowd did not seem particularly friendly, judging by the occasional stares in his direction, yet the females dressed in pumps, pantyhose, and short skirts with slits up to their hips, would appear to be almost beckoning to him.

Totally engrossed now while staring hard at one dark-skinned woman with beautiful mocha legs and black fishnet stockings, he was jarred from his trance by a bump into the side of his leg. "Honey, she can't give you what I can," whispered a young lady dressed in a tight red leather pantsuit. She had pushed her knee suggestively into the side of his leg before slouching down on the barstool right next to him.

Before Joe could even think of what to say, the lady got up off the stool for a minute to lean over the bar and wave to someone she knew at the end of the bar. Joe took note of how incredibly tight her red leather pants were to the point where one could literally and easily imagine exactly what her rear end looked like in the buff. It was an incredibly inviting sight.

Feeling a perceptible stiffness in his loins, he glanced down at his watch and noticed it was past 10:00 p.m. *Christ, here I go again, letting time slip past me. I've got to get home!* He smiled at the lady as he paid his bar tab. "You know some other time I would love to get to know you. I do have to get home."

The lady winked at Joe as Joe took in a heavy whiff of perfume from her presence and responded. "Well, honey, let's not take too long to get to know me. I'm right here every Friday night."

Joe waved at her as he quickly moved to the phone on the wall near the entrance to call Sandi and let her know that once again, time had passed him by.

As he walked out into the warm night air toward the garage, his mind was full of thoughts. He was still flush with the feeling of the liquor and the very attractive lady at the bar. *I shouldn't be too excited about that. It's not like she was actually interested in me because she thought I was an attractive or cool dude—probably just a prostitute looking to get paid for a lay.*

However, as he shifted his thoughts to his phone call to Sandi, reality began to set in on two fronts. She had scolded him for once again letting the time slip by and keeping her and the girls guessing as to his whereabouts. Moreover, he was, after all, still in the hood on a Friday night after 10:00 p.m.

It was amazing how deserted U Street seemed to be in the area where he was heading. Somehow the old feelings of insecurity began to seep in to his consciousness.

As he was about to enter the garage, he stared down the street to his right and noticed the neon sign depicting "Ben's Chili Bowl." That sent a chill up his spine. He was jarred once again, when a man came out of nowhere.

"Mista, you got a dolla you can spare?" It was a homeless man. He had not noticed any homeless people during the daylight hours while he had been in training. Whipping out a dollar bill and slapping it into the homeless man's hand, he moved quickly into the garage. Rather than risk a confrontation with another homeless man or ruffian by walking up the stairs to level three where his Jeep was located, Joe walked up through each level of parked cars. There were only a few left in the garage.

As he moved purposely through the levels, he became steeled in his resolve not to let a lifetime of silly fears ruin the end of his week. *Shit, I'm a Goddamn black belt. I've kicked other black belts' butts many times. I am not the same man I was before I got into karate. This is bullshit whimping out like this. Be real. If I were to come across someone trying to fuck with me, there is no way they are going to have the skills that I have come up against in the dojo.*

He paused for a minute to listen for any sounds. Not hearing even the sound made by a pin drop, he relaxed and resumed his walk, now at a slower, more confident pace. He had psyched himself out of his old fears and knew that he was not the same man he had been before his training.

He rounded the corner to the third level where his Jeep was parked at the very opposite end of where he stood. He was somewhat amazed at how dim the lights were in the garage. Still, he walked resolutely toward his vehicle, the awareness skills he had honed in the martial arts set at a high level. As he walked slowly toward his Jeep, the hair on the back of his neck began to stick out—a certain sign of danger—even though he had not seen or heard anything that would invite alarm.

He stopped suddenly. He could barely make out the sounds of men talking in low voices to one another. It was coming from the general direction of where his Jeep was parked. *Shit, some dudes are over where my Jeep is parked! I better approach cautiously.*

Joe moved with stealth to seek cover from the parked cars that separated him from where his vehicle was parked and himself. He eased slowly forward keeping a low profile, pausing to raise his head slightly to peer in the direction of the voices.

As he quietly moved to the next parked car and slowly raised his head, he became alarmed at what he saw. There were three dudes huddled around the driver's side of his Jeep appearing to attempt to jimmy their way into his ride. They were mumbling to themselves; one dude apparently was fussing with the dude trying to open the Jeep's door to hurry up. Joe knew that even though he was a skilled martial artist, he could be facing experienced criminals who could be armed with knives or guns to ply their trade, negating the advantage he might otherwise have with his martial arts prowess.

He decided in an instant to try a quick ruse to solve his problem. Coming out from behind the parked car, he startled the men. "I'm Metropolitan Police Detective Lieutenant Boyers. Get away from that vehicle, *now*! I have already called for backup. I am going to give you a break; you have about five minutes to get the fuck out of here before you get your butts hauled downtown. Do I make myself clear?"

Turning around and standing to face this "policeman," one of the younger fellows quickly ran down the parking level to leave the premises as fast as his legs could take him. The other two men facing him with a scowl would not budge. The taller of the two walked slowly toward Joe with his right hand out.

I wonder if this guy wants to shake my hand? No way, he probably is up to no good, Joe thought.

While Joe had been in a state of numbed intoxication, his old fears and the sight of people actually trying to steal his Jeep slammed him into sobriety. Hearing a sudden click, Joe noticed a switchblade knife suddenly appear in the man's extended hand with the man giving Joe an ominous warning.

"Man, I am goin to cut you good. I'm goin to make you wish you never set foot here. How I know you the man, motha fucka? You jest a jive ass punk," the big man hissed.

Those were tough words coming from a big, tough-looking dude. The man had noticeable scars on both cheeks probably from knife fights on the street, and his nose was twisted to the side indicating that it had probably been broken one or more times. The man wore a tight muscle shirt and had well-defined, bulging muscles from the tops of his shoulders down to his wrists. He meant business.

At this point Joe was aware that his playacting as a policeman was not going to wash with these dudes and that while he had psyched one of the dudes out to run off, his words meant nothing to the two mean-looking guys he was stuck with.

Instinct took over now from years of punishing martial arts training. He went into action. As the menacing-looking man took another step toward him, Joe quickly switched his stance to have his strong right leg to the rear in a semi-horse stance; and using the tremendous power and speed generated by the blindly swift motion of twisting the hips clockwise so that his body and head seemed to rotate in place, he brought his fully extended rear right leg around in a wide, whip-like motion nearly three hundred and sixty degrees. In less than a second, his foot had connected with the man's right hand sending the switchblade flying in the air and sliding on the concrete harmlessly away. The technique was known in the trade as a spinning back kick, and Joe had executed it in a way that would have made Chuck Norris proud. In the process, the heel of Joe's shoe had smacked the back of the man's hand violently.

"Damn, motha fucka! You bitch!" the man whined as he stumbled back away from the sudden violence exhibited by Joe. However, the man no longer wanted to back up his words. He stepped back further from Joe, clutching his hand in pain, bending over in agony.

Suddenly, the smaller of the two men stepped into the fray. Joe was shocked at what he now was confronted with. Not only did the man ominously wave a small silver-plated automatic pistol at Joe; what really shocked him was the man's face. *Jesus Christ! That looks like the little dude with the buckteeth and bad breath that kicked me in the face!*

There was no apparent recognition from the smaller of the two men that this was the guy he had beat up years earlier. "What you gonna do now? Jes cause you know a little kung fu, you think you gonna Bogart us, asshole?" Buckteeth menacingly said to Joe.

There was a horrific smack of bone against bone as Joe whipped out at blinding speed a left back fist to Buckteeth's face. Stumbling backward towards Joe's Jeep with blood beginning to drip down from his nose onto his stained yellow Tee shirt, Buckteeth held onto his gun and fired a shot that fortunately went over Joe's head. While only a small automatic, the shot had a deafening sound to it.

Reacting totally on instinct once again, Joe knew he had to rid the man of his weapon quickly. He jumped into the man with a lunge punch catching Buckteeth squarely in the mouth. Both of Buckteeth's front teeth were smashed grotesquely inward, severely cutting his lips. While stumbling backward further, he somehow held onto his weapon once again and fired another shot.

At this point both of Joe's callused fists were bleeding and bruised from the fast, powerful strikes he had administered to his foe. Out of the corner of his eye, his peripheral vision honed by the many contests he had fought in karate tournaments, he detected the taller of the two men trying to work his way around to his rear for a surprise attack. To place Buckteeth between Joe and the taller man, he deftly slipped around to the back of Buckteeth and twisted his gun arm around until he heard his elbow break at the joint. Letting out a tremendous howl and dropping the pistol, Buckteeth grasped his broken arm with his other hand and fell on the concrete pavement rolling in severe pain.

Joe quickly picked up the pistol and pointed it at the taller man. The taller man didn't need instructions on what to do next. He ran like the first man as far from the scene as possible.

Buckteeth continued to writhe on the floor in pain. Joe walked up to him and stomp kicked him in the mouth, remembering the kick he had taken in the face while on the ground. Both of Buckteeth's front teeth were now completely knocked out of his mouth, and he slipped into unconsciousness.

Joe lay the pistol down and thought that now was as good a time as any to leave this godforsaken garage. He got into his Jeep and started it up; then he remembered that he had touched the man's gun. *Christ, I touched that gun. What if the cops run a fingerprint check? I might end up being blamed even though I had to defend myself.* He stepped out of his Jeep and walked over to the pistol, pausing to completely wipe it down with his handkerchief. Then he tossed it over the edge of the garage somewhere in the tight space between the building adjoining the garage and the garage itself. He thought that maybe no one would find it and do harm to another innocent person.

Though badly shaken once again from another violent confrontation on the street with his hands bruised and bloody, he thanked God that he had come out on top of this battle. Gripping the steering wheel hard to steady his frayed nerves, he thanked God for his devotion to martial arts and the years of arduous training. Tonight, in a hostile, faraway, dark, forbidden area of town, he had survived—thanks to his training.

As he headed up 16th Street past Arkansas Street near Rock Creek Park, he finally began to settle down as he slowed when two metropolitan police cruisers screamed past him heading in the general direction of 16th and U Street.

Someone must have heard the shots. I sure hope Buckteeth is still around to greet them when they get there!

It was near midnight when Joe pulled into the parking lot at the Rustic Woods apartments. After turning the ignition off and locking his Jeep, Joe began to feel faint as he walked slowly and unsteadily up the walkway toward his apartment. Somehow, he was able to make his way up the stairs to his third-floor apartment and open the door with his key.

Sandi must have been waiting by the door. As soon as she heard the lock, she quickly peered through the door peephole to see her husband in obvious duress. She opened the door only to have Joe fall practically into her arms. "Joe, what happened? Were you mugged again? My God, how do you get into these predicaments?"

Joe struggled to stand upright. "I'm okay, hon. Sandi, you will never believe what happened downtown."

While Sandi applied cold compresses to his damaged hands, between bites from a cold Italian submarine sandwich, he proceeded to describe his bizarre evening on U Street, from the time Pat and he entered the bar and grill, through his exit out of the garage. The last thing he said to Sandi before passing out from fatigue was he hoped that no one had seen his Jeep leaving the garage and recorded his tag number.

As he finally succumbed to sleep, his last thoughts were positive. *I don't care if the police contact me about what happened tonight. I was defending myself and got the upper hand on the bad guys. I certainly wasn't going to wait around that dark garage for the police to show up.*

Chapter 20

Shenandoah National Park—Skyland Resort—North Entrance

It was early December in the park, and a task force of Virginia state police, National Park service personnel, and FBI agents specifically trained in search and rescue had been assembled in a conference room at the lodge at Skyland Resort. It had been acknowledged that a few hikers had been unaccounted for in recent years in the park. After some investigative work by the police and park service personnel, the consensus had been that they had met their demise in the park via unknown causes. It was certainly possible that individuals who entered the park only to never be seen again could become lost, disoriented, or injured for some unknown reason and end up incapacitated. Over a period of time, they could conceivably die and would be given up to the animals in the forest. Suppose a lone hiker in a remote section of the park slipped and broke a back or hip? He or she might not have a way of communicating his or her duress.

A number of carefully scripted tactical searches in the areas of the park where the hikers had last been reported had come up empty handed with absolutely no evidence of any kind. Those few hikers had literally disappeared without a trace. No human remains, infinitesimal shreds of clothing, shoes, boots, or other equipment had ever been found.

Captain Ted Bonner of the Virginia state police had been designated the leader of a combined task force to investigate the recent spate of missing hikers. It had finally been spurred by a frantic phone call a month ago by one Tricia Houchen, the sister of Gina Hodge, one of a family of three hikers from Arlington, Virginia, who had been reported missing by Miss Houchen.

Captain Bonner sat at the head of the conference table which was strewn with folders, case documents, assorted papers, pens and pencils, and a half dozen coffee mugs and other paraphernalia. Members of the task force sitting around the table included Special Agent Bill Smith of the FBI, assisted by

Special Agents Jeb Harper and Joan Harding of the Richmond office, Captain Billy Miller, Chief of the Front Royal police, with his top aide, Mike Wilson, several of Captain Bonner's top lieutenants from around the state, as well as Ron Adelman of the Colorado division of the National Park Service.

"Okay, people, I want to review where we are with the missing hiker case. While we have found nothing regarding the disappearance of Mr. Gooden, I think we have agreed that a more thorough, planned grid search for the missing Hodge family is necessary before we place them in the same category as Mr. Gooden and the two other hikers unaccounted for up to the Hodge incident that are presumed dead. Special Agent Smith should have some input on the planning of that search.

"Bill?"

Agent Bill Smith of the FBI's Richmond field office sat at the other end of the conference table, casually dressed in a dark blue jacket with the gold letters "FBI" emblazoned on the back. He had extensive experience with the FBI's Hostage Rescue Team (HRT) and had assisted other local law enforcement in similar reported incidents on federal parklands throughout the United States. Taking a moment to glance at a document in front of him, he looked up and slowly met the eyes of his audience around the conference table one by one.

"Tomorrow morning, beginning at sunrise, six o'clock Eastern Standard Time, we plan to execute the following plan. The plan is to conduct a coordinated grid search with one half of our teams beginning in the vicinity of the Thornton Gap entrance of the park where the Hodge party had been reported last seen by witnesses in that area."

"The other half of the search party will start a coordinated search effort beginning in the vicinity of the Stony Man trailhead. The Thornton Gap teams will fan out in five groups of fifty personnel each, moving north and west toward the vicinity of Stony Man Mountain, Little Stony Man cliffs, and the Passamaquoddy Trail located near here at Skyland."

"The Stony Man teams will fan out, likewise moving south and west toward Thornton Gap and meet up with the southern group. The search-and-rescue teams will consist of members of the Virginia state police including a large contingent of trainees and designated park service personnel. I will coordinate the overall effort via wireless communications from the Stony Man area."

"If this search does not yield tangible results, two additional searches will be conducted beginning in two days to the north, east, and south of the Stony Man area beginning in the vicinity of the White Oak Canyon region of the park. Everyone has been briefed, and the participating law enforcement agencies have designated this search effort as high priority. Everyone here has specific assignments related to this case."

"Any questions?"

Ron Adelman, a National Park Ranger brought in from the Colorado office, asked the only question. "Agent Smith, are any additional searches in other areas of the park beyond those you mentioned being contemplated at this point?"

Glancing at Ron, Agent Smith responded to his question. "Not at this point. As you know, this area consists of nearly two hundred thousand acres of federal parkland. There is simply no way we can obtain the necessary manpower to search the entire park. Witnesses are a key factor in searches of this type. We must pinpoint specific quadrants in the park and perform coordinated searches using the latest search grid techniques available. There is an effort underway, as we speak, to canvass all law enforcement units in the United States with special search-and-rescue experience as well as units in foreign countries for assistance in resolving this case."

With that last statement, the task force adjourned their meeting hoping to discover anything related to the missing Hodge family beginning early the next morning.

That late afternoon he emerged from the Stony Man trailhead and began his walk down Skyline Drive toward his favorite park service road to drive out of the park. He had noticed recently a large number of Virginia state police cruisers in this region of the park. Somehow it never connected with him; with the trance that took control of him once he entered the park at the Dickey Ridge visitor center what all the fuss was about. Once he left his family's homestead in the mountains and disposed of the bodies, his sense of recent memory dissolved into oblivion.

He had pulled his collar high above his neck and was wearing a Ranger Vietnam era campaign hat pulled down low over his face to make a good description of him impossible. As he neared the park service road and started to walk around the gated entrance, he heard several short abbreviated shrieks from a very slow-moving state police cruiser just behind him. He froze in his tracks.

"Sir, please do not enter that road. That road is for park service personnel only," came the stern warning from the loudspeaker on the cruiser.

Without turning completely around to face the sound coming from the cruiser, he managed a pleasant smile and wave while keeping his head down, uttering the meek words "sorry" in the general direction of the cruiser.

Noting that the man with the large backpack appeared to be just a hiker probably looking for a trailhead, the officer issued the standard warning. "Sir, I don't want to alarm you. I must tell you that there have been several incidents of hikers reported missing in the park recently. I need to caution you to not hike alone, especially this time of the year when there are very few hikers in the park. If you see anything unusual, please report it immediately to the park service personnel at the visitor centers or contact the Virginia state police."

The "hiker," still keeping his head down and cupping a large portion of his face in a casual manner, merely nodded as the cruiser proceeded slowly down Skyline Drive in the direction of Front Royal.

The police officer was miles away near the Dickey Ridge Visitor Center before it dawned on him that he had not obtained a "visual" of the mysterious hiker he had seen near Stony Man. He silently cursed his mistake.

After several days of coordinated searches, the missing hiker task force once again assembled in the designated conference room at the Sky land Resort for an update on the missing hiker search. Captain Bonner began. "As you know, our coordinated searches have yielded some information that may eventually prove helpful in our search for the missing Hodge family. The items of interest reported to me were a strange finding at a remote area in the forest southwest of Stony Man Mountain within walking distance of the old Passamaquoddy Trail. An old cemetery was discovered in the thickets by one of our crews. Certainly there is nothing on the face of that discovery that appears all that unusual. Old cemeteries have been discovered in the park before. The cemetery was clearly very old with the bodies interred sometime around the mid 1950's. This may well have been an old mountain family. Only the first names of a man and woman were apparent on the gravestones, Rebecca and Samuel with the dates of death as I indicated appearing to start with the number 195. The last digit was not readable."

"The really unusual thing though was that there was a bouquet of fresh-cut roses that had been placed on both of the stones. This cemetery is miles off the nearest designated park trails in thick brush—very difficult to access for the ordinary hiker.

"The other reported observation was of an individual who appeared to be a hiker who was seen the other day, the very same day as our planning conference, walking alone on Skyline Drive in this area. A state police officer had spotted him apparently trying to enter the quarry service road not too far from here on the other side of Skyline Drive. There was no indication of foul play; the officer thought that maybe the hiker was looking for a trailhead and had stumbled by accident onto the entrance of the service road. Unfortunately, the officer did not get a facial on the hiker."

Special Agent Bill Smith proceeded to add his input. "I think these two sightings may turn out to be of minimal consequence regarding our hiker searches. Nonetheless, we have received a description and notes of both the cemetery area coordinates, as well as a description of the hiker's general appearance, his clothing, and approximate age, height, and weight. We need to investigate both of these developments further. All relevant personnel have been advised and have the cemetery coordinates and hiker's general description. Unfortunately, we have no idea what became of that hiker after the officer saw him. No one was able to get a make on his vehicle or saw him later that day."

"Regarding the gravesite, other than the flowers on the gravestones, the cemetery appeared to be typical of one that had once probably been established and maintained by immediate family. Over the years, perhaps as the family died off, it simply no longer received proper maintenance. It was in shabby condition. While we have reported the location of the cemetery to the appropriate state people, we have designated the cemetery as off limits to anyone other than members of this search operation. Let me repeat myself; that cemetery is off limits to anyone other than authorized members of this search OP. If someone is visiting the cemetery, and that appears to be obvious, they are making an enormous effort to move off the designated trails into heavy brush and thickets to do so. In my humble opinion, that scenario should be considered and looked at closely. There could be a family member who has located his long-lost, buried loved ones and is paying tribute to them. There is nothing obviously wrong with that per se. I think you all know where I'm coming from with this."

There were nods all around the table.

Jim Carvello, a park ranger, turned in his chair to Agent Smith. "So, we could conceivably have an individual who clearly has disobeyed park policy in the first place by brush busting through the forest way off the beaten path—and this individual just might be that lonely hiker that the officer saw. Even if it's not that particular hiker, for someone to do what's been reported seen at that lost cemetery with the fresh flowers, I agree, that is bizarre. My God, the effort he had to make to get through the terrain and brush just to get there. Any individual capable of doing that could be mentally unstable and dangerous. Imagine if someone or some group of people got lost in that particular area, and this person is tending to the gravesite. What might such a person be capable of doing?"

Again, there were nods all around.

Captain Bonner sat upright in his chair and began to conclude this session. "Exactly, Jim. With the able assistance of Bill Smith and some of our guys, we have decided to provide clandestine surveillance at the cemetery from a short distance just outside of the cemetery walls. It may involve having a few of our people armed in ghillie suits near the area of the cemetery to take a look at just who is visiting that area of the park. We need to closely monitor just what is going on there at the cemetery. Is this individual involved in any suspicious activity or types of behavior other than placing flowers on the gravestones? This OP will have to be extensively planned and will involve a group of heavily armed specialists. We are going to put a hold on any future searches until we have had a chance to thoroughly investigate this situation. We will set up another search conference in the near future."

Ron raised his hand slightly with a question.

"You have a question, Ron?" Captain Bonner asked.

"Ghillie suits—what are they?" he asked.

Bill Smith provided the answer. "Those are specially made outfits that individuals, usually snipers, use for maximum cover during an OP. They are made to closely resemble the surrounding terrain where the sniper would be set up. Some of the suits resemble leaves and brush and are usually various shades of brown and green to blend into that environment.

"On the other hand, some of the suits are designed to blend more into a winter environment and are primarily white and gray in color. We occasionally borrow them from the Marines near our training center in Quantico to use for very specific operations where it would be an advantage to use that type of camouflage. Our hope is that an individual will return to the cemetery totally unaware of our surveillance, and we can capture him without bloodshed."

"I see," Ron replied.

The question having been answered, the meeting was then adjourned.

Chapter 21

Near Luray, Virginia—New Year's Eve

Pouring himself three fingers of Jack Daniel's whiskey into his "Smith and Wesson" mug, a gift from one of that company's representatives during a seminar he had attended in Massachusetts at their headquarters earlier this year, Jimmy Mackenzie assumed a reflective mood as the year neared its end. He sat pensively gazing at the fire from his recently stoked fireplace feeling the tranquil warmth from the hearth.

It's been a great year for the store, especially this fall what with hunting season and folks being scared about the goings on in the park. I hope Mike and Cindy will be able to drop by after their party—kind of lonely this time of year. Damn women; guess they don't like the way I look.

With that last thought, Jimmy fingered the dull white scar on his jaw line as he stoked his pipe with tobacco. Then he reached across the coffee table to pick up the thick folder of his uncle's papers. He had been giving considerable thought recently to reviving his uncle's defunct apple orchard in the back of the house. His uncle had left some notes to that effect. In fact, he had indicated that it would be necessary to use a special fertilizer to turn the ground over before transplanting the young apple trees to his farm.

Jimmy thumbed through some of the other papers and came to a stack with a yellow "post it" label. Feeling a sudden flash of warmth start to come over him, he pushed the folder away and rubbed his temples.

Damn, I feel strange. Shit, I'm getting a fuckin headache. On a night like this, I don't need to be looking through Uncle Ronny's papers.

Thump! Thump! Thump! A loud rapping on his backdoor snapped Jimmy back to reality. *Must be Mike and Cindy*, he thought. Mike and Cindy had decided to drop by after all.

"Hey, Mike, Cindy—Happy New Year to you," Jimmy said as he opened his backdoor to let his company in.

Mike strolled into Jimmy's house, his left arm wrapped around his blond-haired girlfriend, Cindy, who looked no older than twenty-one, and his right paw wrapped around a Seven Eleven "Big Gulp" plastic soda cup filled with Jack Daniel's, ice, and water. Mike was clearly feeling no pain as he stumbled into the kitchen area.

Jimmy used his hands to steady Mike. "Goddamn, Mike, how much drinkin you been doin tonight, buddy?"

Cindy answered for him. "Mike has been doin too much damn drinkin tonight, Jimmy. He done drank nearly a fifth of Jack."

Jimmy looked a bit concerned. "Damn it, Mike, you and Cindy are stayin at my place tonight. That's an order and don't give me any shit about it."

Mike looked lazily over at his boss as if to say whatever and then took a sip out of his plastic cup.

Walking to his kitchen to refill his mug, Jimmy turned back to Cindy. "Hey, Cindy, can I get you something to eat or drink? I know you don't drink booze. You want some juice or soda?"

Brushing her long blond hair away from her brow while she sat on Jimmy's tattered couch with her boyfriend, Cindy responded. "A Coke is fine, if you have one, Jimmy."

"Got you covered," Jimmy replied.

Handing Cindy's Coke to her and sitting down in the rocker near the couch in front of a fireplace now roaring with intensity, Mike leaned over towards Jimmy. "Hey, boss, that fireplace sure feels toasty. It is cold as shit out there."

As Jimmy nodded, Mike took another sip of his drink, unzipped his coat, and stuck his chest out at an angle towards Jimmy and then continued. "Look what I brought with me tonight, boss."

Jimmy peered intently at a nylon shoulder holster with a revolver resting snugly in the rig. "Damn, Mike, what did you buy now? Let me see that."

Mike put his drink down and turned over to Jimmy his new stainless .357 magnum Ruger GP100 revolver with the loaded cylinder swung out. Jimmy took the piece and smiled in admiration. "Ruger does make great guns. This is sweet. I bought one of these myself 'bout five years ago."

Taking his gun back and holstering it, Mike gazed down at the coffee table at Jimmy's uncle's papers. "Are you still thinking about setting up that apple orchard?"

Jimmy had shared with Mike the notes he had discovered sometime ago regarding starting up an apple grove.

"Yeah, I think so, Mike. I think about it a lot lately."

Mike started to ask another question and hesitated; even in his intoxicated state, he did not want to appear too nosy and changed the subject. "Well, Jimmy, shit, in another hour it's going to be midnight, and you know what that means."

Jimmy smiled as Cindy began to frown. Looking over at his girlfriend, Mike continued. "Cindy don't like me pulling out guns all that much. I keep telling her that they are your best friends if someone is trying to attack you. I can't convince either her or her parents to keep one in the house for protection. Doesn't that beat all?"

Jimmy had to agree with Mike, though he chose to strike a balance between Mike and Cindy's opinions on the subject. "Well, Mike, you and I and most others in these parts grew up with guns. We use them to hunt and feed our family with. And we use them to protect our families. Now, if Cindy plum don't like 'em I figure I don't want to force 'em down her throat, and neither should you. Give it time. I believe she will come to believe that in an emergency, a gun can mean the difference between life and death."

Mike stared at Jimmy's pasty white scar while nodding in agreement to Jimmy's advice.

After sharing some of his leftover spaghetti with his visitors, Jimmy looked up at the wall clock in his kitchen. "Cindy, is Mike awake? It's almost midnight."

Out in the living room, Cindy, nearly asleep herself nudged Mike on his arm. "Wake up, Mike; it's almost midnight."

Mike stirred a bit and then mumbled something incoherently. "What you shootin, boss?" Mike had actually fallen back to sleep when suddenly awakened by several loud blasts coming from the back of Jimmy's house.

Walking up beside Jimmy who was blasting away with his .44 magnum revolver, Mike eagerly drew his revolver and aimed it up in the sky toward the trees near the peak of the mountain that bordered Jimmy's property. Holding the revolver with both hands, Mike began to fire away yelling, "Happy New Year!"

After unloading several more cylinders of ammo, Mike turned to Jimmy and said, "Fuck, boss, you think we got any of them vagrants that calls themselves hikers up there? Serve 'em right for hanging around the woods at night up to no good." Then, he blew the smoke still rising from the barrel of his revolver, charged the gun with a new load from his speed loader, and stuffed it in his shoulder rig.

Jimmy never responded to Mike's question as both men retired to Jimmy's house for the evening calling it a day—and a year.

Chapter 22

Shenandoah National Park—Stony Man Mountain Area

This really sucks. Here I am sitting stock still on a tiny wooden stool smothered in camouflage with a wind-chill factor of near zero degrees. What did I do to deserve this? He brought his mike close enough to take a smoky blast from his breath as it met the frigid air.

FBI Special Agent Terry Smothers was freezing even though he was wearing a multi-layered Gortex suit and special insulated gloves to enable him to quickly fire the Heckler and Kock MP5 submachine gun he was huddled with under a "ghillie" suit that covered his clothing and weapons. The suits were specially designed to enable the wearer to blend in with the forest. In a thicket of brown brush, the wearer in most cases was literally indistinguishable from the thick growth of vegetation he had buried himself in. Since these suits were utilized for the most part by U.S. Marine Corps snipers, about the only thing that might appear strange upon close inspection a few feet away from the sniper would be the lethal metal tube protruding slightly from the maze of camouflage that made up the suit.

Terry was one of a contingent of specially trained agents who had been well prepared by the bureau for these types of assignments. He was a sturdy six feet, 175-pound graduate of the FBI's special weapons and tactics (SWAT) school in Quantico, Virginia. He had received excellent training in outdoor survival techniques under adverse weather and other environmental conditions, was a top marksman at the academy's range, and was one of the top hostage rescue team (HRT) operators ever trained at Quantico. It didn't hurt that he just happened to be a black belt in judo where he had taken up the Japanese martial art while a business major at Southeastern University in Washington, D.C. With the MP5 he had scored the highest of his group during the special weapons and tactics training sequences he and his fellow agents had undergone.

His sidearm, a specially designed Springfield Armory .45 caliber automatic, built on the bureau's specifications, rested securely at his side, mounted low with the muzzle just above his kneecap.

He had been selected along with a contingent of nine other men to provide surveillance in this particular area of the Shenandoah National Park that had no trails or other designed public access routes. They were to post themselves in two-man teams sitting directly opposite one another in heavy camouflage, vigilant and well armed. Their mission was to observe the comings and goings of any individual who took it upon himself to visit this area of the park—an old cemetery deep in the wilderness off the designated trails where two individuals had been interred many years earlier, most likely "mountain" folks who had once homesteaded the area.

If such an individual were observed, he would be asked to surrender peacefully to the agents. Failing that, he would have to be taken down by any means necessary. This individual could conceivably be responsible for the deaths of a number of innocent individuals who had just happened to wander accidentally into the vicinity of this area.

The plan was to rotate five two-man teams every day so that in any given five-day period, one team would have four days off before returning to the area. Hopefully, the four off days would work to the advantage of the surveillance teams to provide the sharpest individuals for any given day of this godforsaken assignment.

Because the duty was mentally and physically demanding, only the best had been selected to "volunteer" for this assignment. An individual had to be prepared to sit in extreme cold weather with only the barest of movements allowed for eight-hour periods during randomly selected times of the day. The individual would be well armed, well clothed, and would have been among the highest scorers at the academy in Quantico, Virginia. The individual would also have some dry rations and water for sustenance as well as wireless communications with his partner, sitting approximately thirty yards from his position. Each team member would also be able to communicate with the task force headquarters situated in the Skyland Resort Lodge high up the ridge close to Stony Man Mountain.

Terry had been sitting in this position since 0800 hours this morning having said his good-byes to his wife and four kids who had risen at an ungodly hour to see him off. He had been married eight years to Jennifer, and together they had four beautiful children, two girls and two boys, perfectly spaced at ages two, four, six, and eight years. He smiled to himself as he thought about them—they were his life. He was so fortunate to have been lucky enough to meet and marry his beautiful wife and have some great kids and an exciting job with the Bureau—though at the moment he wasn't so sure about that.

"*Click, click.*" Terry heard the whispered sound of Chad Cummings, his fellow team member across the way. "Hey, Terry, you awake? You look awfully still over there."

Terry leaned into his mike. "Yeah, man—sitting here not being able to stretch or move really is tough."

Chad had to agree. "No question, dude. I would rather be on a forced ten-mile hike any day. I had three cups of coffee this morning, and it's not helping very much at this stage." Chad tried to brighten the conversation with some light-hearted banter. "Well, its ten now; we only have six more hours to go."

Terry grimaced at the thought. "We better tone it down. From what I heard, this dude is a very bad man. Like they said, the hikers didn't know what hit them. Keep an eye out for my six, and I'll do the same with you."

Chad agreed. "You got it. Hang in there, out."

It was just past three in the afternoon as he drove by several police cruisers on his way to the service road. Slowing almost to a crawl, he had quickly gotten out of his vehicle, unhooked the chain at the entrance of the service road, and stashed his sport utility. As he crouched near the entrance of the service road on his way out, he hit the ground fast when he spotted a cruiser rounding the bend to his left. He began to feel as if he were being tracked like an animal and became angry.

This fuckin place is crawling with cops. These sumbitches ain't goin to stop me.

He let a few minutes pass; and when the cruiser was long gone, he quickly came to his feet. He crossed over to the other side of Skyline Drive to start his walk to the Stony Man trailhead. There was no one on the trail. He took note of the cautionary signs posted at different spots on the trail warning of the dangers of hiking alone and that some hikers had been reported missing. At the right place, he slipped into the thick foliage, noting that with the time of the year, the woods had thinned with only the evergreens and the thick brown brush providing adequate cover.

He had stashed in his backpack two bouquets of roses to place on his parents' headstones. He had also brought along his typical hiking implements: K-bar knife, a lethal seven-inch bladed close-in weapon favored by outdoorsmen, SEALS, and soldiers of fortune; a suppressed Hechler and Kock Universal Self-Loading Pistol (USP) in .40 caliber with a TACSTAR laser unit mounted in the slide under the frame of the weapon; some rope, and his sharpened hatchet.

Over the past six months he had tried on several occasions to enter this area of the woods and had turned back. There were just too many strange people roaming the area appearing to be police or government people. He could not risk being caught. He knew that as long as he could find a way to visit his old home, he would always be able to return. With the winter now in full swing, it being late January, he thought that just maybe the time had come to try again. While being dismayed at the still heavy police presence on Skyline Drive, somehow, once he had entered the woods, he had felt more at ease. He noticed this time that the woods were no longer swarming with cops. Still, he had to be vigilant. If he were caught, there would be no more trips to see his ma and pa. Getting caught was not an option.

He moved much more slowly, cautiously scanning the areas from left to right, right to left, and paused intermittently to gaze around to his rear in case they tried to sneak up on him undetected.

The wind began to pick up as the afternoon wore on. Thick clouds were rolling in with the woods not as bright as they had appeared to be that morning. *Alberta Clipper comin in,* he thought to himself. He knew that he would not hear the sound of the waterfall near the gorge; it was frozen over this time of year.

He crept carefully forward, scanning in all directions—his antenna raised to full alert. He could just barely make out the cemetery now.

Wait! Something is wrong!

It had been a very long time since his last visit. It had been hot and miserable in here. Now he was in an arctic wilderness with the occasional shocking blast of cold air swarming through the thickets and evergreens, the sound paradoxically reminding him of a blowing furnace. The branches cracked from the wind, and he could see the floating, spinning remnants of leaves spiraling out of control in a dizzying frenzy among the trees that stood in stark sentry in the area around the cemetery.

The hair began to rise on the back of his neck. He gazed intently a bit to his left some thirty yards ahead and then to his right, and it hit him.

I'll be damned. Them fuckin dudes got ghillie suits on. They ain't foolin me. What the fuck they think they gonna do? Try to stop me from seein my family? I'll fix them bastards.

Terry glanced at his *Luminox* Navy SEAL watch, another of many shivers driving him to scrunch his body up and tense all of his muscles one by one to awaken his numbed senses. Seeing that it was past three, he managed a weak smile to himself knowing that he was finally nearing the end of his "shift."

He was about to click his mike to check on Chad when he heard a muffled "pop" and felt a sudden violent thump in the middle of his back. He appeared stunned and paralyzed from the effects of the CORBON 165 grain .40 plus "P" caliber bullet that immediately began to expand, shattering his backbone and almost immediately taking the life out of him at the still young age of 35, making his family husbandless and fatherless in the span of a few short seconds.

Across the way, Chad had been nodding off when he heard what sounded like a sudden smack of brush dead ahead. He became immediately alarmed when he saw Terry slumped over on his side in the thickets. Then, he relaxed as he uttered to himself, *that son of a bitch has keeled over asleep.*

He pressed his mike. "Hey, Terry, wake up! If I have to get up, I'll blow our cover. Wake up, man!"

He waited. There was no movement from Terry. He had no idea what was going on. He was getting pissed now. How could the man just fall out like that? *Terry probably doesn't have his mike ready to receive,* he thought.

Chad carefully scanned the area as he flicked off the safety on his MP5 and slowly, slowly began to rise up from his stool, his wobbly legs still numb from sitting in the "L" position for so long. He proceeded forward in a crouch, MP5 at the ready heading in the general direction where his partner lay.

Pifft, pifft. Two muffled double-tap shots rang out, the first bullet slamming into the oak just to Chad's right, splinters of wood breaking violently off the tree trunk, the second grazing him just above his right shoulder. He felt a stinging sensation, and a warm liquid beginning to well up in the area of his shoulder. He began to panic with his only thought being to crouch down to protect himself as quickly as possible. Using his training and guile, he desperately tried to get himself together. He was literally scared shitless. *Fuck, I've been hit. Some asshole is shooting at me.*

Peering over to where Terry lay, he didn't know whether he should attempt to yell out to him. Then he noticed a smattering of what appeared to be blood dripping out of the area where Terry's mouth would have been. *Oh no! Somebody out here has killed Terry! Christ!*

Unbeknownst to Chad, no sooner had the man fired his shots, he had circled around and behind Chad to gain the advantage after achieving his intended initial shock effect. Chad's head nearly rolled off his torso, with the clean cut made ear to ear from behind by the KABAR. Having been on his haunches taking cover from the shots, he now slumped face forward onto the forest floor lifeless, the MP5 slipping out of his hands. His neck spurted a Roman candle version of bright red arterial blood.

"Red one, come in. Red one, come in—do you read?" Special Agent Bill Smith was getting frustrated trying to reach the first of the five teams that were to provide surveillance at the old cemetery. He sat in the conference room at the Sky Land Lodge with Captain Bonner of the Virginia state police monitoring the surveillance teams. The two-man teams had been designated "red," "black," "green," "blue," and "purple." They had not heard from the red team at their designated hour to report in. The teams had been told to report in every hour to the lodge on the status of their mission. Specifically, had any activity been noticed in the area of the cemetery?

Since it was a Monday, the "red" team had been the first team sent out for the week. Chad and Terry had been punctual—up to the very time they had been scheduled to return to base at the lodge to conclude the day's surveillance mission. Now it was after five, over one hour past the time they had been ordered to make their last report.

Bill's face had worry written all over it. Looking up from the mike at Sergeant Bonner, he spelled out his concern. "I don't like it, Ted. Something is fishy here. It's not like both Terry and Chad not to report in or respond."

He tried again. "Red one, red one. This is an order. Acknowledge and confirm this message at once! We need to pinpoint your location and situation."

Silence.

Ted made about the only suggestion pragmatic at the time. "Okay, Bill, I'm on it. I'll have a team of our SWAT guys down there right away with a chopper. This is bizarre."

When the police arrived in the area of the cemetery, they found the ghillie suits heavily blood stained in stacks near where the designated FBI sentries had been posted. There was no sign of their bodies, nor were any of the agents' weapons found. One of the SWAT team members, Corporal Rod Kelley, did notice one strange thing about the site. Standing in stark contrast to the brown-and-gray bleak surroundings of the old cemetery in the woods with twilight fast approaching were two bouquets of red roses placed in a halo around each of the ancient headstones.

Chapter 23

Shenandoah National Park—Skyland Resort—North Entrance—
A Day Later

Suddenly, the agenda of the "Missing Hiker" task force had taken on a new dimension; it had been expanded to include a search for two missing, possibly deceased FBI agents. The evil that lurked in the woods in and around the old cemetery was getting very personal with the task force now that they had apparently lost two of their own men. This was not just a case anymore of a bad guy hanging out in the woods attacking innocent hikers. This was a case of a likely serial killer who had the cunning and guile to take out two heavily armed FBI agents during a surveillance mission in the park. The task force had last met a month earlier and had drafted up plans to provide two-man surveillance teams at the old cemetery to observe any activity in or within close proximity of the area. These teams were to be clad in camouflage, specifically the "ghillie suits" often used by military snipers to provide them with total disguise so that their positions could not be "read" by the forces of their intended targets. It certainly would not have been prudent to merely place armed sentries in clear view at the cemetery. Any criminal worth his salt would see the sentries as he made his way into the area and immediately take off—more than likely undetected.

Moreover, the risk factor for the sentries would be substantially increased; they would become intended targets of opportunity themselves. The task force had come to the following consensus:

A. The missing hikers had all been reported lost after having been seen in the vicinity of the same area of the park—somewhere southwest of the Stony Man trailhead and close to the old, barely traveled Passamaquoddy Trail.

B. Extensive searches had already been conducted in that area and adjacent areas of the park.

C. An unknown person was making sporadic visits to an old cemetery. This individual was leaving fresh red roses on the headstones of "mountain" people who had been interred there long ago. This individual had never been observed in or around the area of the cemetery.

D. This cemetery was in the vicinity where the hikers had turned up missing.

E. The next logical move would be to provide surveillance of that area, specifically the old cemetery to observe activity there.

F. It was recommended that rotating two-man surveillance teams be placed in the vicinity of the cemetery in a manner in which their positions would not be revealed to an unknown individual that might be moving into that area.

G. These teams would be heavily armed with wireless communications, well clothed against the elements, well disguised in "ghillie suits," and among the best people the FBI had to offer for this type of mission.

Special Agent Bill Smith spoke first with the crease lines of worry etched across his brow. "People, we have a very serious problem here. As you know, two of my agents have been reported missing on surveillance duty at the old cemetery in question. My worst fears are that they are dead.

"Captain Bonner, can you give us a report on what your people found yesterday?"

Bonner nodded his head slightly. "First of all, Bill, our hearts go out to you and the FBI family. Our assignment looks grim. Corporal Rod Kelley, one of our top woodsmen, and his team spotted the two camouflage suits soaked heavily with blood. From the looks of it, it appears that agents Smothers and Cummings suffered severe, possibly fatal wounds to either the head area or their upper extremities right around the neck area. Neither agent was found. We found no weapons or other evidence that would be useful for this type of investigation. There appears to be a very good possibility that these agents have met the same fate as the hikers. While we are still in a search-and-rescue mode for these agents, the prognosis does not look good. We will continue to grid search the areas and all areas adjacent to the scene."

As Captain Bonner started to continue, he was suddenly interrupted by the violent open palm slam of Bill Smith's hand on the conference table. "Goddamn it, Ted. This isn't good enough. Sure, you can go on and search the area with a few cops. What are you going to find with just a few people?" Sitting erect in his chair with his hands clasped together and elbows on the table, Agent Smith continued. "I put in a call to the director before this meeting to ask that he contact the governor with a request to make available all units of the Virginia National Guard to participate in a massive grid search from the Shenandoah River all the way past Stony Man Mountain. I want that whole area covered with searchers, and we need a lot of manpower. The director agreed and is making the call as we speak. The director has also sent all available agents not on critical assignments in the country to assist in this effort. We are dealing with a serial killer, a man who not only is capable of stalking and killing innocent civilians; he also likely has killed and disposed of two of the bureau's finest agents. These guys were young, strong, well-trained, vigilant, armed-and-tenacious warriors. And, Jesus Christ, just like that, they got taken out by some unknown, smart, crazed son of a bitch."

Ted nodded continuously, eventually holding up his hand. "Bill, believe me, we understand. The scope of the present search is with what we have available to us at the moment. It certainly was not intended that the search be limited in its scope by our state police. We will cooperate with you fellows to the full extent possible. This is the top priority in our state."

Clasping her hands on the table, agent Joan Harding spoke up. "We have received a description, what little the officer was able to give to us, of the strange hiker who was reported on the service road a couple months ago. Also, we are attempting to put together a hypothetical profile, for now, of a possible perpetrator based on all of the facts we know so far regarding this case. We believe that the perpetrator obviously has some connection to the people interred at the cemetery.

"That's not an eye-opening revelation per se. What is damn difficult is getting a decent make on this guy. We feel that he is more than likely an individual highly skilled in wilderness survival techniques, as well as in the tracking and killing of individuals. A .40 caliber bullet was pried out of an oak tree near where one of the agents had been posted.

"Based on the best evidence that we have from the scene, this guy was at the very least armed with a knife and a pistol. The recent, apparent loss of our agents confirms that this fellow has a skill level far above the average dirt-bag killer. This guy possesses serious stealth and lethality capabilities. I want to stress to all of you that this is by no means a complete or final profile. We are working with what we have—which isn't much. And, we are working with what our shrinks think we are dealing with—based on the activities that have occurred in this region on a sporadic basis over the years."

Breaking the ensuing silence, Rod Adelman turned first to Agent Harding and then looked around the room. "So, from what you're saying, we are likely dealing with a highly skilled, very dangerous person with first-rate wilderness survival skills armed to the teeth, who perhaps has an emotional connection to the dead people in the cemetery. Maybe these people were this guy's parents or grandparents, and he is mentally off his rocker—which, of course, makes him even more dangerous."

With heads around the table all nodding in agreement, Captain Bonner proceeded to wrap up the session. "Okay, people, we will meet first thing in the morning to assess where we are with the bureau's request for manpower from the governor. I wish each and every one of you Godspeed in your efforts, and the FBI and the families of the missing agents certainly have our prayers."

The FBI's request for the assistance of the Virginia National Guard to assist in the massive search effort for their missing agents was immediately granted by the governor of Virginia. The next day a massive, coordinated search plan was set up by the task force, and a new phase of the mysterious happenings in this part of the Shenandoah Valley began. It was decided that with the massive influx of the National Guard in the region, it was no longer necessary to continue to post FBI sentries at the cemetery.

Weeks passed with hordes of guardsmen clad in winter attire scouring the side of the ridge from the Little Stony Man cliffs past the Passamaquoddy Trail and much further past the southeastern areas adjacent to the summit of Stony Man Mountain. Winter turned to spring, and spring to summer with not a trace of any human remains discovered.

Sometime during that period, a decision was made to clear the forest around the old cemetery. The tall oaks and chestnut trees were removed, and virtually all of the brush and thickets in the area were destroyed. The area resembled a large area approximately the size of a football field, a hundred yards or so in length and fifty yards in width around the cemetery. This made the cemetery and its immediate surroundings an open, unobstructed area for ground as well as aerial surveillance by state police and FBI helicopters. During this period of change in this area of the park, there were no reported sightings of activity in the area. Indeed, no flowers of any sort were reported seen at the headstones.

A year later with no further reports of a sighting or activity in or around the cemetery, another decision was made. The continued surveillance of the area was taking an enormous toll on the resources of the FBI and the Virginia state police. Therefore, the task force had concluded it might be prudent to simply remove the remains of the mountain people from the cemetery in the hopes that the serial killer would not come into the area again. The FBI profilers had guessed that this individual might be suffering from some sort of dissociative behavior. Perhaps he had a dual personality in which he could be functioning normally in society as one personality. On the other hand he could also appear as a raging serial killer triggered by violent events in his life long ago in his wanderings in the park. It was agreed that the area would still continue to receive random observation and surveillance on an indefinite basis.

The remains of the mountain people were removed and interred at a cemetery with unmarked plaques near Front Royal. The location was not disclosed to the public.

Still another year passed with hikers swarming the mountains without any reported incidents. It truly appeared that since the motive for attacking hikers in the area of the cemetery had been removed, the motive for violence against innocents would cease. While the perpetrator remained at large or possibly deceased; hopefully, no more deaths would occur in the region spurred by the removal of the graves.

Chapter 24

Shenandoah National Park—Stony Man Mountain—Two Years Later

His mind was consumed with a myriad of thoughts as he drove slowly on the Skyline Drive toward Stony Man Mountain. After two years of contemplating a really serious hike in the mountains where he had planned to duplicate Master Toguchi's feat of performing *Sanchin Kata* under a waterfall, Joe Lynch was excited that he was now actually going to undergo this adventure. Joe had talked with Sandi many times in the past several years of his desire to hike to a waterfall in the mountains and perform *Sanchin Kata.* For one reason or another—a plethora of difficult work projects on the job or a demanding martial arts workout regimen—he just had not been able to manage a window of time for the effort.

Now at last his special day had come. He had cleared this weekend for his much talked about hiking adventure. Joe was now ranked Third Dan in Goju-Ryu Karate and was well respected and admired for his martial prowess wherever he trained at karate dojos on the East Coast. He had even been the grand tournament champion at an undisclosed no-holds barred, full contact "all comers invited" kumite in New York City. His participation in the kumite, of course was much to the chagrin of Sensei's Huffman and Hytaga. It was interesting, however, that Huffman had been in Joe's corner at ringside for his matches.

Moreover, Joe was now a Grade 13 at the Civil Service Commission recently renamed the U.S. Office of Personnel Management.

He was very happy with his life, smiling at his wife and children as they waved good-bye to him when he drove away for his great adventure. In thinking about them, his smile quickly faded into sadness. He had always brought his family along with him whenever he went to the mountains. Nicole and Amy had gone on the Fox Family hike with him, and Sandi had tagged along to climb Stony Man just last year despite an injured right knee.

He thought about what it must have been like for the Fox Family back in the early to mid eighteen hundreds when they first entered the mountains. Like most mountain people, it must have been backbreaking work initially for them to clear out their "hollows" with the rude farm implements they had. The soil in these mountains was interwoven with rocks of all sizes. He had noted the mounds of rocks he had seen on some of his hikes. They must have been brave souls to weather the winters here at the higher elevations. Indeed, he was certain that many of the old mountain families had to have been drawn very close to one another facing the uncertain existence that they were a part of.

In those days the families almost certainly would have had to be extremely security conscious, especially with the comings and goings of their women and children. Two—and four-legged predators would have been a constant danger here in the mountain wilderness. For a man to clear the land here for a farm and to set up a home with a wife and children must have brought a measure of satisfaction to that individual knowing that he was surviving the challenges that life brought to him and his family in this mountain wilderness.

Joe's mind shifted to his friend, Jimmy Mackenzie. While he and Jimmy had talked several times since Joe had first reached him a couple of years ago, between his and Jimmy's busy and demanding schedules, neither had been able so far to find time to actually get together for Joe's hike. Joe had been so anxious to finally begin his hike that he had not bothered to stop by Jimmy's sporting goods store on the way to the Stony Man trailhead. Maybe, he would check it out after his hike.

Reflecting back on the courage and strength of the mountain people, his mind quickly reverted to the present. He had also thought that this very special mission had to be performed by him—and him alone. After all, the mountain people had survived their ordeals alone; the master had performed his spiritual trip alone; there could be no other way. In a sense, he thought also that carrying out such a mission alone where the possible, though remote, chance of danger was ever present, would add an element of intrigue and challenge that would not be present otherwise. No, there just wasn't any other way to do this thing.

Joe had wanted for years to do what he was undertaking today, yet had not been able to set aside a window of his time to perform this feat. He knew that he would need an entire weekend. Indeed, he had planned at least two hikes. One was the relatively easy and familiar route to Stony Man's summit to take pictures of the spectacular vista the summit offered. And the other was an extensive, time-consuming trip through the White Oak Canyon portion of the park where there were a number of waterfalls, any one of which might serve as his "*Sanchin* Waterfall." Yes, he had many thoughts this morning, tinged with both happiness and sadness.

However, there was one slightly worrisome thought totally unrelated to the others that had intruded upon his mind. His mind began to drift back to the conversation between Sandi and himself last night.

"You know, hon, the weather report does not look all that promising." Sandi had made that observation to Joe as they sat up in their bed supported by several huge pillows watching the nightly news. Indeed, the television was showing a pictorial of the Atlantic coast where a white cotton-like plume was swirling in a counterclockwise motion as it moved slightly northwest toward the United States near the Carolinas. The latest weather forecast had the storm veering at the last minute back out to sea.

Joe looked over at his wife. "Oh, Sandi, don't worry; that hurricane is supposed to shift to the northeast and stay out in the Atlantic. I have been planning this trip for so long and am really stoked for it. I can't let a questionable forecast stop me."

Looking deeply into her husband's eyes, she rubbed his arm briefly. "I just worry about you, Joe. You really have changed over the years. I remember when you would have said no way would you risk it."

Joe just smiled. "Hon, I'm a changed man. This is what martial arts can do for a person if they dedicate their lives to it. The confidence and serene spirituality that one obtains is all encompassing throughout all of the facets of one's life," he said with a wink.

Sandi nudged Joe on his arm. "Oh, here we go again with the karate recruit speech. You have that down well, Joe."

Joe gave out a hearty laugh. "Give me a break. I really believe and practice the concept daily."

Sandi glanced reflectively at her husband. "You know, Joe, I have to give it to you. Yes, you really have become dedicated to the art—you have changed for the better. I mean that in a positive way. Before, you were Joe, my husband, and a great guy. Now, you're still the same, only you have a wonderful discipline that seems to complement you. I haven't forgotten the times when you used to wear yourself out practicing in the dining room when the temperature was ninety degrees with our air conditioning unit kaput. You impressed me."

Joe reflected back to the previous night's weather report. The sky was somewhat overcast, and the air appeared a bit humid for this time of year in late September. However, his years of martial arts training would not allow him to think negative. He had decided to avoid worrying about the weather forecast by just leaving the radio in his Jeep off on his drive down to the park from his home in Maryland. His mindset was one of thinking positively about any undertaking. In keeping with his training, he would not allow troubling thoughts to enter his consciousness.

Joe pulled into the parking lot where the trailhead to Stony Man began. He had to stifle a brief, heart wrenching thought of the spring before when he and Sandi had slowly hiked this very same trail. *Damn, I miss her*, he thought.

Joe also managed a thought about the reports of missing hikers in the park a couple years ago that had briefly dominated the news at the time. Apparently, those people just disappeared. Who knows, maybe they just had bad accidents. Joe certainly wasn't going to let it bother him at this point.

He turned off the engine and took a deep breath to clear his mind as he took stock of what he had brought for his hikes. A large backpack with bottled water and food rations, a two-man pup tent, a "Rambo" knife that he had bought at the local Sonny's Surplus store, some bear spray, two flashlights, the usual first-aid necessities—Band aids, gauze, alcohol, and a small shovel to assist with his overnight camp preparations. He had also placed in one corner of his knapsack his karate uniform and black belt for the waterfall ceremony.

Joe hopped out of his Jeep Cherokee, grabbed his backpack, and immediately noted the heavy humidity in the mountains. The sky also appeared to be much darker than he would have imagined. He entered the Stony Man trailhead and proceeded quickly through the trail noting all of the familiar sights. Less than an hour later near the summit, he passed the old copper mine on the left and stepped out onto the ridge that was the summit of Stony Man.

Joe was shocked at what he saw. Looking out over the great vista, he saw in the distance from one end of the horizon to the other a wall of black slowly moving in his direction. Reverting back to his pre-karate training days with the old fears and anxieties, he stood frozen and transfixed by the atmospheric spectacle before him. He became gripped by fear.

Shit, that hurricane never veered out to sea. That wicked-looking bastard is bearing down on me, and I am four thousand feet above sea level. My God, what am I going to do?

Smelling the heavy humidity around him now and remembering that he had seen absolutely no one on the trail coming up the mountain, Joe was in the throes of panic. He thought of running back down the trail toward his Jeep in the parking lot. Then his martial-training mindset reflexively began to kick in.

He admonished himself. *You fucking wimp. You're thinking of running like a scared rabbit back to the Jeep and high tailing it out of here. Breathe deeply and settle down. Get yourself together. Think!*

Okay, I don't know what the hell is going on with that storm. Maybe it's not the hurricane after all. Maybe it's just a bad thunderstorm heading this way. Relax and breathe deeply. I am going to need to find some shelter for now where I can ride this thing out and still manage my waterfall hike later. A tree won't cut it. Trees attract lightning. I need to check out that old abandoned copper mine.

Joe quickly moved back away from the edge of the summit overlook and backtracked toward the mine. He crouched down on all fours and felt behind the rocks and bushes that fronted the mineshaft, finally noticing a small break in the rocks where he just might be able to enter for shelter from the storm. Perhaps he could ride this thing out here using the mine to protect him from the encroaching storm.

Feeling a bit more confident now, he remembered that he had brought along his camera to film his waterfall experience and decided to leave his backpack by the mine while he went back up to the summit to film the storm just before it hit.

Standing on the precipice of the summit once again, Joe felt that old familiar spike of fear coursing through his body. *Oh, my God! Look at that. The whole sky is black!*

Beads of perspiration were forming on Joe's brow as he squinted into his camera, pointing it at the huge, black, boiling mass moving toward him. He clicked several pictures and let the camera gently down with the strap around his neck. The wind now was blowing at a furious pace, and he could hear the cracks of thunder all over the mountain range. He gazed at his watch and noted that it was only one o'clock in the afternoon, yet the day was rapidly fading into blackness. He stood mesmerized by this wonder of nature, too numb to think.

Joe once again felt those familiar, warm, tingly sensations in his head that only frayed nerves could bring to him whenever he was caught in the grip of total fear. The hair on his neck stood up as a sudden whip of a huge pocket of air nearly knocked him off his feet into the abyss below Stony Man's visage.

Easing down to all fours now, shaking all over with his camera banging precariously against the large rocks at the summit, he felt he was in grave danger alone against the elements. Joe scurried back away from the summit toward the copper mine as a wicked lightning strike split an oak down the middle just yards away from the mine. His survival instincts had kicked in, and he knew he must make the mine at all costs.

Somehow, Joe had managed to crawl though the slit among the timber and rocks and brush to gain entrance into the old copper mine. He had pulled his backpack in behind him and discovered that in the blackness around him, he was standing on some form of ledge in a vertical shaft. It was early afternoon, yet it might as well have been the early hours of the morning just past midnight. He squirmed around and suddenly fell fifteen feet down the shaft, clutching at anything he could reach along the way to save himself, his body brushing roughly against the sides of the shaft on the way down.

Attempting to regain his composure after landing in a heap at the bottom of the shaft, he reached for his backpack, instinctively feeling for the flashlights he had brought along for his hikes. There, he found one. He immediately flicked on the light as he heard the tempest raging above him. At least he felt safe in here. He panned the flashlight around and noticed that other than this short shaft, there was little left of the mine. Certainly, any other entranceways had long ago been permanently blocked off. That was of no consequence to him now as he was merely looking for shelter from whatever freak of nature that was howling above him. He was just happy to have this narrow shaft covered with stones and timber to protect him.

I wonder if that's the hurricane? Maybe it never veered to the northeast and just came ashore in Virginia? God, I bet Sandi is worried sick. I guess the only thing I can do now is just ride this bad boy out. Maybe tomorrow morning when the weather clears, I can head back down to the Jeep and make my way to the White Oak Canyon trailhead to do the waterfalls. Right now, I am tired. I need to rest.

Joe flicked off his flashlight to conserve the batteries and began to nod off even as the fury of the storm above him increased.

Suddenly, he was awakened with a start to a tremendous vibrating sound and was immediately seized with the fear of being trapped in the mine with the walls of the shaft literally caving in on him. *Christ! I've got to get the fuck out of here!*

He flicked on his flashlight while sliding on his backpack and scrambled with both his legs and elbows against the walls of the shaft desperately driving his body upward for support to reach the surface as quickly as he could. To his dismay, he found that at the top of the shaft, he could not break clear to get back onto the trail. Somehow, a large rock had rolled over to seal the shaft.

Catching his breath and sweating profusely, he leaned in frustration against the wall of the shaft, his rock-hard legs and arms now trembling with fatigue to prevent him from once again sliding down the shaft.

He noticed a strip of lumber protruding near his face that appeared to be a two-by-four. If he could only slide both his arms under the two-by-four, he might be able to use leverage to move the rock away just enough for him to slide out of the mine. Pushing more heavily now against the walls of the shaft with his legs firmly wedging his feet in whatever indentations he could feel in the walls of the sides of the shaft, he put his flashlight into his pants pocket and pushed both his hands and arms under the two-by-four. Then using all of the strength he could muster, Joe finally tipped the rock just enough to where he could crawl out of the shaft, only to be knocked unconscious.

Chapter 25

Shenandoah National Park—Stony Man Mountain—Two Hours Later

Joe Lynch rolled over to face the tempest above him. The right side of his head was throbbing from a horrific blow that had literally knocked him senseless. He could hear a vast, howling roar all around him and felt that he was being dragged to God knows where. He opened his eyes further in a desperate attempt to regain full consciousness as the fear once again began to seep into him.

It was three o'clock in the afternoon, and it was night on the mountain. The trees near him were bending and breaking with startling rapidity much like the rhythmical, staccato fire from a machine gun. There was a deafening, whistling sound that one only hears when winds blow in excess of one hundred plus miles per hour. The weather forecast had indeed proven incorrect, though it had allowed—as many forecasters do—that there was a minuscule chance that the hurricane might suddenly turn west at the mouth of the Chesapeake Bay at the peak of its warm water-driven power.

The storm had done just that—turned west, fueled by the still very warm bay waters of an unusually hot summer that had just concluded. Indeed, Joe and Sandi had heard that the storm had reached category three strength just off the Carolinas the night before.

Unbeknownst to Joe, Sandi and the girls back in Maryland were now in a state of panic learning that the hurricane had targeted the Piedmont region of Virginia and nearby points, including the Shenandoah Valley with its current category-five rating. In fact, this storm far exceeded the minimal requirements for that category with maximum sustained winds of over 160 miles per hour.

Seized by panic once again, Joe had only two thoughts: to forget about the idea of doing his waterfall hike and to get to the safety of his Jeep as quickly as possible. Struggling up only to be swatted down like a half-dead fly to the ground, he contemplated briefly what the hell had happened to his aching head.

It must have been one of the pieces of timber at the top of the shaft that blew down on my head as I was crawling out of there.

He gritted his teeth and willed himself up once again, half-jogging, half-stumbling back down the trail toward the parking area.

Joe was not aware that he had inadvertently caused himself another major problem. The blow had warped his sense of direction causing him to become disoriented. He somehow turned abruptly to his left to enter the Appalachian Trail at the point where it crossed the Stony Man trail, rather than stay on the trail to the parking area. Nonetheless, in the windswept vortex that swarmed through the park, he forged on unbeknownst to him in a direction that was taking him farther and farther away from his parked Jeep.

Joe began to find himself in thick brush. He paused for an instant, grappling at his backpack for his flashlight, remembering that he had forgotten to use it in his mad dash to safety. *How could I be so fucking stupid?*

Flicking on the flashlight and panning it all around the brush surrounding him, he had no earthly idea where he was in these godforsaken woods with this horrendous torrent of Mother Nature's wrath bearing down on him. He gazed up at the bending, cracking trees in the black night of the afternoon. *God, what did I do to deserve this? Shit, I'm probably going to be struck by lightning. I don't care—I have got to keep my ass moving!*

He willed and bulled himself forward as only he could. Joe was in the best condition of his life. He was both admired and feared for his prowess in karate by many of his fellow black belts. To face Joe in a kumite match was itself a humbling experience. His strength and the sheer blinding speed and precision of his techniques alone were legend in the dojos. Several black belts had received broken bones in matches after giving their best against Joe. Many of the older, higher-ranked black belts would find ways to avoid being put into a match with Joe. His *kata* was executed with whip-like ferocity with the sleeves of his *gi* snapping like a bullwhip with every hand strike. While doing *Sanchin Kata*, his breathing technique was so powerful that many a bamboo stick had been broken on his abdomen with Joe barely noticing the effect. Any individual who contemplated a physical confrontation with him had no idea what awaited him. However, like most true karateka, Joe disdained battle on the streets or confrontations of any type. His philosophy was to walk away from a potential encounter, knowing full well that he had no need to prove himself. He had already done so countless times in the dojo.

Straining against the thick brush and the force of the storm round him, he mounted a mighty effort, his body contorting in this enterprise and covered now with welts and ugly scratches from the unyielding thickets. Joe felt the same will that had pushed him relentlessly through *Sanchin* while taking a merciless beating from his fellow karate students with their bamboo sticks and two-by-fours. With his disorientation finally beginning to fade from physical effort, he knew that he was now probably hopelessly lost in the stormy wilderness—though he did not know he was engulfed in the worst hurricane of the century.

After what seemed like hours of thrashing around in the mountain forest, Joe was suddenly blinded and stunned by a violent crack of lightning. Its ensuing thunder caused him to fall forward with no resistance from the thickets into an open area. Before fading once again into unconsciousness, he thought he saw a vision of a man in the wilderness in the bright lights of the clearing with one of his arms held up. His last thought—was this the bright light one sees before passing away? He did not, however, notice the trickle of blood that was now coursing down his face, as his body lay flush on the turf below it.

He had been sitting for hours since mid morning at the cemetery. The sudden surge of the hurricane with the daylight turning to darkness and the ferocity of the wind and rain had no perceptible effect on him. As he sat at the gravesite in a cross-legged position with the rivulets of rain running down his forehead, he merely took it as a sign that some divine power was angry that his family's cemetery had been molested and the gravestones removed. He knew Ma and Pa were still down there. So he had kept coming to pay his respects over the past couple years even after the tumult when he had to kill those government people who were violating his family's homestead.

His visits had become sporadic with the heavy presence of strangers in the area. It was imperative that he not be taken. To be taken would mean that there would be no one left from his family to guard their sacred hollow.

As the intensity of the storm had risen, he had merely decided to just sit at the cemetery and wait it out. Today, he had brought only his .357 magnum Ruger and his KABAR knife with its seven inches of razor sharp blade.

He had almost nodded off in the torrent when his keen senses had alerted him to a crashing sound in the woods almost dead ahead just at the edge of the clearing where the cemetery began. At that point he had once again become very angry.

Them Goddamn agents again, tryin to invade our property. Gonna have to kill them sumbitches all over again.

He had whipped out his revolver, cocked the hammer for a more sure single-action shot with the much lighter trigger pull, and waited for the "agent" to break clear of the brush.

Just as the "agent" had broken out of the thickets coming for him, he had quickly acquired his target—the head—with his sights and pulled the trigger. No sooner had his shot rang out when a loud bang from a nearby lightning strike with its ensuing flash had magnified the effects of his magnum tenfold.

He saw his prey fall and muttered satisfaction to himself. *Got that sumbitch! Now I need to make sure he is dead.*

He quickly holstered his revolver and whipped out his KABAR moving rapidly toward his enemy to finish him off.

Fortunately for Joe, he had not been knocked out very long. The bullet had grazed his right ear, tearing a chunk off. His instincts told him he was in mortal danger at that point. Upon regaining consciousness, his first thought was that he had indeed been struck by lightning and somehow had survived. Rolling over, he felt a painful stinging sensation on his right ear and felt the stickiness of blood on the right side of his face. He was in a thick patch of ferns when he heard what sounded like a man screaming in his direction.

"Where are you, you no good bastard? What the fuck are you doin on my property? I'm gonna kill you, you sumbitch."

In the shocked state he was in, Joe's thoughts now switched to a more immediate concern. Apparently he had not been struck by lightning. Incredibly someone was out here in the woods trying to kill him. Unbelievable! While he had never received combat training, his training credo that there is no advantage to attack first kicked into gear. He had felt a measure of protection from the thick patch of ferns. Indeed, ferns of this type that were found in abundance in numerous areas of the park, had multiple fronds with divided leaflets that would camouflage anyone who chose to seek cover under the plants.

There is a myth that the seeds of the fern plant are supposed to make the possessor invisible. That concept was working well for Joe as he quietly flattened himself in the ferns.

The madman began to kick around in the plants searching for the invader swinging his knife wildly. Joe sensed even in the still horrific weather conditions on the mountain that this crazy person was getting closer to him.

When one of the kicks landed with a thud on his hip, his training instincts kicked in without thinking. One of Master Toguchi's greatest capabilities was his ability to fight while on the ground, and he had shared some of the secrets of defending oneself in this position with his students. Many of the advanced black belts in the Goju system were knowledgeable in this segment of their training.

Joe leaned quickly on his left side while simultaneously pushing away just far enough from his tormentor with the edge of his left foot, and then he clamped both of the crazy man's ankles in an iron grip with his ankles and feet in the classic ground takedown technique. The man fell quickly down in a clump of ferns, losing his knife in the process, with Joe holding on with his ankles in a vise-like grip for dear life. They lingered in that position for what seemed like minutes.

Joe started to ask the man why he had shot him when an awful noise rang out with a chunk of the forest soil and ferns being decimated by a magnum round too close for comfort.

After hesitating for a moment, Joe yelled at the man. "What the fuck is your problem? Why are you shooting at me?"

Another bang from the gun told Joe all he needed to know for his next move. There was now no longer an advantage to holding this man down. He took a chance before the man could get off another shot; and with incredible foot speed, he let go of the man's legs and twisting now to his right, he raised his left foot and brought it swiftly down near the man's head with an ax kick from the heel of his foot. He heard a moan and saw the man rise up out of the ferns with a crazed expression on his face, his revolver pointing toward Joe.

His only thought now with this armed man was to remove himself from the area as quickly as possible. Suddenly, he darted out of the protection of the ferns to run as far away as possible from the deafening sounds from the man's gun. He heard and felt the closeness of the magnum rounds tearing through the thickets inches from his body and the maelstrom of the raging storm around him.

Chapter 26

Shenandoah National Park—Three Hours Later

Joe bulled and crashed his way through the thickets and trees, driving more with fear and the adrenaline surge it brings than anything else. He did in total survival mode at this point, not know if he would live to ever see Sandi and the girls again. He was in the best condition of his life, needing every fiber of that strength to escape from this living nightmare.

While the fury of the hurricane had not yet abated, the sounds of the man's gun had faded as Joe put distance between himself and the crazy man.

He paused to catch his breath, having no idea where he was now in the forest. When he no longer heard any gunfire, he stopped just long enough to whip out his second flashlight to enable him to steer clear of the really heavy brush in his escape. In this part of the forest there were no trails to be seen.

Calming down a bit, he remembered that he had brought a Rambo knife with a compass placed at the end of the handle. He rifled though his backpack as he eased down near a big oak to collect his thoughts, the rain still coming down in buckets. Noting the direction the needle on his knife compass pointed for north, he figured to head in that direction would conceivably take him back in the vicinity of Skyline Drive.

No—he couldn't go back there. He was immediately swept with fear over the idea of heading back in the general direction of the crazed individual with the handgun he had come across in the park. What the hell was that dude doing there in the middle of nowhere armed with a gun in this hellish storm? Had he been hiking like himself and been caught in the tempest? Still, that didn't explain his bizarre behavior. How many hikers carried powerful handguns in the park and shot at people? Perhaps the guy had just brought along a gun for protection in the forest, an idea that had occurred to Joe several times, though he had never owned a firearm. No, that didn't make sense. That crazy dude had yelled something about Joe being on his property. He wondered if the man had ever lived somewhere in the area. In the surreal conditions on the mountain with the wind, noise, and blasts from the storm and the man's gun, he really couldn't make out much about the man's appearance.

His mind was preoccupied with a million questions regarding his violent experience in the forest with this strange person when he thought he heard several large cracks in the brush nearby. Carefully and silently, he unsheathed his knife and placed it in his left hand to keep his stronger right hand free, quietly working himself around the tree to hide behind it while peeking from one side in the direction of the cracks he had heard.

Jesus Christ! There he is! That bastard has been tracking me.

The storm was beginning to calm a bit, and Joe held his breath as he observed the lunatic moving stealthily through the brush in his direction. Since he was at an angle to the approaching man, he decided he must attempt a strike at the man's temple to disable him. He slowly and quietly inserted his knife into the sheath that he had slipped earlier onto his belt. The man still held the revolver in his right hand as he passed slowly by Joe. With the quickness of a Bengal tiger, Joe suddenly sprung from around the oak tree and clocked the crazed man in the left side of his face near the cheekbone with a vicious reverse corkscrew punch. His fist had started out in the classic wrist-up position and turned over until the two large knuckles had collided with the man's face. The man fell in his tracks sprawling forward with his revolver dropping from his hand.

Unlike most men who would have absorbed such a blow, he was not down long, and Joe assumed a kumite stance to deal with this wary and dangerous adversary now upright and glaring menacingly at Joe. Noting the rapid swelling on the man's face made apparent by a moon that was just beginning to break clear from the clouds, he knew that this individual was no patsy. A clean shot to an unsuspecting individual of that magnitude should have been enough to knock most men out. Joe stood slightly at an angle to protect his torso as karate combatants often do in matches with both hands now in a knife-hand position, thumbs tucked into the palms of each hand to strengthen the knife-edge of each hand.

They circled each other in the slight clearing near the big oak, and Joe could see the intensity in the man's eyes and a hideous white scar on his jaw. This was someone who appeared out of his mind. It was a scary sight. More puzzling to him was that this crazy man vaguely resembled someone he might have known from the past. In the chaos, he just couldn't put his finger on whom. He knew the only way he could stop this man would be to render him completely unconscious or kill him. There was no other choice.

The man made a sudden lunge into Joe's midsection and was caught by an instinctive, lightning-quick right punch to his nose. Stopped dead in his tracks from the blow, the man fell backward slightly, bleeding profusely from his nose. Unbeknownst to Joe, this madman now had multiple broken bones in his face and was still attacking!

The man feinted a front kick to Joe's groin and threw a swift lunge punch to Joe's jaw, connecting with the force of a jackhammer. In all of his life, Joe had never been hit with such force to his face. Not even in the tournament in New York when he had stupidly let down his guard, only to be stunned by an opponent's sudden reverse back kick to his jaw that had knocked several of his teeth loose. He stumbled backward, tripping over the brush, nearly knocked out from the horrible blow. He felt no pain, just a numb feeling all over. At this point in the battle with a broken jaw, Joe's karate training was no longer an advantage.

While he was holding onto his consciousness, the man jumped down on him, pinning his shoulders down with both of his legs and began to punch Joe all about his face, chest, and shoulders. He was going for the kill.

With every ounce of his remaining energy, Joe delivered a vicious right-hook punch to the man's left rib cage that elicited a scream of pain. He then rolled the stunned man off him while the man grabbed his side in agony. They both paused in the fight totally exhausted, each man struggling to stand up.

Joe then remembered he had his knife and felt he had no choice other than to stop this fight as soon as he could. While not trained as a knife fighter, he had very quick hands. Joe swiftly whipped out his Rambo knife and lunged at the man's torso, having no idea that the individual he was attacking was himself expertly trained in close quarters knife fighting. In doing so, Joe had gone against the tenets of his training—launching a strike with a weapon he was not specifically trained in. the man parried his thrust, and with both hands, quickly wrested the knife away from Joe.

Joe backed away from the knife-wielding man, finally convinced he was dealing with an adversary who clearly possessed enormous fighting skills and tenacity. They stared warily at one another with only a stiff breeze from a now weakening storm and a full moon as their companions for this night.

Suddenly, Joe bolted as quickly as he could from the scene, tearing through the brush with no idea where he was going.

The fatigue and injuries he had incurred during his prolonged running battle with the crazy man in the mountains had finally taken its toll on Joe. Sensing he was at a disadvantage with a tough, perhaps demented adversary in the wilderness, Joe had been able to summon just enough energy to quickly escape from his tormentor. However, after thrashing again through the brush for what seemed like hours with only the benefit of the full moon for light having lost his backpack in the last fight, he was now virtually depleted of any energy.

He knew that in his weakened state, it would have been suicide to attempt to resume the fight with the man holding his Rambo knife and clearly skilled in knife fighting. This crazy person was obviously a trained street fighter. However, Joe thought it more likely that the man had received formal professional training. There was clearly something about this fellow. He was very cool when attacked and never panicked when caught flush by Joe's wicked karate blows.

Joe's jaw was clearly broken and grotesquely swollen. He was more stumbling through the thickets now than running, holding his right side in pain. When the crazy man had broken his jaw and tumbled on top of him, Joe had been punched repeatedly in his right side. He suspected that he probably had sustained broken ribs from that fusillade of punches. All of the *Sanchin* training in the world could not protect an individual in certain vulnerable areas of their body where bones are near the surface of the skin, and Joe was living proof of that.

He staggered forward and dropped in a clump of bushes rolling over onto his back, his arm lying over his aching forehead. His clothes were now in tatters, and his entire body was striped red from the cuts and scrapes he had incurred in his mad dashes through the woods. Both his face and the right side of his torso were swollen from the horrific blows he had endured.

As Joe squinted between the crack of his arm at the bridge of his nose toward the moon peeking through the overhanging trees and brush, he began, for the first time in years, to question the effectiveness of his training. *I had lulled myself into thinking I was indestructible. Now I am beginning to understand why some of the old masters insisted on training in the harsh conditions of the outdoors. Imagine doing kumite with an opponent in a driving rainstorm in the midst of thickets with thorns and sharp twigs tearing through your flesh. When we do kumite, it is often in an air-conditioned, climate controlled environment on a mat. Sure, our techniques are fast, sharp, and sometimes painful when someone connects. It is nothing like this, though, fighting a monster in the woods. I wonder who that person is?*

With that last thought, Joe drifted off into a fitful sleep.

Joe awoke with a start. He had no idea what had awakened him from his drug-like state. Maybe it was an inborn survival instinct that had revived him. He sat up slowly and looked all around, straining to see or hear anything that might prove ominous to his well being out here in the deep woods. Nothing.

It was still dark with virtually no wind, and the moon had shifted in the sky from the last mental picture he had of it. He had to keep moving. Something was telling him he was still in danger. He eased himself up feeling intensely stiff and sore and kept pushing himself forward. *Where to?* Joe had no idea; he just had to keep moving and hope for the best. He sensed somehow that the terrain had begun to change. There were more trees now and less brush.

After another hour of aimless wandering, he came suddenly to a field. Perhaps he was at a farm where he might be able to find help or call the police. As he struggled on, though, there was no indication of human presence anywhere—no houses or barns. Sighing, he kept moving, scanning the horizon and pausing occasionally to look behind him to see if he was being followed.

Three things now were gradually becoming apparent to him. First, he had sensed that the night was fading; he thought that it must be around five in the morning. That was a good thing. In the daylight he would be able to navigate much more effectively, though the excitement in that thought was quickly extinguished, knowing that the crazy man would benefit from the daylight as well. The other two things would definitely work in his favor. There was a winding road dead ahead; and in the distance, he could make out the sound of rushing water. *Could that be a river?* The road and the river—both were potential escape routes out of this horrendous ordeal.

As Joe approached the road, his first thought was to wait by the side of the road or walk down the side of the road and flag down a motorist. The more he thought about that, the less he liked the idea. He would be clearly visible anywhere near the road. Suppose the crazy man had recovered his gun by now; he would be a sitting duck near the road. No, he would just cross the road and check out the sound of the rushing water. Maybe it was a river, and people would be out fishing in the early hours of the morning.

Joe staggered across the road and glanced to his right where he noticed a gravel road that appeared to head up an incline toward a house. He followed the gravel road up the incline and broke out into a smile.

After taking the knife from the "agent," his first thought had been to immediately follow the man through the brush and kill him. He was confident that it was just a matter of time before he got this man, killed him, and cut him into pieces to feed to the forest. That fellow was clearly beaten and scared. That was why he had turned tail and run. Before pursuing this man, he had a weapon to retrieve—his Ruger revolver. That was too good of a gun to lose in the woods. After taking care of this government agent, he would have to go home and nurse his injuries before resuming his vigil at the cemetery.

Scratching around in the area where he had been ambushed with the sudden punch, he was able to dig out his gun. *Christ, that smarted. That asshole could sure throw a punch,* he thought as he felt the side of his face. Placing the revolver in his shoulder rig, he pushed forward in the direction that the "agent" had taken with the confidence that he would eventually take out this latest intruder.

"Great!" Joe almost shouted. He had stumbled upon a canoe rental company. On the wooden sign read "Shenandoah Canoe Company—We Rent Canoes

And Rafts." What made him really happy was to see the stack of canoes turned upside down in an area of the parking lot. No one was around—at least, not yet.

He summoned renewed energy and jogged to the canoes. After struggling a bit, he was able to pry one from the stack and pull it across the small parking lot to a ridge overlooking a fast-moving river. Fortunately, there were two paddles on board. *"Must be the Shenandoah River,"* he muttered to himself. He had gone through Front Royal several times on his way to the park with his family and had remembered noticing the river south of town in one of his family's back-road adventures.

It was going to be a bear getting the canoe down to the edge of the river. He would do the best he could. The crazy man could be on his heels. Getting to the swift-moving river swollen by the heavy torrent of rain during the past twenty-four hours was imperative. Joe remembered that the Shenandoah River was unusual in that it flowed north, eventually emptying into the Potomac near Harper's Ferry. It would take him past Front Royal and to freedom.

Joe positioned himself behind the canoe and pushed it over the ridge, down toward the edge of the river, hanging on for dear life as both he and the canoe suddenly tumbled uncontrollably down the hill overlooking the river.

"I believe that government feller is heading toward 340, probably trying to find somebody on the road," he muttered to himself. *"Damn, I've got to get to him before he does that."*

Feeling a sense of urgency, he tore through the brush using all of his woods smarts and guile to track and kill the "agent." He knew that with the night all but gone and morning looming fast, he must step up his pace.

Within an hour he had crossed Route 340 south of Front Royal, being very careful not to be observed, and had continued to search for his prey. He paused for a moment to survey the situation, looking slowly left to right and then glancing to his rear. There was no sign of anything.

Looking again to his right, he observed the high ground and ambled up the gravel road toward the canoe place where he surmised he would have a much better view of the surrounding terrain. He could hear the rushing sound of the river, now at a roar with the recent storm causing the river to swell nearly to flood stage. Reaching the parking lot, he glanced over with dismay at the stack of canoes neatly stacked—minus one.

Joe felt that he had probably broken every bone in his body. He had lost control of the canoe thinking somehow that he would be able to hold onto it while guiding it down the hill toward the river. He had no sooner pushed off the canoe when he tripped over a tree stump and found himself holding onto the back of the canoe, as both he and the canoe tumbled uncontrollably down the hill, only to be stopped suddenly by a bone-jarring smash at the base of one of the willow trees hanging over the bank of the river. Fortunately for Joe, the canoe had absorbed most of the hit, bouncing off the tree with no perceptible damage to either Joe or the canoe, other than the fact that he was once again horribly shaken up. His head began to throb again from the latest jarring hit as he struggled to rise again for what seemed like the millionth time since the previous night's ordeal in the mountains.

As he struggled painfully to stand up, he heard a loud boom just up the hill behind him, spontaneously followed by an explosion of tree splinters from the willow tree that stung him on the side of his swollen face.

"What the fuck? That son of a bitch is still after me!" he shouted out loud to no one in particular.

He now knew that the man obviously had found his gun and wanted to finish him off with it.

"Shit, he must have spotted the missing canoe. I have got to get moving—like now," he spat out as he twisted the canoe around and shoved it into the swirling river.

Another shot rang out as a large clump of mud and rock at the edge of the river near where Joe was pushing off was strewn crazily in the air. He nearly misjudged the placement of the canoe in the water as he lunged into it, almost falling short of where he most certainly would have had to watch the canoe disappear around the river bend and lose all hope of survival against his armed assailant.

As Joe paddled the canoe toward the far edge of the river away from where the crazy man was shooting at him, he began to feel a bit more relaxed. The river was running fast and deep, driving him north rapidly. For the past ten minutes, he had heard no sounds of gunfire. Quick glances to the sides and rear of the canoe appeared to confirm that he was the only one in the river at the moment.

He began to feel for the first time a sense of renewed hope. He could visualize himself paddling into Front Royal, docking the canoe, and getting to a hospital to call his family.

What is that? He thought he heard the sound of a car or truck motor on the far riverbank near the road. *Maybe just the morning traffic, nothing to worry about. That actually would be great; maybe the crazy man will stop pursuing me.*

Then, Joe began to hear the sound of someone screaming like a madman from somewhere high up on the riverbank. It sent a spine-tingling chill down his back, and he nearly vomited when another loud magnum round rang out, smashing into the bow of the canoe, splintering it, and sending a swell of icy cold river water up into his face.

He began to paddle furiously, maddeningly attempting to reach the far shore. Joe realized that once again the crazy man had the upper hand. He was using him for target practice now that he was in the river thinking he was safe at last.

"Fuck!" Joe shouted at the swirling, bubbling river. He stared at the distant riverbank and saw the crazed person crouched by a tree taking aim at him with his revolver. Placing both hands around his mouth to direct his voice in the direction of his tormentor, Joe shouted as loudly as he could. "Fuck you, asshole! You'll never get me. Keep on trying, you fuckin nut bag!"

Boom! Another shot split Joe's canoe in two with Joe and both pieces of the canoe now twisting sideways, tumbling crazily over the first large rapids he had come to. Joe tumbled out of the canoe scraping his face and hands on the rocks in the riverbed at the rapids. He found himself struggling in water up to his neck.

Boom! Boom! There were loud smacks in the water all around him as the crazy man on the riverbank resumed his deadly target practice.

He ducked into the cold water to avoid having his head blown off. *"God help me. Somebody help me!"* Joe whimpered to himself.

Five Hundred Yards Up River

"Damn, boss, did you hear that?" Mike Stoner yelled at Jimmy Mackenzie as both were tossing fishing lines over into the fast-moving Shenandoah River while easing toward the center of the river, wearing waders.

"I sure did—the unmistakable sound of gunfire. Tell you what, Mike—that was the reason why I thought we should bring our new forty-fives what with the goings on in the mountains over the past several years. There ain't no telling what lies out here in the woods. We call it home, but it sure attracts some bad apples now and then."

They could still hear the piercing cracks of gunfire just around the bend on the river. Jimmy quickly reeled in his rod and listened intently in the direction of the gunfire. "Fuck, Mike, sounds like a .357 to me. Somebody is packing some big heat!"

Mike reeled in his line as well. They knew they couldn't take any chances caught in waders out in this swirling river holding lines in the water. They could end up being on the wrong end of a shoot-to-kill target session.

The SEAL mentality of Jimmy began to take over as he quickly began to think of a strategy to find out what was going on up river. Maybe someone was out here on the bank of the river just taking target practice. Perhaps they had set up some tin cans or paper targets and were innocently shooting the targets; on the other hand, just maybe they were up to no good. He was going to find out one way or the other.

As Jimmy motioned for Mike that they were going into stealth mode with his finger to his lips, he waved Mike over to the protection of the shoreline where there were clumps of trees. Withdrawing his stainless Kimber .45 ACP pistol from his nylon shoulder rig, he whispered to Mike, "Okay, Mike, you stay right here—don't come for me unless you hear my whistle—or if you don't hear a peep from me in a half hour or so. Just lie low and keep your weapon locked and loaded. I am going to do some sneaking and peeking to see what the fuck is up—got that?"

Mike nodded.

Jimmy racked the slide slowly on his forty-five, flicked the safety on, and started up the bank of the river to higher ground to begin his surveillance of the unseen enemy.

As Joe gulped water, desperately trying to keep his head above the angry river, stumbling and floating north, he had a brief thought of Master Toguchi. He had not been able to experience *Sanchin Kata* with a waterfall cascading over his head and body, yet here he was literally in a waterfall! Somehow, the thought strengthened his resolve to survive. He willed himself to make it to the opposite shore where he knew he could make a much safer escape at this point on land from the crazy man.

That thought was short lived as the swirling river suddenly rose up under him and took him literally off his feet as he attempted desperately to walk along the river bottom, sending him rapidly in the direction of the gunfire.

At this point rather than give up, he steeled himself to take a bullet and end his ordeal in a dignified manner. He was not going to be taken afraid and shivering like a wimp. His martial arts training began to dominate his thoughts. He would survive somehow!

Ten more minutes passed without another shot. Maybe the crazy man was trying to get a really good bead on him for the fatal shot. Better yet, maybe the man had run out of ammo!

He still felt vulnerable, yet somehow his mind had cleared, and he felt at peace as he drifted swiftly in the current toward the hostile shoreline. He thought that at least the moment of truth—the defining point in his life—was nearly at hand. He must prevail.

The sonic booms had abated—at least temporarily. Jimmy stealthily walked toward an unknown enemy with his gun at the ready, crouching low and watching out for twigs that could inadvertently snap to give away his position, and abruptly came to a halt. He was standing behind thick brush high up over a landing that was often used to beach canoes by folks who had completed their trek up river and would wait to be picked up by a driver from the canoe company for their ride back to their vehicles parked at the establishment. He was shocked at what he saw. There was some man dressed in military camouflage taking aim with a large revolver at a man floating precariously in the river.

Jimmy couldn't believe his eyes. *Fuck! That sumbitch is trying to kill that poor man in the river. Must be some kind of argument caused that. I've got to help that man!*

Suddenly for Joe, all hell seemed to break loose. While he rolled, twisted, and turned in the gurgling water occasionally breaking the surface, he could hear gunfire from several directions as if a war had broken out. On the one hand, the closer shots of the magnum that had been dogging him on the river had resumed in a slow, deliberate manner as if the shooter were taking careful aim at his adversary. On the other hand, Joe was now beginning to hear rapid fire from another shooter somewhere to his left further down river. About the only thing good about all of the gunfire was that for the first time, none of it appeared directed towards him.

As suddenly as it had resumed, the closer, magnum gunfire ceased. Joe could still make out the staccato bursts coming from down the river. Suddenly, there was a huge splash and tremendous smack in the water mere inches from his floating body that shook him from his thoughts. He rolled in the water to see for the first time the crazed man with the piercing red eyes, red beard and ugly, pasty white scar along his jaw line with Joe's Rambo knife raised for the kill, ready to plunge the blade into him. He rolled again just in time as the man splashed the knife into the river just a few yards from the riverbank. The man rose up from the river once again with the knife and charged Joe who was now able to stand in the shallow water.

Joe executed a hard block to the man's wrist using the back of his wrist with his fingers pointed down in a chicken-beak manner. This technique, known as a chicken-wrist block and taught to green belts and above in Joe's style of karate, separated the Rambo knife from the crazy man's grip as it fell harmlessly into the murky water swirling around both adversaries.

The man lunged again at Joe only to be caught with a shocking reverse palm strike that drove upward at the base of the man's nose. In some cases when the blow is perfectly delivered, it can cause instantaneous death when the bone of the nose is driven into the brain of the opponent. This, however, was no ordinary individual. The crazed man stumbled backward, momentarily incapacitated by the blow with Joe moving in with a left-ridge hand strike to the neck. At this point the crazed man's face was a bloody mess as he bled profusely though his nose, now a mess of broken bones and cartilage. Still, he lunged again at Joe swinging wildly, catching Joe high up on his damaged ear, opening up the coagulated wound so that it began to bleed again.

Ignoring the blow, Joe summoned every remaining ounce of energy to deliver a devastating reverse punch to the man's abdomen, driving with his right hip all of his internal energy into the blow. The man hesitated for a second and began coughing blood as he sank to his knees and fell forward into the water face first completely submerged at Joe's feet. *Damn, I've killed him,* Joe thought. The adrenaline-induced high of his fight with its inherent lightning bolt surge of strength began slowly to be replaced with sadness. *Oh, my God, I've killed him,* Joe thought again.

He stood there transfixed; the roar of the nearby rapids beginning to be heard only now by Joe as his awareness of his surroundings began to kick in.

Suddenly, Joe found himself thrust violently on his back into the water, floundering wildly in three feet of water as the crazy man had both his hands on Joe's neck with his eyes bulging out and blood dripping profusely into the water; he was strangling Joe with an iron grip.

The crazy man with the red, bulging eyes and the fierce red beard leaned forward into Joe's face and whispered to him, blood and saliva seeping from his mouth. "No way you take a Ranger, son—you just died."

Struggling to keep his head out of the water and prevent himself from being strangled or drowned in the Shenandoah River, Joe could manage just one last thought. *Damn, I'm going to die in this river.* He began to slip into unconsciousness.

EPILOGUE

Fort Lauderdale, Florida - Six Months Later

"*Ah*! *Ah*!" Joe cried out as he swung his Ahab fishing rod in a wide circular arc, attempting with his still painful injuries to place the artificial lure as close to the far bank as possible. That was the area on the canal where they said the bass could be found, feeding and hiding amongst the vegetation close to the shoreline. His near-death encounter with a monster of a man in the mountains of Virginia just a few months earlier had just been brought instantly into focus with the pain in his ribs.

Joe was in Fort Lauderdale, Florida, in the back of his mother's house with one of her patio chairs pulled up to the edge of a canal where the temperature was a warm eighty degrees in late March; he was recovering from the injuries he had received during that fateful encounter in the Shenandoah National Park.

Gazing for a moment up and down the waterway, one could not help but notice the orange trees growing in the backyards of the neighboring houses. While his mother did not grow orange trees, she did have a beautiful old mango tree with its upside-down fluted flowers, pinkish-orange in color to brighten up the scene. In the back of his mother's house was a manmade canal, one of the many artificial waterways connected to the everglades ecosystem, created in Florida to nourish the state.

Joe was doing his favorite leisure-time activity whenever he visited his mom—fishing. While he and a few others in the neighborhood would fish for that elusive bass in the canal, it was rare to catch anything in this particular waterway. It really didn't matter to him. If anything, Joe could practice his casting technique and relax with a beer and a good cigar, and everything would be all right with the world.

Whenever Joe visited his mom, he would often take time to go fishing with his brother Bill in Bill's boat in the nearby everglades. Occasionally, they would go blue-water fishing in the gulf.

After being patched up in the hospital, Joe had put in for an extended period of leave to recuperate mentally and physically from the terrible ordeal he had experienced. He had spent a week in the hospital in Northern Virginia having his injuries repaired. His jaw had to be wired, and he had received a slight concussion from the blow. Three broken ribs were still on the mend, and casting his line had served to remind him of that very painful fact. He had lost several teeth in the encounter and had experienced numerous cuts and abrasions during his nightmare in the mountains.

While the physical injuries would mend, his biggest challenge was overcoming the mental damage he had experienced. Even though Joe had undergone extensive martial arts training in the past several years, no one could imagine being truly prepared to undergo the type of ordeal he had just recently experienced. To be suddenly shot at while peacefully hiking in the mountains and then confronted violently by a skilled, yet mentally unbalanced individual in unbelievable conditions was just too much to fathom.

The hurricane that had suddenly turned west into Virginia near the mouth of the Chesapeake Bay had been designated the most severe of the century by the weather service—more powerful than any category five on record. At the height of the storm, Sandi had desperately tried to reach the Virginia state police to provide a description of her husband hiking alone in the Shenandoah National Park—to no avail.

After Sandi and the girls had arrived at her husband's bedside at the hospital, having eventually been contacted by the state police, she had confided to her still groggy husband that she had been unable to contact the police for the longest time. The storm conditions had caused a number of power outages in the mid-Atlantic region, and the phones were dead.

He had been deep in the mountain woods initially traumatized by the weather event only to confront an evil worse than any hurricane. In a drawn-out battle in the woods and mountains, he had had to do battle with a demented ex-Army Ranger. This guy had been specifically trained to perform at a high level in conditions much like what Joe had experienced in the stormy mountains. That was just the tip of the iceberg. To discover that this individual who once long ago had been his military science professor during his short stint at the Virginia Military Institute was mind boggling. For Colonel Jackson to have severe mental problems—as well as to be surmised by psychiatrists after an analysis was made based on descriptions of his behavior by Joe and others who knew the real Thomas Mosby Jackson, as a person with dual personalities—was too much for him to comprehend.

Of course, one of the very pleasant surprises that came out of that horrendous ordeal was Joe's hooking back up with his long-lost cadet buddy, Jimmy MacKenzie, after over twenty some years. While they had talked over the ensuing years a few times, it was incredible that Jimmy and his store assistant just happened to be fishing in the Shenandoah while his battle with the colonel was nearing its climax.

Lying unconscious in the water and feeling the sting of Jimmy's hand slaps as Jimmy had attempted to revive Joe, and hearing Jimmy's country twang—he thought he had gone back in time or was in a crazy dream. What a coincidence! In some of their talks, both he and Jimmy had wondered what had become of their favorite professor at VMI. For the three of them to wind up engaged in a life-or-death struggle in the Shenandoah River was too overwhelming to comprehend, yet, it had happened.

Joe never imagined that he would meet Jimmy and the colonel after all these years in this set of circumstances.

"Dad, are you okay?" Amy, who was rapidly approaching her eighth birthday, rushed up to Joe to rub his sore ribs. The only thing she had heard about her dad's experience in the mountains was his unfortunate encounter with a bad person while he was hiking and that the weather had been horrible.

"I'm fine, Hon," Joe replied to his youngest daughter as he ran his fingers through her pigtails. Joe liked to occasionally tie the ends of her pigtails together, and Amy would occasionally take a comb and rubber band and put together a short ponytail with what little remained of Joe's hair on the back of his head. Nicole, his teenage daughter, had thought it much more exciting to be over at her Florida girlfriend's house, just down the street from his mom's house, talking about boys. Amy scurried off to play with the family dog, a pretty ginger-colored cocker spaniel named Daphne, who had come along for the trip as well.

He lit a Monte Cristo cigar, savoring for a moment the rich mild flavor, took a sip of his Heineken, and carefully tossed his line into the canal. His mind drifted once again back to the last minutes of the battle in the river. He knew that he had inflicted grave damage to the colonel with the wicked strike to his abdomen in one of the areas known as a "death" spot. Joe had been taught that there were a number of points on the human body where a lethal strike could be administered. If the individual did not die from the blow, the hit at least could seriously incapacitate that person. The colonel had vomited blood shortly after the strike, indicating that he had suffered internal damage. Yet, after summoning up one last shred of effort in his attempt to strangle Joe to death in the river, saying words to the effect that as an Army Ranger he would not be taken, Colonel Jackson had softened his grip on Joe's neck and slumped over dead. He had finally succumbed from Joe's blow.

Joe shivered at the memory of seeing the dead man lying face up just below the river's surface, eyes open in the "death stare" with clouds of blood floating lazily around his head. He would learn much more about Thomas Jackson during several phone conversations with the Virginia state police detective investigating the case. He had so far been unable to talk with his wife in depth about the incident.

"Joe, can we talk?" Startled by Sandi as she came up behind him sitting in the patio chair by the side of the canal in deep thought, Joe winced as he turned slightly in his chair to put his rod down and grab her hand. She had pulled one of the patio chairs nearby closer to her husband and gently kissed him on his sore cheek.

"Yeah, I guess so," he replied.

Sandi looked intently into her husband's eyes. "Honey, can you please tell me what the detective told you about that crazy person who attacked you in the park?"

Joe had not revealed much about his encounter to his family other than the man in the woods had appeared demented and wild. She knew that he had once been Joe's and his old friend Jimmy's professor at VMI, and that he had obviously benefited from the skills he had acquired while a decorated Army Ranger prior to his professorship at the Institute. Sandi was also aware that a passing motorist driving on Route 340 beside the Shenandoah River where Joe and the colonel had fought had called the police to report loud gunshots in the vicinity of the river just south of Front Royal. By the time the police had arrived, it was over. Colonel Jackson lay dead near the bank closest to the road, and Joe was fighting for his life with Jimmy and his fishing buddy attempting to revive him on the bank of the river. He had barely been able to make a short statement to the police of the events that had led up to their final battle in the river before becoming too delirious to speak.

At the time in the river, he had not even recognized Jimmy who had immediately scampered down from his location high up overlooking the river to offer help to Joe once he saw the colonel dive into the river after Joe. Later, at the Fairfax Hospital, he had been able to describe in more detail the traumatic events of the past day.

Jimmy and Mike had dropped by to see him, both meeting Sandi and the girls. Jimmy had been floored to find out that the crazed man at the river was the colonel.

Joe was still in the throes of post-traumatic syndrome, and it had been difficult for him to extensively verbalize what he had learned. He shifted somewhat uncomfortably in his chair and began. "Okay, I'll try. Be patient with me. The detective told me that Colonel Jackson was believed to be someone with a dissociative disorder of some kind."

Sandi interrupted him before he could go on. "Well, he lived a normal life, didn't he? I mean he was once an esteemed professor at VMI and interacted with people. He had friends that he associated with, I am quite sure."

Joe relit his cigar and looked out at the canal. "Yes, he had friends. As a matter of fact one of his very good friends just happened to be the Vice-Chairman of the Joint Chiefs of Staff at the Pentagon. He was shocked when they told him his friend had more than likely killed a number of hikers in the park over a period of several years.

Retired Lieutenant General Gibson had told the police he would never have guessed that Thomas Jackson was the person doing the killing in the park. The detective did tell me some strange things that General Gibson had mentioned to him," Joe said.

"What was that, Hon?" Sandi inquired.

"Well, he said that the general had not seen his friend, the colonel, in years. He said that the colonel had retired from VMI and eventually just dropped out of sight. They had gotten together for a while after the colonel retired. Then, just like that, Colonel Jackson had disappeared. General Gibson had felt that the colonel had become obsessed with getting back at the super at VMI for not pushing his promotion through, and wow, I guess between that and finding out about what happened to his family in the mountains, he just snapped and lost it," Joe explained.

Sandi touched Joe on the arm. "Do they know what made the colonel do this to those people?"

Joe sighed. "Well, from what the detective told me, no one knows one hundred percent for sure what made him tick. They knew that he was originally from that area. As a matter of fact, according to some papers they found in his house in Chevy Chase, he was actually born in one of those hollows in the Shenandoah Park.

"What the psychiatrists believe is that he might have been severely traumatized as a young boy by a violent event that occurred at his parent's home in the mountains. The information is sketchy; it appears that some of the mountain people did not want to leave their homes and land around the time the park was being constructed. The state apparently was fairly lenient toward many of them, letting some of the older residents stay there indefinitely. The notes left by the colonel's uncle indicate that there was violence at his parents' home, and both were killed as a result. Apparently, so I was told, the colonel's uncle had lived with the family in the hollow. The police and state people had visited the home in the mountains, and Colonel Jackson's father supposedly had shot at them. A violent gun battle ensued with both of the colonel's parents losing their lives. The colonel and his uncle were the only survivors at the shootout in the mountains when his parents were killed. Little Thomas Mosby Jackson was gathered up by the police there at the time and turned over to his uncle to be raised by him. Apparently, the police, at the time of the incident, found family papers in the old cabin in the mountains with the names and address of the nearest kin."

Sandi looked puzzled at her husband. "Yes, but he was raised by a good uncle, given loving care. He had a normal life after that. I mean, obviously he was mentally healthy to have gone to VMI, graduated, and later gone on to become an Army Ranger—a decorated one at that. As you indicated, he then later became a military professor at VMI. What happened to him?"

Joe began to look a bit exasperated. "Like I said, Hon, no one knows all of the answers. The only thing I can tell you is what the detective told me. I asked him the same questions. The detective told me that while it is pure speculation, the theory based on their findings is that Colonel Jackson apparently had assumed what they call dissociative behavior early on, and it had been masked until something very traumatic occurred in his adult life. I vaguely remember that he had a running battle with the super at VMI, a power struggle of some sort. He was really out to get the super and vice versa. When he found out that the super reneged on a promise to recommend that he be promoted to full colonel, well, apparently his whole life just caved in. The super had the last laugh, retiring from the Institute without forwarding the colonel's recommendation for promotion. Some of the shrinks believe that after the colonel left in disgust from the Institute, taking early retirement himself, he went into a funk. Somewhere along the line, he found some papers originally from his uncle's house with information about his parents. The boy's trauma had previously led to him disassociating himself—in other words separating himself—from that horrible experience.

"Unfortunately, the end result of that trauma for him led to tremendous anger towards those whom he perceived had brought about the pain in the first place. While he had an abject hate for those who had violated his family in the mountains, no doubt his extreme anger over his demise at the Institute added fuel to his madness. The notes his uncle kept apparently alluded to an approximate area in the park where his parents' old home and cemetery had been. One day—and this was long after he had left the Institute—he decided to try to find his parents' old home in the mountains."

Sandi put her hand on Joe's hand and tugged slightly. "Well, I guess he must have found at least the area where the home was."

Joe nodded. "I'm afraid he did, and that was what triggered the violence. Apparently, whenever he visited the park, he would assume another identity and hang around his family's home. I mean there was a cemetery there at one time, and they have put it together that some hikers stumbled accidentally upon him at his parents' cemetery standing guard. That was a big mistake on their part. God knows why they were way off the beaten path.

"In my case, when the storm hit, I freaked out after spending some time in the abandoned copper mine. I thought that there may have been an earthquake, and the mine was going to cave in on me. Little did I know at the time that the large pieces of timber at the end of the shaft were vibrating violently, creating an illusion of an earthquake for me in the narrow confines of the shaft. I was in a state of panic and simply found myself off the trails."

Thinking more about his nemesis, Joe continued with his narrative. "The colonel was into guns; we used to see him frequently on the range at the Institute when Jimmy and I were there. He hunted and was a great woodsman and expert in wilderness survival. The guy apparently was a legend as an Army Ranger. He had received the Purple Heart award for an injury to his jaw line that he had incurred while engaged in combat. Evidently, he had taken an awful hit to his face by a Viet Cong with a fox hole shovel and shot the dude dead while he was rescuing his company commander."

"Sandi, the man was a great guy at VMI. He was our friend and confidant; we all loved the colonel. He was a southern gentleman, a man of great courage and charisma. To think that I came across him in this state after all of these years, and actually killed him simply blows by mind."

Joe began to shiver uncontrollably, making Sandi concerned.

"Joe, I know it has been difficult for you to share this with me. I had to know more about your awful experience. I just thank God that you survived. You are going to need time."

Joe held his hand up as the shivering began to slowly subside. "The thing is, as terrible as this has been for me, imagine what he had to go through as a young kid. To be traumatized like that as a little tyke. You know that I have read some things about the mountain people that once lived there before the park was built. These were good people struggling to eke out an existence in the mountains. I am sure they sat around in the evening in front of the fireplace and hugged each other. It's just a sad story. I feel horrible knowing I had to kill this man to survive."

Sandi peered intently into her husband's eyes. "Joe, it was either you or the colonel. Please try not to feel too bad about this. I am certain that Thomas Jackson was probably a good little kid. The events surrounding his parents' death and the violence that he experienced as a very young boy made him into a monster. Obviously, the extreme depression he experienced at VMI didn't help. I believe the good Lord selected you to stop this monster. What you had was a good young person who became evil because of the events that he had experienced. He had to eventually be stopped by someone. How many more innocent people was he going to kill in his mental state?"

Joe struggled out of his chair, flicked the stogie into the canal, and hugged his wife. "Thanks, hon. I am glad you were able to get me to open up. I feel so much better."

A few minutes later, Joe's mother opened the side door to her house and leaned out of the door. "Joe, Sandi, dinner's ready," she said.

Joe and Sandi walked arm in arm into his mother's house with Joe sporting a big smile for the first time in several months.